The Land of the Living

Sherie James

Edited by Joy Shields of the Writer's Beacon

Book cover by Della Paul Designs

ISBN-13: 978-0-692-61742-7

ISBN-10: 0-692-61742-6

DEDICATION

For Sierra, my eternal light.

This book is dedicated to all of us who are trying to live in light, love, and the power of discovering the beautiful truth of our existence: that each of us has a unique and wonderful purpose the world is waiting for.

The Musical Companion To This Novel Is Coming Soon!

CONTENTS

CHAPTER ONE— THE UNEXPECTED GUEST

The commotion at the Wright house as they prepared for the dinner party made each of them oblivious to the presence of an unexpected guest standing at the door. "Did Winter get here yet?" Marie Wright asked, rushing up the curved staircase to her bedroom.

"I didn't see her car outside when we brought the groceries in, but she mentioned wanting to visit the Magan's down the street. She usually parks her car there and walks over from their house. Winter calls it her only form of exercise," Marie's daughter, Ella, called up the stairs. "Don't think she was planning on coming to the party tonight."

The person at the door knocked again, and hoped one of the Wright's would answer, but Ella was busy searching through records for party music, Christopher Wright was busy stashing away his sweets from his daughters throughout the house, and Mrs. Wright was getting dressed.

From the kitchen pantry, Winter thought she heard a faint knock on the door. She stopped moving and listened, but the house was quiet. "This house is old. It always makes strange sounds," Winter said aloud. She stood on her tiptoes searching for her father's salted caramels. The unexpected guest knocked a fourth time and realized the door was ajar. She placed a hand on the knob and pushed it open slightly.

"Hello?" She said into an empty entryway.

Aged dark wood floors gleamed in the setting sunlight. A half-moon table sat in the middle of the room beneath a glass vase filled with bright peonies. Inside the pantry, Winter could hear the faint voice of the unexpected guest echo in the foyer. To Winter, there was something strange about that voice. She stopped chewing and became still. *Can't be*, she thought. Upon hearing the voice, Mr. Wright and his eldest daughter, Ella, went to see who had arrived. They entered the foyer and saw a girl with pale blond hair peering around their front door.

"I'm sorry to barge in on you," the girl said, blushing.

No, no, no. Winter gasped with half a caramel in her mouth. The voice belonged to someone she hadn't seen in six years. It was not a voice she could forget. Winter bit the inside of her lower lip and tiptoed out of the pantry with the salted caramels in hand. Avoiding all the creaky floorboards, Winter tilted her head around the corner of the kitchen, just enough to see who stood in the doorway. The flash of distinctively pale blond hair confirmed Winter's fear. It was *her.* Winter melted into the wall.

Winter's teenage years had long passed, but Anna Herald's relentless taunts still rang clear in Winter's mind even as an adult. Anna had lived next door to Winter since they could crawl. She was Winter's self-proclaimed arch-nemesis since the age of nine. Everything Winter tried to do growing up; Anna did it better. She got straight A's to Winter's multi-lettered report card, and Anna always made sure Winter knew how much she fell short. The only times they spoke was when Anna felt Winter was in need of a good taunting.

Mrs. Wright had always referred to Anna as the sweet, smart girl a couple of houses down. Winter never corrected her mother's idea of her arch-nemesis because she feared Anna's retaliation. Growing up, Winter was forced to endure family dinner parties where she was obligated to laugh at Anna's dramatic stories as she stabbed cold peas with her fork. And now here that girl stood in the Wright's entryway. All of a sudden Winter was fourteen again, trying to avoid Anna's steely gaze. Though they hadn't seen one another in years, the last words spoken between them still lived in Winter's mind.

"I'm looking for Winter. Does she live here?"

"Anna!" Marie Wright said, coming down the steps in a fresh change of clothes.

"Hi, Mrs. Wright. It's good to see you. I'm leaving for grad school in a couple days, and I really wanted to see Winter before I go."

Winter's eyes bulged as she looked down at her ripped jeans where her rich brown skin peeked through the holes at her knee caps. A white t-shirt hung loosely on her body, and her coiled hair was pulled into a messy ponytail. Winter had envisioned meeting her former tormentor many times, but not like this. Not with a mouth full of caramel and looking as if she hadn't showered in a week. *What is she even doing here?* Winter thought. *I have to get out of here,* she decided.

She looked around the kitchen, trying to form an escape route. The loudness of the sliding glass doors to the backyard would give her away. Winter grabbed her bag off the counter as she formulated a plan. *The basement!* The basement door wasn't far, just to the right of the pantry. *If I move fast, I can make it.* Winter went to pick up her shoes, but only saw one. *Where is my other shoe?* Winter yelled internally as she turned in a frantic circle, and then the floorboards in the hallway creaked.

Anna was coming, and Winter couldn't face her, not now. There was only one place to go. Winter shuffled back into the pantry and shut the door as softly as possible. Once inside Winter exhaled. *This is so pathetic. I'm still running from her.* Winter had always thought herself a feeble person. Each time she ventured out from beneath her shell, disappointment seemed to greet Winter. Confidence seemed as attainable as grasping a passing breeze, but even this made her feel more cowardly than normal. Shame made her cheeks hot.

"I can try calling her for you Anna," Mrs. Wright offered, taking out her cell phone.

In the pantry Winter swallowed hard and couldn't escape the sensation that she'd just eaten a package of nails. Winter shook her head fervently, knowing her phone's obnoxious ring would betray her hiding place, and being found crouching in a pantry by Anna would be too much embarrassment to withstand. Winter felt she'd already undergone lifetimes of humiliation from the calculating mind of Anna Herald.

"No, her phone is always dead. I've tried her once today," Ella interjected.

Winter clasped her hands in front of her chest, squeezed her eyes shut and passionately whispered, "Thank you" repeatedly.

"I'm so sorry, Anna," Mrs. Wright said. "And you came all this way."

It's two houses, Winter thought. *But at least Anna will go now.* She breathed out in relief. "We're having a party tonight, Anna. Guests should be arriving soon, but you're welcome to stay," Winter's mother said warmly.

"That'd be great. Thanks, Mrs. Wright," Anna replied.

Winter moaned and silently thrashed her body, careful not to bang into the walls stocked with food. On cue, the doorbell rang, and a stream of guests began arriving for the dinner party.

Twenty minutes later most of the guests arrived. Winter could hear loud voices outside the walls of her parents' kitchen pantry and mentally kicked herself for forgetting that the party was tonight. She preferred to dodge a night of questions about the clarity and direction missing from her life, and now she was stuck in a pantry until Anna left.

What have I gotten myself into? Winter groaned, backing into the far corner of the pantry. The L-shaped pantry was an average size. The floor in front of the sweets was more worn than any other part. The lilac paint was fresh. Some of the shelves were in constant disarray, much like Winter's life. *I guess it's not so bad, though,* she thought, eyeing her surroundings. *Another person could even fit in here, well unless they're claustrophobic.*

Music started to play, but over the chorus of guests' voices, Winter heard four awful words. "It's in the pantry!" Winter's face contorted into pure terror as the door handle turned at glacial speed.

CHAPTER TWO—THE QUESTION

Ella pushed open the pantry door, and there was Winter sitting scrunched in the corner, index finger poised pleadingly over her closed lips. She beckoned her sister to stay quiet, to not give her away. Ella grabbed a blue mug from a chipped shelf. She quickly shut the light off and closed the old wooden door, leaving Winter alone in the dark room. She could not believe she was hiding in a pantry so she wouldn't have to face Anna or 'the question,' the one that every graduate or person over twenty-three gets asked. The. Dreaded. Question.

"So, what are you doing these days?"

In other words, what are you doing with yourself? Did you spend that loan money and the past four to six years of your life well? She didn't have a steady job, nor any clue where her life was going. None of her plans or hopes had come to fruition, which is why Winter was hiding from Anna Herald in a pantry. She decided that failure felt heavy, and something needed to change in her life or she would implode beneath the weight of it. Winter crumpled lower against the shelves, and a bag of potato chips fell onto her head. The door opened, and Winter said a silent prayer though she hadn't prayed for months, years even.

"What are you doing in here?" Ella asked, her hands waving in the air.

Winter's eyes bulged as she said, "Anna Herald—my life-long arch-nemesis—is out there. I can't go out there and tell her I'm the failure she always knew I was! Even I have limits for the level of embarrassment I'll inflict on myself."

Ella scoffed. Her bright brown eyes bore into Winter. "You're hiding! This is ridiculous. You can't hide from her, in—a—pantry. Besides this has nothing to do with her."

"Of course it does! Look, go away. I'm fine in here. There's plenty of food," Winter said, picking up the bag of chips that had just assaulted her.

4

"I know you've been dealing with some," Ella paused briefly, searching for the right word, "...difficulties lately. But, Winter, I don't think this is a healthy way of handling your issues. What about this weekend at Sienna's lake house? If somebody asks you what you're doing, are you gonna jump into a cabinet?"

Winter breathed out impatiently. "I don't think now is the best time to talk about it. Just tell me when I can sneak out and go back to my apartment."

"No way. Just come out."

"If you don't tell me, I can't promise those Belgian chocolates you love will survive the night."

"I'll just bring them with me now," Ella said.

"There are thirty people out there. Those chocolates wouldn't stand a chance," Winter shot back.

They eyed each other for a moment before Ella said, "Fine" and shut the door. She returned a half hour later when everyone was outside in the backyard having their mother's homemade lemon meringue pie. It was one of Winter's favorites, but she had no time for pie tonight.

"Everyone's in the backyard. This is your only chance to go unless you want to sleep in there."

Ella walked out of the pantry followed by a cautious Winter.

"I'm starting a new job, Winter, a new phase of my life. I don't need the stress of your crazy dramatics," Ella said, throwing nuts into a glass bowl for the guests outside. They stood at the marbled island in the middle of the kitchen. The floors softly moaned beneath their feet.

"How was flight attendant training? And have you seen my other shoe?" Winter whispered, fearful the guests outside would return to the house.

"How did you lose your shoe?"

"I don't know! The usual way you lose something. You put it somewhere and forget the *where* part."

Ella spoke a bit louder than she normally did. "No, I haven't seen your shoe. Training was good, a lot of work. I start in a couple days." Ella paused for dramatic effect. "And you better behave, or I'll take you off my flight benefits."

"You put me on!" Winter exclaimed, grabbing her sister's arm.

"I did. You owe me one hundred dollars, by the way," she said, popping a cashew into her mouth.

"Thank you, Ella!" Winter said.

"Sure. Anna left a few minutes ago. She asked me to give this to you." Ella handed a piece of paper to Winter.

The words were hastily written on a coupon for a local grocery store Anna had torn down from Winter's parents' refrigerator. Winter frowned. Anna had only ever written notes on Winter's locker or school desk, words that usually had to be wiped off before other children set eyes on Anna's crude but inventive profanities. Ella passed the note to her sister and peered over Winter's shoulder. There, in Anna's perfected handwriting, it said:

Sorry for what I did to you. Will you forgive me? -Anna

Winter's mouth hung open as Ella asked, "Forgive her for what?"

But then the back door began to slide open. Winter hurriedly hugged her sister, mouthed thank you, and ran into the next room. She slipped out the side door and rushed to her car. For the second time that night she prayed, with eyes lifted to the sky as she sprinted across the freshly manicured lawn with only one shoe dangling from her foot. Winter pleaded that nobody's car would be blocking her in. She reached the curb and raised her arms into the air in triumph. Her small red car had just enough room for her to inch out onto the street. She got in and smiled as she shut the door.

Ten minutes later Winter pulled into her parking spot, barely fitting within the white lines. She awkwardly shoved open her broken door handle and stood on the concrete with one shoe on her foot. A cool night air passed over her skin. Winter breathed it in, thankful to be outside the cramped quarters of the pantry. She pulled out her keys from her worn jacket pocket. The keys clanked together, creating a hushed symphony as she walked.

Winter clearly remembered the day she bought the jacket thirteen years ago. Her younger self had pleaded with her mother to let her buy the camouflage coat she now wore. It was far too large for her then, but she told her mother she'd grow into it, and she had. Winter could point out life events from the spills and tears across it.

Part of the stitching on the left sleeve had thinned from Winter's incessant nervous fidgeting. The collars had served as tissues for her tears, at the hopes she had that faded like whispers. The colors had grown dim from walks beneath hot suns and moments spent dancing under the rain. It had the vague scent of campfire nights spent with her best friend, Sienna, too.

But Winter could also remember why she desperately wanted the camouflage jacket to conceal her. It was the events of one torrid summer day thirteen years ago, right before Winter's twelfth birthday, that prompted her to agonize over getting the coat. That was the day she wished, more than anything, would evaporate from her memory; the day when Winter came face to face with hate. But it remained, so instead, she willed herself to think of different times when that memory pushed its way to the surface.

Winter bit her bottom lip and exhaled. It was a quiet, gentle night. The noise from her keys and the chirping of cicadas filled her ears alone. Winter leaned against the building's door for a moment, thinking about her closest childhood friend, Sienna. Every year she went to Sienna's family's lake house. Winter saw Sienna when she visited their hometown, but the lake weekend was special. It was the one time she and Sienna got to see their college friends. They'd all moved across the country after school ended. Life had called Winter's friends to different places.

Throughout college, lake weekends had kept them connected during summers spent apart. Since freshman year, they went to Clearwater for a few days. It was the middle of April now, which was early for a lake weekend. Winter knew she'd be asked the same question that had been posed to her for months now, ever since she lost her job in August and had not found work. More than two years on from school and Winter still had not found her place in the world. For a brief moment full of self-pity and insecurity, Winter contemplated staying home this time. But how could she?

"Hello?! Who's there?!" A woman's voice barked roughly from the intercom. Winter jumped and covered her ear.

"Oh, hi. Sorry, Mrs. Jones. It's just me, Winter. I was leaning against the..." Mrs. Jones cut her off.

"I know just what you were doing! Stop leaning on my buzzer!"

"Sorry, won't happen again," Winter said into the intercom. *For your sake and mine,* she thought, her ear still ringing.

"That's what you said last time. Now I mean it, I was just about to go to bed. Stop it."

"Okay, I promise that I'll only lean on walls with no buttons," Winter chuckled, thinking Mrs. Jones would laugh at her joke, but she'd already stopped listening to Winter.

Winter slouched her shoulders. She unlocked the building's brass door and walked up the sunken stairs to her second-floor apartment. As she climbed the steps, Winter thought of the note in her pocket. Could she forgive Anna Herald? For everything? When she was younger, Winter didn't have the courage to tell anyone in her family, not even Ella, what Anna had done to her over the years, because she feared her wrath. And then life separated their paths. Winter wasn't sure if she could forgive Anna, but she had more urgent questions to think about than forgiving her childhood bully, like what to do with her life.

Winter shook her head, dislodging the thought, and opened her door. She threw her deep green jacket and brown shoulder bag onto the carpet at her feet. Winter stepped further into her apartment and felt a crunch beneath her shoeless foot. A wrinkled, and now flattened, piece of paper lay on the floor. Winter picked it up and unfurled her apartment renewal lease, another reminder that she needed more direction in her life. She held it in her hands, wishing her life could work itself out without her input.

Winter stood in the middle of her studio. Her place was tiny, but she didn't mind. The outdated carpet needed to be swapped for something in the twentieth century, and her white walls were bland, but the far wall had two built-in book shelves. Candles lined each of the four windowsills, and two bamboo plants flourished next to her reading chair. Winter loved her apartment since the day she signed the lease, not because it was spectacular, but because it was her first step into the world on her own.

On Winter's first night in the apartment she didn't have any furniture, so she sat cross-legged and ate pineapple from the can in her graduation dress. It was the only piece of clothing she could find. She later realized that her three boxes of clothes had fallen out of the moving van on the way over. Walking around town the next day, she found a bread trail of her clothing along the town sidewalk, a pair of her shorts on the bench, an old t-shirt next to Golden's Hardware store, and then she stumbled upon the box itself. Now she had a couch and chair, and a small kitchen table. Every piece of furniture in her apartment had come from other people. Discarded bits of their lives sat on her floors, filling up space that was once entirely empty. The thought made Winter wonder when she would be able to fill the space of her own life.

Winter's apartment was more window than anything else, and that's what sold her on the place. At night, she'd turn off all the lights and look out the smudged glass, and the stars, illuminated across a darkened sky, would fill her apartment. At first glance the stars didn't seem connected, but with a deeper look constellations became visible. A map of unseen intricacy and beautiful connection formed, and Winter hoped her life would one day make constellations from its own seemingly disconnected pieces.

Winter grabbed an old duffle bag from her closet and started packing for the weekend. She could already hear her friends' voices as she threw in sweat pants and shorts. "Where is your suit?" Winter didn't own a bathing suit because she could never make sense of getting one when she only swam once a year. She finished packing and lay in the middle of her living room/bedroom floor. Winter gazed outside, taking in the ink black sky sprinkled with pale stars, and fell asleep.

The sun's warmth woke her. She stood and limped to her kitchen, stretching from a night of sleeping on the floor. Winter pulled down a paper bag of fair trade coffee beans that Sienna had sent her from work. She opened the bag and dropped the beans into a coffee grinder her mother had gotten for Winter on her last birthday. The robust smell of brewing coffee filled her small apartment, a blend of deep aromas so fragrant Winter felt she could drink the air itself.

She poured the coffee into a mug and grabbed a frozen blueberry muffin from her freezer. Winter placed it in the oven and jumped into the shower. By the time she finished, the muffin was steaming. She threw her duffle bag strap around her shoulder and walked to her car with full hands. The drive to Sienna's lake house was about two hours. Winter rolled down the windows of her old, hand-me-down car. She had to crank them down manually, putting in a bit more muscle whenever the lever got stuck.

Winter bobbed her head in rhythm to the music on her static-filled radio. She sang out as she drove down secluded two-lane roads, picking notes that blended in harmony with the songs. When she pulled up to the lake house, Sienna came running to her car.

"You're the first one!" She shouted as she neared Winter. They embraced, swaying side to side.

"Do you have a bathing suit?" Sienna asked, knowing what the answer would be.

"I swim once a year, Sienna," Winter said with a smile.

Sienna laughed and asked, "Can I help with your bags?"

"I just have the one," Winter said.

"Okay, I'll take that," Sienna offered, reaching over Winter and grabbing her fraying bag from the car. Sienna was the type of person who always made Winter want to be better, more thoughtful. It seemed to come so easily to Sienna.

"How have you been? I just finished the coffee you sent me. It was seriously good. I drank the whole bag in five days."

"If you ever get sick, the hospital is going to have to hook up your I.V. to caffeinated coffee to bring you back to life! I'm glad you liked it! I'm loving working with Just Coffee. I never thought I'd get the job. I applied on a whim, but it's the best place to work. I get to meet people from all over the world. I was surprised at how many people come to Seattle. It's a dream. With my degree, I'm hoping I'll be able to work my way up and eventually go to the source farms to meet the people who grow the beans and talk about ways to improve the organization. I already have so many ideas," her voice brimmed with pleasure.

"That sounds amazing, Sienna," Winter said, feeling her own life's direction resembled a broken compass. She could see how content her friend was, but her stomach still clenched. She knew the question that was coming next.

"So tell me what's been going on with you. I know you've been having some trouble finding a job."

"Yeah, going on nine months. I'm volunteering a couple times a week, and I started working part-time at this consignment shop. Well, it's a little less than part time, but it's all they could give me. I have more than enough money saved to get me through this bump. It'd be nice to have something permanent. But it's okay. I'm doing okay."

"Hmm," Sienna said, her face indecipherable as she looked towards the shining lake in the distance. Then her friend's gaze turned toward her, and Winter felt Sienna could see parts of her mind even she wasn't privy to.

"What are you thinking?" Winter asked, only partially wanting to know the answer.

The sound of a car made them both turn.

"I know you'll find something, but I want to talk to you before you go. Okay? Let me get my thoughts together, but I think I have an idea for you."

"I'm intrigued," Winter said, wondering what her friend was brewing up.

The other girls arrived within the hour. Screeches of laughter bellowed around the lake.

"You girls ready to get in the water?" Sienna yelled over the ruckus.

She walked to her shed and grabbed four life jackets. Out of her group she was the most comfortable in the water. Sienna had grown up on the lake, and her friends weren't the best swimmers. Maya, Emma, and Ali could stay afloat and swim if they needed to, but Winter couldn't even tread water. It had taken years to get her into the lake and even more time for her to go on a jet ski. Sienna had to attest profusely that Winter would not fall off and die.

"What if I fall off and sink to the bottom and die?" She'd asked.

"You'll have a life jacket on. You'll start to float back to the top, promise," Sienna had said.

She tossed the life jackets to her friends and got out the rafts. Even in April, summer finally felt like it had come to the four of them as they stood beneath the sun at the lake house. Trees in full bloom provided shade, a retreat amid the unexpected heat. Their legs carried them to the water's edge, and soon its calm surface was filled with life.

"This water is too cold! You'd think it'd be warmer than this!" Ali shouted. They all sunk slowly into the cool lake.

"I've missed you guys!" Maya said, splashing water over the raft she was on, trying to adjust to the icy temperature.

"It's been so long since we've all been together," Emma added.

Ali kicked her legs with tranquility beneath the water's surface and then floated peacefully.

"Yeah, I'm just glad we don't have to worry about papers or tests anymore when we come to the lake," Ali said without opening her eyes. "Remember Dr. Reynolds? He always gave out assignments at the start of summer for his fall classes. Ridiculous. I'm still mad about that."

"Now we just have jobs, which is so much better," Maya said sarcastically.

Winter shifted her weight on the raft and tugged a bit at her life jacket. She could feel Sienna's sympathetic gaze on her, and she wondered how long she would elicit those stares that made her feel so innately inadequate.

"Well, we're all finding our way," Sienna said. Winter could feel the collective stares of the group turn towards her.

"Oh, no. I'm sorry, Winter. I didn't mean…" Maya began.

Winter cleared her throat. "No, it's okay. I'm okay. I'm volunteering at this great place, and Anna Herald is moving away." She lifted her hands to the clouds, "and the sun is still shining. Everything is fine. Really. Okay?"

She wished she could close her mouth, but it seemed to function apart from her brain and will. She knew no normal person said 'okay' that many times if she were in reality, okay.

Winter felt hot and knew that even without the sun's rays on her, the heat, which was steadily climbing to her face, would not cease. The internal desire to not be the one everyone pitied, the one whose life seemed to stay still and stagnant while others plowed past her, would not be moved. Winter bit the inside of her lower lip and tried not to sigh too loudly. It was Emma who changed the subject. She couldn't stand pauses or lulls in conversations, no matter who was in her company.

"Anybody want to jump off the high diving board with me?" She asked, a mischievous glint lighting up her eyes.

A black platform lay in the middle of the lake supporting a diving board. Winter wasn't sure how high above the water the board hovered. Her stomach dropped as she took in the foreboding structure. She remembered when her fear of water was born. It was at a family reunion in a Mississippi hotel, on a day even hotter than this one. Winter was eight years old. She was wading in the shallow end of the hotel pool, her arms stuffed in bright orange floats.

The floats were so large that she couldn't put her arms down, so they stuck out from her sides uncomfortably. Her dark skin made it nearly impossible to see her blush, but that didn't stop the chemistry of her body from sending blood rushing to her cheeks. All her older cousins swam in the pool, but not just in any part of the pool. They swam in the deep end— without orange colored floats.

Though Winter was young, she knew she looked odd to her older, far more sophisticated cousins. They didn't wade in the kiddy pool with oversized orange marshmallows impeding the movement of their arms. Winter stood up from the pool's edge and decided to give the deep end a try. She took off the floats. *How hard can it be?*

The answer, she would soon find out, was that it was not hard at all. It was impossible. The closer she got to the deep end, the more she stretched and strained on her toes until nothing but water was beneath them. And then panic set in. Water surrounded Winter. Her body screamed for air as her head bobbed under the water. Winter's arms flailed helplessly.

Every time she surfaced, she tried to scream out for help. Her Uncle Jim jumped in and pulled her shaking body to safety. She walked back to the hotel room with Ella, who insisted her head never went under the surface. This fact remained a point of contention in their relationship to this day because Winter most definitely insisted that her head did go under, because how else did she swallow mouthfuls of chlorine treated water?

"Hey!"

SHERIE JAMES

Winter looked up to see Emma staring at her.

"What do you say, wanna jump off the high board with me?"

"Uh, I think I'll watch," Winter said.

"Oh come on, you can't be afraid of water your entire life. What if you live by the sea one day?" Maya asked.

"I fully doubt that will happen," Winter said plainly.

Ali laughed as she started to swim in slow circles.

"Maybe it's a good idea to try because it makes you nervous," Sienna offered.

Winter wished she could swim so that she could swim away.

"I know it might seem illogical because I have a life jacket, but I don't think I could do it. That sensation when water surrounds you, envelopes you…" Winter shuddered beneath the sun. "I don't think I can. It's one of my longest held fears. That and heights."

"But, you're in the water now," Maya said.

"As long as I don't imagine how deep it is or get completely submerged, I'm fine."

"It's one of your deepest fears, even when you have a life jacket?" Maya asked, her nose turned up in confusion.

"Yes, don't you guys have any fears that might seem irrational to someone else but makes total sense to you?" Winter asked.

"I have one," Emma said. Her eyes darted between her friends. "But you all have to promise not to laugh."

"I do not promise any such thing," Ali said.

Emma rolled her eyes and took a deep breath. "All right, here it is. Worms." She threw her hands in the air as if she was saying, 'Ta-da!'

"What?!" Everyone shouted. "Why worms? They literally can't do a thing to you," Maya cried out.

"I know, but it's the way they look and feel and move. It creeps me out!" Her face was the picture of disgust. "I'd rather hold ten spiders than have half a worm inching its way across my body. Yuck." She shook at the thought and brushed at the imaginary worms on her skin.

"What do you do in the spring when they all surface?" Winter asked.

"I jump around them while having a panic attack. It kind of looks like I'm hyperventilating and playing hopscotch simultaneously, but I've accepted it."

"How did none of us ever catch this?" Sienna looked around at Winter, Ali, and Maya, laughing.

"I've gotten better over the years. When I was young, my fear grew during middle school because some of the kids found out and they started chasing me with worms. It was terrible. They'd dangle their limp bodies in their hands and run to catch up with me. Luckily, they never got me because I started to get pretty fast. Actually, in junior high I tried out for

12

the track team and got one of the fastest times. So in a way, I should thank them all for helping me to discover one of my hidden talents," she joked.

"Okay, so that's Emma's illogical fear—thanks for sharing—and Winter's somewhat illogical fear is water. We have all heard that story, which is why I believe it's only somewhat illogical. What about you two?" Ali asked, pointing to Sienna and Maya.

"Mine is pretty typical. When I was a kid, I thought shadows were monsters out to get me," Maya chuckled. "I'd always ask my mom for extra blankets. I don't know why I thought mounds of excess fabric and cotton would keep me safe, but somehow it made sense to me. The most blankets I ever slept under was twenty-six."

"You didn't faint?" Emma asked. "I'm hot just imagining it," she said, waving a hand at her forehead.

"My mom always snuck in and moved them. For a while I thought it was the monsters eating their way through the stack."

"On no, that's awful," Sienna said sincerely, clapping her hands on either side of her face. The other girls hid a bit of their laughter.

"Your turn, Sienna," Ali yelled dramatically.

"Well, I was afraid of places I didn't know. I had this immobilizing fear of new places. For some reason I thought I might not be able to go back home once I left. It was like new places were portals to some other kind of world. It was actually kind of serious, and my mom, the psychologist, was always using exposure therapy techniques on me. It worked, though, and now new places are my thing."

"That's so true. They are. You've traveled more than any of us. I would never have guessed that it used to be one of your fears," Maya shared.

"Okay, Ali," Emma said, doing a terrible impression of a drumroll. "What's yours?"

"Uhh, I don't have a greatest irrational fear. I mean, I get nervous, and some of the things that give me anxiety aren't rational. I know I won't have a life or death experience when I do public speaking, but I still feel my heart beating as if an angry mob is chasing me. But we all have them. Everyone. I don't believe a single person on this planet is immune to the phenomenon of the illogical fear."

Ali still did laps in the water as she spoke, slowly circling the girls.

"I think our fears serve a purpose, though. I think we're supposed to have them. They act as the stepping stones to conquering mountains of unknown fears in the future. Overcoming them will help to set us along one of the paths we belong on; the paths that are clouded from our vision because our doubts have grown so tall. You have them so you can overcome them, and…grow."

Ali finished with a shrug of her shoulders. The girls all nodded their heads in unison.

"Okay, somebody help me find a worm," Emma shouted.

Everyone laughed. They stayed on the lake until the sun started to set and began casting a golden halo on the tree tops. With pruned skin, the girls got a fire ready and sat encircled around its bright flames. They held sticks with marshmallows over the fire, cooking them until they became crisp and golden from the flames. Maya's caught fire and burnt. She frantically tried to blow it out, but it was too late. It sizzled and fell to the ground. Maya stomped out the small fire and began anew.

Lying on their backs on the grass, they ate s'mores and looked up at the clear sky. Winter took in the stars, the steady breaths of those around her, the peace which filled that moment. She felt dwarfed by the star's absolute magnitude, yet she could not help but stare, couldn't help but imagine herself among the stars. And then it came to her. It was only as clear as a whisper on the softly blowing wind. But it was loud enough for her to hear. She knew what she needed to do. Winter Wright finally had a plan.

CHAPTER THREE—THE BEGINNING

The weekend passed by too quickly for Maya, Emma, Ali, Sienna, and Winter. Huddled at their cars, they told one another to call more often, to get jobs closer to each other. After twenty minutes, the other girls slipped into their vehicles and waved as they drove down the lane away from the lake house. Sienna and Winter stood waving at the edge of the driveway. Once the cars rounded the bend, Sienna grabbed her friend.

"I have an idea for you. It might seem a little out there, but I think it could be brilliant."

"Oookay," Winter said, amazed at how strong Sienna's grip was on her arm.

"I know you've been saving for years. You hardly ever buy anything. I can tell from your duffle bag and your car," Sienna's eyes fluttered across Winter, "and your jacket that you still don't spend a ton.

"Is the point of this to make me not like you? Because if so, let me tell you that you're succeeding spectacularly."

Sienna smiled and took her friends' hand. "No. I remember when we were in college together you were always hanging up pictures of the places you wanted to go one day. You've been out of the country once, right?"

Winter nodded her head. She was only four at the time she'd gone to the Bahamas with her family. All she could remember was being afraid that the dolphins would carry her away and give her to the sharks as ransom for not eating other dolphins.

"Why don't you go somewhere? Sublet that dirt cheap apartment of yours and go. Just go."

"My lease is up at the end of the month," Winter's voice trailed off with the quietness of possibility.

"Even better. Let it go, put your stuff in storage, and go on an adventure."

15

Winter stood transfixed as the words of her closest friend washed over her. Could she pack up and just go? Sienna was right. Winter had worked throughout high school and college. Her savings had grown steadily over the years. The words Winter heard last night while she lay beneath the stars came back to her.

"Maybe you're right. When we were lying next to the campfire, I realized something. I know what the next step for my life needs to be."

Sienna's eyes widened with anticipation as she waited to hear Winter's revelation. "Tell me," she said.

"I can't live in fear any more. My fears have ruled my choices for too long and I need to overcome them."

Sienna nodded her head vigorously, agreeing with Winter's words.

Winter inhaled deeply and said, "Growing up, whenever something outside of my control happened, a crude or upsetting comment, I folded into myself, as if making myself physically smaller would lessen the blow. But I've been doing that for too long now. Last night I woke up and realized I'm barely existing. I mean, who hides in a kitchen pantry because they're afraid of a few words? Have I lost myself so much?"

Winter chewed on her lip as she continued.

"I've let my fears dictate what I do for longer than they have any right to, and now they've become me. If I do this, that will be my hope for the trip, to get rid of as many illogical fears as possible. To conquer them, so that they're the ones who're barely existing, and not me. I don't want to be a stranger to my life anymore."

Sienna looked as if she might cry or burst into yells of encouragement.

"Where do I go?" Winter asked, incredulous. The words didn't feel real to her, but the sheer charge of them did.

"Anywhere. Look at those maps that you had sitting on every free space on your desk or that ratty globe you showed me when we were kids, and pick one."

Winter hugged Sienna. "Thank you, Sienna. Thank you."

"Tell me how the planning goes. I don't want to miss out on any of it!"

Winter let go of Sienna and got into the driver's seat. She cranked down the window with minimal effort this time.

"I'll see you soon, hopefully. Tell me when you're planning your next visit home."

Sienna smiled and wrapped the light sweater she wore around herself. "Definitely! Hopefully, it'll be soon."

Winter waved to Sienna's figure at the end of the drive until she could no longer see her. As trees rolled past her rearview mirrors, Winter thumped her steering wheel. A popular song had come on the radio; one she couldn't quite make out because of the static level. Winter started contemplating what a trip abroad might entail. Was it only a rambunctious idea? Was it something that only characters in movies and novels set out to do? Or could it be a possibility? Winter thought about all the things she'd wanted to do since she was young. The list was long. She'd wanted to be a dancer, study abroad, travel continents. The list grew and expanded to the point that Winter couldn't remember everything.

The only thing that connected them was her fear, which had kept her from trying any of her dreams at all. Her fears had lived under the guise of reason. She'd come up with excuse after excuse why now or then wasn't the time to seek out her hopes. Winter decided right there, as the wind blew into the car, tossing her thick, coiled hair around her face, that she would go. She would find a way to do it. She wanted to live fearlessly and to do that she was going to have to face her fears. Winter stopped into Mariah's Home Bakery on the way home. She picked up a chocolate cream pie and went over to her parent's house where she found her sister in the backyard, feet up, reading a magazine.

"How was your weekend? Did you jump into any cupboards?" Ella asked, without looking up from the pages.

"You are hysterical. Where is everybody?"

"Out."

"Obviously, but where?"

"I don't know, on errands or something."

Winter sat down on the edge of Ella's chair.

"Well, I brought this pie as a sorry for skipping out the other night. One piece is for you, for helping me escape."

"Aww, thanks. You can hide in the pantry from Anna Herald as often as you like if it means I get chocolate pie."

Ella popped the lid off the pie and breathed in deeply.

"I don't know how they do it. If I worked there, they'd have nothing to sell to customers." Ella took her finger and swept up a pile of whipped cream. Her shoulders began to shake with laughter.

"What?" Winter asked.

"I'm sorry," she said, her nose scrunched, her eyes watering. "I just can't believe you hid in a pantry from your arch-nemesis." She was fanning her face now. "I mean, who even has those?"

"All the advanced, mature people of the world. Well, if you're done laughing," Winter joked, "I'm gonna head home. Tell our parents I stopped by."

"Sure. Why off so quickly?"

"Ella, I think I know what my next step is."

"What do you mean?" She asked, eating another dollop of cream.

"I'll tell you more when I've figured out what I'm doing. Oh! But I might need your help, okay? Enjoy the pie."

Winter walked to the front yard and drove home. She moved into her parking spot slowly, trying not to scrape the crooked parker's car. Once inside, she grabbed an old notebook, ripped out a sheet of paper and sat in the middle of her apartment floor. If she was going to leave on a trip to conquer some of her deepest fears, then she needed to name them to face them. She had to stop avoiding them, living under the delusion that they'd disappear on their own. Winter rolled the backend of the pen against her lips.

"Well, water is definitely one," she said aloud as she scribbled black ink across the white paper. She wrote a couple more fears down, and then they began flowing from her pen. "Singing in public. Can't forget that one."

At Winter's ninth grade choir recital, she had a solo. Almost everyone she knew sat in the packed auditorium, including Anna Herald. When the music led into Winter's part, no sound came from her lips. Her mouth hung open in anticipation of notes that never emerged. The only sound that could be heard in the dead silence of the auditorium was the slight croak of fear in Winter's throat. As hard as she tried not to look at Anna Herald, Winter's eyes landed on her. On Anna's face, from cheek to cheek, was a snide smile.

Winter felt hot tears come to her eyes, but she blinked them back ferociously. The pianist led Winter into her solo again. Winter averted her eyes from Anna and opened her quivering mouth once more, but nothing came. On the pianist's third attempt, laughter started to break out from among the other choir members.

The instructor's eyes became so wide that Winter feared they might pop out of her head. Winter scuttled off the stage as quickly as she could, but her legs tangled in her black robes. Her tears had blurred her vision so badly that she ended up crying in the boys' bathroom for an hour. It was her sister Ella that thought to look in the men's room. Since that night, Winter promised not to put herself in that fear inducing position again.

Soon, the paper's barren surface became filled with black markings. 'My List of Illogical Logical Fears' was written neatly across the top of the page. Some fears were based in truth, but Winter had let them expand to unreal proportions through her worries. When she finished, she lifted the pen from the paper and stared down at it, at the list that she'd allowed to hold her back, at the things that she'd let take her place in her life. The list stopped at fifteen, and to Winter the number seemed insurmountable. All she'd done was write down her fears and already she could feel her heart beating harder. She ran her finger lightly over the paper and read out her fears.

My List of Illogical Logical Fears
1. Bodies of water (and being lost underwater).
2. Heights that are above my own.

3. The future. Where am I going?
4. Singing in public.
5. Being alone in a foreign country where I don't know anyone.
6. Getting rejected and being vulnerable.
7. Not finding true happiness.
8. Looking and sounding incredibly stupid.
9. Getting out of my comfort zone.
10. Self-consciousness growing larger in my life.
11. Failing to find the road that leads to the path I'm meant to be on in life.
12. Never accomplishing my dreams.
13. Reliving the sadness of my past.
14. Living a small life.
15. Having hate find me again.

Winter went to her front closet and began to search for the globe she'd had since she was a kid. It had gold thumbtacks stuck into the places she'd dreamt of traveling to one day. Some had been put in the middle of oceans, but Winter ignored those pins her young fingers had once eagerly placed down. Parts of the globe were completely covered in gold. Winter folded her legs and sat turning the earth in her slender hands, noticing the scratches and dents from the times she'd dropped it.

It used to sit on her father's desk in his study. As a little girl she often snuck into his office, grabbed the globe, and took it upstairs to her bedroom. With her abundance of childhood imagination, Winter pretended she was an ancient traveler setting sail to explore the world. She always tried to sneak it back before he realized it was missing.

Her father would play along, pretending not to notice its absence from his desk. When her parents drove away from dropping her off at college, Winter walked to her dorm room to unpack with a stomach full of nerves. There, at the bottom of one of her boxes was the globe with a note.

I think you've gotten more use out of this than I have. Can't wait to see where you end up. Love you, Dad.

Winter hugged the old globe to her body for a moment before she anxiously checked her savings account. It was barely enough for a global trot. One ticket, maybe two. Depending on where she went and her accommodations. Winter believed she could make that time stretch. *Maybe that will be enough.*

Winter decided to give herself a solid three months' time to figure her life out; she would have ninety days before life's more realistic burdens came calling for her. She had three months to confront her deepest fears. Three months to begin existing.

"Three months," she repeated to herself, "I'm ready to meet my life."

CHAPTER FOUR—ADVENTURE CALLS

Winter picked up the globe and stood against her window. It was early. The sun's bright rays were still rising on Hill Lane. To Winter, it seemed as if the whole town was sleeping, as if she and the sun were the only ones awake. Winter knew if her plan was going to work she would need Ella's help, so she picked up her phone and dialed her sister's number.

"Can you explain how the flight benefits work?" Winter asked.

"I can…" Ella responded.

"Hmph, Ella, will you explain to me how the benefits work?"

"Why, yes. Of course!" Winter rolled her eyes at her older sister. Only a year and three months separated their ages, but Ella milked every opportunity to remind Winter that she was the younger sister.

"At my airline, employees' parents fly free or at a reduced price, and we get two companion slots. People use it for spouses or relatives. Because you are my only sister, I have chosen you. I thought I might give the other spot to Anna Herald. What do you think?"

"I'm laughing so hard," Winter said in a deadpan voice, but Ella just kept going. "On international flights you only have to pay taxes. One of my friends recently flew to Scotland for one hundred dollars. One hundred dollars and she sat in first class! Can you believe that? I'm going to go all over the world! I have the best job in existence."

"That doesn't even sound real," Winter said.

"I know, but it is. The only hang-up is this: you can only get on a flight if there are open seats since you haven't paid full price. So you could be waiting ten minutes or days. It depends. I know you can be uptight, so understand that flying non-reservation is the opposite of having your plans set. It might put a wrench in the middle of your itinerary. So don't have an anxiety attack if that happens. Be ready to have to fly somewhere else if you can't get on a plane."

Winter recoiled at the thought of being stranded in a foreign airport with no destination or point of return.

"I'll give you the login information. You need to do a bit of paperwork, but that's simple. With the login, you can check the flight loads to see if there are empty seats and register for your ticket. After you do that, you'll be in the system. When you leave for your flight, just go to the kiosk at the airport and print off your temporary ticket. You'll turn the old one in for a new ticket at your gate if there's a seat available for you."

"That doesn't sound too hard."

"It isn't. Where are you going?"

"Not sure yet, but wherever I end up my goal will be to face my fears. You know more than anyone else how much they've taken over my life."

"Maybe lots of people run into pantries during house parties." Ella teased. Then she cleared her throat and said, "I have a question for you, though."

"What is it?" Winter asked.

There was a pause and then Ella asked, "Why do you dislike Anna Herald so much?"

Winter rarely dwelled on the grounds of her disliking Anna. Anna Herald had harassed Winter nearly every day, but there were two distinct experiences which made Winter harbor life-long resentment towards her bully. Anna was part of the reason for 'The Unspeakable Day,' which Winter seldom mentioned.

The incidents leading up to that dreadful day, and those that followed, were the reasons Anna had become Winter's bane. Winter referred to the other event as her 'Grand Failure.' It was the last time Winter had been subjected to Anna's antics, but the memory clung to Winter like dead weight on a sinking boat.

"I'll tell you another time," Winter said.

"All right. Oh! One last thing."

"What is it? Another scathing remark?"

"I'm happy for you, Winter. I'm glad you're doing this."

"Thanks, Ella," Winter said, taken pleasantly aback.

"Okay, I need to go. My show is back on."

Winter laughed and sat back in disbelief. One hundred dollars to go abroad. Being on the benefits meant that Winter's budget had just grown exponentially, from implausibility to realistic possibility. She still wasn't sure how many places she could afford to go, or how long she would be able to stay. *Perhaps until my money runs out, or as long as the place I'm in is pushing me towards my fears*, Winter thought. She turned the earth in her hands and glanced down at the gold pin beneath her forefinger. Winter had held the globe so many times that she was familiar with its grooves. So when she raised her hand, she knew what country lay beneath her finger.

There in chipped, aged paint was the green island of Ireland. Winter felt her heart thump a bit harder in her chest. Images of stone castles and the Irish Sea began flooding her mind's eye. She didn't know if the images she conjured up were true to life or not, but the idea of Ireland made her open up her computer and start dreaming. Her screen filled with pictures of lush green land, cobbled streets, rugged and towering black cliffs, and bridges suspended above turquoise waters. Belfast, in Northern Ireland and Dublin, the heart of the Irish Republic, seemed to be the places that travelers were rhapsodizing.

Winter pushed her chair away from her computer. She didn't want to make a payment for a room in case she couldn't get on the flight, but she knew herself. She had to make a move before she came up with a convincing reason not to. She booked her airplane ticket for three weeks from that morning, and found a list of hotels in the Belfast area she could walk to once in the city. In two weeks, her lease would be up. The lease paper sat blank on her desk, in need of her signature. Winter eyed her living space.

An old chair sat against her far wall. Her day bed was beneath one of the smaller windows with her messy white linen thrown across it haphazardly. The tip of her sheets touched the un-vacuumed floor. Packing up the apartment wasn't going to take long. So Winter stood, grabbed the lease paper, and began to pack the belongings of the last two years of her life in that apartment. The next evening, she drove over to her parent's house for dinner and shared her new plan. Christopher and Marie Wright were skeptical but supportive.

"You're positive you want to do this?" Her mother asked as she bent over her garden pulling dark pink radishes from the dirt bed.

"I am. I already called my boss at the consignment shop. She said if I come back and still want to work less than part-time at the shop, she'll try to help."

Her mother's eyes grew.

"Mom, I'm coming back. I'll be traveling for a few months. You won't even notice."

"I'd feel better if you had a real ticket. What if you get stranded?" She asked, digging up the soil as she pulled at a deep rooted plant.

"I'll just have to use my critical thinking skills," Winter quipped. "Besides, flying on the benefits is the only way I can afford it. If I do have an emergency, I'll have enough to buy a ticket home right away."

"When do you leave?" Her father asked. He stood next to her mother holding a blue umbrella over her head. A light rain had started falling that morning. It was a gray, bleary day. Beads of clear water dripped down the umbrella onto the plants beneath.

"The first week of next month. The first week of May. I want to get my things into storage. Can I stay here for my last week in the states?"

"Of course you can," her mother said, her voice cracking a bit.

Winter hugged her parents and assured them she'd be fine. She drove back home, and her mind wandered. *What will the next three months have in store for me?* She genuinely hoped her reassuring words to her family were true.

***

The days leading up to Winter's departure were a haze. The reality that she was leaving had not sunk in yet. From the moment she'd decided 'yes,' her life felt like it had been set ablaze. Plans came to fruition. Her apartment was packed; she'd worked her last day at the consignment shop, eaten as many desserts from Mariah's Home Bakery as possible, and tried to convince herself that this was in fact happening and that she could release her fears. A couple days before her departure flight, a package came for Winter at her parent's house. Ella tossed the brown parcel on the foot of Winter's childhood bed.

"Special Delivery," she called out as the package made its landing.

"Oh, thanks, I didn't think I ordered anything else." Winter said as she wrapped her fingers around a string that held the brown paper together. She pulled and the string unraveled, letting the paper fall to reveal a light purple box. Winter picked up the box and shook it.

"It's not Christmas, open it," Ella said.

Winter peeled back the lid and inside she found a journal and a stack of letters bound in the same string as the package. Two sticky notes lay on top of the letters. Written on one in bold blue lettering were the words, DO NOT OPEN. She looked up at her sister who smiled slyly down at her.

"You know what this is?"

"Of course I do," Ella said as she walked towards the door. "And make sure you bring me something good back," she added before gently closing the bedroom door. Winter recognized her closest friend's handwriting on the note. The package was from Sienna. Winter's eyes moved to the other sticky note and read the words written on them for her.

Winter, this journal is for you. I know how you process the world around you. As you journey across the world, try to remember as much of it as you can. The stack of letters is from all the people in your life. There are words of encouragement and wisdom (from the older crowd, of course) and words of laughter and hope. The letters are to give you courage as you face your fears and conquer the illogical. You can't open them until you leave, until you know it's time to hear a voice from home.

Good luck, your friend Sienna

Winter held up the stack of letters, amazed at how many words Sienna could fit onto one sticky note. She ran a hand over the journal. It was a deep blue color with an old proverb etched on the front in white, curved lettering:

"Just when the caterpillar thought the world was over, it became a butterfly."
—Anonymous.

Winter pulled the book up to her chin and flipped through the hundreds of blank pages. They fluttered past her, a blur of white background and blue lines. Empty. Anticipating. Waiting for her to put a pen to their smooth surfaces and make life out of nothing. That's what writing sometimes felt like to Winter, giving presence and breath to things that otherwise would never have had the chance to rise into existence. Her hand hovered over the pages for a moment. Then she turned, grabbed a pen, and started writing her first entry.

I'm leaving in a couple days. It hasn't quite hit me yet. My friends have been asking me how I feel about going, and there's one thought that passes through my mind when they ask me that question. One of the things that scares me the most is imagining my life five years from now and seeing that it's still the same, that I've not changed or moved at all. I don't want to live a 'What If Life' anymore. I don't want to look back at my life with regret-filled wonder. I don't want to ask myself 'What if I'd been brave enough to chase my dreams?' or 'What if I'd been brave enough to stop living my life ruled by my fears?' I don't want a What If Life. I want an 'I Did Life.' I did chase my hopes. I did live in spite of fear. I did try those dreams and fail at some. I Did Live. I can't live a lukewarm existence anymore, a 'barely there' life. So, here is to seeking a bigger life.

Until then, Winter

***

The day before Winter left she was unbearably nervous. She lay awake in the twilight hours of the night. In less than six hours she'd be going to the airport to fly to another continent where she'd unearth her fears. Winter had decided that if she couldn't get a seat to Ireland, she'd just pick another country. Either way, Winter wanted to get off the continent she was on. As she lay there alone in the dark quiet of her childhood bedroom, she could sense a slight shift in her heart. Winter knew that whatever transformation was coming would not be easy. But the chance Winter had could be life-changing, and to her, that was worth the risk

CHAPTER FIVE—THE PAST RETURNS

Inside O'Hare International Airport, passengers rushed to catch their flights. Men in suits pushed past people, forcefully making their way through the crowded terminal. Winter moved out of the way of a family of six shuffling across the wide, expansive hall. She had already checked in at the kiosk and printed off her temporary pass.

Winter looked down at her ticket, which she'd crushed from the pressure of her hand. Her nervousness exuded from her being, claiming the integrity of her ticket. If she could get on her flight to New Jersey, from there, she would fly to Belfast. Winter rolled her only bag of luggage to Terminal C. As the wheels clicked on the linoleum floor, it sounded strangely loud to Winter. She only had the one bag. Winter packed as light as her needs allowed. Gate 9 was mildly full. With sweaty palms, she walked up to the counter, her bottom lip lodged between her teeth.

"Excuse me? Hi, I'm flying non-reservation to New Jersey. Are there any seats available?" Winter managed to say the entire sentence in one anxious breath.

The woman at the desk looked up at Winter from the bright computer screen below. She hit a few buttons and told Winter to hold on.

"There are a few seats. Can I have the ticket you printed off at the kiosk?" She asked, her voice firm.

"Yes," Winter said breathlessly. She fidgeted as she passed the rumpled paper over the counter. Before setting it down, she tried to smooth it out on her green jacket. The woman eyed Winter, and then the ticket, before looking back down at the screen. After hitting another series of buttons, she started to speak again.

"Here's your ticket. Enjoy your flight."

Winter stared at the woman for a moment, confused as to why the attendant didn't seem as thrilled as she felt. She'd just provided the first stepping stone to Winter beginning her journey.

"It does look like the flight might be grounded, though. The weather is getting choppy. I'm not sure if you'll make your connecting flight at the New Jersey airport," she said without making eye contact. On the taxi ride over, much to Winter's dismay, rain started to fall.

Her chest deflated. "Can I sleep in the airport? I mean if I get stuck?"

The woman raised an eyebrow at her. Winter took her ticket and muttered an inaudible thank you. She chose a low, gray seat by the window. The clouds outside were beginning to darken. They rolled in the sky, threatening to end Winter's trip before it began. Winter tried to convince herself that the sky would clear, and the flight would take off to Newark, New Jersey at any moment. *I will make it, even if that means I have to go to every gate in this airport*, she chanted internally.

Winter peered around the terminal, noticing full bags and tilted heads. She began to pull at a fraying string on that weathered old jacket, a distraction while she waited for news about the flight. A worn hole was above her left pocket. She was cautious when she put anything into that pocket. Too many times before she let things slip into the hole, never to be seen again. Winter envisioned boxes filled with the items she'd lost over the years. As she examined the weathered coat, the memory of why she wanted it came to the surface. Winter tried to push the unpleasant thought away, but the past had already returned...

"You don't fit into it. It's three sizes too big for you," her mother, Marie Wright, had said.

"I'll fit, I promise. I need it. That coat is supposed to be mine. It was made for me." When Winter saw that her words had little effect, she switched tactics. "It is my birthday..." Twelve-year-old Winter pleaded with her hands folded in front of her chest.

"Why do you want a camouflage jacket so badly?" Her mother had asked.

Winter didn't answer, but they left the store with an oversized jacket Winter promised she'd grow into, and she did. She'd worn it ever since. It was no longer the lively color it once was. Now the patches blended, forming a faded dark green color. Her camouflage jacket no longer held the distinction of being camouflage. It was entirely unable to serve the purpose once intended. As she sat in the terminal, the memory of the warm summer morning that hate entered boldly into Winter Wright's life came flooding back. She'd seen veiled messages of prejudice before this encounter, but this day was different. Despite the barriers, the memory seeped through the cracks in her facade.

Winter had just finished the sixth grade. Her best friend at the time, Leyla, yelled out to her. "Come on! Keep up!" Leyla's long hair whipped behind her as she peddled. They pulled into Leyla's driveway telling jokes and planning their night. They leapt off their bikes with the freedom that could only be felt in the summer months.

Winter and Leyla's entire summer break consisted of taking bike rides down streets with outstretched arms, playing cards, having four-night sleepovers, and dreading the start of school in the fall. Winter loved spending time at Leyla's, and they reveled in their summertime adventures. Winter wheeled her bike to the back of her friend's house, as she usually did, and set it against the chain linked fence. And then she saw him.

As Winter came around the front of the house, she noticed a man standing across the street. His thick arms were folded hard across his broad chest. Tendons pulsed beneath his skin. Winter began to nibble on her bottom lip. She had seen this man before because every time she came over he made himself visible. His presence was an undeniable force, but today was different.

Sometimes when Winter came, he'd be working outside on a vintage car that sat in his garage. Upon noticing her, he would roll from underneath the powder blue hooded vehicle, drop his tools to the ground, and with his eyes fixed on Winter, he'd enter his house, slamming the door hard behind him.

Other times he would come out and glare, but return to his work, shaking his head back and forth as he did so. That day, however, he didn't adhere to his usual routine. Instead of watching from behind open blinds, he stood openly at the end of his driveway and faced her. The atmosphere transformed as he positioned himself parallel to Winter on the street. The air became heavy, steeped in tension. Winter had thought him an odd man, but today there was something about him that made the hairs on Winter's arms stand up.

And when they locked eyes, something about his gaze made Winter feel fear, pure and unadulterated fear. The sun beat down heavily on Winter's back. She wanted to get inside. The concrete road was the only thing that separated him from her. He opened his mouth, and a string of lowly spoken words escaped.

"Black people coming here...all the same...destroy everything...just need to leave...disgusting." Winter only caught some of his words, but then he raised his voice and said clearly, with a force that felt like a physical blow to Winter, "I hate them."

She cowered under his gaze, turning away from the look that permeated his face and the words that spilled from his mouth. She could still feel his eyes on her small frame as she retreated, burning holes into her skin.

Leyla returned from the backyard, unaware of what was taking place. Winter walked quickly into her home and ran upstairs to her friend's bedroom with wobbling legs. Sweat trickled down the smooth skin of her forehead. Winter was unsure whether her perspiration was induced by heat or terror. She tried to ignore the fear in her gut, the dread she felt rising like bile in her throat. She looked down at her brown skin and wondered what was wrong with it, what about it could make that man hate her. For a few glorious, strained minutes Winter pretended nothing had happened. She attempted to forget about the man across the street. But then Leyla stopped what she was doing and looked into Winter's dark eyes.

"You know that man…the one who lives in the red and white house across the street?" She asked.

"Hmm," Winter said, barely opening her mouth, not wanting to talk about him.

"He came over yesterday to yell at my parents…about you." Winter could feel Leyla's eyes on her.

"Oh…" Winter said, looking at her friend, yet wishing deeply she could avoid her eyes.

"Yeah," she continued, "he told them that we shouldn't have you over, or let you in our house because you're black. He started to shout."

She began to act out the conversation between the man and her parents, the words shared.

"And then he said, 'Don't let that nigger in your house or on our street!' And then my parents told him that he needed to leave."

Leyla's eyes got wide at the conclusion of her words. Winter sat in silence. But her heart rapidly beat in her chest. Her eyes became hot, threatening to unleash a stream of tears. Winter took a shivering breath, but it did nothing to abate the influx of trepidation. Leyla changed the subject, asking Winter if she wanted to play another game of cards. After a while, she laughed and made no mention of the man, or the story she had told, and Winter wished she too could forget so easily.

As Winter left that hot afternoon, she did so cautiously. She looked out to make sure the man was inside his house. Only then did she put on her helmet and jump on her bike. Winter quickly pumped her legs to disappear around the corner of Leyla's street. She heard a car door open behind her and rode the bike harder.

Once on the main street, she looked over her shoulder to make sure he wasn't there, and when she turned her head, the bike hit a rock. Winter flew forward onto the rough asphalt, scraping her cheek and skinning both of her knees badly. Blood dripped down her legs from the fresh cuts. Winter's tears began to fall, but she swept them away and hurriedly climbed back onto her bike. The blood from her cuts trickled onto her light blue socks, staining them, but Winter didn't stop moving her legs until she was more than halfway home.

That was the day Winter learned about prejudice. Winter realized the feelings she invoked in some people: loathing, anger, and hate. Winter was young, simply a girl riding a bike in the freedom of summer, when this reality solidified for her. Now she was keenly aware of the truth that had been laid bare, and the innate belief of goodness she had in people began to dwindle.

Her world changed that afternoon. Though there had been whispers throughout her young life, that the skin she resides in was not good enough, that day she couldn't avoid it. Hate had found her in a place she thought she was safe. The world settled into startling clarity for Winter. Everything in her life shifted that hot summer day, just one day before her twelfth birthday. Little by little Winter began closing out a bit of life. Something significant happened to Winter when she learned that she was the object of someone's unfettered, and undeserving, disdain.

The string Winter played with on her old jacket broke between her fingers. Winter released her bottom lip from between her teeth. She still bore the scar on her left knee from her fall. Her body had done its best to repair the broken skin, but the real wound still festered within her. The true scars, though unseen, bore deeper than the wounds on her skin; trauma to the soul takes far longer to heal.

Winter looked down at the gift she still wore, the jacket she pleaded for her mother to buy. As a young girl she wouldn't cry about it, because she didn't want to feel the pain, but it pressed upon her nonetheless, like stones being thrown onto her chest. She didn't cry that day, nor any day since.

In a way this method of avoidance helped, but it also meant that Winter kept other emotions at bay, and was blocked from experiencing their full depth as well. Every time she avoided this memory, another rock was thrown on top of the others. Winter's chest felt tight, as if it was under a mountain of pressure. She took in a shallow breath. It amazed her how much the memory still affected her, how much it still touched her. But of course she still felt the weight of her first encounter with hate, because it changed who Winter Wright was, and who she would become.

And now just a thought could send her back and make her feel the handlebars of the bike beneath her palms, the fresh air that seemed to choke her. Almost thirteen years later, in a busy airport terminal about to make her way across the world, and she still found it hard to breathe. She knew it wouldn't be easy to change the way she'd lived for most of her life, in fearful wait of hate finding her, but she needed to give it a chance.

Winter wanted to defeat all of her fears, but it was her fear of hate that had invaded her life the most. And if she could overcome the others, perhaps that meant she could find a way to defeat the worst of them all, the one that had stopped her from living. Winter could no longer stand isolation and pain as her lonely companions. She had to try to stop shutting life out in pursuit of the protection of her heart.

Winter picked at her fingernails with one leg crossed over the other, and tried to get comfortable. She left her tin of snacks on the kitchen counter, and imagined Ella taking the container and enjoying its contents in one sitting. Her stomach began to grumble. She placed a hand over her gut, embarrassed.

"All right, Group A may begin boarding."

The woman's voice came from the speakers above. Winter sat up straighter. *It's beginning*, she thought. The rain outside had not stopped, but it didn't need to. It just couldn't get any heavier. Winter waited, leg bouncing up and down in anticipation, and then her group was called. She jumped up, luggage in hand, and took a place in line. Winter could see the jet way, the white walls, and flat carpet leading to the plane. She gave her boarding pass to the attendant, watched it get scanned with the red, striped lights, and wheeled her luggage towards the hall, her heart beating wildly.

Winter charged down the jet way and got onto the plane. She found her seat towards the back and heaved her luggage into the overhead bin. With wet palms, she sat down and clicked her seat buckle together. Outside the small window, Winter could see planes preparing to take off into the clouds. Against her hopes and expectations, the rain was getting worse.

"We have a small problem. The weather is getting worse. We are going to stay on the taxiway until we hear otherwise." A collective clamor of disappointment filled the cabin. Winter anxiously tapped the surface of her seat belt.

"I have to make it off the ground," she whispered, unsure of who she was talking to or when the fire to move had begun to burn so fiercely inside of her. Winter started to conceive a new plan when the voice of the captain filled the space.

"We are third in line. Prepare for take-off."

Winter beamed. *Prepare for takeoff*, she repeated silently. *I'm coming for you, fears*. She dug inside her bag and pulled out the journal Sienna had sent her. Winter had rewritten her list of fears inside its pages. Number five (Being alone in a foreign country) and nine (Getting out of my comfort zone) stuck out to Winter. But then she set down the journal, her attention taken by the plane bounding down the runway.

It rose steadily from the ground and ascended into the misty clouds. Past the glass of her window, lightning flashed across the sky, making it appear boundless, vast, and terrifying. Her eyes moved to the strikes of lightning running through the sky, creating shadows and pockets of light across the coming darkness. She leaned her head against her seat, her soft hair creating a pillow. In less than twelve hours, she'd be in Ireland.

CHAPTER SIX—PERFECT TIMING

Winter woke up to a light tapping on her shoulder. "Plane's landed," the person in the seat next to her said. He stood above her, grabbing suitcases from the overhead bin. Winter bolted upright in her seat. She grabbed both hand rests, the tips of her fingers pressed into the bland colored fabric. For a moment, Winter dreamt she'd missed her connecting flight in New Jersey. But as the fog of sleep lifted, she remembered boarding the flight from Newark International Airport bound for Ireland.

"We're here!" She said, full of relief. The man stared at her with a slight crease in his brow. Winter composed herself as best she could and eagerly pulled her luggage down. She stepped off the plane and into Belfast International Airport. She walked by tall glass windows, colorful ads, and Irish shops. Winter stopped at the first information desk she saw.

"Hi, are there any hotels or hostels nearby?" Winter inquired, barely able to contain her excitement and coinciding terror. A woman whose name tag read Aileen gave Winter a bright smile.

"Oh, yes, there are taxis just outside that will take you wherever you need to go. If you're staying in Belfast, I'm sure you'll be going near the city center. Make sure to have a look at the pamphlets." She lifted her hand, pointed behind Winter, and said, "On the back wall we have brochures of tours you can take while you're here. Hope you have a lovely time."

Winter turned and saw a wall filled with pamphlets. She picked up one of every kind. As Aileen said, there were tours of Ireland's coast and countryside. Folded books featured Ireland's most iconic castles and museums, and stacks were dedicated to restaurants and pubs. Winter's hands were full by the time she made it to the street. A line of buses and taxis sat in front. She walked over to a black cab. The man faced the parking lot.

"H...H...Hello, are you available to drive me?"

The man had a broad smile and silvering hair. "Where to?" He asked warmly in an Irish accent.

"I'm not sure actually," Winter said. "I'm looking for a place to stay."

"There are loads of hotels close by, inside the city center and surrounding it. It won't be hard to find a place. Quite the adventurer, eh? Coming to a new country with only your bag on your back!"

"Adventurer, crazy person, I'm pretty sure the two are interchangeable," Winter said.

The man smiled and placed Winter's bags into the back of the cab. She hopped in and closed the door. Winter felt elated as the lightness that coincides with gratitude lifted her spirits.

"Where else are you going while you're here?" The driver asked Winter.

"I don't know where I'll go next, but I'm gonna be here for a few weeks or more."

"You mean you came just to see Ireland?" A smile began to show on his acutely shocked face.

"Belfast and Dublin," Winter said with confidence that surprised her.

"That's wonderful!"

Winter leaned forward in her seat and said, "I can hardly believe I'm here. Are there any places I should be sure to visit?"

The man started listing off so many sites and country sides that Winter could barely keep track. What she could remember was Crown's Pub and the Titanic museum.

"We have a saying around here about that ship: The Irish built it, and the British sank it," he said.

He dropped her off at a hotel he was sure would have openings. Before walking in, Winter stared at the curving lanes and trees in full bloom. Pubs sat on street corners, and the welcoming scent of hearty Irish food poured out onto the road. The sun was shining, but Belfast was chilly. Winter buttoned up her jacket, smiled softly at the scene before her, and went inside.

At the front desk Winter learned the hotel was booked. One of the employees told her to go down the road. There were at least four other hotels and a few hostels. Winter marched outside, still on a positive high. But when the fourth hotel didn't have a single empty room, the other hotels above Winter's price range, and the hostels full, she started to panic.

"Why didn't I book something? Why am I such a fool?" She muttered to herself, collecting stares from passersby. She tripped over a break in the sidewalk, and the wheel on her suitcase snapped off. Winter moaned, threw her hands to her sides, and tried to contain her frustration. Her foot started to throb. She limped down the stone sidewalk, rolling her bag on one decently working wheel, wishing she'd opted for the more expensive four-wheeled suitcase. Winter wrapped her hand firmly around the handle of her suitcase and half-dragged, half-rolled it behind her tense figure.

After forty-five minutes, Winter still hadn't found a place, and she seriously contemplated curling up in a ball and rocking back and forth on the street. Every hostel, boutique, hotel—none had any available rooms, and the people she spoke to all pointed her further away from the city center.

When Winter felt she might have a breakdown, she walked into a place out of her price range just to see if they knew of anything with open rooms and lower prices. Inside, the hotel was plush; extravagant furnishings sat on gleaming hardwood floors, paintings covered every wall, and a chandelier hung from the ceiling. Winter hobbled through on her one good leg, her broken wheel clicked on the marble floor, echoing in the open space. A desk attendant dressed in black with perfectly coifed hair watched Winter's trek.

"Can you point me in the direction of a hotel with average affordability?"

"Yes, but you don't have to whisper," the woman said.

"Oh, right, sure. Okay," Winter said, awkwardly resting her face on her palms as she waited. The smooth desk was freshly polished, so Winter's elbows slipped, dropping her face onto the shiny surface of the desk. The oily print of Winter's chin glistened on the desk.

"I can clean that," Winter said, taking her jacket sleeve and wiping hastily.

"There's no need to do that," the woman said as Winter drug her sleeve across the desk. "Really, they wipe it very often."

"Oh, good," Winter said, slowly removing her arm and placing it at her side.

"There's a new guesthouse that opened rather recently. Keep walking down the lane. It's toward the end. I believe it's called The Gregory."

"Thank you!" Winter said. She turned and tried to walk outside with as much poise as was possible in her current circumstances.

Winter pressed on. She wanted to find a bed, a very large one, with fresh sheets, and more pillows than necessary. She walked down the lane and thought for certain there would never be an end to the street. And then she found her destination, a rich green yard enclosed by a pristine black fence connected to a place called The Gregory. She opened the gate and walked past red bricks stacked high and neatly. The windows started low to the ground and reached half the height of the building. Winter could see a quaint dining room through the clear, clean glass of the windows.

Winter pulled her bags inside the entryway and into the light of The Gregory. A woman sat at the front desk. She had dark brown hair and wore a mint colored sweater that almost matched the color of her eyes. Her voice was chipper and made Winter feel at home immediately. Calm poured over her tense body.

"I was wondering if you had any rooms available," Winter said, desperately hoping they would have something. As she spoke, Winter could hear a phone ring in a room behind the front desk.

"As a matter of fact we do. Is it just you?" She asked.

"Yes, just me."

"Ooh, we have one single room left." Mrs. Thompson's price for the room was ideal and made Winter want to scream out in happiness. "Would you like it?" She asked.

"That would be amazing, yes, yes I would," the words spilled from Winter's mouth in their haste to be heard.

"All right. How many nights?" Winter hadn't any idea.

"One week. Maybe more, but for now a week," she said.

"Let me get that squared away for you."

She hit a series of keys and asked for Winter's card, which she gladly handed over.

"One second, I'm new at this...ah, let me get my husband. Peter!"

She turned around, and as she did her husband emerged from behind the door, a large smile covering his face.

"Janette, we just got a call for our last single room!" He said.

"I just gave it to this young lady," she said, pointing her hand in Winter's direction.

Yes! Winter yelled inside.

"Oh, great, well, I'll let them know," he said.

He turned quickly on his heel and went back into the office. Winter could hear him pick up the receiver and start dialing.

"Perfect timing," Janette stated.

"I'd have to agree," Winter said with relief.

CHAPTER SEVEN—THE FIRST FEAR

Peter and Janette Thompson helped Winter carry her bags up the winding staircase. Winter's gaze was sporadic as she tried to capture all the beauty of this novel region.

"How long have you been open?"

"Only six weeks. We lived in the country for most of our married life, but I've wanted to have a bed and breakfast since I was young. It's also family run, which is nice. You'll meet our daughter, Lilly, tomorrow morning. She helps serve breakfast, among many other things, and our son is usually floating around here somewhere."

Janette handed a piece of thick, cream colored paper with maroon borders to Winter.

"This is the breakfast menu," she said.

"Wow, thanks," Winter said. As her eyes passed over the paper, her mouth began to water.

Porridge with Fresh Berry Compote
Ulster Fry with Sausage, Bacon, and Potato Bread
Mushrooms and Fried Eggs
Eggs Benedict
Scrambled Eggs with Smoked Salmon and Toast
Vegetarian Breakfast: Potato Bread, Pancakes, Mushrooms, and Beans

The menu had dishes that made Winter's stomach grumble. She could smell fresh bread baking downstairs. Peter unlocked her room door and set her belongings inside. Winter stepped into the bedroom.

"Let us know if you need anything," Janette said, closing the door with a warm grin on her face. Winter's room had high ceilings, sweeping windows, and the bed of her dreams. It looked as grand as a castle but was as inviting as her mother's home on a leisurely Sunday afternoon.

Winter opened her pitiful suitcase and began to unpack, surprised at how ordinary her first task was in a new country. Winter had no idea what to do next. She placed the blue notebook on her bed, and it flopped open to the page full of Winter's fears. Her nerves were still raging, but she'd done it, crossed the ocean. And now she was lying on a bed of fresh linen in Belfast. Winter stood and stretched. She raised her hands high above her head and glanced below at the street.

Across the way were houses nestled closely to one another. Bright lawns covered both sides of the sloping road. Winter went over to her wardrobe door and pulled it open. Treats filled the cabinet shelves. An electric tea pot, tea bags, and packaged cookies sat on the shelves. Winter picked up the kettle and filled it with water. She made herself a cup of tea as the afternoon sun shone into the room. Her eyelids drooped as she sipped on the tea.

Her jet-lagged body longed to sink into the bed and rest there for hours. But Winter was not going to allow herself to sleep away her first afternoon in Belfast. She sent a quick text to her family to let them know where she was staying before grabbing her bag. Winter buttoned up her green jacket and made her way down the stairs, a slight bounce in her step. Peter Thompson was placing books in the guesthouse sitting room. Warm afternoon light poured in through the uncovered windows.

"Are you going out?" He asked Winter, straightening the pile of books he'd set down.

"I thought I'd walk around the city, get acquainted," Winter said.

"There's a bus down the street that'll take you to the city center. You'll be able to find loads to do there."

He stood and reached his hands into his pocket. In his palm were three shining pounds that reflected the daylight. They hit Winter's hand with a thud. The coins felt heavy with the weight of history. They were a reminder to Winter of the island's former times, of the decades' long struggle of Ireland to escape British rule. After long warfare the free Republic of Ireland formed, while Northern Ireland remained part of the U.K. Winter thought about her own country's past, and the indelible and deep marks conflict leaves in its wake.

"Do you have these yet?" He asked, bringing Winter back to the present.

Winter felt dense for not getting her money converted at the airport.

"Uh, not yet," she muttered under her breath.

He started walking to the front desk, calling out his wife's name.

"Honey, do you have a few extra pounds?"

Janette searched her pockets. "I used the last ones. Let me ask Tobias."

She called up from the bottom of the winding staircase for her son. "He's always listening to music with his headphones on. Hold on a wee moment."

Minutes later she returned with coins in hand. "Here you are. Have fun and make sure you're back before curfew!" She said in jest.

"Thank you, I…I'll return this as soon as I get my money converted," Winter said as Peter Thompson placed more pounds in her hands.

Winter laughed, stunned by their kindness, and the natural warmth that emanated from their spirits. Mr. Thompson showed Winter the way to the bus. Outside the welcoming walls of the guesthouse, Winter was met with a gleaming, stark blue sky and full, white clouds. For a moment, Winter stood beneath the sun and breathed in cool, life invigorating air. She already felt more alive.

It was a short walk to the bus stop. After a few minutes, a bus rolled up, and Winter stepped on after a group of school girls. They laughed and talked about their excitement that school was over. They made plans for the weekend the whole bus ride. Winter smiled into her jacket. She remembered being that young, feeling that exuberant. They couldn't have been older than ten. Winter watched as they talked with otherworldly animation.

As joy filled their expressions, Winter looked on and pondered what it must be like to feel that sensation. Their joy seemed unreal to Winter. It had been so long since she'd experienced true joy, filled with depth and sincerity. She'd been happy, sure, but it sometimes felt to Winter that she wasn't living in true happiness, in joy. She could clearly recall the day it left her, the day it slipped from her grasp as she rode her bike away from that man's street.

Since that day she'd been running from hate, and her own hidden worry that the person she was born to be was not good enough. Every detail of that day was clear, but joy seemed unattainable, simply a faraway notion. Winter closed her eyes briefly and tried to recall the feeling, reclaim its being, but she wasn't able to. The memory of that distant day began to form, but Winter shivered the thought away and turned her attention outside the bus window.

Belfast in the early days of May was captivating to Winter. The city center was full of people dressed in sophisticated and fashionable clothing with shopping bags on their arms. To Winter, everyone seemed enamored with their companions as they strolled the busy, cobblestone streets. Belfast city hall sat in the distance, acting as a beautiful backdrop. Off the bus, Winter placed her chilled hands in her pockets. She didn't mind the cold, but she did want an umbrella.

A steady rain had begun, wetting the pavement. Winter ducked into the first shop she saw. Drops of water poured from the front of her aged coat. Winter adjusted herself in the entryway, shaking off the excess water with her palms. When she looked up, she caught the eyes of a man in a tweed coat with thinning gray hair staring at her.

"How would you like to go on a wee tour?" He asked enthusiastically.

"What gave me away?" Winter asked with a wide smile, her hands still buried in her pockets.

"You're in Belfast, and you don't have an umbrella or a raincoat!" He shouted.

"Oh, right," Winter said, shaking water off her shoulders. "You're selling a tour?"

"Indeed I am."

"I'd love to go. I don't know how else I'll see the country since I don't trust myself to drive here. I'm more than positive I'd go off a cliff. You don't mean right this minute, though," Winter said, glancing around the building she'd entered.

"We have tours almost every day. How long are you in Ireland?" He asked.

"Not sure yet, depends on how far my money stretches," Winter said, feeling a light twinge of adrenaline rush throughout her body. She was starting to sense how adventurous she was for the first time in her life.

"Well, take a look at this!" The man said cheerfully.

He pointed to a wall filled with pictures of Ireland's most glorious natural wonders. Winter's eyes fell upon cliff faces, clear, endless waters, and crisp skies. An image of a bridge suspended over water drew Winter's gaze. She recognized it from an Irish tourism website she'd found a few weeks earlier. Two of her fears stared back at her from the blotted paper. The man took notice of what she was looking at and began to speak.

"That is the Carrick-a-Rede Rope Bridge. It's almost one hundred feet in the air! It's a very popular tour."

"What is that tour called?" Winter asked. Her breath was short as she stared at the bridge, as she pictured herself a hundred feet in the air over rocky waters.

"That, my dear, is the Giant's Causeway tour. It's often called the eighth natural wonder of the world." He smiled.

"I'll take that one," Winter said straightaway, both proud and terrified at the prospect of facing her fears so soon into her trip. Something in her questioned whether or not she should buy a tour from the first person to offer, but she pushed the thought aside. Winter paid the man who passed her a yellow ticket stub.

"The bus will pick you up…uh…where are you staying?"

"The Gregory."

"It will come for you at The Gregory in the morning at nine a.m."

"Okay," Winter said, a smile reaching across her face. "I'll be ready."

CHAPTER EIGHT—THE CARRICK-A-REDE ROPE BRIDGE

Winter woke early the next morning charged for her day. She rewrote her list of fears from the blue notebook and placed the copy in her coat pocket. This afternoon she was going to take on new fears. The mere thought of facing her fear of heights sent electricity throughout her body. Her hand slid down the smooth dark wood of the banister on her way to breakfast. Winter could hear the soft clinking of china and smell the alluring scent of baking pastries.

The dining room had eight tables bathing in early morning Belfast sunlight. Regal flowers had been stitched onto crisp white tablecloths. Stenciled teapots and gold rimmed tea cups sat upon flowered saucers. Winter chose a table by the windows so that she could look outside and admire her first Ireland morning. A girl with an apron tied tidily around her waist approached Winter's table.

"Morning! What can I get you for breakfast?" She asked. The girl's voice and demeanor were naturally mellifluous. Winter perused the menu and ordered the vegetable omelet with toast. "How about a wee cuppa?" She asked, smiling.

"Sorry, a what?" Winter asked, her mind attempting to work out what the girl had said.

"A cup of tea," she laughed. "A wee cuppa."

"I'd love some, thank you," Winter said, committing the words to her memory. *A wee cuppa. I love that*, she thought.

"I'll be right back with the kettle. My name's Lily. Let me know if you need anything."

She walked away towards the kitchen leaving Winter to look outside the ornate windows. Lily Thompson came back minutes later with a teapot in

39

hand.

"It's very warm," she cautioned. "Here's your cream and sugar."

She set down a bowl filled with white and brown cubes of sugar. Winter thanked her and poured herself some steaming tea. She dropped in two lumps of brown sugar and poured cream into the cup. The cream swirled into the rich brown hue of the tea. She placed her hand on the delicate handle and brought it to her lips. Winter took a deep drink, and tasted a perfect blend of flavors. She sat still as she gazed out the window reveling in her cup of tea. Winter was amazed that these two simple things could make her feel so content.

Maybe I'll just stay here all day. The bridge isn't going anywhere, she said to herself, knowing she was going to walk to the curb and get on that bus in thirty minutes. Lily came to the table with arms full of decadent savory foods. Her hair fell across her face as she set Winter's plates down.

"Oh!" Winter said, startling Lily. "I borrowed this from your parents yesterday." Winter searched for some of the pounds she'd converted the day before from a pocket in her green jacket.

Lily waved one hand in the air and said, "Don't even think about it."

Winter stretched out her hand to Lily. The money sat in her open palm. "I just needed to get it converted."

Lily remained benevolently stoic. "I am not taking that money. Do you need anything else?"

Winter shook her head. "Thank you," she said again.

Lily left the table with an affectionate nod. Winter stared down at her plate. The last real meal she'd had was on the plane. After exploring the town yesterday, she'd fallen into bed. Jet lag claimed her first night in Belfast. She tried to eat leisurely but couldn't escape the feeling that she resembled a rabid hyena that hadn't eaten in weeks.

At eight fifty she went to the curb and waited for the tour bus to pick her up. Her stomach dropped when she thought of the bridge, of the water too many feet below the swaying wood. *It'll be over before I know it*, Winter lied to herself.

She glanced at the time on her phone's screen. The tour bus was running late. Winter leaned against the black fence. The sloping road that led to the bus stop was quiet that morning. After twenty minutes of waiting, Winter began to fidget with the largest hole in her jacket. It was a feeble effort at distraction.

"Did I really give away my money my first afternoon here to a complete stranger in return for a ripped piece of paper?" Winter said aloud, too distressed to care if she looked questionable to the people who walked around her. She turned to go inside when an orange van with the words, 'The Colossal Tours of Belfast' written in cursive, looping black lettering on the sides, pulled up to the curb. She let out a sigh of relief and started towards the bus, but the man said, "Sorry, wrong address," and promptly shut the doors in her face.

Winter thought about falling to her knees in an epic display of regret. She imagined cursing her actions as she clenched her fists and yelled to the heavens, "What have I done?!" But then a rusted white van pulled up to the curb saving Winter from making a spectacle of herself. A large man got out and pulled open the rusted van door.

"Giant's Causeway tour?" He asked in a Scottish accent. The man had broad shoulders and a strong, rumbling voice.

"That's me," she replied.

"In ya get," he said.

Winter looked around the cabin. It was a small van, with bolted down seats and what appeared to be a banana peel on the floor.

"This is just the shuttle bus. I'll take you where you need to be. Sorry for being late! I had a lot of groups to pick up this morning," he called back to her.

"Oh, I don't mind," Winter said, grateful he'd shown up at all.

The man dropped Winter off a few streets over in front of two large tour buses. Lines of people were boarding with cameras and umbrellas in hand. It was sunny at the moment, and Winter wondered if it would stay that way. But as she got on the bus the weather shifted. Raindrops ran in small streams down the windows.

"That didn't last long," she said to herself.

She looked around the bus and noticed that most everyone was in pairs or groups. Winter sat in a two-person seat alone. She picked at a few loose strings on her coat and fleetingly wished she hadn't come by herself. *I refuse to feel sorry for myself. This is part of the reason I'm here! Stretch yourself,* she thought. Her insecurities had been given abundant life over the years, growing steadily along with her fears. She reminded herself that the point of this trip was to silence their voices and deny them a front row seat in her life. In the reflection of the window, Winter could see the outline of someone coming around the corner.

"Wait!" A girl with wavy brown hair was running down the street. "Wait!" She called. The bus driver opened the door for her. "I've been chasing these white vans since they left the main street. I'm going on the tour, too," she panted. Her face was flushed, her cheeks red.

The man driving the bus clapped her heartily on the back. "Sorry for that!"

"No worries. I woke up late," she said. "Besides this isn't the first time this has happened, or the second, or the third," the girl confessed.

Winter couldn't place where the girl was from because her lightly accented English was entirely unfamiliar to Winter. She was able to decipher that the girl was on her own, too. Winter could tell because she looked like herself. The stranger searched for a place on the bus. But the girl struck Winter because she appeared completely confident, lively. Simply walking down the aisle of the tour bus, this girl seemed as though she was the holder of some secret to living. Winter thought to offer the seat next to her. The notion reminded her of being in a school yard trying to find a new friend. It made her recall standing in a frilly pink dress with folded hands and intertwined fingers wiggling with uncertainty, and the encroaching fear of being told no.

Winter cleared her throat. "This seat's free."

"Thank you!" The girl said.

"I'm Winter," Winter said, extending her hand.

"Marieleen," she said, shaking Winter's hand.

"Nice to meet you. Where are you from?"

"The Netherlands," she said, as she unwrapped a long gray scarf from around her neck and pushed her brown hair off her face. "And you?"

"Chicago," Winter said.

"Ooh, I've always wanted to go to Chicago. People usually want to go to New York when they talk about America, but I'd love to see Chicago. But I'd go either place if I got the chance! What brought you over?"

"I wanted to do some traveling. I haven't been out of the country since I was four and thought it might be time. You?"

"I'm in between years in University. I found a program online that lets me live and work at a hostel here in Belfast. I want to practice my English this summer. That's a huge part of why I'm here."

"How long have you been learning English?"

"Since I was young. The lessons started early in school, but I need to practice a bit more, though, because I still get some words confused," Marieleen said.

"If I could speak another language as well as you I'd be so over the moon pleased with myself. I took four years of Spanish in high school. If I went to a Spanish-speaking country today, I'd get lost and go without food for weeks. I'd probably never find my way home."

Marieleen held her stomach and laughed. "That's not so good. Maybe you shouldn't go."

"I know, right, that's what I'm saying!" Winter answered with a chuckle.

"It's really about immersion, though, being around the language as much as possible," she said. "That's the best way to learn. Perhaps you'd survive."

"Knowing myself I'm not sure it'd be wise to test it."

"But you know, we learn English so young. It's not quite fair, but it's a language you have to know. And please correct me if I make a mistake!"

"I'll try, but I might need you to do the same for me," Winter said with an earnest laugh.

"I can't wait to go on the Carrick-a-Rede rope bridge," Marieleen said, shifting with eagerness in the seat.

Winter managed a rather unconvincing smile in Marieleen's direction. On the ride, Winter watched the weather take another definitive turn. The clouds darkened, blocking out the sun's encouraging light. When the tour bus came to a stop, Winter's hands shook at her sides. She could see the bright pink ropes of the bridge in the distance. It both captivated and horrified Winter. The Carrick-a-Rede rope bridge was suspended ninety-eight feet in the air over a chasm of water between two sheer rock faces. Winter took a hard swallow as she exited the bus and felt the spongey earth under her feet.

She and Marieleen talked as they made their way to the line, but Winter barely registered the words shared between them. Her heart felt like it was in her throat, trying to beat its way out of her. Her legs seemed to be a separate entity from her body. Every time she told them to stop moving they ignored her orders. Winter's hands froze in the cold Ireland morning.

"I thought it was supposed to be spring here," she said, looking to Marieleen.

"I don't think Ireland knows that," she answered.

Winter shoved her hands into her thin pockets and berated herself for bringing a light jacket and translucent scarf to keep warm. She searched her bag frantically for another layer and yelped when she found a crumpled, dark gray beanie. The ropes of the bridge stood out to Winter as they neared. They strongly contrasted the natural colors surrounding its man-made vibrancy. The planks dangled high above the water, higher than Winter realized. She laughed inwardly, a manic laugh of panic mingled with desperation.

I can do this. I'm seeking a bigger life. I'm going to overcome my fears, and once I do that, I'll see how small some of them are, she said to herself.

Marieleen and Winter arrived at the front of the line. Seconds later Winter's hand was gripping the guard rail just before the bridge. And now she was looking down over the inclined edge of the rock's steep surface. Marieleen placed a foot on the bridge first. Winter followed, the pit of her stomach dropping. Marieleen turned, a slight crease on her brow, and asked, "Are you nervous?"

Winter couldn't help but notice that Marieleen's movement made the bridge sway unevenly. She took a sharp breath and said, "I'm alright, I just, I'm afraid of heights." Winter forced a smile. She was sure Marieleen could see through its lack of authenticity. Winter thought falsity always had a way of showing despite genuine efforts to conceal it.

"I just need to go across a little slowly," she managed to say. "I'm trying to overcome some of my fears. Heights is one. I have quite a few," Winter quipped.

Winter didn't know it, but Marieleen could see slivers of her former self looking out from Winter's eyes. Marieleen could glimpse in Winter what she used to recognize in herself. It wasn't just timidity that was clear in Winter's soft gaze. Marieleen also used to be someone so fraught with worries that life escaped her, too. In Winter's fumbling movements, in the unsureness that accompanied her every step, even off the bridge, Marieleen perceived a girl who felt lost. But in the glint of Winter's eyes Marieleen could see past her blundering exterior and into the person that wanted to break free like she once did.

Marieleen had also tried to disrupt the mold she'd fallen into and overcome the uncertainty that ruled her former self. And the only thing that worked was doing the very things that made her limbs quake. Now, that was how Marieleen moved through her life, with presence and fullness, risk and spontaneity. She felt every moment was one to be captured. Anyone she met moving through life the same way she once did, became her mission in a way, her undertaking, even if just for a short time, to bring them through the tangled web of fear that once ruled her life, too. Marieleen peered over the side of the bridge and looked back at Winter.

"Oh, I understand. Here," she extended her arm, closing the space between them.

"Take my hand. I'll guide you across."

Winter fought better judgment and raw insecurity. Taking both hands off the side railings seemed a bad idea, but she wasn't sure if her body would move without a little help. And something about Marieleen made Winter feel slightly more at ease. Winter reached out her arm, grasped Marieleen's open hand, and felt immediately better. She pushed aside thoughts of the planks beneath her breaking. She quieted notions of falling and trying to catch herself on the sharp rock, and only concentrated on getting across. That's all she had to do.

"I used to be nervous about heights, too, but now I kind of like them. The feeling you get in the pit of your stomach used to cripple me, but these days I find it exhilarating. So tell me, what do you do at home? I can guess you don't walk across high bridges very often," she said, a smile alive in her eyes.

"I'm looking for a job. Ah…" Winter tried not to look down. "But I'm having a hard time."

"Sorry, I meant what types of things do you love doing at home. Any hobbies?"

"Oh," Winter's face scrunched up. "I like to dance, and I take classes at home. I started a little while ago. When I was a kid, I was in ballet, but I quit because the other girls would taunt me. I was the only dancer without a tutu with volume. Apparently that was highly valued among those pink tutu loving assassins masquerading as ballerinas." Winter tried to breathe deeply.

"And then during a recital my tights split while I was doing a jet`e and I hobbled off the stage holding the hole, hoping it didn't spread. It did. I stopped taking dance after that, but over the years I was always drawn back to it. I love to watch dance. So a couple of years ago I figured that if I loved watching it so much I'd probably like doing it even more. So why not take it up again? I can't be a professional or anything, but I like the idea that it's never too late to find your life's passion." She took another breath. "And there are so many things I wish I'd done sooner that I never even touched. So now I go once a week to this old studio, and I dance. I, uh, haven't told anyone that. It's a bit embarrassing watching myself in the mirror, but I just close my eyes to spare myself."

Marieleen looked bemused by Winter's ramblings, at her frantically darting eyes. "I like that," she said, tilting her head gently to the side. "Photography is the thing I love to do. I take pictures everywhere I go. A while ago one of my pictures was hung up at a local cafe. It still hangs right by the window."

Winter could see Marieleen's eyes envisioning the photograph in the cafe.

"There was a time where I thought I needed to concentrate on a more stable future. My parents and some of my friends thought I was crazy to want to be a photographer. They told me being a photographer is too unstable, and that I should focus on building a better foundation. So I stopped taking photos and worked on getting a job with more security. But it felt like torture seeing my camera sitting neglected in the corner. And then I started wondering if I was still able to take photos like I had before. I started to try again, but the pictures never lived up to what I wanted. I was heartbroken. Sometimes I'd walk by the cafe just to look at the photo and remind myself that it still exists, that it is possible for me to create something that I love. Something beautiful."

They were halfway across the bridge.

"I'm getting back into photography," Marieleen declared, peering at the landscape surrounding the bridge. She inhaled a breath of salty ocean air and said, "I want to remember what it's like to have a passion again. I want that sense of direction where the only certainty I have is my love for what I'm doing and my belief in its importance."

"What do you take pictures of?" Winter asked, enthralled by Marieleen's words.

"Everything, but mostly people. When they're in their natural environments, I feel that's when they're their truest selves. That's what I love to capture. I was in India a little while ago, and I took a trip to the Himalayas. While I was there, I took some photos of kids playing with a ball made of scraps. The sun was setting, and it cast this amazing orange color over the open valley. They played beneath it laughing and running. Sometimes when I look at the picture I'm right there again, next to mountains topped with snow."

"That sounds beautiful," Winter said, feeling transported to the base of the Himalayan mountains. She could feel the wind at her back, see the glow of the setting sun. They were almost off the bridge. At first Winter knew Marieleen was trying to take her attention away from what she was doing. But as Marieleen spoke Winter became lost among the brush strokes on the canvas she painted. And then, because Winter could see the end of the bridge, she could allow herself to look around.

So she moved her eyes from their downcast position and looked at where she was. Clear, turquoise, glimmering water, and the most vivid blue hues enveloped the land around the grass-covered boulders. The North Atlantic Ocean was behind her, and she could hear the splashing of waves meeting a shoreline of jagged rocks.

Within seconds, her boots settled onto solid ground once again. Winter almost tipped over when she looked at the bridge she'd just exited. And then Winter realized it was over. "I made it!" She stammered. "Ah! I'm still alive! The bridge didn't snap!" She yelled, too thrilled to care about the people staring at the shouting girl. "I can't believe it's over!" She called out, gripping Marieleen's hands. Winter shut her eyes tightly before looking to the sky. "Thank you, thank you!" Then her eyes settled on Marieleen.

"Thank you for that. I'm sure you didn't think you'd be a babysitter today."

Marieleen chortled and then squinted her eyes as she asked Winter a question.

"Why did you come onto the bridge if it makes you so nervous? You mentioned something about fears on the bridge."

Winter rubbed her hands together trying to return warmth to her cold, numb fingers, which started to tingle as blood rushed through her veins. "Well, I have this self-appointed task to face a list of my fears, my deepest, most life-inhibiting fears. Water and heights are two of them."

"You just did two in one! A bridge over water!" She exclaimed. An inquisitive look came across her face.

"Wow. I don't know if I could do that. Can I see your list?"

"Yeah," Winter said, surprised at her willingness to share her deepest fears with someone she'd only known for two hours. But Marieleen didn't feel like an utter stranger anymore. Winter brought out the folded piece of paper she'd copied from her journal that morning and passed it to her new friend. The list of illogical logical fears landed in Marieleen's hands.

My List of Illogical Logical Fears

1.   Bodies of water (and being lost underwater).
2.   Heights that are above my own.
3.   The future. Where am I going?

4. Singing in public.
5. Being alone in a foreign country where I don't know anyone.
6. Getting rejected and being vulnerable.
7. Not finding true happiness.
8. Looking and sounding incredibly stupid.
9. Getting out of my comfort zone.
10. Self-consciousness growing larger in my life.
11. Failing to find the road that leads to the path I'm meant to be on in life.
12. Never accomplishing my dreams.
13. Reliving the sadness of my past.
14. Living a small life.
15. Having hate find me again.

As her eyes scanned the slightly crushed paper, she made noises like, "Hmmm and ah and yeees." Then she looked up at Winter. "What's the title?"

"Oh, it's my list of illogical logical fears."

"How do you mean?"

"Um, I mean that some of the fears on my list are rational and make sense on some level. But in a way they're fears with roots that have grown larger than they have any right to."

She glanced back down at the list. "Singing in public?" She asked, wrinkling her nose.

"Yeah, it's a weird one, but ever since I was fourteen, I've had this extreme phobia about it. I had a solo at a concert once, and I forgot my words. No sound came out of my mouth. It was awful. And my arch-nemesis was in the audience."

"Your what?"

"Oh, shoot, my life-long enemy. She wasn't the most civil. It sounds a little dramatic but—"

"I got it, a—a rude person. Maybe someone who's not very nice."

"Yes! Exactly! A life-long rude person."

"Okay, keep going."

"She was in the audience enjoying my misery. I just stood there like an idiot with the spotlight glaring down on me. Then I ran off the stage crying. I've never been able to even try to sing in front of other people since then."

"Oh my gosh!" Marieleen said, holding either side of her face, her eyes huge.

"Hmm, Christmas caroling is a no go for me. I only mouth the words even to songs on the radio, unless I'm by myself. This probably sounds so strange to you," Winter said, shaking her head at her words.

"Hey, I'm not judging," she said, raising her arms outwards. Her eyes returned to the list of fears. "That's a long list, a good one, but a long one. What do you mean by hate?"

Winter's mind flashed to her 11-year-old-self riding a bike down the roads of her small suburban town. She swallowed and shoved the memory from her conscious mind and further down into the chasm of pain she ignored. "I guess I just mean intolerance of any sort," she offered.

"I see," Marieleen said, passing the list back to Winter. "I suppose I should tell you some of my fears since you told me some of yours." She inclined her head to the sky and held up her fingers, counting off the fears she was about to name. "I don't like birds, especially pigeons. They swoop down, and I always think they are going to beak me to death or go to the bathroom in my hair."

"Has that happened to you before?"

"It has. A pigeon flew over me while I was camping with some friends and it went to the bathroom in my hair. I had to stick my head in this river, and I fell in. I cannot stand pigeons. My biggest fear is that I might not succeed as a photographer and that maybe that one photo was the only good one I'll ever produce. How's that?"

"Valid fears, I'd say."

"Good," Marieleen said with a curt nod.

The tour guide yelled in the distance that time was up. The two of them trudged back to the bus, unbelieving that it was already time to go. Marieleen dozed off in the seat after a few minutes. The drive was like a trance. They drove along turning roads that Winter thought they might tip off of and narrow lanes that didn't seem wide enough for the tour bus, let alone another vehicle. It made Winter glad that she hadn't rented a car because she knew she would have driven off a cliff.

The bus was headed to the Giant's Causeway on the coast of Antrim in Northern Ireland, a natural wonder produced by volcanic eruptions that made interlocking basalt columns. The causeway was a thing of myth and legend. A story of giants. The tour guide stood at the front of bus with a microphone.

"Now, I have a wee story to tell you all about our next destination. I'm going to tell you how the Giant's Causeway came to be. Our story begins with two giants. Their names were Fionn Mac Cumhaill and his Scottish rival, Benandonner. Legend says that the giants were going to fight one another in an epic test of strength, and Fionn built the Causeway to serve as a bridge between their homes. But in a twist of fear and self-preservation the fight never occurred. One night, the Irish Giant was asleep on the bridge when pounding footsteps awoke him. He opened his eyes and saw his Scottish adversary approaching, and he was two times larger than Fionn."

The tour guide's hands told the story. They waved in the air theatrically, his face displayed a bevy of emotions, making Winter sure this was not his first telling of the story.

"Fionn ran home to his wife, Oogna, and told her what he saw. Knowing he couldn't win the battle using strength alone, his wife instead used wits. She wrapped her husband in blankets and put him in a cradle by the fire. When Benandonner arrived, Oogna welcomed him and said her husband would be back soon. She led him to the fire and told him not to wake their baby."

The tour guide began to walk up and down the aisle, acting the story out.

"Upon seeing his adversary's baby, Benandonner was struck with fear. The Scottish giant left immediately. If Fionn's child was that large, Benandonner couldn't imagine how large his opponent would be. As he fled, he broke the bridge between their homes to make sure Fionn could never cross it. The broken remnants of the Causeway alone remain. And that is how you tell a story!" He concluded brightly, and then he bowed low. The bus was full of jovial tourists who clapped loudly.

When the bus drove up to the Causeway, Winter's breath caught in her chest. She pressed her face against the glass, creating unattractive streaks on its unblemished surface. Mountains hugged in willowy green grasses, and sparkling, incandescent ocean waves filled Winter's vision.

She and Marieleen stepped off the bus. The Causeway was covered in almost perfectly symmetrical hexagonal shapes of deviating heights and sizes that formed natural steps. Winter placed her hands on the pieces nature had called into being over hundreds of years. She climbed up a wall of the natural wonders to the other side where the ocean lay peacefully. Winter rubbed her hands against the tops of the structures brought to life by volcanic eruptions that happened long before her time. It was smoother to the touch than she imagined.

"Do you want to sit here?" Marieleen asked, pointing to two stumps on the edge overlooking the water. They sat on the shapes, which also made comfortable seats, and looked out across the water, at the magnificent and serene view that surrounded them on every side.

"Are you hungry?" Marieleen asked.

Winter placed a hand on her stomach. "I am. I hadn't even noticed."

"It's all that adrenaline pumping!" Marieleen opened her bag and passed Winter a plump orange and grabbed a banana for herself. With contented smiles, they ate ripe fruit by the water, as the salty wind blew across their faces.

"So, what happens with your list after you finish a fear?"

"I hadn't thought about that," Winter said, her brow furrowing. "I think I'll cross it out," she said with a smile.

"Do you have a pen?" Marieleen asked.

"I don't think I do," Winter twisted around, hoping to locate a pen in the depths of her bag, but Marieleen was prepared. She pulled a pen out of her pocket.

"I think you should do the honors," Marieleen said, passing Winter the pen.

Winter straightened out the list and ran the black ink of the pen across the letters that composed her fear of heights and water.

My List of Illogical Logical Fears

1. ~~Bodies of water (and being lost underwater)~~.
2. ~~Heights that are above my own~~.
3. The future. Where am I going?
4. Singing in public.
5. ~~Being alone in a foreign country where I don't know anyone~~.
6. Getting rejected and being vulnerable.
7. Not finding true happiness.
8. Looking and sounding incredibly stupid.
9. Getting out of my comfort zone.
10. Self-consciousness growing larger in my life.
11. Failing to find the road that leads to the path I'm meant to be on in life.
12. Never accomplishing my dreams.
13. Reliving the sadness of my past.
14. Living a small life.
15. Having hate find me again.

Winter crossed out number 5 as well. She'd already found a friend. Marieleen clapped her hands together and let out a "Woot! Woot!"

"I'm not sure I could have done it alone. They would have had to pry my lifeless fingers off those pink ropes if it wasn't for you, Marieleen!"

She swallowed a bite of banana and said, "I think you would have surprised yourself."

"Maybe I would have," Winter said, feeling a sprinkling of the sea on her skin. "That's three down. Twelve to go."

"How long are you here for?" Marieleen asked.

"I'm not sure, but probably a few weeks. I want to fit in as much fear conquering and life living as I can."

Unbeknown to Winter, Marieleen was an architect for creating moments, and immediately upon seeing the list of fears, a scheme had settled into place.

"Congratulations, Winter," she said, nudging into her new friend.

Winter Wright was indeed seeking a bigger life

CHAPTER NINE—THE PUB SURPRISE

The night of the Causeway Tour, Winter and Marieleen made plans for the next evening. They met late afternoon at the Botanical Gardens, a twenty-eight-acre park next to Queen's University. Winter, arriving first, sat on a wooden bench in front of the park. It was a few minutes before she saw a long gray scarf and wavy brown hair whipping in the wind.

"Hope you weren't waiting long! I was cleaning at the hostel as fast as I could."

Marieleen gave Winter a hug and then said, "I'm starving. I've been dying for a burger! Do you have any place you want to go?"

"No, I don't have a clue," Winter said.

"Why don't we grab some food first at Maggie Mays and then I want to take you to this pub that has live music. I love the, um, how do you say you love the feel of something?"

"Uh, atmosphere," Winter said.

"I love the atmosphere. Does that sound good?" Marieleen asked, a carefree smile on her face.

"Sounds awesome to me," Winter replied. It was day three, Winter had already faced some of her fears and though her body still tingled at the mere thought of the bridge, she'd made it across. And now she was about to have dinner in a restaurant in Ireland. By her standards, she was doing well.

"Good. But we need to leave soon because the line at the pub gets so long. The live music nights are popular."

The walk over to the restaurant was brisk. They practically ran, hunger pushing their limbs quickly towards the establishment's doors. The place was dimly lit. Winter ordered fish and chips while Marieleen got a beer and a burger. They ate without much talk, quieting their hunger with every bite. Marieleen looked at a large clock hanging on the far wall of the room.

Winter noticed she'd been doing it almost since they arrived.

"Ah, it's time to go if we want a nice spot in line."

Winter pushed her seat out, taking one last bite of food before leaving money on the table. They arrived at the pub, and a line was outside already. It wasn't too long, but the buzzing of voices inside could be heard out on the pavement. A blackboard outside showed the pub's live music line up for the evening. Winter's eyes moved down the list, and she stopped dead in her tracks. Her feet became heavy as stone, impossibly still. Written in white chalk on the board was her name. She looked to Marieleen, her eyes huge, anxiety rippling in waves through her unsuspecting body.

"What?" Winter managed to ask. Marieleen's eyes glowed with triumph, pleasure, and pride at what she'd done.

"You told me you came here for this so let's do it. You're second, as you can see," she said, pointing to Winter's name on the board. "I called ahead. It's open mic tonight. There are some professionals booked as well, and there was a cancelation. I might have said you were a solo act."

Winter opened her mouth. Her throat felt dry. "But…I need time to think of a song and…and time to practice! I needed a warning or something. I can't just… just do it."

Her voice didn't sound like her own. It felt detached from her. Winter's hands groped the air searching for an excuse, for a reason that this couldn't happen. She began to chew on that bottom lip, which cried out for mercy.

Marieleen leaned closer to Winter, that glow still evident, and asked her, "Why?"

Before Winter spoke, Marieleen answered her own question. "Winter, life doesn't give you the luxury of time. You don't get to practice. You don't get a warning. You have your one chance, and then it's gone. I've been there, and I wish someone would have pushed me when I let fear steal moments of life from me. If you don't take it, that might be it. It's passed. It's over. That moment might never present itself again. Before you know it you'll be looking back at your life and wondering where it went. And then you'll realize that you never lived. You'll see that life was always right in front of you, that it never went anywhere because you never did."

She pulled the doors open for Winter, offering her an opportunity.

"This chance is yours. It's waiting. Will you take it or will you let fear stop you?"

Winter couldn't tell how long she stood there with Marieleen holding the door open. Winter's chest rose and lowered unsteadily. People passed around them and through the pub doors. This was why she'd come, and Winter knew what she had to do. Her decision had, in fact, been made, but it didn't make it any less difficult. *I can do this. I'm seeking a bigger life*, she told herself. She breathed out heavily. Winter knew she'd already let her life move without her full presence, and Winter wanted a turn at life, at *her* life.

"Okay," she finally said, trembling. Her voice was shallow, full of resistance.

Marieleen smiled. "Okay. After you."

Winter moved through the open doors and she couldn't help feeling like part of her life was waiting for her on the other side. She swallowed hard and as arduous as it was; she put one foot in front of the other. Winter stepped across the threshold of the pub where she hoped to conquer another fear. The lights inside emitted an amber luminescence, casting faces in warm shades. A man stood on the stage, facing the crowd of people sitting on wooden bar stools. "To start the night off right, we have Connor O'Grady!" He called out.

A tall guy with black hair and a vine of tattoos up both his arms walked on stage. He carried a midnight blue guitar in one hand and looked effortless both on and off stage. His level of comfort made it appear like he was in his living room, and the one-hundred people in the audience were simply his house guests. He strummed a few chords, bringing them into tune before he opened his mouth to speak. From the cheers of the crowd Winter knew he was not an everyday walk-on.

"Thanks for havin' me. I'm called Connor. Ah, this is an original. I hope you all enjoy it."

He began to play and the notes of his song floated into the air, landing softly on the ears of the people in the room. Within seconds the crowd was transfixed by the haunting tale of heartache and hope he sung about. His voice was deep and bellowing. It expanded into the room as people moved to the rhythm of his lyrics. Some people even sang along to the words, cementing the thought in Winter's mind that he was a professional. Winter believed it was rare to find new messages and inspiration hidden among the lyrics of one song each time it's played, but she knew Connor's music held undiscovered stories. Winter felt like the song was for her, and she had no doubt that every other listener also believed the words had been crafted with their unique heart in mind. At the chorus, he raised his hands above his head, clapping at the song's bridge, and Winter swore her knees would give out. She didn't want his songs to end because she was up next.

"I'm so nervous," Winter said as she tried to fight panic.

Marieleen smiled at Winter and said, "I don't see your arch—," She snapped her fingers as she tried to recall the word. "Your arch—"

"Arch-nemesis, haha, very funny." Beads of sweat began to accumulate on Winter's forehead. "I feel so stupid right now. I came all this way to face my fears, and three days in I'm already wanting to run away."

Marieleen placed her hands on Winter's shoulders. "You're here. You can do it. Take a breath and pick a song."

"Are you gonna sing?" Winter asked.

"What, are you kidding me? Not a chance. I'd rather face a pigeon."

"I don't even have a guitar!" Winter said.

Marieleen turned her head, a look of unmovable determination in her features. "I'll be right back! Don't move."

"Not a problem. Don't think I could if I wanted to."

With that, she moved confidently into the crowd and disappeared, leaving Winter in a corner to have a panic attack alone and in relative peace. Connor moved on to a new song, one with an upbeat tempo. A few people began to dance as he played rhythmic staccato notes. The whole room followed his commands; heads bobbed, and hands came together, reflecting his movements. Winter scanned the crowd for Marieleen, but after two more songs she still couldn't spot her friend. She swallowed hard and began to chew on her bottom lip.

From the stage Connor said, "Cheers. Thanks for havin' me. You've been too kind. I'm playing Whelan's in a couple of weeks. Come out and see me if you can."

Winter froze. *He's done!* Connor began to walk off the stage. There were howls of approval along with shouts of disappointment that his set had ended. As he moved into the crowd, Winter felt a hand on her shoulder. It was Marieleen with a guitar in hand.

"We have to give it right back when you finish. What are you singing?" She asked.

Winter could barely hear her over the noise in the bar and her own beating heart, which rang like a clanging bell in her head. Marieleen placed a hand on Winter's back.

"If you face this fear, it gets you closer to the others, and I saw that list. You should get moving," she said with a teasing wink.

"I only know one song on the guitar. I just hope I don't faint before I get up there," she said, lifting a hand to wipe away the perspiration from her forehead.

The announcer for the night came back to the stage. "That was brilliant, Connor! Go out and see him at Whelan's if you can! Next up we have Winter."

Winter felt butterflies erupt in her chest and then wondered why they were called butterflies when to her they resembled bats with sharp talons and dripping fangs. Her eyes filled with worry. *What am I about to do? Why am I going to increase this to a global level of embarrassment?* She wished fiercely that this was not her fear, or that she could magically transport herself anywhere else in the world instead of being in that pub. Heights was one thing, but to put herself at the mercy of a room full of people was an entirely different level of vulnerability.

"Winter? Are you here?" The guy holding the guest list called out to the noisy crowd from the stage.

For a second Winter contemplated staying exactly where she was; when the man continued calling out her name, she'd look around the room like everyone else, with brows furrowed, and say, "Where is this Winter person?" After the third time he called her name, Marieleen gave her a push. Winter had almost forgotten about her. Marieleen would never let her stay in the crowd blissfully and fearfully silent.

Winter started walking towards the stage. Her hands clung to the neck of the guitar so tightly that her fingertips turned blotchy red. And she thought to herself, *when did I become this person? I mean, I hide in pantries because I'm too afraid to let myself be embarrassed, too nervous to face Anna and people's questions about where my life is going. I can do this, even if it's terrible, which judging by my last efforts, it most likely will be. I can do this. I can do this. I will do this.*

She repeated those last words to herself until she reached the middle of the stage floor. Winter cleared her throat. Being elevated above the audience made her thankful for the blinding lights. The glare made it nearly impossible for Winter to see the faces in the crowd. At that moment, standing on stage, she felt totally out of control, completely exposed and utterly vulnerable. Naked before a room of fully clothed people.

"Hi, I'm Winter. I'm just gonna play a quick song for you. Please don't boo. It'll be over soon," she said with a shaky voice, unsure anything could calm her continually heightening nerves.

A bit of laughter broke out, but Winter couldn't hear it. She didn't know if silence or laughter followed her words. All she knew was that she was on stage: she was that much closer to conquering a fear, even though she felt nothing like a conqueror. Winter lifted her hand and started to play. Her fingers fell clumsily over the strings. Winter's heart was beating so heavily in her chest she wasn't sure if words would come.

She played the last few chords of the intro. It was almost time to sing. Winter swallowed hard and released her bottom lip from her teeth. She could feel the sweat growing on her brow from nerves and the bright stage lights. Winter took a breath, her mouth formed the shape of the words, but nothing came from Winter's lips. Like a heat wave overwhelming her body, Winter could feel her embarrassment swelling. She caught eyes with Marieleen, who gave her the nod, telling her to keep going.

She replayed the chords, fighting the urge to run off stage like she had before. Anna Herald wasn't in the audience this time to laugh at her, but that thought hardly provided comfort. The intro ended for the second time, and Winter opened her mouth once more, but not a sound came out. It was happening all over again. Heads in the crowd started to turn as Winter stood on that stage. What was she so afraid of? Winter always ran away from attention. She feared people labeling her, she feared not being good enough, she feared failing at something again. But this was a brand new chance, a gift waiting to be unwrapped. She knew what it was like to run away in fear, but Winter hadn't a clue of what it felt like to stay, to stand your ground. And that's what pushed her now.

Winter played the intro one last time. When the chords led into the first verse of the song for the third time, Winter opened her mouth and sang. Her voice was raspy. It shook as the words emerged from her lips, but Winter kept going. As she played a song about home, her muscle's memory returned to her hands. The chords became crisper and stronger though her voice still trembled. Before singing the next verse, a calming thought entered her mind.

You're at home, by yourself, and no one is watching. It's just you in a room full of sunlight.

That's what she told her shaking body. And then she began to sing again. The words of the song sank into Winter. She sang about how home can be an ever-shifting thing. Winter wanted deeply to be at home in herself, to be grounded in who she was, and be wholly content in her skin. Her failures felt so invincible to her as if she'd fallen too low to find a way out of the depth of her defeat. But as she played under the hot lights of the pub stage, Winter began to see that she was not the sum of what she'd done or experienced, and that there is only one direction dire failure can lead to; whichever direction she chose.

Winter sang the last note of the song. The chords faded into the air slowly. There was a moment of silence that seemed suspended in time for Winter. Then clapping filled the room. It wasn't like in the movies where you know everyone loved it. That wasn't the point or the reason Winter had climbed those stairs. She stepped off the stage, feeling light though she still shook. She was glad it was over, but a small part of her didn't want to leave the stage where she'd overcome a fear. *I did it. I sang, and words eventually followed! Take that Anna Herald,* she thought triumphantly. Almost a decade-long fear, one Winter had come to accept over the years, had just been quieted.

Her eyes met Marieleen's, whose face was full of emotion, her hands folded beneath her chin. Though small, Marieleen could sense the metamorphosis of Winter.

"Beautiful," she said when Winter reached her. "The list?" Marieleen asked. Winter produced the list of her illogical logical fears. Marieleen passed her a neon pen. "I thought you needed a little more color."

Winter brought the tip of the pen across another fear.

"I'm glad I met you, Marieleen," Winter said, feeling tears rim her eyes.

"Yeah, I am pretty cool," she said, and they both laughed.

Winter and Marieleen linked arms and swayed together to the next singer. And Winter knew at that moment that she'd come face to face with bliss in the back of a dark pub in Ireland.

CHAPTER TEN—THE UNSPEAKABLE DAY

Winter spent the next week drinking copious amounts of tea, spending time inside the Titanic Museum, visiting the Belfast Opera House, walking around the city center, and frequenting Maggie Mays, a cafe with unbelievably good ice cream. As she walked home after a day spent exploring Belfast, Winter felt the slightest pang of homesickness. She didn't want to leave Belfast, but sometimes she wished her friends could be there to experience the country with her.

Winter gasped. She'd forgotten about the letters. Her time in Ireland, and her attempts to overcome her fears had made their existence pass from her mind entirely. It was what would satiate her yearning. Winter raced upstairs to her room and fumbled at the lock before shoving the door open. Winter didn't locate the letters immediately, but after a bit of rifling through a mess of clothing her hands found the stack of notes.

Winter picked up the letters and brought them level with her eyes. There were thirteen letters concealed in envelopes of various shades and textures. She picked up a blue-colored envelope with grooves running throughout the paper. *I know whose letter you are,* she said, peering at the note. *I know exactly.* She thought it appropriate to open this particular letter first. It was the one she most wanted to read. Winter ripped it open and peeled back the layers of the folded note when her phone buzzed suddenly, making her jump and drop it from her hands.

"Hello?"

"Hey! It's Marieleen. I just remembered I didn't give you directions!"

"Oh, right," Winter said, looking at the time on her phone. She was already late for Marieleen's dinner.

"Sorry, I'm not very good at doing a lot of things at once. What's the English word for that?"

"Multitasking," Winter stated.

"Yes, that. I'm not good at that."

Marieleen quickly gave directions to the hostel. Winter jotted it down on the back of the blue envelope and said she'd be there soon. She tucked the note into her coat pocket, making sure it couldn't slip out, and bounded down the stairs. The address Marieleen gave was close to the Manor, but that didn't stop Winter from taking a wrong turn (or two).

As she hurriedly walked, she caught a glimpse of her silhouette in a window. Her thick curls and coils blew high that windy evening. Her big hair used to be such a worry. The unspeakable day Winter cut off most of her hair was one she could now look back on with dramatic details, making listeners laugh. But laughter was the farthest emotion Winter felt the day it happened. And the years leading up to that moment entirely lacked comedy. Winter twisted a button on her jacket as a childhood memory resurfaced.

Two slim ballet teachers stared at Winter. Their black tights and leotards made them look unexplainably tall to Winter's six-year-old self. "I just don't know what to do with her hair. It won't lay flat. There's too much of it to fit into a bun. I need a power tool to get this into shape." The woman shook her head. "Didn't her parents think to do her hair before sending her?"

Winter's head turned to her teacher as she spoke. Winter was confused. She remembered sitting at her mother's feet as she gently placed her hair into a bun for the recital. Winter, who's front teeth were missing, tried to speak, but the women kept talking and staring at Winter's hair.

She stood between her two ballet instructors, looking up at them as they talked back and forth about her hair, which they kept calling problematic. And then their hands moved toward Winter's head, undoing the care-filled work her mother had done. By the time they'd finished, Winter's hair was pulled back so tightly she found it hard to blink.

"Is it presentable now?" The taller teacher asked the other.

"I think that's the best we can do," the other replied.

That night she danced her recital, but all she wanted to do was yank her coils out of that hair tie. At the end of the night, Winter, though young, could tell her mother was irritated. But Winter was simply happy that her hair could come down and that she hadn't made many mistakes during the show.

The button on Winter's camouflage coat almost fell off in her hand. It was connected by one last thin piece of string. She released it and turned away from her reflection and kept walking. She didn't want to arrive even later for dinner at Marieleen's. Before coming to Ireland, Winter was nervous about meeting people, but now she was on her way to a friend's place for dinner. She smiled to herself. Winter sometimes forgot to recognize small movement in her life. A stranger walking past Winter stared at her hair tossing in the wind. Winter's stomach clenched, but the woman said, "I love your hair! It's huge!"

"Oh, thank you!" Winter called out, surprised. If only Winter could have heard similar sentiments growing up, or at least not believed the negative ones. Again, she recalled the events leading up to that unspeakable day when her mother drove her to a beautician to cut off her hair.

Three years after her recital, Winter sat in her fourth-grade classroom. She chewed on the back of her pencil as the teacher taught multiplication across the board. The students sat on a carpet beneath the windows for the morning lesson. It was a warm day. All the windows were cracked, allowing a cool breeze to pass into the hot room. Winter was trying to concentrate on the class when someone tapped her on the shoulder.

"Winter, can you move? I can't see over your hair. It looks like you got electrocuted or something." Laughter erupted around Winter while the girl smirked at the reaction she received. Winter's cheeks burned as she tried to blink back her tears.

"This is how my hair grows from my head. It doesn't look electrocuted," she managed to say. The girl leaned forward and whispered in Winter's ear, "Could have fooled me." She sat back in her seat and rested her feet on the base of Winter's chair. Then the girl raised her hand high into the air.

"Excuse me, Mr. Johnson! I can't see the board because of Winter's hair."

"Anna, you can move to the front of the room if you'd like," the teacher said, but then he eyed Winter momentarily. "Perhaps you can pull your hair up, Winter. Do you have a scrunchy?"

"No, I'm not two," Winter replied.

"Winter, please do not be difficult. It will help if you put it up."

Winter felt as though she was made of lead. With the eyes of her classmates on her, Winter stood, walked over to her book bag, and pulled out a hair tie. She grabbed her hair and placed it into a ponytail. Winter walked back over quietly and took her seat.

"Thank you, Winter," the teacher said before turning back to the board to teach.

Anna Herald leaned forward in her seat, getting close to Winter. "That barely helped."

Winter wanted to sink into her chair as her classmates snickered. She wanted to disappear like the numbers erased from the blackboard. That was the day Anna Herald began her reign as Winter's rival. She represented what Winter was already beginning to fear. She sat straight and tried to focus on the rest of the lesson, but all she concluded was this; something is wrong with Winter Wright.

***

The steps to the hostel were lopsided, and the custom made sign had a misspelled word. It read, 'The Traverser's Lodge: Kosy, Warm, and Ready for Your Traveling Needs.' Winter smiled. She already liked this place. She rose her hand and brought it down on the peeling purple paint of the hostel's front door. Winter could hear the stampede of several pairs of feet behind the entryway. There was a bit of rustling and then Marieleen swung the door open.

"You made it!" She said, her hands squeezed into fists beneath her chin. "Were my directions helpful? Did you get lost?"

"Lost? No, I didn't get lost. However, I did decide to take the scenic route over."

"Ah, I see. Good choice," Marieleen said, nodding her head.

"What happened to the sign?" Winter asked, pointing a finger at the word kosy.

"Oh," Marieleen rolled her eyes. "The guy who made it spelled cozy wrong, but we kept it because we thought it added character."

"It does," Winter said with a smile.

"Well come in, come in!" She said, waving her hand to Winter. She shut the door and stepped around her guest. The hostel was a small place with low brick walls and rooms that shot off the hallway.

"I'll give you a tour!" Marieleen said, brimming with enthusiasm. "This is the sitting room. There's lots of magazines and books for people. You're allowed to take a book as long as you leave one. We've got stories from all over the world, and in almost every language, sitting on that coffee table."

"That's amazing. Maybe I'll swap one," Winter said, admiring the intermingling books and the cultures from which they hailed.

"It's tiny in here, but it's also really cozy, with a K." She gave Winter a playful smile. "We serve tea and coffee in the morning for the guests. Up those stairs are the rooms. They're all full right now, which is good. Keeps me employed. I do wish there was an open spot now so you could stay here with me. You'd love it here! If a room opens up, I'll tell you right away." She led Winter down a narrow hall.

Marieleen pushed open a door to her right and walked through. They were standing inside another very small room. A coal fire crackled happily in the background. To Winter's right, a desk, covered in loose papers, was snuggled against the wall. A round table with mismatched chairs sat beneath an open window. The table looked oddly large in the space. Winter turned and found a map of Ireland hanging up. Sea, coast, and land covered every bit of available wall. She walked up to the map, trying to locate the Causeway.

"What a beautiful place," she said, looking at the island of Ireland.

"Yeah, it is. The cliffs and stretches of open land are gorgeous. In the Netherlands, we have rows of trees planted. It doesn't look very natural," she laughed.

"I'd like to see that one day."

"You can visit me anytime I'm home!"

"Same to you," Winter said, amazed at how close she already felt with Marieleen.

"Do you like working here?" Winter asked, imagining herself working at the hostel.

"I think so, yes. Seeing what kinds of guests come, and hearing the stories they have to tell, is the most intriguing part."

They walked through a side door from the small room with a crackling fire and into the compact kitchen. Large pots rattled on the stovetop. "This isn't part of the tour. It's not that interesting," Marieleen decided, waving her hand in the general direction of the kitchen. "But you can smell what I'm making," she said, raising an eyebrow. Winter turned her eyes to the rattling pots. Steam was rising into the air. Whatever was cooking smelled wonderful to Winter.

"I thought since it's so beautiful tonight, it might be nice to eat in the backyard."

"I'd love that," Winter said genuinely, glad for the rainless night. "It's like a maze in here," Winter said.

"Yeah, and sometimes the doors in this never-ending maze get stuck, so you have to give it a little shove." Marieleen banged on the door, unjamming it, and led them outside.

A small garden grew in the backyard, and white flowers in red pots lined one side of the brick wall. Thin, green vines grew up the rust-colored bricks. Hanging lights dangled from tall, wooden awnings. The little bulbs twinkled and blew like wind chimes as they glinted in the cool night air. A family of garden gnomes sat in the back, each with colorful hats painted onto their stout heads.

"My friend Rosamund grew everything you see. When she started working here, she said the plants were inhaling their last breath. She's inside somewhere, and she'll be joining us for dinner."

"Did I hear my name?"

Winter turned and saw a girl with short, dark blonde hair standing in the doorway. She wore a red sweater and chipped, black nail polish covered her fingernails.

"Hi, you must be Winter. I'm Rosamund."

"Nice to meet you. Your garden is beautiful," Winter said.

"Aw, thanks, darlin. I don't like to admit it, but I have a knack for gardening."

"Rosamund, you're strange. If I could keep something alive other than myself, I'd be proud. Don't you think, Winter?"

Winter nodded in agreement. "I'm still working on keeping myself in decent enough shape. So, yes."

Rosamund chuckled and said, "Maybe I'll reconsider then. Are you guys ready to eat? Food's about done."

Marieleen answered first. "I am! After a long day of work, I'm ready to relax. I'll get plates and drinks."

"Can I help with anything?" Winter chimed in.

"Um, can you pull those chairs around the table while we get the food?" Marieleen asked.

"Sure," Winter said, moving three folded, white chairs from against the gate. She set the chairs around the table and took a seat while the other two walked into the kitchen. A few minutes later Rosamund came out first, carrying a deep pot.

"This is one of Marieleen's specialties," she said as she moved closer. "Between you and me, I think 'speciality' is code for 'the only thing I can make.' But it's still one more dish than I can cook." Winter laughed and leaned forward in her seat as Rosamund lifted the lid off the pot. Winter breathed in the pleasant scents and felt her stomach begin to speak.

"I can't wait to try it," she said, her hunger growing.

Rosamund smiled down at Winter. "I can't wait to eat it again."

"Here we go," Marieleen said. She carried another pan and set it down in front of Rosamund and Winter.

"I left the wine on the counter! I'll be right back," Rosamund announced. She pushed the door open and disappeared into the kitchen. She emerged with a tall bottle of red wine and three glasses. Marieleen set the dishes down and began to spoon heaps of food onto each plate. Fluffy, hot rice and sautéed vegetables, covered with freshly grated cheese, filled Rosamund's plate.

"Cheers, but ah, are you trying to put me into a food coma?" Rosamund asked.

"What? That's a normal amount of food!" Marieleen said, holding the serving spoon in the air. She shrugged her shoulders. "At least it is to me," she said with a smirk as she continued to pile food onto the dishes. They ate slowly in the backyard, exchanging stories about life at home between bites of food.

"What do you mean you can't swim?" Rosamund sputtered. "When I was a baby my parents threw me into the water. I took off like a dolphin."

"That sounds absolutely terrifying," Marieleen uttered.

"It was, but now I can swim, and I don't have to worry about drowning. That's what's terrifying."

"This is true," Winter said.

"We should jump in some water. I'll teach you," Rosamund said.

"I can only agree to that if I can practice at the Causeway," Winter joked. "I guess you're used to that kind of beauty, being from Ireland."

"A wee bit, but the magnitude of its beauty still catches me sometimes,"

Rosamund said.

"The Causeway was breathtaking." Marieleen said. "I left my camera that morning. I was so annoyed with myself."

"Have you traveled much since coming to Northern Ireland, Marieleen? Have you been able to get other pictures?" Winter inquired.

"The tour we went on together was my first venture," she answered. "But I want to go back with my camera. We'll see if I have the time."

"I hope you find some time. The Causeway was one of the most naturally striking things I've ever seen. And it had been so long since I'd gone on a road trip," Winter reminisced.

"I once went on a road trip when I was in America. I drove with some friends from Ohio to California. It took a ghastly amount of days," Rosamund said.

"Rosamund isn't a fan of long road trips," Marieleen explained.

"Why's that?" Winter asked, perplexed.

"Living in Ireland, a typical road trip is forty-five minutes, three hours tops. The island is not massive. When I was in America and people wanted to go on nineteen-hour drives I thought they were losing their grasp on reality. That's a whole day of life! That's just my opinion, though. I don't like long drives, but I'm always available for random travel on planes. One time I went to Australia because I didn't have anything planned for the summer. I just packed my bags and camped in the outback. It's the craziest thing I've ever done."

"Ooooh, what was it like?" Winter asked, fascinated.

"Unbelievable. We camped by waterfalls and cooked over fires. I've never seen so many stars in the sky. Last minute and random have been a winning combination for me."

They laughed and then Marieleen asked, "What's the craziest thing you've ever done, Winter?"

Winter knew the answer. The 'Unspeakable Day' was by far the craziest and most regret filled act she'd ever committed. Winter subconsciously picked up the button hanging by one last thread, and began to twist.

The day that Winter had to cut off her hair didn't come until four years after Anna Herald christened Winter electro girl. Kids stuck with the name because they all agreed with Anna. Winter Wright's hair made her look like she'd been electrocuted. No matter how many times Winter said, "This is how my hair grows," she couldn't escape the label. It followed her to junior high. At thirteen, Winter was exhausted. She was tired of magazine racks, movies, and billboards that told her she didn't have a reflection worth showing, and after a while she started to believe it was true. Many of the black girls at her junior high had perms. They'd stand at their lockers with freshly done hair, and Winter would drool. Her first few weeks of eighth grade, deliverance seemed to appear in the form of a tall girl with long, straight, permed hair. After class, she pulled Winter aside.

"You're Winter, right?"

"Yeah," Winter answered.

"I'm Amy. I've noticed you around before because of your hair. You really need a perm. I've been getting one since I was five. Why don't you have one?" The girl asked, her eyes were probing. Winter was thoroughly bewildered.

"What's…what's wrong with it?" Winter asked. Wondering if she was doing something wrong. The girl started to laugh.

"It's so frizzy and big. It looks like you lived in a desert for a hundred years. Look, if you want to be pretty you have to straighten it," the girl finally said. "I mean how many people do you see who look like you? Look around!"

Winter thought about the women she saw on magazine covers and billboards; she thought about the characters she read about in her favorite novels, and the films she always pulled out to watch. Light skin and straight hair are what she always saw, and these images coalesced into an undeniable and distinct message to those young eyes watching, to those young minds being shaped. By the exclusion of people who resembled Winter, she received this message: "You are not worth showing." It was erasure by omission.

"Basically no one is the answer," the girl said. Winter took a step back. She desperately didn't want to believe the girl's words. Winter had family members who had straight, curly, and wavy hair, and they were all pretty to her, more than pretty, they were smart and good, valuable people, but Winter couldn't deny that the girls words spoke to her on some level. Noticing the look on Winter's face the girl used a softer tone.

"I'm just trying to help. If you want to keep wearing your hair that way, go ahead. But if you want to look good, I can hook you up. Let me know."

Winter watched the girl walk away. Her hair shone as the lights from above hit it. What Winter wanted was not to be in the spotlight and sometimes she felt like her hair was a stage light beating down upon her head. *A perm.* She rolled the word around in her head. Two class periods later, Winter decided she'd try to convince her parents to let her get one. At dinner that night she chewed on her bottom lip and ignored talk about how Anna Herald was growing into such a beautiful girl. She waited for the opportunity to ask her parents the question consuming her brain. Winter planned on biding her time, but when a break in the conversation came, she just blurted the question out.

"Can I get a perm?" Both her parents looked at Winter. Ella's head popped up from her plate.

"Winter, you know the rule. You have to wait until you're sixteen. If you still want one in three years then we can talk about it," her mother said.

"I'm thirteen. That's a long time to wait," Winter said, moving a dinner roll across her plate. "I'm not sure I can wait that long," she said under her breath.

"Well, you're just going to have to, because that's your only option," her father stated.

Winter mumbled, "Fine." But as she looked down at her plate, one word dominated her thoughts; option. Winter did have another option.

The next day at school Winter peered over heads and around lockers looking for Amy. She found her after fourth period standing at the vending machines. Winter felt awkward and unsure walking up to the girl.

"Hi, um, can you hook me up?" She asked. The words felt strange coming from her mouth; Amy seemed to agree, but she ignored Winter's failed efforts.

"Winter! I can. Come to my house after school tomorrow. Bring fifty dollars."

"That's a lot of money," Winter said.

"It's a business! I'm saving up for college. I'm trying to go to an Ivy League. I'm top of the class but I need that extra bit to push my application over the top." Winter weighed her mental scales.

"I can figure something out," Winter said.

At home, Winter dug through her drawers. She emptied out the piggy bank she'd had since she was seven and found seventeen dollars in coins in its hollow belly. Winter opened birthday cards from grandparents, which brought her total to thirty-two dollars, but she couldn't find any more money. Winter slumped in the middle of her bedroom floor. She hadn't felt this desperate since she begged her mother for the camouflage jacket on her twelfth birthday.

And then she remembered the money her mother had tucked away after Winter babysat for the neighbors. She snuck into her parent's room while they talked in the backyard. Winter could hear their voices as she lifted stacks of paper, and slowly slid open drawers until she found the stash. Three weeks' worth of babysitting money lay in the envelope. She only took what she needed. Winter slipped out eighteen dollars and tucked it in her backpack. When she finished, she went to the backyard and sat on the deck where her parents sat sipping coffee.

"Can I go to Sienna's tomorrow?"

"Of course, honey. Do you want a ride?" Her mother asked.

"No, but thanks. I'm going to take my bike."

"Just be back by eight-thirty, sweetheart," her father said.

The next evening, after a long day of staring at the clock during classes, Winter hopped on her bike and pedaled to Amy's house. Winter smiled as she rode her bike. In a couple of hours, she would be like the people she saw in the movies, and she'd no longer be called electro girl. Maybe people would stop labeling her kind of different as bad. She would fit in just a bit more, even with the people who looked like her. That's what propelled Winter down those streets, those longing thoughts of acceptance, of relief.

The first thing Winter noticed about Amy's house was its size. Walking up the stone steps to use the gold lion knocker on the large doors was intimidating. Winter rose a hesitant hand and knocked on the door. Seconds later, Amy pulled the door open.

"Winter, ready to meet the new you?" She asked, a hand on her hip.

"I am," Winter said, excitement building in her.

Amy led her to the basement where a swivel chair sat in front of a large mirror with uncovered light bulbs lining its sides.

"Have a seat, Winter. My sister Lena will be down momentarily," Amy said in a polished, professional voice.

"Oh, you don't do it?"

"No, I'm not much older than you! I get the customers, and my sister does their hair. She's seventeen."

"Oh, ok," Winter said. Amy's older sister came down the steps carrying a white tub of cream in her hands. She had a nose ring and striking, almond shaped eyes.

"You must be Winter. I'm Lena. I love a newbie. You guys have the best reactions when I turn you around and you see your reflection for the first time," she said, slapping on plastic gloves.

Winter shifted in her chair. She was beginning to feel uneasy. The sound of the gloves made Winter think of surgery. A perm was permanent, and that scared her, but she wanted this too much to leave now.

"I'm going to start. This is your last chance to change your mind," Lena said.

Winter took a breath and bit her bottom lip. "Do it," she said.

The girl began to apply cold relaxer to Winter's scalp. She sectioned her hair and pulled the white cream throughout Winter's curls and coils. It was like a potion to Winter. As the girl pulled the comb through Winter's strands, she could see them losing their curl. Lena's tongue stuck out as she concentrated on perming Winter's hair.

"You have a ton of hair. It might take some time for the relaxer to work."

Just then there was a knock on the upstairs door. Lena turned to her younger sister. "What?" Amy frowned at Lena from the couch.

"Can you get that?" Lena asked, exasperated. Amy rolled her eyes and went upstairs. The door opened and a boy's voice could be heard.

"Lena!" Amy called down to the basement from the landing. "It's your boyfriend! I knew it would be," she muttered.

"He is not my boyfriend! Tell him to leave!" Lena shouted back.

"He said he wants to talk to you," Amy told her.

"Ahh, Winter, I'll be right back. If it starts to burn come and get me," Lena said.

She set the comb down and took off the gloves. Lena walked up the stairs, leaving Winter alone to stare at her reflection in the mirror. Her head was completely covered in the white relaxer. Winter smiled at herself, wondering what she'd look like when Lena finished. As she stared in the mirror, Winter could feel a tingle begin, but it didn't burn. So Winter waited, but after a few more minutes the tingle increased to an itch. Winter tried to ignore it, but as more time passed the itching increased.

"I'll just give it a light scratch," she said to herself as she reached forward and grabbed a comb from the beauty stand. Winter put the teeth of the comb to her scalp and rubbed it back and forth wherever she felt the need to scratch. For a moment the sensation stopped, but it was utterly temporary.

The harsh and quick turnaround was hardly worth the relief. Winter's head started to burn and throb. She felt like someone had taken an iron to her scalp. Maybe this is normal, she thought, her fear escalating. The burning became so intense that tears came to her eyes. Winter leaped from the chair and ran upstairs to find Lena. She was there at the door talking to a boy in a leather jacket with big, apologetic eyes.

"Is it supposed to burn?" She asked Lena, whose back was to Winter.

"It burns a little, but" Lena stopped talking once she saw Winter's face. "What did you do?"

"I scratched it because it was itching!" Winter said.

"Are you serious? Where are you from? You can't scratch your head when it's full of a chemical relaxer!" She shouted.

Lena rushed Winter down the steps, stuck her head under the sink, and began to rinse away the relaxer from her head. Even the water hurt Winter's scalp, and the soft pads of Lena's fingers felt like nails. Winter balled her hands into fists as the chemical cream fell to the bottom of the sink. Lena finished rinsing and wrapped a towel around Winter's head to dry her hair. When Lena removed the towel she gasped.

"What? What is it?" Winter asked. For a moment Lena didn't speak.

"...Since you scratched your scalp we had to rinse the relaxer out, otherwise, you'd get a chemical burn. But the relaxer didn't set completely because we had to rinse it out so fast."

"Let me see," Winter said.

Lena slowly turned the chair so that Winter could face the mirror. Winter held her breath as she looked at her reflection. She didn't recognize the person she saw. Some parts of her hair were straight, but other sections needed more time. Clumps of the same strands, at different points along the hair shaft, were both permed and natural. Winter's hair looked awful. It stuck out from her head limply. Parts fell where the perm had taken while other sections stood up where the perm hadn't altered her hair structure entirely.

Now I do look like I've been electrocuted, she thought. As Winter stared in the mirror, she began to cry. *This wasn't supposed to happen*, she thought, shaking her head as she looked at herself.

"I'm so sorry! You don't have to pay me," Lena said, and then she turned to her sister and hit her arm. "Amy! You should've chosen a better customer!"

"Hey! She's supposed to be black! How could I have known she wouldn't know not to scratch her scalp? It's so basic," Amy retorted.

Winter barely heard them. She was staring at her hair.

"Should we call your parents?" Lena asked. With that, Winter broke down. She'd forgotten about them, about the fact that she was there against their wishes. Winter shook her head, and without speaking, she rose from the chair. The two girls watched Winter anxiously as she left their house and closed the door behind her. She walked outside calmly, picked up her bike, and rode it home. It was her mother who first saw Winter that night. She was stooped in the garden on the side of the house, planting seeds, when Winter arrived.

"You're back from Sienna's already?" She asked. She stood, looked at Winter, and dropped the box of seeds in her hands. They fell to the ground with a thud.

"Wha...Winter, what have you done to your hair?" She asked, shocked.

Winter was honest when she answered her mother.

"I was tired of being me, Mom. I..." Winter was choking back sobs. "I just wanted to be seen as normal for once. I don't want to stick out anymore. I...I wanted to fix myself. I didn't want to be stared at another day. I took money from your drawer."

When Winter stopped talking, she could barely look her mother in the eye. Her shame was all encompassing. It was then, as she stood with an aching scalp in her mother's garden, that she first had the inkling that her life was not being lived. Winter was beginning to see that she was trying to slip through life. She simply wanted to exist without acquiring more scars.

Winter's mother leaned down and hugged her daughter. "Honey, your value doesn't lay in how many people choose to see your worth. You are loved. You are valued. You are an unbelievably special girl because you are Winter Wright. Don't allow yourself for one moment, to believe any differently."

Winter nodded her head and tried to believe her mother's words. Marie Wright placed a kiss on her forehead and then they walked to the car. Winter dropped herself into the passenger's seat and rested her head against the window. As they rode down the street, Winter saw Anna Herald leaving her house. Winter ducked low into her seat, fearful of being seen by Anna.

Winter knew her arch-nemesis would be merciless. They drove in silence to the hairdresser. Inside the salon, Winter didn't even try to hide as stranger's eyes gawked in her direction. She took her seat in the beautician's chair, and as she turned Winter towards the mirror, Winter stopped her.

"I, um, I don't want to see myself," she said. The beautician honored Winter's request and began to examine her hair with Winter facing away from the mirror.

"Your scalp has a lot of cuts. They're going to ooze and scab over the next couple of days. It's a chemical burn so there's a lot of damage here. I can cut some of it or all of it. If I cut all the damage off now, it'll grow better, but it will be very, very short. You'll have to start over. What are you comfortable with?"

Winter exhaled deeply. "It can all go."

When Winter left the beauticians that unspeakable day, she couldn't have felt smaller. It wasn't the length that bothered her; it was the pursuit of an ideal she would never fit, and the steps she'd taken seeking it, that made her sink low in the car on the drive home. At her next birthday party, as she stood over the burning candles, Winter didn't wish for clothes or movies. She wished for the world to all look the same, act the same, and be the same so that the idea that someone was born wrong would cease to be.

"Winter, what's the craziest thing you've ever done?" Rosamund repeated the question.

Winter continued to twist the button on her jacket, but it couldn't hold on any longer. The string keeping it attached tore suddenly, disconnecting the button for good. Winter collected herself. To the unknowing eye, she could laugh off the instance she was about to share.

"Once, I had to shave my head because I wanted straight hair. I tried to get my hair permed by a high schooler. It didn't work out."

Both girls' eyes grew large with shock.

"What? I wish had the volume you have!" Marieleen exclaimed.

"That's rough," Rosamund said, resting her chin on her hands. "How did you feel about it then?" She asked.

"Terrible. I haven't put chemicals to it since."

"So, a perm straightens your hair?" Marieleen asked.

"Hmmhmm. This one didn't, but they're supposed to."

"I bet you looked good with a shaved head," Rosamund said.

"You are not entirely wrong," Winter responded with a smile.

"That was more than I was expecting for crazy stories!" Rosamund declared.

As she spoke, she popped the cork off the bottle of wine and poured it into their stemless glasses. Rosamund and Marieleen each took sips and settled further into their chairs. Winter brought the glass to her nose, as she'd seen people do in films, and took a small drink. It burned her throat before settling unceremoniously in her stomach.

"What do you think?" Rosamund asked.

"Mmmm," Winter said through pursed, tingling lips.

"I didn't give you enough," she said, pouring more into Winter's glass. Her eyes bulged, but she picked the glass up once again. The same thing occurred. An uncomfortable burning sensation appeared in her throat, followed by a rumbling stomach.

Marieleen chuckled. "Rosamund, she doesn't like it! Every time she drinks, she looks like this." Marieleen proceeded to scrunch her nose unpleasantly and wrinkle her face. Marieleen poured Winter's wine into their cups and said, "We have other drinks. Please don't force it down."

"That would be great," Winter smiled sheepishly as she played with a deep chip on the table. Small, fragmented spots covered it, hinting of a long life lived. Winter wondered how many meals had been shared around the table, how many stories told and life lived at its aging surface. As if reading her mind, Marieleen began to speak.

"My grandmother had a table like this when I was a little girl," she said, lightly touching the grains in the wood. "Once a week, my whole family would go to her house for dinner. She'd make mountains of food and she always snuck me extra sweets. I'd get home, and in the bottom of my bag I always found two pieces of chocolate wrapped in gold paper. One time I accidentally put a dent in the table. I was so afraid I'd get in trouble that I hid from everyone. She found me and told me it was fine, that it would remind her of all the good memories we made together over the years. A week later, when my brothers broke two of the legs, we put the table away, of course."

The three of them laughed, and Rosamund leaned back in her chair. "It's such a beautiful night. Do you guys want to go on a wee walk?" Winter and Marieleen were a chorus of two. "Yes!"

"Let's go to the river," Marieleen added.

"I'll grab dessert from inside."

The girls cleared the table and made their way to Clarendon Dock. Winter placed her hands into her coat pockets as she walked, shielding them against the faint coolness of the night. Her fingers slid over smooth paper, and she remembered that the note lay in her pocket. Winter knew the letter's author. She could tell from the writing and the simple blue stationary. Quiet and unassuming strength. Winter played with the bent edge and imagined what words awaited her. By the time they reached the dock, the night had become colder, but not unbearably so. It made Winter's breaths chilled.

"Look," Marieleen said, drawing their attention.

One side of the dock was covered in locks with initials scrawled across their fronts. For a few minutes, they looked at the initials of those who once stood in the same spot as them, declaring devotion next to loved ones. They sat down on the dock and watched the gentle waves lapping against the river bank.

Rosamund lifted a box of chocolates from her bag while they dangled their feet over the dock and looked out across the water. The sun was setting in the distance. The quietness of day as it turned seamlessly into night made Winter feel at peace. Rosamund uncovered the candies and held them out.

"Anyone care for a chocolate?" She asked.

"Is that question even necessary?" Marieleen asked in jest. She chose two and passed one to Winter. Next to the river bank they picked up candies with mystery contents beneath a dark chocolate coating.

"Oh no, I got a coconut one. Somebody switch with me," Marieleen shouted.

"I'll take your coconut if you take this orange peel monstrosity," Rosamund said.

"Done," stated Marieleen.

"I like them all," Winter said, which was only a subtle exaggeration of the truth. She could have eaten the whole box on her own.

"So, Winter, Marieleen told me you've come here to face your fears. Why Ireland?"

"I've never been out of the country on my own, which kind of makes me ancy, so I thought I'd start there. I recently decided I'm seeking a bigger life than what I've grown accustomed to living. Ireland has always sparked intrigue for me. There's a family tree that traces an ancestor of mine back to this Island. Who knows if it's true, but it's an enthralling prospect to visit places where you potentially have roots. But I just want to conquer my fears, and taking myself out of my comfort zone seemed the best route. I thought traveling while fear conquering would be the most challenging, and hopefully, because of that, the most rewarding."

"Now that's brave," Rosamund said.

"I'm not sure what it is. I didn't look or feel brave on that bridge or at the pub. Marieleen can attest to that," Winter said, glancing at Marieleen, who smirked from behind her scarf.

"You weren't that bad on the bridge," she said, and then she bugged her eyes out, teasing her new friend.

"Uh huh," Winter laughed, before continuing. "But this journey has taken me places I would never have gone. Sometimes I look around and I'm shocked by where I am, but I'm so glad to be here."

Rosamund nodded as she listened, a small smile danced across her lips. "It is brave. I think it earns you another chocolate."

"I won't argue with that!" Winter said, reaching for another candy.

"You know what I love?" Marieleen interjected.

"No, because you haven't told us," Rosamund joked. Marieleen shot her a look of feigned offense.

"I love moments like this, simple moments that make up your life. I always forget to be thankful for them until they've passed. But they're precious and important."

Rosamund groaned, "Well I can't make fun of that."

***

Winter fell into bed that night and read the note by the dim glow of her bedside lamp. She took a breath as she lifted the paper to reveal the note inside. Winter wasn't sure why she felt so nervous. Sienna's handwriting was there in pale silver ink. Her words glinted in the soft light of the room.

Winter,

I'm so proud of you for doing this. I know you've been having a hard time getting a job lately, but I also know what's been causing deeper heartache for you. I think it's great that you're facing your fears. Since you are, I thought I'd share one fear I have for you, Winter. I'm worried that you've let all the hurt from your past define you. I don't think that's how you should be, how life should be. I want to see you interact with your own existence. Don't go through the motions. Life can be hard. Sometimes it seems like people believe that if they stay still enough, if they don't rock the proverbial boat, that everything will work out. But it takes courage and effort to have the life you want. At times, life's burdens might seem unscalable, but we're not meant to climb over life. We're meant to connect to each other and make it through hardship together. I need you to remember not to lose yourself in the familiar ache of your pain.

Winter, there is humanity in those you don't know, and some of the people you've met have failed to see yours: to really see it, respect it, trust it, and believe in it. But that has nothing to do with you. Don't live your life diminished because someone else has failed to acknowledge your beautiful humanity. You can't wave the white flag on your own life. I've been doing a list of promises to myself for the past few months. Mostly, they're little hopes I want to achieve in my life, ones I'm nervous I won't try unless I remind myself, and I think you should start, too. After talking with you, I kept thinking about something you said. You told me that your fear had grown larger than it had any right to. So, I added one more line to my practice.

I don't know where you are in your journey, but I do know that you're on it. I know that it's not easy to take that first step into the unknown that life has to offer, and that you have to offer life, but you have. Sometimes, as strange as it is, we become comfortable in our pain because it saves us from being vulnerable again, from having to risk further heartache. We stay in our boxes, in the familiar sting of hurt, and become too cautious of happiness and too afraid to chance change. Be brave enough to be happy, Winter. Be strong enough to believe in people again. I wrote this out for you. I don't know what you'll fill in, but promise you'll at least try. Oh, and write back.

Love your dear, wonderful, most amazing and irreplaceable friend, Sienna

On this day, I make a promise to myself. I choose to trust in my own worth and value. Because of this I know my potential is limitless. To unlock it and to take that first step, I promise to conquer that which has held me captive for longer than it has any right to. This is my promise to myself: _____

Winter didn't stare at the blank line for long. She had known before she finished reading what words she would write. She felt something aligning within her spirit. Winter looked down at the empty line and filled it in.

<u>To Live Fully</u>

CHAPTER ELEVEN—THE BLOOM OF FRIENDSHIP

The next morning Winter got up early. She stretched on her bed as she listened to the faint chirping of birds. Even at this distance Winter could hear the clear sound of their music. She leaped out of bed and put on an old white t-shirt and black jeans. Winter pulled her hair into a loose bun and grabbed her phone. There was a missed call from Ella, so she got out her calling card and dialed her sister's number. On the third ring Ella's voice answered.

"Hello? Have you forgotten the time change?"

"Hey, Ella! Maybe for a second, sorry. I'm calling you back!"

"I called you yesterday. You can't call me before the sun is up."

"The sun is up here, and you should probably be getting up anyway. You should be thanking me."

"It's four-thirteen a.m."

"Just thought you might want to hear about some of the fear conquering I've done," Winter said, knowing her sister's curiosity would be enlivened.

"Oh my gosh! Are you changed yet? Have you ascended into the heavenly realm of fearlessness?" Winter smiled, she hadn't realized she missed her annoying older sister.

"Yes, actually I have. It's glorious. You should join me here."

"I've been to the realm of perfection actually, thanks for the offer, though. Perfection is tiresome. You'll see," she joked. "Tell me about Ireland! What's it like? Have you taken down any fears?

"Well, I walked over this sky-high bridge, and Ella, I sang in public at a pub. And get this, there were actual people in the pub when I sang!"

"Who are you?!" Ella yelled. "Are you the same girl who hid in our parent's pantry? You cannot be. What's happened to you over there?"

"I don't know Ella. Sometimes it doesn't seem like I've changed at all, because my fears are still just beneath the surface. But then I look around and see where I am and what I'm doing, and the only answer that feels true is that I am changing. It's been nerve wrecking, but each time I push through my fear, I can feel my life expand a little bit more."

"Wow. Keep it up, girl. I'm proud of you."

"Thanks, Ella."

"I know you've missed me terribly."

"Excruciatingly. I can barely get out of bed."

"I believe it. I have that effect on people," Ella quipped back.

"How is everyone?" Winter asked, laughing. "I haven't been gone too long, so I can't imagine much has changed."

"Things have changed. Mom asks me every other minute if I've heard from you. You need to text them or email them or something so they can relax. They're making me crazy asking me if I've heard from you, Winter. Be better at communication." Winter laughed again.

"I'll try. Do you like your job?"

"I adore being a flight attendant. People are incessantly rude to you and the other day someone sneezed in my face and spilled ketchup on my new white, work shirt. A woman who told me to bring her nuts and fruit yelled at me because the nuts were touching the fruit. I mean, I believe I've found my life calling, Winter."

"You're not the least bit dramatic, Ella," Winter chuckled.

"I know it. Honestly, besides the crazy passengers it's been awesome. I'm always going to new places, and I want to get on international flights one day, so my layovers will rock. It's the perfect job for me right now. I actually have to get going because I have an early start time this morning."

"So you should thank me for calling this early!" Winter yelled.

"No. However, I'm glad you called because I wanted to tell you I found something for you."

"What?"

"A support group for people who hide in pantries during house parties. You'd be surprised how many there are. You go on fun trips and—"

"Ella, I'm hanging up on you."

"Wait! I'm not done."

"Do you want a souvenir?"

"I'm completely finished. I'm done. Hang up and bring me back something good," Ella teased.

Winter hung up and laughed right as her stomach grumbled. Before leaving her room, she grabbed one more note from home. Winter didn't know who the letter was from this time. The mystery of it appealed to her. She went down to breakfast with her fingers crossed, hoping that her favorite table would be open. Winter rounded the corner into the dining room and looked at the empty table with a smile. She ordered the porridge with fresh berry compote. Winter picked something new every morning since she'd been in Belfast. The only choice that remained the same was her cup of tea.

She took out her list and looked at what fears she had left. The first few had gone better than she'd hoped and Winter was anxious to know how she would face the rest of them. She didn't have the answer, but Winter did know that as she attempted to conquer her fears, failure would eventually show itself. Winter wanted to stay strong in the midst of its inevitable return.

Grand failure was familiar to Winter, and her most grand of failures had been inextricably linked to Anna Herald. Electro girl had only been the beginning of their years long battle, and Winter's Grand Failure was the final war fought between the pair. Winter shoved the thought of Anna and her grand failure away and peered at her fears.

My List of Illogical Logical Fears
1. ~~Bodies of water (and being lost underwater).~~
2. ~~Heights that are above my own.~~
3. The future. Where am I going?
4. ~~Singing in public.~~
5. ~~Being alone in a foreign country where I don't know anyone.~~
6. Getting rejected and being vulnerable.
7. Not finding true happiness.
8. Looking and sounding incredibly stupid.
9. Getting out of my comfort zone.
10. Self-consciousness growing larger in my life.
11. Failing to find the road that leads to the path I'm meant to be on in life.
12. Never accomplishing my dreams.
13. Reliving the sadness of my past.
14. Living a small life.
15. Having hate find me again.

She stopped looking at the list and closed the journal on her page of fears. Winter finished breakfast and waved to the Thompson's as she left. The morning was calm, the sun shone down brightly. Winter decided on a leisure walk instead of taking a bus to the city center. She headed to a coffee shop on the main road, her notebook from Sienna in hand. The coffee shop's exterior was completely glass. Inside, Winter could see that it was not too crowded. She danced up the steps, ordered a cappuccino, and sat in a corner booth overlooking the busy main street. The coffee was strong, which was a necessity by Winter's standards for hot morning beverages. Winter pulled out her notebook, sprawled it across the table, and rested her back against the booth.

I could get used to this, she thought, as she watched life moving outside the windows.

A few tables around her spoke with accents; others had multilingual conversations. She welcomed the orchestra of languages as she sipped her morning cappuccino. She took the letter from between the pages of the journal and ripped off the envelope. The outside of the note read: Disclaimer: ALL results and consequences of taking the following advice are the sole responsibility of the user

Ali, Winter thought. *This is your letter.*

Dear Winter,

It's raining here. I'm writing by the window we broke. Do you remember that? I thought my parents were going to send us back into the universe from whence we came! When Sienna said to write something for you, I wasn't sure what to say. I've never been the best with words, but I'll just give you some encouragement that I always find helpful. Here it is. I'd say every experience you have, try to experience it to the fullest. If you're swimming in the ocean, or in your case, cautiously sticking your toe in, feel the water on your skin. If you're laughing, notice how your whole body joins in and shakes with bouts of joy.

When you stand at the corner of a street in Chicago or on those Irish cliffs you dream about, feel the wind on your skin. Breathe in deeply. Be in every experience. Don't think about the things you have to do or need to get done, or the list of blah, blah, blah. I know you worry about tomorrow every day, but it can all wait for you to have an experience. Because they are the things that make up, well, our lives. My cat is trying to eat my ankle right now, and I guess that's all I've got. That's all of my wisdom, Winter. Proceed with caution and use it wisely.

Love, Ali

P.S. Sienna told me to remind you to write in your journal so you don't forget anything. So, write Winter, write!

P.S.S. Never noticed that sounds exactly like your last name. Well, I gotta go. The quality of the letter is severely declining. Write.

Winter laughed loudly in her corner booth. Ali could always make her laugh. She felt the pocket of her green jacket buzzing and picked up her phone. Its screen was lit up with a new message. It was Marieleen asking if she wanted to go to Maggie Mays for milkshakes and a walk in Botanical Gardens. Winter cleaned up her mess and headed to the restaurant.

Marieleen and Rosamund waited outside, both bundled up in scarves. Winter made an unspoken resolution that she would stop eating so much ice cream when she returned home, but until then, she would go to Maggie

Mays every day if the craving arrived. After ordering inside the packed shop, they stood outside on the curb filling their mouths with ice cream. Marieleen's eyes rolled as she drank her dark chocolate milkshake with ribbons of caramel.

"Can I try yours?" Rosamund asked.

"Of course. Dig in," Marieleen said, handing the cup to her.

"Oh, that's good. Winter, you should try it," Rosamund said, her eyebrows furrowed. Exceptional ice cream was a serious matter, and Winter obliged without any hesitation.

"So, I don't believe I've seen the whole list. I only heard about the bridge," Rosamund said.

"Oh, well here. Feast your eyes," Winter said, placing the list in her hands. She could feel heat rising to her cheeks as Rosamund stared down at the list.

"Ha!" She shouted. A few heads turned to examine them. "I have this one too, the um, singing in public.

"Do not say that out loud and in front of Marieleen," Winter cautioned.

"Why?" She asked, a smile turning up the corners of her mouth.

"She didn't tell you? She forced me to sing on stage. I thought we were going to listen to professionals, and my name was spread across the line-up," Winter laughed.

"She told me you sang, but she gave me the impression it was your idea."

"And so it was. In a way," Marieleen said, licking her spoon clean.

"That's grand. Now anytime we go out I'm going to wonder if you're tricking me into public embarrassment."

"I will only do it if you want me to," Marieleen responded.

"That's a relief," Rosamund said, her smile still present.

"Don't trust it," Winter joked.

"Do you come across this last fear, the fear of hate, often?" Rosamund asked, frowning.

"I guess I do. It comes in so many shapes."

"What kinds?" Marieleen asked.

"Are you sure you want to talk about it?" Winter asked. The other two looked at one another.

"Life isn't just the happy parts. We've got to be open to hearing about the parts of life we don't know about. That's what I think," Marieleen said.

"I'd have to agree," Rosamund said.

Winter narrowed her eyes, remembering. Most people Winter encountered squirmed when the conversation turned to color. Some denied that racism was still a problem, so Marieleen and Rosamund's openness to simply listen, encouraged Winter's soul, because Winter didn't know a life separate from prejudice.

"Sometimes it's quiet, as light as a feather, so light you think it's you who's making it up. There are doubled sided comments that uphold and cut down in one breath, 'you're smart for, you're pretty for, you're cool for...' and most of the times people don't mean to perpetuate stereotypes or prejudice. And that can make it hurt more, because it's implicit; it's accepted without question. Other times there are definite moments when it's more undeniable. In college one of my professors, as she was standing in front of the class during my first week in school, told me she thought the only way I'd made it there, into that collegiate seat, was because I'd gone to a predominantly white school.

"That's appalling!" Rosamund shouted.

"You'd think that kind of thinking would have evolved by now," Marieleen commented.

"She made it seem as though the entirety of my achievements were the result of someone else's proximity to me. I didn't go to a school like that, and the thought that the sum of my accomplishments were not my own, because of my skin tone, was a sentiment I'd heard all my life. Growing up, I could see other students of all backgrounds believing teachers who didn't believe in them. I saw some of them just crumble over the years. Sometimes those notions of doubt never leave you once planted. You always have to prove yourself before you've even opened your mouth. That's a small part of it, I guess."

Winter stopped speaking, but Marieleen told her to keep going.

"I'm trying to push against the implicit, and sometimes accepted idea, that what and who I am is naturally a deficit. It's been a struggle, and it constantly makes me cautious of other people, because I'm not sure I'm strong enough to face more prejudice. And the chance is always there. But I've come to a point in life where I'm tired of being told I don't belong. I feel suffocated by the message that I don't have a right to exist exactly as I am: not in a shared space, not in my body as it is, not in my home. I'm not less than anyone else, and beliefs like that one can be dangerous. Perceptions can alter lives and take them. The idea of not having a right to belong and be in this world, as I am, is overwhelming at the least of times. I walk into a room and wonder if people are making assumptions about my abilities, my character, and my worth based off of superficiality. It's always in the back of my mind. Does someone in here believe I'm inferior? Better yet, are they aware that they might? So much of the prejudice I've encountered is small judgments, little actions. But that's why I'm here. I'm in pursuit of a bigger life. I want to live my life not so fearful of hate finding me because it always will. I've let it stop me from being truly alive for too long. What's the point of life if you won't live it? I'm trying to instill in myself the fact that this is my world too, and I don't need permission to occupy it. I have a right to."

They fell silent for a moment. Winter wiped the condensation from her ice cream cup off on her jacket.

"Well, I couldn't agree with you more. This is your world, too," Marieleen said.

"And give people the chance to surprise you," Rosamund offered. "As people we get caught up in concepts that are meant to separate us, to divide us and pit us against each other. If we were given the choice between hatred and peace, I think most people would try to live out of goodness," Rosamund contributed. Winter nodded slowly. She wanted to believe that, but she wasn't sure if she could yet, at least not completely. But then Winter's mind drifted to the first time she remembered hope being extended to her.

Winter was hiding in the bathroom crying after Anna Herald told the class it looked like she'd been electrocuted. She sat on the cold toilet seat cover and muffled the sound of her sobs as she shed her tears. The bathroom monitor for the week walked up to the stall and knocked on the door.

"Excuse me. Is anyone in here? Mr. Johnson said I have to do a check." The voice startled Winter.

"I'm coming out," Winter said, wiping her eyes. She stood and exited the stall after wiping her face with the back of her hand. A girl from Winter's class stood in the bathroom with her. She wore blue tights and black shoes with silver buckles.

"Were you crying?" She asked. Her head was inclined to the side as she posed the question to Winter.

"Um," Winter frowned. She didn't want to admit that she had been crying, but her cheeks were still wet with her tears.

"I don't think your hair looks bad," the little girl said, taking a step forward.

"Last week Anna Herald made fun of me too. She said I smell funny, and she always makes fun of what I bring in my lunches. I told her she should try it before making fun of it, and then she pretended to gag. Once, I asked my mom if I could bring normal food in my lunches and she told me that my food is normal because it's a part of my Mexican-Filipino culture, and I shouldn't have to change that to fit in. I think that maybe it's the same for you. Your hair is different, but you shouldn't have to change it because its apart of you." She smiled at the conclusion of her words.

"I'm Sienna," she said, extending a hand with sparkly blue nail polish.

"Hi, Sienna. I'm Winter, and I don't think you smell weird at all." The two girls giggled in the bathroom as they spoke to each other.

"Just because we don't look like her or eat the same food as her doesn't mean we look the wrong way or eat the wrong way," Sienna said, and then she ran into one of the stalls and grabbed Winter some tissue. "Here you go," she said, smiling as she handed the wrinkled toilet paper to Winter.

"Thanks," Winter said, blowing her nose into the tissue. "I like your skirt and your blue nail polish," Winter said. Sienna smiled.

"Blue is my favorite color."

"Mine too," Winter said, drying her tears.

"Do you want to come over to my house after school?" Sienna asked.

"I'll ask my parents," Winter said happily.

When school ended, Winter's parents drove her to Sienna's house. They walked inside, and an aroma of new spices met them. The Magans insisted the Wrights stay for dinner. Ella wanted to go home and watch the season premiere of her favorite show, but when the food arrived on the table, she stopped sulking. They sat around the Magans table and ate pancit and shanghai. Winter filled her mouth with soft noodles and flavorful meat wrapped in crispy batter. She ate until her stomach became round and then she and Sienna played explorer in the backyard until dusk.

Winter's mind slowly came back to the present. She cleared her throat. "What about you Rosamund? What are some of your strange fears?" Winter asked, shifting the focus of the conversation from herself.

"Hmm, well my sister doesn't like people dressed in costumes, like mascots. She nearly cries around them and they always seem to find her. You'd be amazed. But for me..." She said, tapping the side of her cup. "I cannot stand anything with a tail, especially when it looks like it shouldn't have one. On a more serious note, I think I'm afraid of one of the same things you wrote down. It's a bit different for me, though. You're afraid that you'll never accomplish your dreams, and I fear I'll never know what mine are. Perhaps that's part of life, though. Maybe the more you live and do things, the more you collect memories like treasures, and then happiness fills your life. I think it's important to find what you're passionate about, but I've also seen people get bogged down by trying to find a dream so thoroughly that they forget to live. And that's the only place your dreams can reside. In life, in living it. Maybe that's my real dream, to live a happy and fulfilled life. At the end of my life, I want to be able to look back at chests filled with memories, and not hollow, empty boxes."

Marieleen rose her ice cream into the air. "Here's to collecting chests of unforgettable memories."

Rosamund and Winter knocked their cups together and said, "Here, here!"

And then they turned and walked beneath the black gates into the garden, welcomed by the fragrant scent of blooming flowers.

CHAPTER TWELVE—DUBLIN

A couple days later, Winter walked back to the guesthouse after a day spent touring the countryside with Rosamund and Marieleen. Winter had an inkling that this weekend would be one of her last in Belfast. Winter wanted to make sure she had enough money left for new places, for more fear conquering on other continent's terrain.

It wasn't just because of the money that Winter felt her time in Ireland was coming to an end. Winter's intuition told her she'd done all the fear conquering here she could. As the thought passed over her, she realized she hadn't written in her journal once since coming to Ireland. She could picture Sienna's face asking her if she'd used the gift yet. Fraught with guilt, Winter finally opened the deep blue journal and put pen to paper.

I've faced four of my fears since arriving in Belfast. Even though I almost peed myself in front of someone who, only two hours before was a total stranger, I still feel like a champion. My legs were shaking, and my hands were sweaty, but I moved, and that matters. I sang, actually sang, and words came out of my mouth! Not just croaks, words!

I'm in a new country and every day is a journey outside the limited zone of comfort I've set for myself. I've spent so much of life half awake, and over the past couple weeks I've felt my eyes opening. Every fear I take on seems smaller once I've finished it. I was so afraid to leave home, but I could hear the voice of righteous reason yelling down at me, "What are you doing, Winter?"

But too much of my existence has been distance and redirection. I've run from everything, and distanced myself from living. I've done that for so long now and after facing these fears, I've come to the conclusion that I've got to be okay with being seen for exactly who I am. I can't allow other people's perception of me, good or bad, to create the foundation for my life. And I know what a road that will be for those words to become truths in my actual life. I'll have to take on more formidable fears to achieve that. I made a declaration to live fully. I long for that to be a constant truth.

The urge to retreat from the world can be so tempting. Sometimes it seems I make a decision, and subsequent events strip me of hope. But I want to live a large life. I'm ready to live a large life. The idea makes me nervous because I don't know what that will look like, but I do believe I won't regret the effort. So, here is to seeking a bigger life.

Until then,

Winter

Winter sat on the edge of her bed. She'd been in Northern Ireland for almost two weeks now. Winter went over the funds she had in her mind again. She still wanted to make it to Dublin, which meant now was the time to go. Winter picked up her phone. She texted a message to her friends and had a response less than a minute later.

Hey, Marieleen and Rosamund. Want to go to Dublin for the weekend?

She was met with an exuberant yes, so Winter booked a hostel for two nights. She hit a pen against the pages of her journal as she contemplated where to go after Ireland. Winter picked up a travel book from the bag next to her bed and extended the built-in map. It covered the rectangular bedside table. Winter's eyes glossed over the map, over countries and continents. After thirty minutes of looking, she attempted to fold the map back up, but Winter couldn't get it to return to its proper shape, so she just left it open on the nightstand. She shut the light off and thought of Ali's advice as she drifted slowly, and peacefully, to sleep.

Winter wanted to experience every moment she had.

In the morning Winter packed. She was full of eagerness as she got ready for the weekend trip, wondering if Dublin would lead her in a new direction. She ate breakfast in the dining room by her favorite window overlooking the town. She'd be gone a couple days, so Winter made sure to book the same room at the guesthouse to stay in after returning from Dublin, and before leaving the Island of Ireland, in pursuit of her fear conquering. Winter grabbed her passport, pounds to convert into euros, and stopped by the shop across the street for food. That morning, the three of them met at the black benches outside Botanical Gardens before setting off for the Republic of Ireland.

CHAPTER THIRTEEN—A NEW PATH REVEALED

Dublin felt entirely different to Winter. They got off the steps of the bus on O'Connell Street where a silver spire stood in the center of the road. The monument, made of stainless steel, reached high into the sky. Winter raised her hand and shielded her eyes from the sun's rays to see its top far above her.

"I saw some things online that are must-sees here in Dublin!" Marieleen said. She pulled out a brochure and began reading the list of activities she'd circled.

"We can't leave without seeing the countryside, and Whelan's is a famous pub I thought we could go to. One of my favorite movies was filmed there!" Her voice held a euphoric amount of delight. "I think we should check out who's playing Whelan's tonight, and tomorrow we can have an early breakfast and go to the Cliffs of Moher. Oh! And maybe the next day we can do a tour of Wicklow Mountains National Park. I want to see the mountains covered in purple flowers." She shut her eyes tightly and clenched her hands into eager fists. "I can see the pictures! Do you think the flowers are in bloom? I can't wait to get some shots." Marieleen looked up from the pages when she finished.

"What do you guys think?"

"Lead and I will follow tour guide," Rosamund said. "Whenever I come to Dublin I stick to the same places. Whelan's is one of them. I can get there from any and every direction. Plop me anywhere and I'll find it. Besides," she said, looking at Marieleen's pamphlets covered in writing, "You came so much more prepared than me. I just thought we could go to some pubs, maybe watch some rugby;" she said, her neck still arched as she peered at the spire.

They found a restaurant for lunch and settled into a deep leather booth. The waiter was an older man with a belly that protruded beneath his apron.

"Hello! What can I get for you all?"

"What do you recommend?" Winter asked.

He patted his stomach and said, "It was a great idea to ask me." He bent down, taking a close look at the menu, and listed off the dishes he thought were particularly pleasing. All three settled on fish and chips with cold beers. Winter made it through half of her beer before Marieleen and Rosamund. They stared at her with wide eyes.

"I guess this agrees with you more than the wine," Marieleen said. Winter bit into her food and took another swallow of her Guinness.

"I guess so," she said with a mouth full of food. After they'd devoured their meal, the waiter came to clear their plates.

"Where are you ladies headed today?" He asked, placing their plates on an empty tray.

"We're going to Whelan's tonight," Rosamund answered.

"Ah, very nice."

"Do you have any suggestions?" Marieleen asked.

"Well, as a matter of fact I do. I think you should take a stroll over to Trinity College. There's an exhibition going on with the Book of Kells that you might enjoy, and if you don't know what that is, it means you definitely have to go. Can't leave the country without taking a look at its history," he explained.

"Thank you," Winter said.

"My pleasure. Enjoy your day!" He said, walking away with a smile.

"That was so good. I don't think I can move." Rosamund leaned back in her chair, a look of utter satisfaction spread across her features.

"Really? Because on our way in I saw a dessert place I want to try." Marieleen's eyes moved in the direction of the shop.

"I can move for sweets," Rosamund said, sitting up.

"Try jumping up and down," Marieleen said.

"Why?" Rosamund frowned.

"I don't know. Maybe it will push all the food down."

"Or push it up," Winter laughed.

In the late afternoon, they walked over to Trinity College's Library to see the Book of Kell's, a ninth century text of the four gospels full of artistic imagery depicting scenes of the New Testament. The manuscript was written in Latin and heavily rooted in Ireland's history. The exhibition was named 'Turning Darkness into Light.' Winter thought it an intriguing title. The Book of Kells was on an upper level in a dark room. Winter felt transported to ancient times as she looked down at artfully decorated paper that had seen more life than her. Marieleen kept whispering, "I wish I could take a picture!"

"The Library is supposed to be stunning too, and you're allowed to take pictures up there," Winter said.

The girls left the room and walked upstairs to Trinity College's Library. When they stepped over the threshold, Winter thought she might never leave. An expansive vaulted ceiling of rich mahogany wood seemed to float overhead. Ivory busts of Ireland's prominent historical figures lined the room and from parallel walls emerged two-story bookshelves, filled with ancient texts. Long, sturdy ladders connected to every shelf. Winter imagined climbing on and sliding across the shelves as she got lost in the pages of the books. Inside, she felt the need to stand up a bit straighter, speak a bit softer.

Winter walked through quietly and contemplated how many words filled the walls of the library. *Is it more than millions?* Winter pondered how many collective hours was spent by the writers, how much life had been given to make this place a reality. She could sense the old sting of inadequacy returning. Over the years, she'd had so many interests, but she saw few of those hopes come alive outside of her mind.

After her Grand Failure, Winter had stopped trying as much. Something broke in her that day she failed spectacularly, that last day she saw Anna Herald six years ago. Winter turned her attention back to the towering rows of books that held the history of a nation. *Have I done enough in my life?* She thought.

Winter had quieted her hopes far more than she tried to seek them out, and that's what made her feel her failures so keenly. She was too afraid to move at all and consequently failed by inaction. That's why people who chased their dreams without abandon, with steady and unfailing determination, seemed like puzzle pieces Winter couldn't put together. Winter absentmindedly played with the fraying sleeve on her jacket. She felt a tugging in her gut as she raised another question. *Where am I going next?* The question filled her with tingling suspense.

By the time they finished at the college, early evening was descending upon them. Pale pinks and dark blues colored the sky. They dropped off their bags at the hostel. It was tucked away on a street just off the main road. Strings of orange flags hung from the tops of the buildings, creating a canopy of color above the road.

"Whelan's is a twenty-minute walk from here," Marieleen said, looking at directions on her phone. Rosamund glanced at the phone and then said, "Follow me!"

After ten minutes of walking Marieleen panted, "This is the most exercise I've had in a while."

Winter laughed and said, "That's bad. I'd scold you if the same wasn't true for me."

With Rosamund as their guide they didn't get lost once. When they reached their destination, it was evident to Winter that Whelan's was more than popular. It was an institution. The line outside reflected the pub's appeal. Inside was filled to the brim with people waiting to listen to live music. Winter wasn't sure if anyone else could fit into the building. Whelan's interior was dark. Red lights lit up the bar's sign. The three of them stood in a huddle off to the left side of the stage, and Winter tried her best to avoid getting pushed, elbowed, kneed, kicked and stepped on as people moved through the crowd. Knocking into strangers was inevitable.

"Whoever this guy is, he better be good since we're enduring torture to hear him!" Rosamund yelled out to Winter.

"Stop complaining you two!" Marieleen shouted. The crowd began to erupt into staggered cheers, and then everyone started clapping. With hands raised into the air, they welcomed the singer on stage. He was the main act of the night, the one most people had come to hear. It took Winter until the chorus on his fourth song for her to recognize the performer.

Marieleen turned to her saying, "Hey! Do you see who it is?"

"It's the guy from the pub in Belfast with the live music! Right?" Winter asked.

"Yes! That's that one."

From the stage, he spoke to the crowd. "Cheers. This next song is my last. It's inspired by this past year of my insane life. I've been able to achieve some of my wildest dreams. I recently got signed on with a record label, and I'm stunned by it all. So if there are any dreamers out there, keep at it. You'll make it. I hope you enjoy."

He began to sing. The song was melodic and soft. It settled over the crowd like a spell. At the end of the song he waved to the crowd and stepped off stage. The audience cheered loudly, calling him back to stand beneath the spotlight. Winter could make out his name from the chants. "Connor!" They called.

Winter cupped her mouth with her hands and shouted out along with the crowd. His words inspired Winter. They were air to a dying flame. That was what Winter was after, living a life so full and intentional that your dreams have no choice but to materialize. Over the last couple of years, most everything she attempted fell through.

Winter never got call backs for the jobs she wanted, no matter how long she toiled over the applications. She'd fallen into a mediocre job after college and was let go when they lost funding. It was a fear that she wouldn't achieve her hopes, and sometimes she worried she would only ever dream. But now here she was beginning to live, and it gave Winter belief in her ability to replicate a new dawn where she most desired it.

The next singer approached the stage. Their set was mostly slow songs and mellow rhythms. As Winter listened to the singer, she saw the guy from the pub in Belfast walk outside, and her mind suddenly flooded with an idea. Her desperation made her bold. She pushed her way out of the bar and stepped out of the double doors. Winter peered down the street until she saw him, a black shirt and arms covered in tattoos. She jogged towards him, not entirely sure of what she was doing.

"Excuse me," Winter called. He turned to look at her, his face the picture of confusion and intrigue. "I heard you play just now, and in Belfast, too. You have a lot of talent."

"Cheers, darlin'. Thanks very much," he said. As he looked at Winter, his eyes narrowed while his mind searched for a connection. "Didn't you play that night?" He snapped his fingers as the memory of Winter returned with a vigor that made her cringe. "You were the nervous girl who asked everyone not to boo."

"Well, I didn't think I'd see anyone in that room ever again, so…"

"Everything's a possibility. That's the scary and amazing thing about life."

"That's true, I guess. Just so you know, it was a total surprise to me that I was playing that night, so I had extra nerves. Otherwise, I would have…," Winter searched for a word before settling on the truth. "I still would have been just as nervous."

"You weren't bad. You have a nice voice. All you need is a bit of confidence and practice being under the spotlight."

"Thanks," Winter said, blinking excessively at the unexpected words he spoke.

Then he crossed his arms, a look of amusement on his face. "How can it be a surprise if you have to sign up for it?" He asked.

"My friend signed me up!" She remarked. "Look, singing in public is one of my biggest fears. It induces a ton of anxiety," she said, tucking her hair behind her ear, unsure of what else to do with her limbs. She could feel a nervous tangle of words about to tumble from her mouth. "That's why I'm here actually. I'm trying to conquer some of my deepest fears." Winter had started rambling, try as she might she couldn't make her mouth stop moving.

He pushed the corners of his mouth down, mulling over Winter's words. "And what fears have you faced in my homeland?" He asked, spreading his arms to his sides as if he was fitting all of Ireland between their span.

"Heights, singing in public, and water," Winter listed.

"Did you swim in the cold Irish Sea then?" He asked, folding his tattooed arms. Winter noticed that one tattoo was an arrow with two heads pointing in different directions.

"No, I walked across a bridge that was over water."

He snorted and said, "Does it count if you don't get into the water?"

Winter opened her mouth to speak and then shut it before saying, "I'm reassessing whether I like your songs anymore, and yes, I think it does," she said unconvincingly, without making direct eye contact.

He stared, waiting for her to continue, and Winter remembered why she'd followed him in the first place.

"This might seem strange, but if you don't mind, I wondered if you could answer a question for me."

"Please, go ahead," he said. Winter pushed past feeling vulnerable and ludicrous and asked the question that pushed her to leave the pub.

"You said your last song was inspired by achieving a dream. I wondered, have you always known what you wanted to do? And how did you get where you are now? If that's too personal, you don't have to answer."

He tilted his mouth into a smile. "Do you often chase strangers in pursuit of life advice?"

"I try not to make a habit out of it," Winter replied. He laughed and shoved his hands into his jeans.

"I respect your tenacity, and what you've set out to do, honestly. What's your name?"

"Winter."

"That's an interesting name," he said as he rubbed his jaw, thinking. "I didn't always know. I picked up the guitar when I was quite young. It was just something I always returned to after failed attempts at other things. It always felt like home. Maybe it's the same for you. I think by living you'll find things you're passionate about. But maybe you're like me. Perhaps your dream is so a part of you that you haven't quite figured it out yet. And as far as trying to achieve it…ah…I think you've just got to go for it. I've been told no far more times than I've been given a yes. You've got to believe in what you're doing and not be seduced by the easiness of giving up."

Even though she'd chased him out of the pub and asked him to do this, she couldn't believe that he'd given his opinion and that it was legitimately inspiring.

"You aren't like, touched in the head or anything, right?"

"No, I promise," Winter said.

"I don't condone following strangers," he said, a bright smile reached his eyes.

"I will keep that in mind," Winter bantered back.

Winter recalled his name from the chants and said, "Thank you, Connor. I appreciate it."

"Be honest. Are you stalking me?" He joked.

"No, I'm really not," Winter chuckled. "If I were I would've stayed in the shadows."

Winter had to fight the urge to throw her face into her hands. Awkward words, which she often regretted saying, seemed to spill from her mouth in constant, unrelenting streams.

But he laughed and said, "Cheers. Happy to help. Hope all goes well." And then he waved and began to walk away.

Already, Dublin began to make its unique footprint on Winter's journey. Winter stood on the corner and wondered if the same would be true for her. Was her dream so deeply ingrained into her being that it had eluded her? Or was she too fearful to name it? If Winter searched deep enough into herself, she'd find what she was seeking. She knew that one day in her future she'd have to be brave enough to speak her hopes aloud, and therefore, uncover and give life to her deepest held dream.

***

Back at the hostel that night, after talking with Connor, Winter went online to check her email in the lobby. She sat between Marieleen and Rosamund as she typed in her password and opened her account. There were a couple emails from her parents telling her to call. She wrote down a reminder to herself in her blue notebook. An email from Sienna was at the top of Winter's inbox and below it was one from Ali. Both updated Winter on their lives and asked how she was doing. Winter scrolled through Sienna's email and gasped.

"What?" Marieleen and Rosamund leaned forward.

"I think I know where I'm going next!"

"What do you mean, next?" Rosamund asked.

"You're going to stay here with us," Marieleen said with authority.

Winter grinned and kept reading the email. Sienna wrote that she recently ran into their old college professors, the Rangers, and they asked Sienna to say hello to Winter for them. Just Coffee, where Sienna worked, was going to be partnering with the non-profit cafe the Rangers had started in Jinja, Uganda over ten years ago.

Winter typed in the name of the cafe the Rangers had founded, The Life Cafe. Their picture and biography stared back at her from the illuminated screen. Winter couldn't believe it hadn't crossed her mind to contact the Rangers. In college, they sent students abroad to live and work in the cafe. Everyone always raved about the experiences they had while they lived on the other side of the world, working in the cafe. The program stopped the year Winter was able to apply, but she wondered if they'd be willing to take a volunteer on at the cafe. Winter typed away at the keyboard and wrote an email to the Rangers.

Good Morning Rangers Family!

I hope you are both well! It was so nice of you to say hello. I'm thinking about going to Jinja. I know you both spent a lot of time in Uganda because of the cafe, and I wondered if you could use any extra help. I can pay my way. I'd love to be an extra pair of hands and help out for however long I'm able. Thanks so much, can't wait to hear back from you.

Sincerely, Winter Wright

For a moment, Winter's finger hovered over the keyboard. *Who emails people you haven't seen in months and asks for a place to stay?* The question ran through Winter's mind on a perpetual loop, but she pushed past the excuses shrouded under the guise of reason and pressed send before going upstairs and heading to bed. Winter didn't know if her plan was going to work, but it was liberating to put her ideas in motion. It was something Winter was glad to say was becoming a habit.

CHAPTER FOURTEEN—A SECOND CHANCE

The Cliffs of Moher made Winter want to rethink her life plans. *Maybe I could live by the sea after all*, she thought. She stood with outstretched arms above white tipped waves. Marieleen was stretched out on the ground taking pictures. Her fingers moved rapidly on the shutter button as she collected photos. Winter didn't believe any picture taken of the cliffs could look less than spectacular. She didn't mind the three-hour drive from Dublin to the Atlantic coast on the west of Ireland.

"Winter, don't move," Marieleen said. "I want your picture."

Winter stood at the edge of a rocky cliff with her arms extended out to her sides, eyes looking towards the sky. Marieleen snapped the picture. Winter tilted her head back, letting the sun hit her exposed skin.

"Got it," Marieleen smiled. "Now both of you."

Rosamund reluctantly moved toward the edge. "I better not die for this shot of yours," Rosamund said, peering over the rock's edge.

Marieleen took the picture and a smile full of calm reached across her face.

"That's it."

"Let me see what masterpiece I'm a part of," Rosamund said.

"It's not digital. There's something about film that digital cannot capture. Give me your addresses and I'll send the photos to you both when I get them developed."

The three of them sat down on the grassy side and looked out over the sea. Something about Ireland made Winter feel more alive, more in awe of the earth and its unparalleled beauty and strength. The exposed cliffs, the fields of green with roaming sheep, and the yellow flowers that peeked out from tall grass made Winter settle into the present moment. It quieted her thoughts and the noise that often filled her mind.

At home, Winter would ignore her feelings by filling her day. Her mind fluttered from one distraction to the next. She was an expert at stowing away the things that made her heart ache. Winter realized how much noise she'd filled her life with before leaving. There was noise to block out feelings of discontent and fear, noise to occupy herself, to rage on in her mind, enabling her to neglect the things she so desperately needed to face. Now, Winter knew the noise was simply blocking out the whispers urging her to do something more. And the longer she waited, the more she silenced her hopes, the unhappier she became. Winter wanted to lean in, decipher the whispers, and cancel out the noise that told her she wasn't enough.

Here, she could hear the noise lessening. In the quiet serenity of the Irish Coast, Winter was meeting the person she was before fear, prejudice, insecurity, and the desire for protection infiltrated her true self. Slowly, ever so slowly, Winter was making it back to the self she barely knew.

The sky seemed bluer and the clouds more radiant than usual. Winter reminded herself that this ethereal beauty probably existed at home in some form too, though in a different way. There was simplistic splendor in the flat farmland of her home, in the wheat that grew from the soft soil, and the cornstalks that swayed in the breeze.

Winter didn't want to lose what she was gaining from Ireland. She wanted to wrap it up, bring it back home, and bestow the gift of being present in your life to everyone she knew. On the bus ride back to Dublin, Winter checked her email from her phone. The response from the Rangers had already come.

It's great to hear from you, Winter! We're glad you're doing well. We have a few volunteers there now who are working at the cafe, and we cover living and food expenses. They shadow our people to learn about the work we do apart from the cafe through a grant we have that funds improvement projects in local villages. You'd be very welcome to join if they need the help. There are only a few staff members so we're pretty positive they'd welcome extra hands! We'll have them reach out to you.

The Rangers

Winter smiled in her seat and began pumping her arms and legs into the air with excitement at the possibility.

"Are you all right?" Marieleen asked, staring at Winter as she contorted her body in her seat.

"I might be going to Uganda!" Winter sang out. Marieleen and Rosamund looked to one another.

"Don't tell us about any plans you have for leaving," Rosamund said.

"After you told us about the email last night, we decided that we won't support any plans you have that involve abandoning us," Marieleen concluded.

Winter laughed and said, "You could always come with."

Winter's time in Dublin lasted a few days, but its impression on her was far reaching. It was there that she began to have the first inklings of a dream she was not yet brave enough to proclaim. When she and her friends returned to Belfast early the next morning, they parted ways and Winter walked back to The Gregory, back to a familiar place. Once in her room, Winter saw a new email in her inbox. Winter sat down as she read the email from her phone's screen.

Hi, Winter. My name's Simon. I work for The Life Cafe's Community Project Program. I handle volunteers and interns as well. We have two people here now and could use another if you're available. The Rangers spoke highly of you! The work won't be glamorous. We need help with odd jobs like cataloging the cafe library, working in the cafe store, and cleaning. If you're interested, some days you can come to different villages to learn about the programs and partnerships we have with local communities. We can cover living costs, but it will be unpaid. Interns and volunteers live above the cafe. I interned here five years ago, and it was the best decision I've made for myself. Let me know soon if you would like to come.

Peace to you, Simon

Winter leaned back in her chair incredulous. Her heart beat hard in her chest as she chewed on her bottom lip. Providence seemed to be working in Winter's life. The thought of Uganda filled Winter with a sense of inquisitiveness she wanted to explore. Winter started looking up attractions in the country. She gazed at images of roaring waters beneath rafts that seemed flimsy and unreliable in her fear-filled opinion. To Winter, the only reliable thing about water was the hard ground that surrounded it.

Winter thought back to the last time she talked to her closest friend Sienna at the lake house. Before leaving to conquer to her fears abroad, Winter tried to confront her fear of water that very day.

Winter had made sure she was the first to wake up that morning at Sienna's lake house. She soundlessly closed the back door and walked outside towards the shed where the life jackets were stored. Winter was going to jump from the black diving board floating high above the water. It was before six a.m., and the lake was cold as she pushed herself through the velvety waters to the black platform in the center. The sun was rising, casting light on the trees, making it appear as if Winter was wading into the water on a chilly autumn morning. Specs of coming blue sky could be seen emerging through a cascade of leaves. She climbed onto the raft and shuddered. The bars of the ladder felt wintery against her bare feet. Her toes tingled with nervous energy.

Winter stared over the steady water from the top of the plank. She and the lake were completely still in that silent moment of daybreak. Her life jacket was secured around her body so tightly it threatened to hinder her breathing, but that didn't stop Winter from tugging at those straps just a bit more. She probably stood towards the back of that diving board for over ten minutes, by herself, staring at her solitary reflection in the water. Winter inched forward and felt her stomach plummet as her toes moved to the end of the plank. *You can do it. You'll pop right back up*, she told herself, but then she remembered thrashing in the pool as a child, the endeavor breathing became as water surrounded her body.

Eventually, Winter climbed down the ladder and pushed her body through the ripples, gradually, until she reached the bank. She sat on the edge of the lake with her arms wrapped around her knees. She'd failed her first attempt at conquering a fear. Winter imagined what the water would feel like if she didn't fear it, if it didn't make her heart pound in her chest. *Weightless*, she had thought. Winter believed it would feel as if she could fly away at any moment, just lift her arms and ascend gracefully and fearlessly into the sky. It'd be pure freedom, no barriers, nothing to weigh her down, only her and the endless heights to which she could fly.

Winter wanted to overcome her fear alone, to make that leap through willpower. She didn't want to be persuaded to jump or comforted by her friends if she failed. But she couldn't bring herself to launch her body from the plank. The memories of Winter's head sinking beneath the surface, and being unable to find her way to the top as her body screamed for air, had rendered her immovable. Her fears had been heard that morning.

Winter stood up from the edge of her bed at The Gregory and paced the room. The picture of that clear water slowly moving around her, while she stared into the dark depths of the lake, made her contemplate one fear she'd checked off. Her fear of water was submersion. To check it off, and feel good about it, she knew she'd have to face her fear of water again. Every travel website Winter visited, she came across the same picture; she knew how she was going to face this fear. Winter was going to raft the Nile.

She shot off an email to Simon and the Rangers saying she was ready any day they needed her, and then Winter started getting ready for the morning. She had to fight the urge to sit staring at the computer screen waiting for a response. Winter knew a reply wasn't going to be immediate. The room was quiet as she packed her bag for a day out with friends. One of the strangest things about being in a different country on her own were moments of solitude. At home, someone was always a phone call away or a quick drive down the street. Here, she'd had to depend more on herself in her quiet moments when Marieleen and Rosamund were busy.

Contrary to her experiences, Winter was finding out that she was just that. Enough. It amazed her how quickly she'd made friends that felt like family. She'd lived more life in the last week than she had in the last few years. Winter hastily grabbed her journal and flipped to a fresh page.

I'm going to Uganda. Those words don't feel like reality, but it's true. I can barely believe all that I've done since hiding in that pantry. I'm facing my fears, and I can feel myself breaking free from the existence that's been suffocating me. My breaths are still shallow, but I finally have air. Here's to seeking a bigger life.

Until then, Winter

Winter closed the journal. She placed that same old green coat onto her body and rubbed a hand over the sleeve, remembering why she'd bought it for her twelfth birthday. She'd wanted to be invisible after that day, able to camouflage herself from unforeseeable hurt, from hate. Winter learned that day that an attack could come in any form, at any time. She'd kept it all these years, and as she stood in her bedroom at The Gregory, she knew that one day she would have to let the jacket, and all it represented, go.

Winter headed to Maggie Mays to meet Marieleen and Rosamund. She picked a table by the window, her mind abuzz. Winter wanted to stay in Belfast and have dinners in the garden, ice cream runs to Maggie Mays, and walks along sandy coasts. But she also wanted to challenge herself to go someplace new. Winter was ready to see what she'd gain from time in Uganda. She laughed inwardly, astonished at the change. If she knew months ago that she would be traversing the world with no destination in sight, she'd have fainted. Now, it brought a sense of liveliness to her limbs. Marieleen came through the door then, the same scarf wrapped around her neck, buffering her skin from the chill. Rosamund followed closely behind, her black nail polish fresh.

"I can't believe you're making plans to go," Marieleen said, upon hugging Winter.

"I know. I can't quite comprehend it myself. But I've got more fears to face," Winter responded, without breaking their embrace.

The waiter came over to the table, pen in hand.

"Marieleen, which one do you always get?" Rosamund asked.

"Dark chocolate with caramel!" she answered.

"I'll give that one a go,"

"I will too," Winter said.

Winter searched in her bag for her wallet and pulled out her journal in the process. She'd been carrying it in her bag so that she could write in it whenever she felt the need to immortalize a memory. One of her letters fell from between the pages and Marieleen picked it up.

"What's this? Is it a note from home?"

Winter furrowed her brow. "Yeah. It is, but I came with them. One of my friends had everyone write letters of advice and encouragement to me. I'm sure some of those letters also detail what a lunatic I am for doing this."

"I love that. Not the lunatic part, but how sweet that must be to read those words," Marieleen said. She turned and hit Rosamund on the shoulder and asked, "Don't you love that, Rosamund?"

"You're going to start making me miss my family, and they don't even live very far from me. How many have you read?"

"I've only read a couple, but they've been so helpful to me."

The waiter came back over then. "That was fast!" Rosamund said.

"Sorry ladies, but we ran out of milk. If you're willing to wait, I can run to the shop across the street and grab some more."

"We don't mind at all. Do you know how long we would wait for one of these milkshakes?" Rosamund asked. He laughed and said he'd be back soon. They watched him race across the street and into the store. Winter turned to Marieleen and Rosamund. "I'm gonna miss this place."

***

Winter got back to the guesthouse late that night after dinner in the courtyard and a long walk through town. She sat at the edge of her bed and pulled out her phone. Winter leaned down and re-read the email from Simon three times over. They said she could come. They had a place for her. Winter recalled the globe that sat in her old apartment back home, which now seemed like a distant lifetime, and the picture of the African continent came into her mind's eye. A new story was beginning, and Winter Wright was determined to make it exceptional.

CHAPTER FIFTEEN—THE BILLBOARD

Winter frequented her most loved places in Belfast over the next two days, and packed for Uganda. On a hazy morning, when the sun hid behind steel-colored clouds, Winter slowly rolled her bags down the steps of The Gregory. Mrs. Thompson had already arranged a ride for Winter. A black taxi, similar to the one that introduced her to Belfast, was parked on the curb.

In keeping with Belfast tradition, it began to rain lightly, but Winter was prepared. She pulled out her umbrella. The Thompsons helped Winter load her things into the back of the cab.

"Come again, please," they said with genuine smiles.

"I will. I couldn't imagine staying anywhere else," she confessed.

Winter took a long look at the guesthouse. Her eyes gazed at the green lawn and red bricks that had become her home over the past three weeks. She said goodbye to the Thompson's and was just about to get into the taxi when she heard yelling.

"Wait!" Winter turned and saw Marieleen and Rosamund running down the street. A smile brightened Winter's face as her friend's approached.

"I know we already said our goodbyes, but we wanted to wave you off," Marieleen said. The girls fell into a hug.

"Thanks for everything. You guys made my trip," Winter said with a tight chest.

"Don't forget to tell us about how rafting goes," Rosamund said. "I want to know if you survive the Nile."

"I just hope I don't get kicked out the country for making too many cultural faux pas. I know I'll make them."

"We were pretty close to making you leave Ireland," Rosamund said.

"See!" Winter shouted with laughter.

"Here," Marieleen handed two letters to Winter. "We wanted to write something, too."

"I don't know what you'll do without us. We were so paramount in helping you overcome some of the things on that list of yours," Rosamund joked, making Winter laugh loudly.

"You're right. I don't know how I'll finish my list. Thanks for everything," Winter said more seriously.

"Don't forget us," Marieleen said.

"Not possible," Winter managed to say.

"Collect as many good memories as you can. Fill that treasure chest of experiences to the brim, friend." Rosamund said.

They hugged one last time and Winter got into the back of the cab. She pushed the door shut and the car began to move away from the curb. Winter rolled the window down and popped her head out. "Goodbye!" She said. But the word got caught in her throat, her eyes burned hot with tears.

The two of them stood in the middle of the street. Rosamund smiled lightly. Marieleen's face was red, flushed from emotion. They lifted their hands in unison and waved goodbye to their friend. Winter waved until the downward slope in the road slowly blocked them from her vision. It wasn't until the driver turned the corner that Winter stopped looking back.

"How long have you been friends?" He asked, looking at Winter from the rearview mirror.

Winter roughly wiped at her tears and answered, "Feels like lifetimes."

The driver smiled and put his eyes back on the road.

Winter bit her lip and sighed softly. It would be so easy to stay, but in her pocket was her flight information and the phone number of the person who was going to pick her up. Her fear conquering was calling out to her. Winter was already gone.

The cab driver made conversation with Winter as they headed to the airport. He spoke openly as he told her about his years working as a tour guide. Then Winter's eyes happened upon a billboard out in the distance, and her heart dropped to her gut. A slight perspiration formed on her brow as her addled mind tried to shape the letters into something else, but they would not budge. Written on the sign in stark, white letters were these words: "No Irish, No Jews, No Blacks, No Dogs."

Winter swallowed and moved her mouth to speak, but realized she didn't know what to say. The cab driver was still talking as they passed the Belfast City Cemetery. "And this graveyard over here," he said, pointing a thick finger outwards, "There's a wall underground separating the Catholics from the Protestants. They said they were separate in life and wanted to be separate in death also."

"Why?"

"It goes back far into our history. There's tension between Protestants and Catholics that dates back to the 1800's and still lingers to this day. Back then religion decided lives and people separated themselves along political and religious lines."

She swallowed again, and for a time, that was the only act she thought her body capable of performing. Winter wanted to learn more about what the man spoke of, but her shock had overcome her. When they pulled to the curb at the airport, the man told Winter to come back to Belfast. His smile was genuine and his demeanor jovial.

Winter shook her head at the juxtaposition of the morning. She thought to ask him about the sign. *What brought it about? Who put it up? Who was being affected by it?* Another question entered Winter's mind. *But will he feel uncomfortable?* She worried about burdening him with the weight of having to answer the question, with the possible discomfort that would follow, so she decided to stay quiet.

Winter walked into the airport slightly dazed, wondering why hate always took her by surprise. *Why does it shock me?* She asked herself. Winter stood in line waiting to go through security. She walked to the front of the line and a man stepped up to her. He wore a uniform, clothes that intimidated Winter. In his presence, she felt the need to stand up straighter and push her shoulders back from their hunched-back position. It felt awkward and unnatural to stand up straight and with confidence.

"Where are you coming from?"

"Uh, I was in Belfast for a few weeks. I arrived the third and I'm leaving today, the 24th, but you probably already know today is May 24th," she said, tripping over her tongue. She scolded herself for stumbling over her words.

"What were you here for?"

Do not ramble. Do not ramble, she thought. "I was here for vacation."

He just shook his head up and down, listening.

"Um, that's all I was here for."

"Do you have any weapons on you?" He asked abruptly.

"Do tweezers count?" She said, wanting to be forthcoming.

He inclined his head as he said, "Depends on how scrappy you are with them. You're fine. Go ahead."

His formal demeanor dropped, and Winter felt at ease once again. She went through security and breathed a little as she set off to find her gate. Her broken wheel clicked on the tile, making Winter's bag roll lopsided. She found her gate and checked in at the desk. Winter was grateful to learn there were plenty of stand-by seats available. Winter sat down and took out her journal. She flipped through its pages until she found a blank sheet. Winter held the pen above the paper as her thoughts expanded.

The images of her last moments in Belfast inundated Winter. Most of her time in Ireland was beautiful, and yet she could feel shame rising. The internalization of someone else's loathing was a constant battle. The weight of feeling unworthy for simply existing as she was, made her chest tighten. She took in shallow breaths, but no amount of air could rescue her from the suffocating reality of hate. Winter couldn't understand why her skin made people think less of her, why differences in culture, ethnicity, and religion, made someone erect a sign of hatred.

I can't believe how different my life looks compared to a few short weeks ago. My time in Ireland wasn't without it's prickles, but I will learn how to deal with their sting. My hope is that one day, I'll be able to withstand the thorns and begin to shift my focus to the beautiful and full bloom my life is beginning to resemble. Here's to seeking a bigger life.

Until then, Winter

Winter dropped the pen into her bag, and then all at once her mind flooded with the mental picture of that billboard. She gazed, her eyes an empty void, across the terminal. Though Winter didn't know it then, her most entrenched trepidation was looming on the horizon of her life, waiting. Every step brought Winter closer to her fear of hate.

CHAPTER SIXTEEN—THE OTHER SIDE OF THE WORLD

The flight from Belfast to Jinja Uganda was lost in Winter's wholehearted curiosity. She barely slept. She hadn't a hint of what the coming weeks would bring, and that fact filled Winter with miraculous wonder. She laid back in her seat as the captain's voice rang clearly throughout the large cabin.

"We will be landing shortly."

Winter lifted the plastic shades to look out her window and gasped reflexively. The scene beneath Winter was majestic. The sun was rising from behind a landscape of mountains. Its rays set the sky ablaze and illuminated the dark silhouettes of the mountain range, of rugged, untouched earth that seemed to rise and greet Winter to this new country.

The plane landed and Winter made her way outside. She had looked at The Life Cafe's website enough times to recognize the faces of the interns and employees. It was a small staff. So when Simon Stone rolled into the parking lot in a large, white suburban, Winter knew her ride had arrived.

"You must be Winter! I'm Simon," he called out from the window as he drove into an open spot. He wore black rimmed glasses and a white button down shirt. Simon pulled to a stop and three car doors opened.

A short girl wearing a stack of threaded bracelets on her arm and a tall guy with fraying pant legs jumped out of the car. Winter shook her head yes.

"I am. Something keeps giving me away. People seem to know when I'm a foreigner. How could you tell I'm new here?"

"You're the only one that looks completely intrigued by what she sees," he said as he shut the car door. Simon strode towards Winter with a bright smile covering his face.

"We're glad you're here. We always love having new hands around the cafe," he said, pointing to the other two. The girl stepped forward.

"I'm Alexis," she said, extending her arms to embrace Winter. "I'm more of a hugger," the girl said with a smile. "I've been anticipating your arrival because I need help keeping this one in check," she said, casting her eyes toward the guy next to her.

"I'm Michael," he said with a crooked grin. "And don't listen to her. If she gives you any trouble, come to me."

Simon rolled his eyes playfully. "You'll get used to them; God knows I've had to. Are these all your bags?" Simon asked, looking at Winter's bag and broken suitcase.

"Hmm. That's it," Winter replied, adding, "One of my bags is compromised, though. The wheel broke."

"I'll be careful with it," Simon said, leaning down to grab the case.

"How was your flight?" Alexis asked as they walked towards the car.

Winter smiled and said, "Long but beautiful. I came in next to a sunrise."

Simon understood the dreamy look in Winter's face. "Ah, the mountains. They are something to see."

"I'm from the flatlands of the Midwest. Anything bigger than a mound is something to see," Winter said.

Simon laughed loudly. "I can understand that. Michael and I are from the Midwest as well. There's nothing but farmland where we lived. Our old town is called Archer Hills, but there's not a hill in sight."

"That sounds about right," Winter said, nodding. Simon placed Winter's bag in the back of the suburban.

"How long have you all been working at The Life Cafe?" Winter asked.

"I'm going on four years," Simon replied, shutting the trunk door. "I worked as an intern for a year before I got the job. I don't think I'll ever leave."

"I got here a few weeks ago. I was doing some traveling in Asia when Simon said he could use me here," Michael said, climbing into the back of the suburban. "He's my older, decrepit brother."

Winter laughed and said, "That's how I'm going to start referring to my older sister from now on."

"Happy to be of service to another younger sibling," Michael said.

Alexis pursed her lips as she thought. "I've been here for a month. I heard about the cafe from a friend who interned there when she was in college. I can't believe I've been here that long. It doesn't feel like it!" Alexis said.

"It does to me," Michael half-whispered, making sure his hushed voice was loud enough for Alexis to hear.

"Michael, annoy me, and I will wax your eyebrows off in your sleep!" Alexis warned.

"Winter," Simon began, "Usually one tires out and they call it a tie before the rematch begins. I place bets on them. You're welcome to join me."

"Who do you bet for? Winter asked.

"Alexis, of course," Simon said coolly.

"Thanks, brother," Michael said, shaking his head back and forth. "You see how they treat me, Winter! I need you on my team."

"Let me think about it and get back to you," Winter said in jest.

"Remember the abuse we suffer as younger siblings," he said.

"Now that's a good point," Winter said, and then she turned her attention to Simon.

"You've been here a long time. Do you miss home often?" Winter asked, curious.

The other two looked to Simon.

"I do, but this is home now. As terrible as this may sound, I sometimes miss the food I can't have here more than some people," Simon joked.

"You're right. That does sound terrible," Winter said with a laugh.

"I warned you," he said.

"You did."

"I'll probably retire here, but you'll get to decide how you feel about the place very soon." His mouth turned upwards into a soft grin. "It's a long ride to the compound, but it's a great introduction to Jinja. All newcomers get the front seat."

They all piled into the suburban and rolled out of the parking lot and onto the long, winding red dirt streets of Uganda. Winter looked at tall trees and the outlines of mountains in the distance as she mused over what kind of mark Jinja was going to leave on her. The deep red dirt of the streets covered the suburban's black tires. Winter dared not move her eyes from the window as they passed homes and shops that resembled nothing her eyes had seen before. Pieces of tarp and metal came together to make roofs. Planks of broken wood joined to create countertops for small store fronts. People leaned over the counters and watched as the large white car, painted in red, drove past.

Simon brought the car to a stop to let a cow and its owner walk across the road, and as they waited, a man came up to the car and began knocking hard on the window, startling Winter. He was offering grilled chicken. Winter thought she might be conjuring up the image in her mind, but Simon turned to them and asked, "Do you want any?"

"Of course!" Michael called out, hitting his brother hard on the arm.

"I'm still a vegetarian but thank you," Alexis said.

"Winter?" Simon asked.

"Uh…"

"You have to," Michael told her.

"All right. Thanks," Winter said.

"Roadside chicken is the only way to go," Simon said with a smile. "You'll fall in love with it—unless you're like Alexis."

Simon turned back to the man selling hot food. "I'll take three. Thanks. What else do you have?" He asked, leaning out the window. Simon ended up buying steaming chicken, fire roasted corn, bread that reminded Winter of tortillas, and what looked like a triangle shaped pastry.

"Webale!" Simon called out as the man walked away.

"Kale!" The vendor shouted back.

Simon laid the food on the console between them and began pointing. "So, this corn is called maize. It's not sweet like the corn at home, and it has a bit of a bite to it. The bread is called chapati, and it comes with a warning I give to everyone who tries it. Ready?"

"Yeah," Winter laughed.

Simon raised his hands with caution and said, "Once you taste it, no other bread will compare. I'm sorry about that."

Alexis leaned forward from the middle seat. "It's true. I too have been forever changed by its perfection."

Winter chuckled as Simon continued. She was already beginning to feel at home amongst these new people.

"These little triangles are called samosas. I'll let you experience those on your own."

An aroma of fresh spices and the scents of roasted food filled Winter's nose. Her mouth watered. She picked up a piece of the golden bread first. Winter brought the food to her lips and began to chew on the soft, buttery bread. She took another bite and then reached for one of the samosas. Inside the crispy breading were seasoned veggies and tender meat.

"I understand what you mean entirely," she said, looking to Simon and Alexis as she swallowed a mouthful of food. "I could live off the chapati and samosas. No problem," Winter declared.

Alexis and Simon laughed heartily. Michael was lost in a world of food. He smirked as he picked up a samosa and ate it in two large bites. Winter tried the maize next. She bit into it and began to chew slowly, very slowly. The hard kernels were blackened from the open flames that had cooked them. Simon laughed next to her.

"I'll take that with no complaint," he said. Winter wondered if his face was always painted with that grin. She handed Simon the corn. Simon ate the corn as he stared ahead at the road. "It's definitely the best part of the drive. These two would have you believe they rode to the airport to meet you, but they came for the food," Simon said with a wink.

"I don't think I can blame them," Winter said.

She picked up another samosa, along with a bit of bread, and returned her gaze to the streets and mountains that passed by too quickly. She watched as cattle and sheep roamed freely. Young women walked with effortless grace as they balanced large jugs of water on top of heads adorned with colorful scarves.

"I don't think I could do that," she said, entranced by the natural elegance of their every step. "If I did try I wouldn't look like that." They all followed the direction of Winter's eyes, and Simon cleared his throat to speak.

"Oh, I know I couldn't do that because I tried my first year here. I was out at a village learning about the partnerships between the cafe and local farmers, when someone asked me if I wanted to try. I dropped the bucket onto my foot and ended up fracturing two of my toes. No one has let me near another bucket since."

Michael burst out laughing, he slapped his leg and almost dropped his chicken. Winter tried to hide her laughter, but Simon exclaimed, "That story often gets me a laugh. It's not usually as robust as Michael's," he said, staring at his brother.

"I'm sure of that," Winter said.

"Have you ever worked at a cafe before?" Alexis asked.

"No, I haven't," Winter said, excitement coursing through her.

"The cafe work can be slow sometimes but you get to meet people from all over the world," Simon offered, drumming his fingers on the steering wheel.

Winter was already envisioning herself serving food to vagabonds and locals alike, and then she remembered the Nile. Winter felt less calm just thinking about it.

"What have you two done during your free time?" Winter asked, turning to face Michael and Alexis from the front seat.

"We haven't had much free time yet," Michael said. "Was there something you were thinking of specifically?"

Images of the Nile filled Winter's mind. Winter shifted a knob on the half-working air conditioner, so that the slightly cool air blowing out could reach her.

"I was wondering about rafting the Nile. Have any of you done that?" Winter asked. Michael and Alexis both looked to each other.

"You've asked the right people, Winter," Michael said.

"We're planning on going Friday afternoon. Do you want to come? We can still get you signed up," Alexis offered.

"What about the cafe?" Winter questioned.

"You can get a day off to raft," Simon said.

"Besides, it feels like initiation and we have yet to do it," Alexis said. "Simon went his first week in Jinja! I've been here a month. Want to go?" she asked again.

Every fear-conquering opportunity Winter sought out still filled her with the urge to run away, but standing her ground in the midst of fear was showing Winter that she had unexpected reserves of strength, and she was going to need them.

"Friday afternoon?" Winter asked. That gave her three days.

"That's right," Alexis said.

With bated, determined breath Winter said, "I'm in."

CHAPTER SEVENTEEN—I'M HERE

The reverberation of the city ripped Winter from sleep. Honking and the sound of tires moving against the hard ground flooded her ears. The intermingling smell of fresh dirt and exhaust made Winter sit up in her seat to take in her new surroundings. She saw billboards overhead advertising a range of skin lightening products. Blue and white vans shuttled people across lanes as bikers found pathways between cars.

Vehicles moved in almost every direction, and open spaces on the roads were crowded with pedestrians. Dust from the street billowed into the air outside her window. Winter noticed people with thin clothing draped over their frames begin to move towards the suburban.

A group of men, women, and children began knocking on the windows. They gestured towards Winter, extending empty hands outwards. This wasn't Winter's first brush with poverty. She'd seen people during brutal Chicago winters hiding from the hard bite of winter's bone-chilling cold beneath car tunnels. When Winter was young she met the Green family.

The Green's couldn't pay their water and electric bills and often came over for dinner at Winter's house. The daughter of the family always ate half her food and put the rest in her pockets when she thought no one was watching. On cold nights, they'd sleep in the Wright's house until their heat came back on. Poverty, Winter knew, touched every continent. She locked eyes with a man outside and a thought, so brief but all encompassing, washed over her. She felt cold, as if the blood in her body was draining from her veins.

The gulf between the reality of he and Winter's worlds was so wide, and yet it was connected by one glaring and evident truth, their common humanity. The realization that this man who stood before her lived a reality so starkly opposing to her own, and that lives this uneven could exist on this shared earth, filled Winter with a longing to close that divide in some way.

"It's a lot to take in," Simon said.

"Yeah...," Winter replied with a shallow breath.

They pulled into the compound ten minutes later. The thick wheels of the suburban drove across the gravel driveway and came to a slow stop in front of The Life Cafe. Winter stepped out of the car and felt the gray pebbles dig into the soles of her shoes, which had become worn and thin from traversing the rocks and cliffs of Ireland. She closed her eyes briefly to remember the crashing sea, the smell of the air. The scents were different from the air Winter now inhaled, and she was looking forward to uncovering the layers of this new place.

Winter could hear barking coming from behind the house. A small dog rounded the corner and Winter suddenly had a flashback to her seven-year-old self. Her skinny ankles had been covered in frilly socks when the neighbors Chihuahua started racing towards her, teeth dripping with anticipation. This new dog barked at her ankles, and Winter jumped. The dog was minuscule, but it still had teeth. Its size didn't prevent Winter from wanting to climb onto the car's hood.

"You look like you're on a pogo stick. I promise he won't hurt you. He might take a nibble, but it'll be gone by the end of the day," Simon said.

Winter eyed Simon. Harmless laughter was clear in his eyes. The Chihuahua had also nibbled her, and its teeth marks resulted in six stitches on Winter's leg. The ghostly trace of the scar still lingered on her ankle. Simon leaned down and grabbed the dog.

"What's his name?" Winter asked, trying to calm her fear.

Alexis walked over and rubbed the dog's scrunched face. "Harrison III," she said. "But we call him Harri. He's the cafe dog. We all pitch in and take care of him. At one point, we had to start a feeding schedule because we were all feeding him three meals a day."

Winter laughed and asked, "Where'd you get him?"

"He was an orphaned puppy on the streets. We've had him for a year now," Simon said. Then he motioned towards the doors. "Shall we?" He asked, pointing to The Life Cafe.

"We shall," Winter replied.

Simon grabbed Winter's luggage and walked toward the cafe. The cafe was over ten years old, but its care-takers kept it up beautifully despite the harsh, unrelenting sun. Above the double doors, on the second level, Winter could see a living room through the open window.

This is going to be my home for a little while, she thought.

Just outside the yard there was a decorated sidewalk. The logo of the cafe was painted in green and blue: The Life Cafe. A few windows lined the shop's exterior, and an old wooden sign hung from a post, moving in the wind. Simon opened the door for Winter, Alexis, and Michael.

"Your humble abode awaits," Alexis said.

Winter peered around the corner as she stepped across the threshold. Inside the cafe, the steady humming of an outdated air conditioner rattled. Winter's eyes landed on vintage chairs of various sizes and shades hugging jewel toned tables. The counter where customers ordered was yellow, and the walls were painted light blue. Dark wooden beams rose up from the floor. Windows were on every visible wall.

The cafe store to Winter's right held racks with intricately beaded necklaces, ornately decorated scarves, and baskets weaved with an array of yellow, purple, black, and white straw. Across from the store was a door to a small library with stacks of books piled high on the floor. Dust floated in the air highlighted by a stream of sunlight. The Life Cafe's tiles were an auburn color with faded grout running between the square pieces.

"I'm gonna head out. I have a few things to get done," Simon told the group. He clapped his brother on the back. "Glad to have you with us, Winter."

"Thanks for picking me up."

"Of course," he said with a smile. "Alexis and Michael can answer any other questions you have. See you all later," he said.

Alexis spun around and started to point with her index fingers. "So, there's a kitchen in back and the cafe shop is over there. There's a courtyard behind the kitchen. Michael and I have our breaks back there during the day. Michael, is there anything I'm forgetting?"

"The cash register sticks."

"That's not exactly what I was going for," Alexis said, folding her hands together.

Michael raised an eyebrow at Winter. "She is impossible to please sometimes," he said. "How about this? We keep a couple guitars in the courtyard for people to play. If you ever want one, feel free to grab it."

"That's better," Alexis said. "Do you play Winter?"

Winter thought back to the crowded pub in Belfast and recalled the taut strings beneath her fingertips.

"A little," she answered.

"The living space is upstairs," Alexis said, unlocking a door in the back of the cafe next to the courtyard. Winter followed Michael and Alexis up the stairs to the living quarters, but her gaze was concentrated on the cafe. Its name seemed to speak truth. It felt alive and full of energy despite its current emptiness.

"Why is the cafe so empty?"

"We're usually closed one day a week so that employees can go out to the source farms. That's Simon's main job, and sometimes we get to shadow him," Alexis said, and then she opened the door leading to the living quarters.

The upstairs in no way resembled the lower level. The quaint living room was painted deep red and tan. A couch and chair sat next to a handmade wooden side table. A single black and white picture of a cliff face, with thundering waves, hung on the far wall. Double doors were to the side of the room, which led outside to a small balcony overlooking the cafe's courtyard. Two sides of the courtyard were enclosed in pale stone while the rest of the yard was open to the abundant plant life of Jinja.

"Your room is up the winding stairs. Just go through the kitchen," Alexis said.

"And come down quickly or Alexis is gonna eat all the cake Sandy made us yesterday," Michael said.

Alexis hit him in the gut and said, "No rush."

Winter took her bag and carried it through the dining room. A striking mahogany table covered in grooves sat in the center of the room. Two long benches lined the table. Winter went to the foot of the stairs. The steps leading to her room were high and narrow, reminding Winter of a tower. Winter lifted her things and began to climb the steps to her bedroom. Through her shoes, Winter could feel the coolness of the stone steps on her feet. Once on the landing, she found herself standing in a dimly lit hallway the color of cement. A closet was on her right up ahead and next to it was a slim white door. It was cracked open, letting a fragment of golden sunshine flow into the short hallway.

She set her luggage down in the closet and moved a basket on the floor out of the way, but something was underneath the bin. Winter stumbled backward when she realized what her hand had touched. A dead gecko lay in a corner of the closet.

"Gross! Gross!" Winter shouted.

She jumped up and down and repeatedly wiped her fingers on her clothing. She was glad no one was there to see her so afraid of a dried up lizard. Winter picked up her luggage and decided to store her things in the bedroom, instead of the geckos resting place.

Winter gently pushed the door open and stepped inside. Two twin beds, neatly made, with blue blankets and cream colored sheets sat on opposite sides of the room. Three windows let in soft rings of light that wrapped the entire room in the sun's warming rays. A small window sat on top of a bench built into the wall. Its triangular shape looked down into the backyard of the house. She opened the window and a gust of fragrant air passed over her.

A line of clothes hung outside drying in the heat. Lush trees and bushes soaked in the warmth of Jinja. Their purple and orange leaves drank in beams of sunlight. Tall trees with colossal leaves curved elegantly. Plump fruit sat beneath leaves relishing the shade. Harri ran in the lawn and Winter worried that he might get lost in the swaying blades of grass, but he leaped onto a porch that held two chairs and stole a pillow with pink and purple flowers. He began to bite at it, appearing triumphant at being able to leap that high. The pillow's fabric was torn, and Winter imagined that wasn't the first time he'd taken it captive.

She unpacked leisurely, looking out the window every couple of minutes as her eyes caught new wonders to behold. She didn't have many things to unpack. When Winter finished, she rested her hands on her waist and bit her bottom lip. She looked around the compact room and took a deep, slow breath inward before deciding to pick a new letter from home to read. Winter knew the note was from her sister because Ella had used Winter's personalized stationary to write the letter. Winter shook her head and clicked her tongue in disapproval as she opened it.

Dear Little Sister,

Sienna told me to write you a letter. I told her that if I'm writing one no one else really needs to because I'll cover every base there is. The rest would simply be repetition, and nobody likes a scratched C.D. Right? I'm supposed to give you advice or encouragement or something. I should probably charge you, but I'm not unfeeling. I can give you this one for free. However, being the older sister, I've given so much advice to you over the years and, I've got to tell you, Winter, it's gone largely unheeded.

The one piece of advice I'd tell you is this; learn to love, fully, and uncompromisingly, who you are. You have to embrace yourself. You have to find the core of your worth and never let anyone shake it, move it, or break it. Forgive, Winter and watch how it moves you forward in magical ways. I'm glad you abandoned that pantry in favor of the world, Winter. I know you're equipped to do whatever you choose. You just have to believe it, too.

I remember how you used to love going to church. You'd sing the loudest out of all the kids, and I'd always be embarrassed. You let hate take so much from you. Your encounter with that man scarred more than your knees; it robbed you of the life meant for you. Don't let anyone, including Anna Herald, that racist man, or yourself, take any more from you. Wherever you are in the world, I know that place is better off cause it's got you there.

Love, Ella

P.S. Bring me an awesome souvenir or don't come back home at all.

Seriously. Never.

Winter doubled over in laughter and tucked the letter away. "I miss you, Ella," she said aloud, wishing her sister was sitting right next to her. Winter swallowed hard, trying to escape the arrival of tears. She had indeed given up that pantry in favor of the world. Now, she was on the other side of the earth.

"I'm here," she said to herself, still disbelieving the veracity of those words. "I'm here."

***

Later that evening the three of them sat on the living room floor. It was completely dark outside. "It's been nice to be in one place," Alexis said, drinking a cup of chai. "I've traveled so much over the last year. Being able to soak in one place has been good for me."

"Where have you gone?" Winter asked.

Alexis began to list off her destinations, the continents and countries she'd seen. "India, France, England, Italy, South America, Germany, Thailand, Australia, Scotland, Ireland, and a few other places. I tried to go to as many countries and cities as I could," she said. "I loved finding small towns hidden between larger cities."

"That's a ton of traveling," Winter said. "What about you, Michael?"

"I've got three continents left. South America, Australia, and Antarctica, which I'll probably never go to because I'd only have penguins for neighbors."

"I'm a little behind. This is pretty much my first abroad excursion," Winter confessed.

Alexis shook her head. "You're never behind. You just have to make sure to get out into the world and travel at least once in your life," Alexis said, glancing at her watch. "We should probably head to bed soon. We're going out to a village tomorrow that sources coffee beans to the cafe, but it's two hours away."

"Who will be here in the cafe?"

"Sandy and a couple other people. Sandy is this amazing Ugandan woman who cooks in the cafe and practically runs it as well. I don't know how she gets it all done. Simon usually does work outside the cafe and that's who we shadow mostly, but don't worry, you'll get some cafe days."

Winter thought of Sienna and her dream to go to source farms through her work at Just Coffee.

"Going to different villages has been our highlight," Alexis said as she stood and stretched. "All the kids come running up to you with these wide smiles on their faces," she said.

"It's impossible not to smile, even for a stoic man like myself," Michael said, leaning back against the couch. Alexis threw a pillow at his face.

Winter said goodnight and headed upstairs. She pulled out her journal, but she could feel her eyes growing heavy. They'd been open for so long. Her hand hovered above the blue cover of the journal and then Winter's head dropped. Her battle with sleep had been lost.

113

CHAPTER EIGHTEEN—INVISIBLE

Winter woke with Anna's handwriting running across her mind. She found the idea of forgiving Anna Herald harder to swallow than barbed wire. *The experience of trying to forgive Anna would probably be considerably less pleasant and far less manageable than the wire*, she thought.

Winter was confused as to why, after all these years, Anna had asked for forgiveness now. To Winter, it was awful timing. She was trying to move her life forward, and Anna's note only reminded Winter of the pain she'd endured, of the pain pointlessly inflicted. The day after Winter cut off her hair she stayed home from school. She didn't want to face Anna Herald. Winter knew Anna would be merciless, but she could not have foreseen what would happen. Winter squeezed her eyes shut, wincing from the pain the memory brought back.

Anna Herald sat on the benches outside of school, waiting for the bell to ring. It was Winter's first day back since the unspeakable day she'd lost her hair. Winter walked to the front doors, hoping to go past Anna without being noticed. Winter adjusted the baseball cap she wore on her head as she passed her arch-nemesis. Anna was talking with her friends and was entirely unaware of Winter's presence. Winter reached out her hand to pull open the door. She was so close, but then one of the girls pointed her out. Anna spit out the orange juice she was drinking.

"Winter? Is that you? Oh my gosh! I didn't think my day could get any better! Electro-girl, what did you do to yourself? What should we call you now? How about Malcolm or Dwight? I like Dwight. Dwight Wright." Anna's eyes teared up as she laughed at her words. "You could barely claim to be a girl before, but now…man!"

"A lot of women have short hair, or no hair, Anna. That doesn't make them less of a girl," Winter snapped.

"Touchy, touchy! So what happened to you, electro-girl? Did your hair finally explode off your head?"

Winter charged past Anna and into the school. Sienna was away visiting her grandmother, which meant Winter didn't have a single friend. A boy passing Winter in the hall stared at her newly shaven head. "Are you sick, Winter?" He asked.

"No, I'm not," Winter said, not wanting to explain.

Winter went to her classroom and sat down. The baseball cap she wore was not allowed indoors, but she hoped Ms. Steward wouldn't notice. At her desk, Winter nervously bounced her leg up and down. Anna came to class soon after and took her seat on the opposite wall. Winter kept her eyes down. Whenever she looked up, she caught someone staring at her, but it was Anna's gaze Winter most wanted to avoid. Winter's trepidation also dealt with the roll-call. The moment Ms. Steward began taking attendance, Winter's name would eventually be called, and everyone's eyes would drift to her as she said, "I'm here."

She didn't want the attention of the room pressing in on her, dissecting her newly hairless head. Winter wanted to stay home another day so she wouldn't have to suffer through the agony of daily attendance. But as long as she could wear her hat, Winter thought she could survive it. The teacher walked into the room then and lifted the clipboard for roll-call.

"Morning, everyone. Let's see who's present before we start class."

And so it began.

"Daniel Abbott...Monica East...Lisa Grant..." Each student called out present or here as their name was spoken. Winter bit her bottom lip and fidgeted with her fingers.

"Anna Herald," Ms. Steward said.

"Here, and Ms. Steward, as the student body president, I thought I should bring it to your attention that hats are not permitted indoors."

Ms. Steward was a rare person. She wasn't fooled by Anna's ability to pull people in with sweet words and toothy smiles, but Anna was right; it was the rule.

"Winter, can you remove your hat?" Ms. Steward asked, her eyes kind. Winter's heart plummeted. She slid off the baseball cap she'd taken from her father's closet, and set it on her desk. Mouths hung open and whispers erupted across the room.

"That's enough class. Let's continue with roll-call."

On it went and Winter had to wrestle the urge to sink into the abyss of her despair.

Mortification and embarrassment seemed to follow her every step. When Ms. Steward got to the W's Winter could feel more eyes fall upon her figure. She wanted to run home. She wanted to bolt from her seat and leave the school. Winter didn't want to be Winter Wright anymore; she didn't want to own that name and the person who belonged to it. It wouldn't be hard to leave, and she didn't live far away, but Winter didn't move. She was tiring of running, of giving in, so she decided to stay in her seat and wait for her name to be called.

"Winter Wright," Ms. Steward called out.

"Here," Winter said quietly. "I'm here."

"Nice to have you back. We're glad you're feeling better," she said. Winter exhaled. It was one of the first moments she'd shown herself that strength resided within her though it proved near impossible to find.

Winter opened her eyes. Her chest rattled unsteadily as she exhaled. She was still angered by the past, still chained to it. Winter got dressed and decided not to think about Anna's note for the rest of the day.

I have more important things to do than put your mind at ease, she thought resentfully.

Winter believed it followed suit that Anna would choose now, when Winter was trying to put her life right, to commandeer her mind. Winter wasn't even sure if she could forgive Anna. Winter felt her life had been made smaller because of people like her. Anna had deliberately and meticulously tortured Winter for as long as she could remember and it didn't stop until they both left for college. Distance was Winter's savior.

Winter didn't know what a world with a forgiven Anna looked like because she'd never shown remorse before. Winter sighed and pushed the thoughts away, turning her attention to the present day. Despite her current mindset, Winter was ecstatic about going to a Ugandan village. She had no idea what to expect and couldn't believe that this day was where her fear conquering had led. Winter walked past her suitcase and saw the sleeve of her camouflage jacket sticking out. She pulled it out and laid it across the extra bed in her room.

"I won't be needing you in this heat," she said, running a hand over the old fabric.

Winter thought about the fact that she would be rafting the Nile in a few days and nervousness began to course throughout her body. Winter hoped that this time when she faced her fear of water, she wouldn't fail. Downstairs Alexis sat at the dining room table eating a blueberry muffin with chai tea.

"Morning! There are muffins," Alexis said, pointing to a bowl on the table. "And tea is on the stove in the kitchen. I already grabbed mugs."

"Woah," Winter said, surprised. "Thanks, Alexis. It smells so good."

"Don't thank me. I found them in the fridge. Sandy, the amazing and abnormally kind cook in the cafe, made them for us."

"I will thank Sandy as soon as I meet her."

Winter grabbed a napkin for her muffin from the table and retrieved tea from the stove.

"How did you sleep?" Alexis asked, raising a cup to her lips.

"Pretty well, although I couldn't remember where I was for a second."

"That's happened a lot to me over the last year," Alexis said, her face full of joyful reminiscing. "There was a period where I went to sixteen cities in a month and a half. Almost every morning I'd wake up with no memory of what country I was in. I'd bolt up in bed and scream 'Where am I today?' It usually came to me. If not, I'd ask someone outside."

"I can't imagine traveling that much," Winter said.

"It's a joy and a struggle," Alexis stated.

"How long have you known Michael?" Winter asked.

"A few weeks," Alexis answered.

"Oh, you two seem close," Winter said, taking a bite of her muffin.

"Sometimes you just click with people, ya know? He's like the brother I always knew I never wanted."

"I can't stand when you lie. I'm the brother you always knew your life would never be complete without," Michael said, walking into the kitchen, sleep still in his eyes. He grabbed a muffin, and put his head on the table.

"Not a morning person, Michael?" Winter asked.

"Coffee enables me to be a morning person, Winter."

"Hey Drama-King, Simon said he'd bring his French press over for you today," Alexis said. "He usually brings a cup over for Michael in the mornings if he remembers." On cue, Simon knocked at the door of the upstairs house. Michael sprinted to the door and pulled it open. Simon stepped inside carrying three large mugs of coffee.

"Bless you, you beautiful, beautiful man," Michael said, grabbing Simon into a one-armed embrace.

"I thought you might want this as well," he said, gesturing to the French press in his bag. "Sorry that it took me so long to remember," Simon said.

"No worries," Michael replied, lifting the lid and taking a deep drink of the hot coffee.

"I brought extra coffee for anyone who wants it.

"Thanks, Simon," Alexis said.

"Of course. Winter, how was your first night here?" Simon asked.

"Nice, but I could do without the jet lag."

"In time," he said. "If you're all ready we can head out."

The four of them left the cafe armed with freshly brewed coffee and homemade bread.

The white suburban sat in the parking lot waiting to be driven. She climbed into the back seat and banged her head on the ceiling in the process. Winter's jet lag made her movements clumsy. During the night Winter woke up at odd times without a trace of sleep in her eyes, but she smiled despite her fatigue.

I'm going to collect another experience, another treasure, Winter thought, reminding herself of the time she spent with Rosamund and Marieleen.

They drove for over an hour until they reached what appeared to be an endless field. High grass, almost as tall as the car, reached up towards the sky. A forest of tan blades, their tips kissed by the sun's light, stretched towards the heavens. The car rolled through the meadow and came to a stop.

Simon turned to Winter. "One thing I forgot to mention is that you'll all have to introduce yourself. When you do, say this: "Erinnya lyange nze." That means my name is. And then you can say, "N'va America," which tells everyone where you're from." Simon wrote it down on a piece of paper and passed it to Winter to look over. Winter's stomach fluttered at the thought of having to stand before a crowd of people. All eyes on her was an idea that never appealed to Winter.

"Can I have a look, Winter? I've done the intro in Lusoga a couple times, but I always get a few words mixed up," Michael asked.

They hung their heads over the paper, trying to commit the words to memory. Simon got out the car and knocked on the window from outside, telling them to get out. They exited the car and shut the doors, eyes still glued to the paper. The crisp collision of carefully placed metal brought heads peeking out from doorways. Winter's gaze shifted around, taking in the village before her eyes. A common area, built with sturdy handmade mud bricks, sat in the center of the village.

A cluster of homes was off to Winter's left. People came from inside their houses and into the vacant space. A tall man with narrow shoulders walked up to Simon.

"Simon, it is good to see you," he said.

"And you, Thomas. I'm glad to have you as a partner and mentor. I'm looking forward to learning about your plans for living improvements."

Winter was enthralled by her new surroundings, and then she heard the distant sound of bare feet on solid ground getting closer. The soft patter of soles on impressionable earth became louder as a large group of about twenty children rounded the corner. The four of them looked to one another as smiling faces rushed towards them. Winter stood between Michael and Alexis.

She could feel the elation brewing between their bodies. But then something happened Winter didn't anticipate. As the group neared, those smiling faces ran to either side of her and into the arms of her friends. She was Moses parting a sea of children. They passed around Winter as if an undetectable barrier diverted them away from her.

Winter stood alone, looking quite comical, with her arms somewhat outstretched. She pulled herself up from the stooping position she'd just occupied, and watched as the children laughed and played with Michael, Alexis, and Simon. Her brows furrowed in confusion.

She smiled awkwardly and waited until Simon began to walk towards the common space. The kids trailed behind the three of them on their way to the pavilion. By then the whole village had gathered to welcome their visitors. Winter took a seat next to Alexis on a wooden bench at the front of the room as a group of children got up to sing.

Their clear smiles were beautiful and giddy. Winter sat on the edge of the bench as the children sang. Their small voices filled the pavilion and beyond. They danced with their hands floating into the air, matching the rhythm of the songs. When they finished, they rose their hands above them, their palms facing outward, fingers spread gleefully. Winter, Simon, Alexis, and Michael showed their gratitude by clapping robustly, thanking them for the warm welcome. The man who greeted Simon lifted himself up from a thin bench. He spoke in Lusoga to the crowd and then Simon stood.

"I have some new visitors with me today," he said to the faces that made up the crowd. "Michael, why don't you start."

Michael stood to share his name and where he was from, his tongue tripping over the new shapes and sounds he spoke. Winter's heart beat a little harder. *All I have to do is say my name and where I'm from,* Winter told herself. Alexis rose from the bench and introduced herself. When she sat down, Winter took a breath. She started to stand but the man clapped for Alexis and Michael, and then turned to speak to the crowd that had assembled.

Winter stood uneasily and began to sit down as Simon politely interrupted and said, "Actually, Thomas, we have one more."

Both men looked at her. The eyes of everyone there turned cautiously to Winter, who wished she could melt on the spot. Winter could feel the heat of the sun on her uncovered neck, the sweat that steadily formed across her brow as she stood and said in Lusoga, "My name is Winter. I'm from America."

She sat back down, a growing feeling of misplacement building, which Winter was trying to fight off. Thomas, their guide for the day, turned and pointed at Winter, making her heart skip a beat, possibly two.

"She is an African Mzungu!" He exclaimed.

Simon leaned over to Winter and said quietly, "You're redefining the word Mzungu."

"What does it mean?"

"Mzungu is a word meant to describe someone of western descent, someone usually thought to look white," he answered. But Winter believed the word meant more than what it imbued on the surface. She could see it, and was starting to feel it in a tangible way.

"Oh," she said, shifting in her chair. Winter wanted to know more about what that phrase meant, but she only perceived the slightest of ripples that afternoon.

They spent the day as Simon's shadow, following him around to meetings with village leaders, watching silently. Villagers showed them where they grew crops, which kinds of buds were peeking through the dirt and prospering, and what plants had neglected the idea of growth no matter how much care and attention they received. Winter could see the genuine interest on her companion's faces as they learned that day. When they stopped for tea and food in the afternoon, a few people came in to meet the four of them.

A mother and her daughter shuffled inside. The young girl wasn't older than five. Her hair was cut short to her head. She wore a dress that was slightly ripped and approached them with her eyes cast toward the ground. The little girl stooped down low to signify respect as she greeted them, lowering herself to the dirt floor.

Alexis wiggled uncomfortably at the greeting, but smiled warmly at the girl, as did Michael. When the girl approached Winter, her young eyes glazed over her. She turned and ran back to her mother whose expression was full of embarrassment. With a wave of her hand, she told her daughter to go back and greet Winter as well.

Winter wondered how often the girl saw someone who looked like her honored in the ways visitors from the West are. She was so young, but she already had a routine. She knew who to greet in particular ways. The girl walked back over to repeat the greeting she gave to those Winter sat next to, her eyes curious.

Then a woman came around the circle with a bowl of water and soap. Each person dipped their hands into the clear water and rubbed soap between their palms. A whole fish in a watery red sauce and a bowl of millet were placed on a rickety wooden table.

Simon leaned over and said, "It's communal style eating. Make sure you use your left hand to eat. The right is used for tasks associated with uncleanliness."

"Gotcha," Winter said, understanding.

The meal was blessed by a village leader, and then they all began to eat. Winter worked through her plate, silencing her picky taste buds. After the meal, they stood, and Simon continued his walk with Thomas, the village leader. All day Thomas and Simon walked around the village with purpose and passion. It did not change or fade as they stood outside the latrine doors. Winter stepped inside and the floor sank low, cradling her sandals.

"One of the projects Thomas and I have been working on together involve making choas safer. We're updating some of them by replacing the wood with cement," Simon said.

"One man fell in last year. He didn't go far before we retrieved him, but these older wooden choas aren't as safe," Thomas added. Thomas spoke to them about the man's fall while their eyes lingered on the creaking latrine floors.

"Choa renovations, exciting stuff, toilets," Simon said.

Within a couple of hours, they had seen the entire village. Simon thanked Thomas and a few other men. They clapped forearms and smiled deeply at one another. They all said their goodbyes and Simon, Michael, Alexis, and Winter walked back to the car. Those they met throughout the morning had gathered at the car to say goodbye. Before they climbed inside the suburban, a woman from the village came up to the car. She seemed relieved that the truck still sat in its place. The woman approached them grinning and reached into a bag at her side. She smiled at Michael, who stood to Winter's left, and passed him a gift. The woman took his hand firmly within both of her own, expressing gratitude for his visit.

Then, slowly, she looked at Winter, and her smile faded. She blinked once and turned her attention to Alexis. She passed her a gift and hugged her before passing a parcel to Simon. Then, after one last blank look at Winter, she left. The three of them shifted their eyes towards Winter.

"I wonder what that was about," Alexis said, setting her gift inside the car.

Michael turned to face Winter. "I'm sorry you got dissed, Winter."

Winter shrugged her shoulders, wondering about it herself, a growing inclination rooting itself in her subconscious. The entire day she'd been ignored. She was seen but remained invisible to most everyone she met. Simon began to drive, and Winter could feel herself deflating. She was annoyed at herself for being hurt by what happened. Winter didn't ride out to the village that day to become consumed by her feelings.

This wasn't the memory she'd wanted to stow away in her mental treasure chest. But try as she might, Winter could not push it away, and then she realized what was bothering her. The nefarious roots of colonialism were at work.

Colonizers, whether in America, Africa, or India, often used the deathly fabrication of racial superiority to divide and conquer native inhabitants in pursuit of personal power and riches. Often, light was pitted against dark and the results of this were imbedded deep into the culture and psyche of people. They mirrored people's lives at home in America as well. Remnants of that truth surrounded Winter. She'd passed countless Ugandan billboards promoting skin bleaching since she arrived.

Winter knew black girls, and other girls with dark skin, who feared the sun as if it was poison, instead of the life-giving star it is. It was colonialism reborn into the colonized, and shame and self-hate were the haunting outcome. Though it perhaps was not present in her interactions the whole day at the village, Winter could see a strand of similarity. The woman who, assuming Winter was from another Ugandan village, ignored Winter because she had the coveted spot of traveling with the Westerners, or at least those who embodied the stereotypical idea of a Westerner, was a prime example. Winter shuddered as she sat there in the car, as she tried to make sense of what happened. She twisted her fingers anxiously, recalling the sinking feeling in her heart as the woman's warmth left her eyes when they focused on Winter. Inwardly, she wondered if she would ever be free of the burden of other people's bias, because her soul was finding it hard to bear the weight. Winter quietly contemplated how many people had lost their identities, had never learned to value their inherent and beautiful worth, because of how the world viewed them. That was all Winter could think about on the long drive home down empty, winding roads.

That night Winter sat in her room, staring at her list of fears. It was strange the ways her ultimate fear could morph into different shapes, and that's what scared her most about it. How do you overcome a beast with so many faces? Hate wasn't something only experienced at the hand of another soul, hate could also be internalized, without the person fully realizing it. Winter looked towards her window. It was raining outside, and the water streamed down her bedroom window, reminding Winter of an old memory of Anna.

It was raining outside Madison Junior High. For the first time in months, Winter had forgotten her camouflage jacket at home as she hurried to make it to soccer practice on time. She rushed up to the glass doors and pulled the handle, but the door didn't budge. Winter peered inside with cupped hands as raindrops fell onto her skin. Winter could see the outline of a few people sitting on a bench in the lobby. She rose her hand and knocked on the door. The people turned around and then Winter saw who they were.

It was Anna Herald and her friends. Anna looked at Winter from inside and smiled as she tapped her friends. They all began to mimic Winter knocking outside in the rain, holding their stomachs as they laughed. A new teacher walked past the doors and opened one for Winter. Winter muttered her thanks and then turned to Anna and her group.

"You guys are jerks," Winter said, walking past them towards the gym.

Anna's eyes narrowed at Winter's words. She lifted herself from the bench slowly and motioned for her friends to follow. In the hallway outside the gym, Anna grabbed Winter's arm.

"Do I have to open the door for you?" She asked, getting in Winter's face.

"No, but decency— "

"Don't you dare call me anything other than my name or I'll take your ass out in school tomorrow." The girls around Winter snickered. "Am I clear?" Anna asked. Winter said nothing, so Anna took one step closer. "I said, am I clear?" Anna enunciated every syllable.

"I heard you, Anna," Winter said through gritted teeth, ashamed at her inability to stand up for herself.

"Wonderful. Next time bring an umbrella," Anna said as she shoved roughly past Winter.

Following Anna's lead, each of the girls bumped into Winter as they left. Winter rubbed her wet shoulder in the hallway and imagined telling her parents or a teacher the truth about Anna, but Winter knew Anna would only make her life worse. She took a deep breath, released her bottom lip, and walked into the gym for soccer practice.

It was in high school that Winter wanted to move away. She often daydreamed about going to Hawaii or New Zealand, anywhere that got her further away from her nemesis, and the growing feeling that something must be wrong with Winter herself. That evening she'd spoken with Sienna on the phone. Sienna was who Winter turned to for help. Sienna was the person who always offered Winter a hand when she needed to be picked up.

"She did what to you? Oh my gosh! I cannot believe that! The nerve of that rat-faced troll! She's the nastiest person I've ever met. What kind of human won't open a door for someone standing out in the rain? That makes me absolutely furious. Winter, I'm so sorry that happened to you."

"Yeah, it wasn't the best experience," Winter said, fighting back tears of anger and hurt at the way she'd been treated.

"And she won't beat you up. You know that, right? You sound nervous to me."

Winter paused before saying, "Do you think she'd get one of her friends to? That one girl looks eternally angry."

"I don't, but I do think you should tell your parents."

"No way, then she really would. I don't really know how to fight. Maybe I should buy a kickboxing dvd tonight."

"Winter, I know she's got influence but no one will beat you up. Anna wouldn't compromise getting suspended and ruining her glorious plans for her pretentious future. That girl only has venomous words and awful beliefs as her ammunition."

"Nothing bad has ever come from that lethal combination," Winter interjected.

"That is a pretty deathly pairing, but Anna just gets some sick psychotic pleasure from intimidating people until they pee themselves, but that's it."

"Oh, we'll just have to start saving money for the regular therapy sessions we'll need from the mental trauma she's caused for us."

"Exactly, and we can find a good therapist together. Besides, if she did try anything I'd jump in the ring, and we could take her together," Sienna said.

"Sienna, you always know what to say to make me feel better," Winter remarked.

"That's my job as your best and truest friend. Your job as my best and truest friend is to tell me when I have toilet paper stuck to the bottom of my shoe, or when I tuck my shirt into my underwear. You sure you're all right?"

"I'll be fine. I just need to get my mind off her. You want to go to Mariah's before they close? We could get a whole pie to ourselves! I've got an hour before curfew," Winter said.

"Let's do it. My treat. I'll hold every door we pass open for you!"

A faint smile played across Winter's lips. The girls hung up and Winter took off her wet clothes as she battled the feelings Anna Herald always brought surging to the forefront of Winter's mind. She found her green jacket and went to meet Sienna.

Winter heard a knock on her door.

"Is anybody home?" Alexis asked.

"Come in!" Winter called out from her bed.

"I come bearing chai tea and poshco chips," Alexis said.

Winter stood and went to help Alexis carry her bounty into the room. The awkwardness of the day hovered in the air, but Alexis melted it away with her kindness. Winter took the cups and set them on her nightstand. Alexis moved Winter's jacket over and laid herself on the extra bed. She crossed her legs and bit into a crispy posho chip, while Winter took a sip of the creamy tea.

"Simon made a potful of chai downstairs. He was going to call you down before he left for home, but I offered to bring it up."

"Thank you," Winter said. Winter was beginning to isolate herself, to withdraw from her fears and the pain of reliving her memories.

"Not a problem," she said, drinking the tea. "Tomorrow we're going to the Clang Clang. Simon has some people he wants to meet with, and there are enough workers for the cafe, so he said we could go."

"What's the Clang Clang?" Winter asked, picking up a chip.

"It's an outdoor work yard," Alexis said, setting her tea down. "That's all I know."

Winter chewed on the chip as a thought drifted into her head.

"How have you liked traveling on your own? Have you felt safe?"

"Not always a hundred percent, but there's a website that gives women tips when they're traveling solo that I check out occasionally. I despise that this is true, but I do feel safer when I'm with friends that are guys. Regardless of the country, men don't bother me as much when I'm with another man. One of the tips on the website for girls traveling solo is to wear wedding rings because it makes people think twice about harming you if you're married to a guy. One time this dude started catcalling me, and this other man shouted at him to stop because he saw the ring. Not everyone stops, but it lessens the chances. It makes me so angry. It's awful."

"That is," Winter agreed.

"But traveling, like anything, has its ups and downs. I love it too much to give it up."

"What's that like? Traveling so much?" Winter asked, planting her elbows on her knees and cupping her face between her palms.

"Hmmm." Alexis exhaled slowly. "It's enriching. It's tiring. It expands your horizons. It's been an education that I've been honored to have." She lifted her hands into the air and formed them into the shape of a sphere as she said, "The world is so different from what I thought it would be. Traveling has taught me so much. It's allowed me to embrace new cultures and new ways of life and thinking."

She rested her hands on her lap. "Sometimes it's exhausting to the bone, and the sight of a plane makes me want to settle down in one place for a long while. I miss family and friends, but then I remember that I'm doing something innate to my being. That's what traveling is to me. It's not merely a hobby. Seeing the world and learning from other cultures is more than something I love to do. It's like drinking water. It's living a dream, something I don't believe I'd be complete without. It's a part of me. I wouldn't let myself give that up."

Winter wanted to know what it felt like to be fully alive in that way, entwined in your dreams, living them out instead of sitting idly or simply imagining them becoming real one day. Winter thought about the hours she'd spent imagining what life would look like if she followed her dreams. *In all that time perhaps I could have achieved one*, she thought.

"What about you?" Alexis asked, pulling Winter out of her mind. "Is there anything you feel called to do? A passion project or a burning desire?"

Winter dropped her hands from her face. "Too many to count. Hopefully I'll get one of them accomplished." Winter took a breath before speaking. Her dreams had become entangled with her worries, which made Winter hesitant to share. To her, fears were intimate things, lone footprints treading on the broken paths of a heart's vulnerabilities.

"I can tell you're thinking about something. Come on. Share it with the class, Winter."

Winter laughed. "Sometimes I feel like I've made too many missteps, like I'll always be catching up," she said, remembering her Grand Failure. "I'm sure it's only doubt, but it's just enough doubt to hold me back."

"Any bit of doubt can do that. Can I tell you what I believe?" Alexis asked, her eyebrows raised.

"What do you believe?" Winter asked with a small smile.

"You have to make a few left turns before you make the right one, and some of those left turns are leading you down paths that are marked for you, getting you closer with every supposed mistake you make. The missteps you learn from make you steadier. Each time you stumble, and choose to get up, you're made stronger. You'll learn to see that every day you're given a journey. There is no endpoint, no destination. When you realize that every day can be a twenty-four-hour expedition, you can sit back, feet up in your favorite recliner, and enjoy the ride."

Winter admired Alexis. She appreciated her new friend and the words she spoke, the life philosophy she embraced. Alexis reminded Winter of what some people might call bohemian, perhaps so that they could idolize and dismiss her in the same breath. The true purpose of a label, of an idea and not a person.

"Are you ready to raft the Nile in couple days?" Alexis asked, smiling brightly.

"No," Winter said immediately. "But I've found that I never feel ready before I face something that scares me."

"What scares you about it?" She asked, taking a drink of her tea.

"I can't swim and when I was eight I almost drowned in the deep end of a pool. I was surrounded by family so I wouldn't have actually died, but I didn't know that then."

"Oh! So you have a real reason! Why do you want to go rafting then?"

"Well, I'm on this trip to face my deepest fears. I have a ridiculously long list of them," she laughed.

"Woah," Alexis said, uncrossing her legs and rising to her feet. "Woah. That…that…is unbelievable! I think facing your fears is great," she said, furrowing her eyebrows in deep thought.

Winter didn't expect such a large reaction from Alexis. Winter's eyes grew as Alexis raised her arms into the air.

"What a personal revolution you're embarking on! That's what it's about. Don't you think so? Discovering who you are at your core is so important. Once you open yourself to that you can do anything: find your calling, help people, and ultimately live, unencumbered, the life meant for you," Alexis said.

"You say it so well," Winter said.

"Thanks. I appreciate that. Some people think I'm too much to handle."

"No way. Your liveliness could only avert people who are averse to living," Winter declared. Alexis sat down and grabbed another chip and tossed it into her mouth.

"Are you nervous about the water at all?" Winter asked.

"No. I feel completely at home in the water," she shook her head slowly.

A breeze blew in through an open window. The sound of trees dancing in the wind made them both still.

"So, I'm not the best at transitioning during conversation, but the reason I wanted to come up here was to make sure you're all right, which I'm sure you know. I hope that what happened today didn't bring you down too much. It was like you were invisible," Alexis said. Winter nodded.

"I really, really appreciate that, Alexis. It's just a bit disheartening, ya know, to see the sentiment exists so broadly.

"What sentiment?"

"I was unseen because of who I was next to, that's all."

Alexis' eyes were concentrated on Winter as she spoke. "I'm part Native American and my grandfather lived his whole life on a reservation before he died. Sometimes, I feel that being Native in America is like being the forgotten. People romanticize our culture and don't think of the actual people who exist in today's world, the struggles we face. A lot of us don't live on reservations anymore, but did you know some reservations in America are as poor or poorer than parts of the global south? I know the two situations are different, but I guess I'm just saying if people valued one another for who they are, if they took the time to get to know one another as people and not ideas, we'd all be better off."

Winter smiled at her words. "I need some of that to rub off on me," she said. Winter too often perceived people only according to the potential pain they could cause.

"I'll try my best to make that happen," Alexis said, finishing her tea and rising from the bed. "I'll see you in the morning. Be sure to get some rest for the day ahead. You'll need it."

"Thanks, Alexis."

Alexis winked and said, "You can pay me back later."

Winter smiled and pulled out her journal as Alexis closed the door.

I made it to Uganda and it's already proving to be a teacher. To be honest, I'm scared. Today was so strange and I'm afraid of my fears expanding while I'm here instead of lessening. I can already feel it happening. Maybe it's bound to happen. Perhaps they'll get bigger before they pass. But I can already sense that I'm starting to lose myself to them again, and I know that's not the right route. I just pray I have enough hope and motivation in me to see this journey through. I still have so far to go. Here is to seeking a bigger life.

Until then, Winter

CHAPTER NINETEEN—THE GULF

Winter fought to stay upright as they drove to the work yard, and after a half hour of driving, Winter heard the Clang Clang before she saw it. The sounds of the work yard lifted Winter faintly out of her resting state. She opened her eyes and immediately knew the location of their destination.

An outdoor workshop was across the busy street from Winter. Thick smoke rose from the work yard. Black and gray clouds formed a heavy blanket over the sound of clanking metal and tools being sharpened. Winter understood how the place had earned its name. A man in a blue and white button up shirt and long black pants rolled up to his ankles, walked up to Simon. They spoke rapidly to one another in Lusoga and English, switching back so quickly and effortlessly that it made Winter's mind feel tired and lazy.

"Would you like to meet our newcomer?" Simon asked.

"Yes, yes," he answered with a smile.

"Winter, this is Isaiah. He's taught me almost everything I know." Isaiah was an older Ugandan man with a gravelly voice and warm eyes.

"Yes, that is true. However, I only take credit for the good things!" Isaiah said, looking at his friend.

"Nice to see you again, Isaiah," Alexis said. Michael reached out his arm for a handshake and Winter returned her eyes to the yard. Some people had cloth masks over their faces, covering their lungs from the dense, smoky, metallic air. Deep black stains covered shirts, calloused hands wrapped around hard tools. Her senses were overcome with the noise and metallic scents of the yard.

She felt odd walking around a space that seemed to be private. Winter could catch a few words passing between Isaiah and Simon, but she still wasn't sure what they were meant to be doing there. She tried to keep her gaze respectful as they moved through, following their guides.

"The people who work here are paid two to three dollars each day," Isaiah called out to the three of them.

Men and boys hunched low over work benches. Smoke assaulted their lungs as they tried to produce items that would enable them to provide life to themselves and their families. Winter recalled the beautiful Ugandan homes she'd passed, the hotels that looked like island paradises. Overabundance and bare minimum right next door.

A sudden and sharp metal clanking sound trampled Winter's thoughts. She rose her hands instinctively to shield her ears from the sound, but no one working even flinched at the ear-shattering sounds. Winter kept walking, but her foot got caught on a bin collecting water. She stumbled over the bucket, trying desperately not to tip it over. She fell forward into the mud, wet from rain that had fallen the previous night. Some of those working looked at Winter's fumbling movements with wide, sympathetic eyes. Michael, who was just in front of Winter, quickly pulled her up.

"Careful. Are you all right?" Isaiah asked.

Winter nodded her head yes. Her cheeks grew hot from embarrassment.

"Thanks, Michael," Winter said.

"Of course. Like I said before, I'm always willing to be of service to another youngest sibling. If you were a middle child or the oldest, I'd have let you eat the mud," he said, winking playfully.

"Here you go," Alexis said, handing Winter a couple tissues from her bag.

"Thank you, Alexis," Winter said, taking the napkins.

"No problem. Try to stay upright," she joked.

Winter smiled and wiped the mud off her body. People in the yard had already returned to their work. She finished cleaning herself off and looked up. Past the dense smoke of the yard Winter could see small homes in the distance. They were poorly built and looked as though a flood or harsh wind might overturn them.

"It's like they're being held up with tarp and hope," Winter said aloud. Michael and Alexis followed Winter's gaze, but both remained silent. That day the three of them listened, they looked, and they learned deeply in that moment, face to face, of the privilege they'd acquired simply because of their birthplace.

To Winter, people sometimes believed that privilege negated what they lived through, or tarnished and undermined things they achieved. *But maybe privilege is being able not to wonder where your next drink is coming from, and knowing that your school is around the corner from your house. Perhaps, privilege is being able to walk down a street without being judged, to walk into a space and not be questioned for being there, to be valued at face value; to have your human rights intact and unquestioned at all times.*

Winter hoped they didn't feel exploited by their gazes, laid bare as foreigners eyes fell upon them. As she walked, Winter began to notice that she seemed to be collecting more stares from those she passed. Eventually, a man approached with wide, unmoving eyes. He stared until he got close enough to speak.

"Are you a Mzungu or are you leading the group?" He asked with probing eyes. Winter was last in line, trailing far behind the three people she'd come with. Michael laughed and shrugged his shoulders in confusion.

"I'm with the group," she said. The man didn't move or speak. It seemed as if he wanted to hear different words, a certain set of words. Winter waited a second, thinking he might leave, but he continued to stare so she said, "I'm a Mzungu."

He became giddy with what she'd shared. Winter watched the man walk away and share the information with some of those who gave long looks her way. Others leaned forward as they too tried to hear what this man had uncovered. He returned again and began to match Winter's pace.

"How are you black and in America?" He asked. The words rushed out quickly, so quickly that Winter had to ask him to repeat them. "How are you black and in America?" the man asked again.

Winter wasn't sure how to respond. Uncertainty of what to share and how to share it made her tongue feel heavy. In truth she didn't know her family's history. It was something her country's history denied her. A great-great grandfather had come from Ireland to America, and fell in love with a woman from the Choctaw tribe. Their children married black Americans. That was only on Winter's mother's side, and she didn't know what was myth and what was fact. She had no idea about her father's side.

Words escaped her. She thought of the school lessons spread out across her childhood, lessons that only gave glimpses into struggle, into one period that marked a darkness over her country, but forgot to tell the unfiltered history of a nation's past. Winter heard stories that told one narrow narrative of a rich story that, in reality, spanned across not one period, but lifetimes.

She stood dumbfounded, eyebrows creased, and then someone called his name, freeing her from having to answer. She exhaled as heat rose to her cheeks. In the same way that she'd only been allowed to exist from one facet in school, in some places it seemed she didn't exist at all. Winter was being stretched. Her understanding was broadening through exposure to the differing histories that prevailed in the world.

"Winter." Simon was calling her name. "It's time to go."

Winter was soon going to become used to her name being called and her body responding apart from her mind. Winter moved her legs slowly. Her head was filling up with questions.

"Are we heading back to the cafe?" She asked.

"No, we're going to go to a local hospital," Simon said. "There is someone there I need to meet with."

"Oh," Winter's voice trailed off.

Winter climbed into the car and looked back on the work yard covered in smoke. Some faces, stained from the work, stayed on Winter's mind. After fifteen minutes of driving, Simon spoke to them from the driver's seat.

"There's a different kind of poverty here than at home. Some of what you'll encounter will be hard to deal with, but try to be open and ready to see challenging truths. Because you all will."

As they drove, Winter's eyes landed on a street of empty, extravagant houses. No one had lived in the homes for some time. Winter also noticed a plain, white abandoned building with someone's name written in old, faded markings. A dark streak of paint had been painted over it to cross out the name, but Winter could still make it out.

"Have you heard of Idi Amin?" Simon asked, noticing the building.

"A little. Not much," she responded.

"He's known for the tyrannical and oppressive regime he ran. He joined the British Colonial Army as a cook and rose to the highest position allowed for a black man at that time. Years after, he successfully staged a coup on a Ugandan leader called Prime Minister Obote. After he came into power, he began a brutal reign over Uganda and its surrounding countries. He was responsible for a lot of deaths. Some decisions he made still impact Uganda today. I have a book about it if you want to learn more," he said, returning his eyes to the dusty road.

They drove past empty streets and to Winter it was a reminder of lives lost to hate under his rule, and of the fact that the past contains an eerie power to affect present life. Winter thought of America and of the stories she'd heard from great aunts and uncles, from grandparents who lived through a different America, one still struggling to bring reconciliation to its present day. She recalled their fear as her own from the stories they told. She could feel their joy for the changes that came, and their regret at the hollowness of some of the transformations promised but never delivered. Their stories had become Winter's, too.

"I hope that all of you will make time to speak with the people who live here. One of the most beautiful lessons I've learned since moving here is people's resilience and gratitude for life in the midst of hardship. To come here and not get to know anyone would be such a loss," Simon said from the driver's seat.

With that, Simon pulled into the yard at the hospital. They'd made it to their next stop. The hospital was a concrete building that wrapped around a vast yard covered in dead grass. A woman stood outside the building waiting for them.

Simon led the way to her. "This is Sarah. She works with the cafe's improvement program and as a nurse. I'm going to leave you all in her care for a bit." Sarah was a round woman dressed in delicate blues and silver. Her demeanor was calm and her accented voice soft.

"Hello. I'm very pleased to meet you all. Simon asked me to tell you about some of the work I do. I work for the improvement program as Simon mentioned. Some of the most common cases that come to the hospital are young children with severe burns," she said as she walked. "Many people out in the villages cook over open fires and children fall over the flames. One of the projects I do at the cafe involves working to bring enclosed clay ovens to those who want and need them," Sarah said.

Sarah led them to the maternity ward and then into an unnamed section of the hospital. Winter was out of her element, removed from everything familiar to her. Her breathing picked up as they rounded the corner. Her mind feared for her eye's sight, for the realities she'd absorb and wouldn't be able to let go of. Winter's nose was immediately invaded by the strong smell of blood, body waste, and medicinal blends. The hallway they were in connected two rooms, each lined with full beds.

From the hall Winter saw an elderly woman immobile on the ground. She called out to them in Lusoga so Alexis walked over to her, saying, "Ndi keewga olusoga--I cannot speak Lusoga." She disregarded their words and motioned for Winter to feel her leg. A large growth sat underneath taut skin. The woman pulled Winter's hands over her calf and Winter realized she was crying. Winter didn't know when the tears had come, but they filled her eyes, blurring her vision.

"Her nurse is coming," Sarah told them. "Come."

Winter followed Sarah and walked past a man holding his fist. Three of his fingers were wrapped in a thin cloth stained crimson red. The deep color spread over the white napkin and dripped steadily down his brown hand. His face twisted in quiet agony as they moved past him. A nurse walked hurriedly in front of the four of them, trying to attend to the needs of ten injured people who lay on the floor, and in chairs along the wall.

"This way," Sarah said, leading them to a room with small cots. People were everywhere and flies buzzed around the heads of the wounded. Feet that were split apart hung in weak looking slings and babies with severe burns wailed. Winter went through the hospital in silence. A child cried by a bed on the south wall of the room. The child's mother smiled at Alexis so she walked over, Winter and Michael followed close behind. Alexis rubbed the child's back and the mother's smile widened.

They started to attract a small group of women as they stood in the core of the ward. Winter moved away, feeling strangely, as if her senses were lagging one step behind her mind. When she looked up, a stranger was beckoning her over. An aged man with silvering hair motioned for Winter to draw nearer. He spoke to her in Lusoga, in words she could not make out. He touched his throat.

"Is he in pain? Is he thirsty?" Winter asked aloud. Her voice was rough and small sounding, even to her.

I don't know what to do. Winter turned her body in every direction looking for a nurse. She stood by his side and tried to communicate with him without the presence of shared words, and soon a nurse came over and began speaking with the man, who lay still and quiet.

Alexis and Michael continued to attract attention. Mothers continually passed babies to them. Alexis' arms were never empty. She held yet another crying child she'd been passed. New life was given to her as soon as another left her embrace. Michael was also handed small children, but he held them awkwardly, unsure of where and how to place his arms.

Winter looked around and saw that Simon had appeared again. Sarah spoke to Simon in a hushed voice. "We have a lack of medicine and the hospital needs better transportation, more reliable transportation. We are making good progress, but too many are affected by sicknesses that are preventable. Diarrhea, Malaria. You understand, Simon."

Winter was immersed in a tangle of her thoughts. The environment engulfed her, but everything ceased when she noticed someone at the end of the room on a bed in the farthest corner. The room went still for Winter. It all froze. Time itself halted. Winter moved swiftly to the area, drawn to it in an inexplicable way. And who she saw on that bed, on that day, is someone Winter will never forget.

A small boy occupied the deteriorating cot. He was morbidly thin and his eyes rolled in his head. He laid on his side with one arm tucked underneath his cheek while the other dangled limply over the cot. His features were contorted by the pain that consumed his body. All he did was look up at Winter, but the look in his eyes was pleading, full of meanings she couldn't discern. Winter took her hand and reached for his own, not sure if she was allowed, not caring at all if she couldn't. She wrapped her hand around his and held it between her palms. At that moment, she wanted to give him human contact, touch.

They stayed that way, speaking across language barriers, connecting despite divergent cultures, linked regardless of age; humanity connected them. His skin was thin under her fingers. His eyes stayed fixed upon Winter's own and never left them. Winter swatted at flies that came too close to his body. She tried to let him know that she saw him, cared for him, and then it was time to go. Just like that. *I can't go,* she tried to say, but the words were held prisoner in her throat.

She moved towards the car in unreal silence. Winter was in a daze. She couldn't reconcile what she'd seen. She struggled to understand how it could exist in the same world in which she also resided. Winter knew vaguely of the historical significance that aided in the stripping of resources from the global south in the name of colonialism. She knew in America of the denial of healthcare and the prevalence of food deserts in impoverished neighborhoods, where the only medical aid buildings were shut down, and grocery stores didn't exist, leaving people without proper care or real food. But that day it hit Winter, harder than it had before. One pervasive thought inundated Winter. *The gulf between lives on this planet shouldn't be this at odds.* She sat motionless as they drove back to the house. Silent tears fell down her cheeks, warmed from the impenetrable heat that surrounded her that hot Ugandan afternoon.

***

Winter was sitting on the porch that evening alone when Simon came out with tea in hand. The night was cool. Her camouflage jacket was draped over her arms. "Tomorrow will be a little less...busy." Winter shook her head without speaking. Her chin rested on her hand. Simon moved closer and passed Winter a mug of tea. "I always like to debrief with people over chai."

"Oh, thank you," Winter said. Simon nodded his head in response. His presence reminded Winter of Sienna. He exhibited a unique warmth and compassion, like sun rays shining light into the shadows. Simon leaned against the beam and took a drink. His gaze watched the distant tree line. Winter took a sip, but she barely tasted the smooth blend.

Simon cleared his throat and said, "I remember the first time I saw deep poverty. I was at home, maybe around fourteen. There was this homeless man who would wander the streets. Sometimes I saw him digging in dumpsters behind restaurants. I followed him once to see where he lived. He was staying in a small abandoned building a mile or so from my house. When I looked inside, I saw him with his hands above a fire he made in an old garbage can. It was the only source of light in the whole place. I didn't go in."

Simon spoke with his hands. They mapped out the scene for Winter. She could see where the garbage can was, how the man hunched over the fire in search of warmth.

"The building was so broken down. I was afraid the roof would fall if either of us moved. So I stood there and just watched him. His skin was covered in dirt and his clothes were blackened. When he looked up at me, I ran. I ran as if he was chasing me. It wasn't until a few years later that I realized I wasn't running from him. I was running from myself. I wanted to shield myself from the pain I could see him facing, from the hardship that scarred his face and stole the joy from his eyes. I ran because I didn't want to look too deeply," Simon confessed. He rubbed the rim of his cup.

"Before college, I wanted to acknowledge that part of me that sought to distance myself from the difficult parts of life, because it required more of

134

me than I was willing to give. It's hard. But I knew I'd rather be aware on some level, then know nothing of life outside myself, that I'd rather encounter glimpses of truth then remain unable to see past what I recognize," he finished.

Winter's eyes were drawn to the moonlight that shone upon the dewy grass as she listened. Winter knew poverty was not the face of the African continent. It was not the defining feature of numerous countries, cultures, and languages that belonged to people living on the largest and most diverse continent in the world, but the poverty Winter saw was still overwhelming to witness.

"It is difficult," she said. "So much of what I saw felt innately heavy and overburdening, as if each encounter occupies a space just above my heart, impeding my ability to take in breath, but it's necessary isn't it?" Winter said, looking up at Simon. "It's necessary to glimpse the truth of other people's existence."

"Yes. I believe it is," Simon offered in encouragement.

"Thanks, Simon," Winter said. She let out a breath, not of relief, but of gratitude for the companionship forged in life.

"Anytime," he said, looking into his cup. He pulled out a chair and sat down next to Winter. "Your rafting adventure is right around the corner."

"It is. Have you been?"

"Only once."

"Are you going on Friday?"

"No," he said, elongating the word. "Once was more than enough for me." They sat that way for a while, talking. When the moon rose higher into the sky, Simon stood, adjusted his black rimmed glasses, and said, "Night, Winter. I'm glad you're here."

"Me too. Good night," Winter replied softly.

She finished her tea and went up to her room. She pulled out her notebook and accessed her list of fears. Some of those fears seemed so small now. What were once caverns of fear and doubt were now small holes of insecurity. She picked up her pen and drew a line through number nine, and looked at the other fears she'd faced.

My List of Illogical Logical Fears
1. ~~Bodies of water (and being lost underwater).~~
2. ~~Heights that are above my own.~~
3. The future. Where am I going?
4. ~~Singing in public.~~
5. ~~Being alone in a foreign country where I don't know anyone.~~
6. Getting rejected and being vulnerable.
7. Not finding true happiness.
8. Looking and sounding incredibly stupid.

9. ~~Getting out of my comfort zone~~.
10. Self-consciousness growing larger in my life.
11. Failing to find the road that leads to the path I'm meant to be on in life.
12. Never accomplishing my dreams.
13. Reliving the sadness of my past.
14. Living a small life.
15. Having hate find me again.

Her list was dwindling with the passing weeks, but she noticed that she was stuck. Winter saw that the fears left had a certain commonality. These were the deep fears rooted in truth and given larger life through denial. They were memories Winter had locked away for fear they would consume and destroy her, slowly eroding her conscious mind into a pit of bitterness, void of hope, yet brimming with despair.

In some ways, a few of them had escaped the mental prison she'd placed them in over time. They came out, occasionally showing their power over aspects of her life throughout the years. Hate had formed the fears remaining. It was the root of the fears left now. It bred self-consciousness like a weed in her soul. Winter's fear of future lied in her worry that it would resemble the past she'd tried so hard to live apart from, but the message that she lacked worth always resurfaced in small, yet immense ways.

The job interviewer who told Winter her hair was untidy, the English teacher who always questioned the integrity of her papers. Winter's fear of the past was that the hate, which made her want to crawl into herself and disappear, would return and continue to keep her stagnant, unable and afraid to move in any direction at all that might resemble the days she'd wished had never come into actuality. The marks left on Winter from the man who spewed his hate at an eleven-year-old girl, and Anna who waved her hate like a banner, didn't seem possible to overcome, let alone forgive.

Winter saw that never accomplishing her dreams stood apart from the fears left. Since Winter believed her first racist encounter lay at the roots of trying to abolish her fears, she knew she'd have to confront the moment her life first shifted. Somehow she'd have to return to the warm summer day that hate entered boldly into her life, and conquer it.

But not tonight, she thought. Tonight her lids were heavy, the aftermath of the weight of realization. Winter lifted the box of notes from beneath the bed and found the letter from her mother. She peeled the paper back and pulled out her mother's words.

To my daughter,

Winter, I haven't told you the origins of your name. When I turned seventeen my parents told me it was time to get out of the house and be on my own. All of a sudden I was an adult, but I didn't feel like it yet. I was so afraid, Winter. I didn't have faith in myself to know I could survive and thrive on my own. I didn't have a job or a car, not even a driver's license yet! I applied for so many jobs and finally booked one at a temp agency. After a couple years of walking to the job, I finally saved enough money to purchase a vehicle. I walked to the dealership and the man who sold me my car drove me to the DMV where I took my driver's test and passed.

Over those two years, before I had a car, many of those mornings when I walked to work were cold. I feared the Winter season. The fabric on my gloves had holes all over them and seemed to always acquire new gaps. I remember holding my hands up to my mouth to harbor them from the chill that I felt in my bones. Some of those days I didn't want to leave my apartment to venture out into the snow-filled streets, but I did. I did it because I knew that time of my life was just that; a season. And seasons always pass and bring new life and new beginnings. Honey, I made it through my winter and it showed me strength I feared I didn't possess.

It showed me that brighter days are always around the corner and that if you look deeply enough into today, even in your winter the sun can shine and melt away the cold. It can bring warmth and light. Even in the dead of winter, life still manages to make it through, and when the cold melts away life is stronger, fuller, and brighter than before. And that's what I hope for you. Make it through this season stronger, fuller, and brighter, more joyous than when you left. I know you can do it, and I'll be in my garden with a cup of coffee for you, waiting to hear about the end of this season and the start of a fresh one.

I love you, Mom.

Winter leaned over and shut off the lamp as a tear fell down her cheek. Moonbeams trickled into the room. Winter turned her face towards them, welcoming the persistence of light.

CHAPTER TWENTY—THE NILE

"Change of plans!" Alexis was banging on Winter's door so loudly she fell out of the bed. Winter crawled to the door and yanked on the handle. All social etiquette escaped her as she pulled open the door on all fours.

"Are you trying to kill me?" She asked.

"Not even a little," Alexis said.

Winter rubbed her eyes and yawned.

"I got our rafting time confused. I booked it for Thursday morning, this morning, not Friday afternoon, and we've got to sign you up still. We leave in an hour!"

Winter swallowed hard. *One hour!* Fear was rising up to be heard and listened to, to stop her from moving. Winter straightened herself out and fought against that too familiar voice of doubt in her head. That first day on the bridge in Ireland, Winter's nerves had been heightened, and she could feel that fear amplified now. But she'd already faced some of her fears, and that gave her a strength she didn't have before.

This was the morning Winter would attempt to conquer the fear she couldn't face that warm day at Sienna's lake house. It was time for Winter to raft the Nile River. Winter dressed and walked downstairs. Alexis was sitting at the dining room table.

"We have banana bread for breakfast!" She pushed the bread to Winter, who cut a piece for herself. She popped chunks of the bread into her mouth.

"I don't feel hungry," Winter stated.

"But you'll need energy to get through rafting today. There's some fresh chai," Alexis said. "Everything will work out today!"

Winter grabbed a white mug and filled it with chai. She sat down on the bench and took a sip of the creamy drink. It reminded her of The Gregory, the first place on her journey where she had a comforting cup of tea and part of Winter wished she could go back to escape. Michael came into the room with this fists pumped high into the air.

"Winter Wright! Are you ready?" He called out like a gameshow host.

"No! But I'm going anyways!" She yelled back.

"What do you mean no?" He asked. He cut himself a large piece of bread and ripped into it.

"I'm a little nervous around water," Winter said, severely undercutting the truth.

"Why's that? I thought you were excited to go," he said, taking another bite out of the bread.

"I can't swim," Winter answered.

"Oh," he said with a casual shrug of his shoulders. "You know what? That doesn't matter. If any of us falls out today, our ability to swim will be useless anyways." A stunned look of disturbance covered Alexis' face. She hit Michael hard on his arm.

"Are you trying to make her more afraid?"

"No! Less afraid. I thought it'd be helpful to know that your level of experience is irrelevant. We'll be together in that sense. That's all I'm saying. If we die, we'll all die together."

"Good grief man! It'll be fine, Winter."

"That's basically what I said," Michael responded. "That only makes me like you more, Winter. I'm a fan of someone who charges on in the face of fear," Michael laughed.

"Michael's a thrill-seeker. He thrives off adrenaline," Alexis said.

"Let's do this before I change my mind," Winter muttered.

"Don't worry. It's going to be good!" Alexis responded.

Winter nodded weakly, slightly uplifted by Alexis' words.

"It's going to be out of this world!" Michael continued, yelling loudly.

His whole body overflowed with energy. Winter wanted some of it to transfer to her.

"I bet growing up with you was an adventure," Winter said.

A roguish grin lifted the corners of Michael's mouth as he said, "Most definitely."

It was only a five-minute drive to the rafting site. On the way over, Winter noticed a couple more billboards promoting skin lightening. She'd heard horror stories about girls putting toxic chemicals on their skin to lighten the tone and irreversibly damaging their bodies. Winter took a breath and concentrated her attention on the fear she wanted to overcome today.

They pulled into the parking lot, and Winter could hear the water rising and rushing. The Nile's powerful waves raged past the white building. Luscious tropical trees and low growing plants hugged the building's sides. It sat in red dirt, making it look remarkably similar to the suburban. Michael practically ran inside while Alexis and Winter trailed far behind. The registration room had a ceiling fan that clicked as it circled above, blowing wafts of hot air around.

Winter's breathing was hard. Her courage came in waves. They checked in and went out back to wait for the next set of available rafts. Rows of picnic tables lined the yard where groups of travelers were getting ready for their time out on the water. They grabbed life jackets from a pile on the ground and sat down at a free table. Something about seeing the rafts, how small they were, made all of Winter's strength evaporate into the hot air. Winter's heart began thumping harder in her chest, vibrating from her anxiety.

"I know we're here, but if you're too nervous you can hang back," Alexis said, upon seeing the look on Winter's face.

"I won't judge you too harshly," Michael joked.

"I can't stay. I have to try. I'm too close," Winter said to Alexis.

"All right. I support you either way," she said.

"Am I missing something? Why do you have to go?" Michael asked, confused.

"You're usually missing something, Michael," Alexis teased.

"Don't blame me if you accidentally fall out of the raft today," Michael said, putting air quotes around the word accidentally.

"You two are crazy," Winter laughed. "The reason I'm traveling is to face my deepest fears and water is up there with some of my most immobilizing ones. I have to go," Winter said, more to herself than anyone else.

"So you're feeling ready then?" Alexis asked, her brown eyes were soft, her face bright and hopeful.

"I'm feeling as ready as I can be," Winter said weakly, twisting her shaking fingers in her lap and gnawing on her bottom lip. Her answer must have been more convincing than she realized, because Alexis clapped her on the back and said, "Awesome, it's gonna be insane."

"I thought Michael was the thrill seeker," Winter said.

She shrugged her shoulders and said, "Gotta jump in for some of the fun."

Alexis' previous words set Winter's mind on a tangent. *It's going to be insane. When you can't swim and get into a river with raging waters, that is certifiably insane. That word is used too loosely and broadly today, but what I'm doing is a true form of insanity. I shouldn't be here. I should be in a white room with heavy padding. That's where I belong*, she thought.

"Winter, you can stick close to us today," Michael said from across the table, his eyes warm.

"Thanks," Winter breathed out.

"I have to say that because you look like you're marching to your funeral," he said.

"Do you hear the words you speak when you speak them, or do you get a more tactful translation in your head?" Alexis asked.

"I'm definitely going to toss you in today," Michael said with a smirk.

"Not if I get you first," Alexis replied.

Michael leaned forward with his elbows on the table's edge. He looked around the yard, at the adventurers, and said, "I can't get enough of this."

"What other life-threatening activities have you participated in?" Winter asked.

"I've been bungee jumping, skydiving, rappelling, and rock climbing. I'm not far off from becoming a skydiving instructor. I'm actually certified in a few of those things. But with all the traveling, I've had to put it on hold. Every adrenaline rush I can get my hands on I go after. Perhaps after today you'll feel the same," he teased.

"I think something is wrong with you," Winter said.

"You're feisty when you're nervous!" He said, laughing heartily and clapping his hands together. Winter smiled. Despite her evident fear, Michael's happiness was infectious.

"What do you like about it so much?" She asked. Her stomach had dropped with every death-skimming activity he mentioned.

He looked up at her, and with invigorating simplicity he said, "Because I feel so alive, but not because they're dangerous. Nature is compelling to me. It's powerful, and you get to be a part of this astounding force. Wildlife is a wildcard. You never know what you're going to get. To make it out mostly unscathed you have to submit to and respect its strength. I get nervous sometimes, but out there the only choice I have is to push through. It never ceases to amaze me what you're capable of when you give yourself the chance to push through hard circumstances. What's more exciting than that?"

While Michael spoke, a Ugandan man with a round, kind face walked up to their table. "Hello everyone. My name is Henry. I will be your guide on the river today. I have been on the rapids countless times. You will be safe with me." Winter thought about running, not just back to the cafe, but back home. She could pack her bags and be on the next flight out. *Who says you can't live a full life when you're full of fears?"*

"These ladies will be joining your group," he said. "This is Emily and Tina."

Two girls stood at Henry's side and waved. Everyone shook hands, and Winter wondered if her palms were sweaty, but then she realized everyone was sweating in the heat of the early Ugandan morning. They all walked to the calm mouth of the river and stepped inside of the raft. The raft began to float along, past tall trees with exposed roots showing through the vibrant soil.

Winter thought to herself, *this may not be so bad after all*. Her paddle lay across her lap, and the waters were not too rough. She let herself breathe, but then the rafting guide said eight awful words.

"It's time to practice. Prepare to jump off." To Winter, those words sounded eerily similar to unavoidable doom.

"Okay!" Henry said, sitting at the top of the raft. "We will practice before we start the larger rapids, and there will be food for you during the rest times. It's important to keep your spirits up for the rapids!"

If anyone was looking at Winter, it wouldn't have been difficult to read her thoughts at that moment. Her eyes widened to a point they never had before, and the lump in her throat felt less like the golf ball it had earlier in the morning. Now it resembled a basketball, or volleyball, anything large that could restrict her lungs access to air.

"We're going to be on here all day?" She gasped to Alexis, trying hard to make her voice sound like a whisper, instead of the desperate plea it truly was.

"Until the evening," Alexis whispered back.

Winter had thought rafting would take forty-five minutes. She'd hop on, spend some time battling the waves, and hop off. She'd go over a couple raging, white water waves, call it day and knock water off her list. But rafting was an entire day. A whole day. An event. Winter's heart started to beat faster as Henry told them to jump out and hold onto the ropes on the outside of the raft. *The outside*, she thought frantically.

"You are going to jump out, upturn the float, and practice getting it upright with your bodies inside."

"None of those words make sense to me," Winter mumbled.

Everyone leaped out of the raft. Alexis glided into the rough waters, seeming at home. Winter watched with admiration and dread. She shakily slid out of the raft and grabbed onto the rope so hard that the tips of her fingers turned red.

"Okay! This side will go under first," Henry said, pointing to the right side where Winter clung to the rope.

To flip the raft over, Winter's side of the raft would be dragged under water. At that point Winter knew she would end up having a heart attack or a panic attack that would debilitate her. If not now, then at some point during the day. Maybe it was going to happen while she was in the water if she was unlucky enough to fall out of the raft. She wondered rather dejectedly, *If I die while trying to conquer my fears, does that mean I succeeded or failed?*

When Winter was still home, she imagined conquering her fears as something that would be immensely exciting. She dreamed of overcoming her fears with victory and grace, but the actual moment before you encounter your fear, before you face it, is overwhelming. Her mind didn't work the same way as when she'd pulled up to the parking lot that morning. A strange mixture of wanting to survive, of her body trying to take over and calm her panic-stricken mind, was beginning to shape Winter's actions.

"Okay! We are going to pull the right side of the raft under the water. Hold on tight. If we flip on the waves, you must grab hold of the rope that encircles the raft. It will save you. Okay? Go!" He shouted.

Before Winter could think about it, her head was submerged and pulled under the water. Her eyes were shut tight; her hands constricted around the rope. The strange swelling sound of water around her ears filled Winter's head. The current dragged Winter beneath the water for only a few seconds, but it felt infinite. She popped out of the water looking and feeling like a cat in a bathtub.

Alexis and Michael looked at each other briefly, smiling so intensely that they seemed to be sharing an unspoken secret, an unmatched love of nature and adventure.

"That was cool," Alexis said.

"Winter, how are you holding up?" Michael asked, turning to face her.

"All right, I'm in no rush to do it again, but I didn't let go of the rope. I made it."

Michael smiled at Winter's words and gave her a side hug as he said, "You did great."

"Okay!" Henry shouted. "Now we are going to practice positions that will help you if you fall out and can't get hold of the rope." He spread his arms out to his sides and straightened his legs. "This T position will save you. Each of you is going to float into that level one rapid to give this a try."

Oh no, no, no, she thought. Winter attempted to practice the position with one hand firmly on the rope, her other arm irrevocably stiff. Her legs seemed to be searching for something solid to appear beneath them, making her body resemble a J far more than a T.

"Now, let go of the rope," Henry said plainly. "You, nervous girl, let go and drift into those waters."

He was pointing at Winter, and all she could think was this: *Get. Me. Out. Of. Here.*

"Me? Oh...are you sure?" Winter asked, knowing full well where his gaze was aimed.

"Yes, you."

Winter had to fight the urge to kick her guide who used the word okay far too often in her opinion. But she reminded herself that she needed him to survive this day and that kicking, while it would alleviate some of her growing frustration towards him, would be rude.

Winter released the rope and let herself drift into the level one rapid. Winter felt that this fear was helping her conquer a couple others on her list: fear of the unknown and fear of looking like a complete fool. Winter knew with undeniable clarity that she looked incredibly and utterly outlandish as her rigid body moved in the fluid, shifting waters.

When her body dipped into the rapid, she wasn't able to execute any of the guide's words. Her arms didn't spread out to her sides, and she couldn't even make a J shape. Her limbs flailed in the air as her feet kicked around. Winter tried to the very best of her ability to keep her head above water.

"Keep calm!" Henry yelled from the boat.

Winter tried to heed his words because she didn't want to be a liability to anyone else that morning, but her body, like her mind, had escaped her. She made it through the rough waters and out of Winter's peripheral she could see swift arms coming in her direction. Alexis swam over and pulled her towards the raft. Winter climbed back inside and sat down, breathing roughly, and laughing softly at the spectacle she undoubtedly knew she was.

"Thank you, Alexis," Winter said between, shallow, embarrassed breaths.

"No problem. I grew up on the water." She leaned closer and said, "Really, don't worry about it. I'm happy to dust off the old skills. Besides I want you to make it. So if I can help, I will."

The others on the raft went through the level one rapid calmly. None looked as odd or uncomfortable as Winter. Though she felt like a spectacle, Winter was also experiencing the arrival of motivation. She'd been scared, but she wasn't alone, and that was something to celebrate. Alexis nudged Winter's shoulder roughly and leaned back against the raft, welcoming the sun on her skin. Winter leaned back awkwardly, trying to replicate Alexis' ease. She already felt she'd done sufficient conquering for the morning, but from the corner of her eye Winter could see the white foam of a new rapid appearing. She could hear the waves crashing over jagged, sharp rocks. The orange raft floated to the rapid with turbulence.

"Okay! Get ready to paddle!"

The water began to push the raft where it wanted to take them, but they had to stay on course. They crashed into the rapid hard. Walls of water flew upwards towards the sky before crashing back down, covering Winter and everyone else. She had to fight the urge to stand up, to seek air, when the raft was entirely submerged underneath the Nile's forceful surface. After they had passed through the first rapid, Winter looked around and saw gleeful, manic grins surrounding her.

"That was amazing!" Michael said.

"You are brave rafters! Well done!" Henry shouted.

Winter's stomach churned. Brave was the least of things Winter felt she was. Her lips turned into a hollow smile, but internally she hoped Henry was right. *Relax, Winter. Trust the process. You're with experts.* She took a breath, feeling comforted by the thought, and then she felt herself falling backward.

An Australian guy leading another raft full of people had grabbed her life jacket, tipping her back and almost into the water. He smiled mischievously.

I'm at least with people who know what they're doing, she said instead.

And so the day of rafting the Nile truly began. They went on rapid upon rapid, trying to stay afloat. They all paddled as quickly as their bodies would allow. Long limbs flew from the raft as they pushed the water behind them, propelling themselves along the rapids.

White waves hammered them, knocking the raft around, throwing their bodies, demanding more from their aching muscles. When they hit the longest rapid of the day, Henry instructed them on what to do. Water poured down his face. At the front of the raft, he yelled to be heard over the thunderous waves.

"Grab onto the rope if you fall out, or if we get flipped. DO. NOT. LET. GO!"

He bounced at the nose of the raft and looked behind him at the rapids they rushed towards. Now Winter was soaking wet. Her shorts stuck to her wet skin, her hair was plastered to her head, and she was determined in a way she hadn't been when they first set out. No one spoke. They all concentrated on their bodies staying out of the water, except for Michael who wanted to be thrown in. The raft in front of them passed through the rapid and then it was their turn.

Over the waves Henry yelled, "Paddle! Paddle!" Their arms pushed the paddles through the opposing waters. "Left! Right! Lean!" Henry shouted with authority. With a magnificent amount of speed, their raft was launched forward. They tried to move against the strong currents without getting overturned. Winter's eyes landed upon a sharp dip in the waters ahead where a small waterfall awaited them. Her stomach dropped. She could sense what was coming. They hit the rocky waterfall hard and then with a sudden jerk, Winter was tossed out of the raft.

The water whipped her body underneath the rapid's strong tides. Winter was turned in any direction the currents chose to take her. Her ankle hit a bit of out-jutted rock, cutting her skin instantaneously. She fought the need to gasp with an open mouth. Winter knew the cut wouldn't be deep, but the shock of it was alarming.

Just when she started to worry, she resurfaced and saw a kayaker coming to help her. She smiled, but her relief was felt too soon. She was pulled under once more and became hysterical. Winter immediately wanted to feel hard, solid, immovable earth beneath her feet not forceful, altering waves around her body, but Winter was trapped for the day.

The kayaker paddled to her, and in her hectic state of mind, Winter accidentally flipped over the kayaker who had come to row her to the emergency raft, which was about eight times the size of the other rafts. She spilled out a string of apologies for over tipping him. His brows were

145

creased in anger as he paddled to the boat. Winter climbed into the emergency raft where Michael already sat. He was not at all flustered by being tossed into the Nile.

"Winter!" He called out.

"Hi, Michael," she said between breaths.

"You do not look good, my friend," he said.

"I cannot say the same for you. Kind of wish I could so I wouldn't seem so out of place," Winter replied.

"Come here and have a seat," he said. Winter's legs wobbled towards him. "I've rafted before, and I'm sure we're almost there. We'll have a break soon and after a few more rapids it'll be over."

Winter nodded. His words calmed her rapidly beating heart.

"There's our raft," Winter said.

Michael stood and waved his arms in the air. The emergency boat rowed along the water towards their raft. Winter climbed in slowly, feeling like she'd just learned to walk. When her feet landed in the raft, everyone clapped. Winter looked up, taken by total surprise. Everyone, including Michael, clapped for her. She smiled bashfully. Her throat was tight, but this time it wasn't because of fear; it was due to the incredible gratitude Winter felt for the people on that raft.

Part of Winter felt guilty for coming that day, for possibly impeding on their experiences, but that's not where their hearts were. They had become her companions on the river instead of people she'd inconvenienced with her fears. These people were becoming a part of Winter's journey towards overcoming. They were glad to see she made it mostly unharmed, and Winter shared their sentiment. Henry gave Winter a pat on the back and a large smile as she passed him on her way to her seat.

The group came to a rest period after that last rapid. Harold pulled out cookies and fresh pineapple already cut into large chunks. Winter welcomed the moment of peace. Everyone on the boat grabbed pieces of fruit and baked cookies. They bit into the pineapple, and their gazes shifted to one another unbelieving. Alexis, with a mouthful of ripe pineapple, said, "Holy crap. This is the best pineapple I've ever had."

Winter took another bite, savoring the intensity of the fruit's tangy sweetness. It was the most flavorful pineapple she'd ever bitten into. The group all rested against the sides of the raft and talked as the wind gently blew around their heads. To Winter, the moment was so tranquil it didn't seem to belong to the day. She was astonished that such a blissful interlude could exist in harmony with the feral waters of the Nile. Tina and Emily scooted closer to Winter as she bit into another piece of the pineapple.

"When you were practicing in the level one rapid, Alexis told us you're afraid of water," Tina shared.

"I guess I looked pretty crazy earlier," Winter said.

"You totally didn't look comfortable in the water. So, when I saw you go under the water my stomach dropped. I couldn't find you anywhere," Emily said. They talked as pineapple juice dripped from their fingers.

"It was nerve-wracking," Winter said. "But that's a few rapids down!"

Though they were strangers, this girl, and the others on the raft exhibited a level of caring and concern that humbled and challenged Winter's notion of people. Their conversation was cut short as Henry turned to the group.

"Finish everything. It's time."

He led them down three more rapids. One was another waterfall that claimed the raft before them. The wide raft, carrying six people, got caught on slabs of uneven rock faces. The people had pumped their arms, trying to use their paddles to get down the waterfall. With red faces, they pushed themselves over and plunged into the watery abyss.

To Winter's great relief, her raft passed over the fall smoothly. It flew into the water in one downward motion, going completely under before popping out onto the water's ragged surface. The entire group cheered and raised their voices high into the air at having made it. They saluted their combined success. Emily, Tina, Henry, Alexis, and Michael's voices rang loudly, but Winter's was the loudest.

Henry swiveled around to face them. "We have one last rapid until the day's end."

Winter couldn't believe it was almost over. *My first fear is almost completed*, she thought with wonderment. She'd even enjoyed parts of the day, and that was something she didn't believe was possible.

"This is a level five rapid!" Henry shouted over the waves. They became deafeningly louder as they got closer to the roughest part of the Nile. "But do not hold on if you fall off. Not this time or you will become stuck under the waves, and you will drown," he stated. His words were matter-of-fact. "To go down this last rapid, though, we must get out of the rafts. A level six rapid separates us from our last rapid. It is too dangerous to pass through. We will walk alongside the mountain, and you will have a choice. You will have the option to stay on land or get back into the water," Henry said.

And then he pointed to safe, high ground. Winter mulled the thought over in her head. *I could be done*, she contemplated quietly. The rafts were all led to the steep, rocky mountainside where groups stepped out of the rafts. People's feet landed hard on solid earth, and everyone began walking around to the other side of the mountain where the last rapid lay in wait. Winter saw several people opting out of riding that final rapid. The number of people staying on land grew as more chose the comfort of land over the uncertainty of water. A guy in the raft behind Winter climbed out of the boat saying, "I'm done for the day. I've had my fill."

Alexis turned her gaze to Winter and asked with pressing eyes, "Are you going to stay?" It didn't take Winter long to answer, and her reply didn't fill her with as much fear as before. She had to see this fear through to its completion.

"I've made it this far. I can't stop now," Winter said.

Alexis pumped her fist into the air and yelped her approval. Howls of support erupted from the group that had now been bonded together from the day spent on the Nile. They got out and walked along the red, rock-filled path to the last rapid. Together, they piled back onto the raft quickly, brimming with nervous anticipation. They were ready for that last rapid, but Winter didn't know what was about to happen. The raft settled into the waves and every person held their paddle closely. Michael and Alexis told Winter to stay close.

Henry called out directions like a sergeant, and they obeyed, putting forth their best efforts from the day worth of lessons they'd received. Water crashed on every side of the raft. Each face was the picture of concentration. They ducked and weaved as water came down in crashing, relentless waves upon their heads, and then it happened. A wave higher than Winter's eyes could see fell over their heads and she was knocked off. She recalled Henry's words and released the rope from her grip.

Her body was immediately pulled through the water with a force that shocked Winter. She tried to keep her eyes above the waves, but it was no use. This was not the hotel pool she'd fallen into during a family reunion party, when she first fought against water. Winter was jerked from current to current, switching directions as a fluid stream of forceful water treated her body like a rag doll. She was utterly helpless.

Again, Winter remembered what she was told by Henry: if you get pulled into currents this strong stay calm. Winter tried to be calm. She closed her eyes when submerged and when Winter felt the air on her skin she opened her eyes, took a breath, spread her body in the shape of a T, and prepared herself for the next wave that would certainly come crashing down on top of her. The waves were so high they seemed to drop from the sky above. It was as if the white, voluminous clouds were raining walls of water.

She twirled and twisted in the Nile and eventually Winter was thrown out into soft waves. She lifted her eyes to the sky, her body still spread into a tight T. It was strange how serene the sky appeared, soft blue and white clouds dwelling above torrid water. She looked to the shoreline and could see a kayaker not far off. The current had pushed Winter to isolated waters a mile out.

Don't tip this kayaker over, she said to herself.

"I'm Reginald," the kayaker said gently as he neared Winter. He spoke delicately upon seeing her quivering fingers, sensing that she was new to the rapids. Winter grabbed hold of the kayak's front and Reginald began to pull her back to shore, talking to her, quieting the wild beating of her heart.

After that last rapid, Winter's anxiety began to recede. She had made it through one of her worst fears, and she was still here, still whole. She let out breaths of sweet relief as she came up to the rocky hillside. Despite her aching body, and the fast pumping of her heart from the exertion required of her fatigued limbs, Winter was intoxicated by her triumph. She trembled with joy.

Alexis' words spilled genuinely from her mouth. "When I saw you go under, I seriously thought that might be the end."

Winter smiled and leaned over to catch her breath, not realizing how much it had escaped her. Winter had made it through something she wasn't sure she could overcome, and it hit Winter that she never once didn't feel fear. *But maybe,* she thought, *it isn't about conquering fear. Maybe the real triumph is in meeting your fears face to face. Maybe they are just meant to be seen, looked in the eye, and told "I see you. I know you are there, and I'm going to exist boldly with the knowledge of your presence, which no longer holds me back."*

And then Winter laughed. She bent over, hands on her knees, her head thrown back into the air in complete surrender to the emotion. On the side of a mountain in Uganda, Winter laughed until tears filled her eyes and wet her cheeks. The others watched her before joining in, their voices growing as each of them laughed from deep within. The six of them talked about that last and final rapid, reveling in the time they shared on the Nile. Already, they began to reminisce about the day as they walked through red dirt, on the side of a cliff, to make their way back to the place that was becoming home for Winter.

CHAPTER TWENTY-ONE—THE FACE OF JOY

"Bungee jumping is next," Michael said.

"Let's catch our breaths first!" Alexis replied.

They sat in the backyard that evening, still wet from the waves. The cafe was closed for the night, and Simon was the only person left there. He closed up the cafe and sat on the back porch next to Michael. Alexis had convinced him to stay for the evening and make all of them tea and Michael a strong cup of coffee. Winter laid on her side on the grass, wearing her camouflage jacket and drinking hot chai to warm her body. Simon strummed a guitar from the porch.

"I can't believe you did that today, Winter," Michael said. Winter's cheeks warmed. She wasn't sure she deserved the influx of praise she was receiving.

"Winter Wright's personal revolution! You're on the road of life!" Alexis shouted out.

"I wonder why more people don't go after what they want in life," Michael said, lightly resting his head on his arms.

"Fear of failure, the stress of economic insecurity, the responsibility of family demands…" Alexis began to answer.

A smile turned up the corners of his mouth. "I wasn't asking for a list, Alexis," he laughed.

"Listen, I'm a hands-on kind of person. Give me a task and I'll complete it."

Michael lifted his head, his eyes filled with deep contemplation. "I've always imagined the world in a certain way. To me, everyone has an individual contribution that they can make, only them, and if we all fulfilled it then it'd have an irreplaceable impact on the world," Michael said.

"Sometimes I forget why I'm your friend, and then you say stuff like that," Alexis said. Michael threw a pillow at her.

"Michael, I would never forget why I'm your friend," Simon said.

"Thanks, brother," Michael said. Winter laughed and took another sip of her tea.

She rested her head on the cool grass and looked up at the sky, at the stars above. She'd never thought of it that way, that each person might be bestowed with a gift, individual to them, and once given to the world, it is changed. Simon continued to strum the taut strings of the guitar, creating notes. They all laid beneath a canvas of stars and Winter heard a collection of notes she knew.

"I sang that song in Belfast!" She said, sitting up a bit.

"I had a feeling you might have good taste in music," Simon smiled.

Winter hummed to the tune of one of her favorites songs, one that always comforted and inspired her. She listened to the bellow of the chords as a cool night breeze passed over her skin. Moonlight shone down on the four of them as the sounds of the night moved around their group, and the fullness of that moment was enough for Winter.

***

Winter woke up to a body that twanged but didn't hurt. She felt that her muscles were singing out. She'd earned her rest for that night. Winter pulled her journal from the bedside table and took out the pen Marieleen had given her. Winter brought the pen down firmly on the paper, drawing another line through her fear of water. Winter took a shower in cold water that made her body shiver and her teeth chatter. When she came downstairs, she found Michael and Alexis at the table.

"Morning Fearless One," Michael said. This morning he wore black-rimmed glasses and a pen rested behind his ear, making him look fiercely similar to Simon.

"Oh gosh. That name won't last long, especially if I find another gecko; dead or alive."

Alexis chuckled as she sipped her tea. "It's your first cafe day! But before you start, Simon needs us to go to the market for Sandy. I don't know if you remember me mentioning her. Sandy manages the cafe and she cooks a lot of the food. She's running low on some essentials."

"We already ate, Winter. We can leave when you're ready," Michael said, his likeliness to his brother increasing. Winter grabbed a pineapple muffin.

"Do I need to bring anything?"

"Just some change for our ride over," Alexis said as they walked downstairs, making their way to the street. On the curb, Winter turned around and looked at the cafe, at the place that would fill her coming days. A flutter of excitement rose up in her being.

"Sandy gave me the list this week," Michael said. He waved it in the air.

"Anything new on there?" Alexis asked, grabbing it from his hand.

"Same as last week. Termite, pineapple, matoke…" she went on reading.

151

Winter chewed her breakfast and glanced around, sealing this morning in her memory. She wanted to be able to recall how bright the sun was, how the heat embraced her skin too tightly, the sight of palm trees and their leaves blowing in a wind that did nothing to abate the heat. She wanted to emblazon this morning in her mind, the memories of her first days in Jinja.

Winter kicked at a few pebbles as they made their way to the end of the road. Up ahead, Winter could make out a few men standing next to bicycles, talking amongst one another. The men resembled Michael in their build: tall, lean, and lanky. Winter recalled riding bikes at Sienna's lake house, bounding down streets with her arms out to her sides. She continued walking past the men and their bikes, but then she heard Alexis' voice.

"Winter, this is it." Winter turned to Alexis.

"What do you mean?" She asked her.

"These are our rides," Alexis said. She began to speak with one of the men and he motioned for them to hop onto a bike. Alexis could read the apprehension in Winter's eyes. She smiled as she explained. "These are boda-bodas. They're bicycle taxis. I'm sure it's a little less cover then what you're used to."

Winter's mind flashed back to the hectic streets she'd seen on her arrival day. She imagined being on a bike entrenched in heavy, erratic traffic. Winter's feet tingled with the urge to run in the opposite direction. Her eyes took in the slender wheels and the rusting bike chains. She swallowed hard.

"Just hold on tight. Girls have to sit sideways on the back," she said.

"Wait, what?" Winter's eyes grew so large she felt they might have temporarily disconnected from her skull.

"What year is this? I have to ride side saddle? How do you balance?"

All cultural awareness exited her. Alexis held back a grin and led Winter over to the bikes. Michael's smile spread across his face.

"What are you laughing at?" Alexis asked.

"I do feel a bit bad for you, but you have to admit that it's funny. I mean, your hesitation is probably the equivalent of someone cautiously putting one foot in a taxi at home, and then running away." Winter stared at Michael. "I'm trying to make it easier with humor. Is it not working?"

"You are not very gifted in that area, man. Ignore our well intentioned friend, Winter. You put your foot here." She showed Winter a piece of metal no longer than an inch.

"What are you pointing at?" Winter asked, being slightly dramatic. "Are you sure something is there?"

Alexis let out a splash of laughter and said, "It took me a while to get the hang of it too, but you have to ride side saddle behind a male driver. The other way insinuates some cultural taboos you don't want insinuated."

"Oh, all right. Are there any other cultural no-no's I should know about?"

"I have one. Don't say maybe because here that is interpreted as yes, and don't point your finger at people because it's considered very rude," Michael said.

"People usually gesture with their faces. They move their eyebrows up and down. I've seen people have whole conversations without opening their mouths. It's a super power," Alexis added.

"It's true," Michael confirmed.

"I'll try to remember," Winter said.

She took a deep breath and climbed onto the back of the bike. The slim metal seat appeared insubstantial to carry all 5'7 of Winter through the weaving traffic of Jinja. She lifted herself slowly and unsteadily to sit down. Before she could get her bearings the bike pulled away. It moved slowly at first, giving Winter just enough time to adjust her feet on the metal piece. When they reached the main road, it began. They tilted and sped between motorcycles, vans, and cars. Winter's driver rang a bell on his bike to ere his frustrations at other drivers who cut them off. He seemed determined to unnerve her.

If she moved her legs and arms the slightest bit outward, she could touch traffic on almost every side of her. The man rode in the tiny spaces between vehicles, and was reasonably proud at his own skill to keep the bike upward in the onslaught of cars. It was a feat, but one Winter wished he wouldn't attempt. She missed sidewalks. Her foot kept slipping and out the corner of her eye she saw Alexis who seemed born to ride a bike side saddle.

Alexis was the type of person who could adapt to any situation. Her chin was in the air as she took in the scenery. Winter did no such thing. She was convinced that one movement to look at the rushing scenery would end with that scenery being her last sight. Her heart jolted at every bump in the road that sent her flying a few inches off her seat.

When they reached the main road in Jinja the driver stopped hard. Winter fell forward, but balanced herself before tumbling off the bike. They'd made it to the market. Winter had the strong urge to bend down, raise her hands to God, and kiss the dirt and cement beneath her feet.

Instead, she dusted the dirt off her body and let her legs shake quietly under the long, beaded, purple skirt she was wearing. She looked over to see which coins Simon and Alexis passed to their driver's and copied. Her hand shook slightly as she passed her coins to the driver. She wiped the sweat from her palms down the front of her skirt and turned to see the market.

Winter's mouth hung open. An expanse of wooden awnings hovering over hundreds of different stands stood in front of her. It reminded her of a microscopic town in size and breadth. A short set of stairs led them down to the market where people's gazes followed their three-person group.

Simon and Alexis walked through with ease. They knew which stands to go to and they were greeted kindly at each one.

Winter spun her body around to see what was being sold at the stands. At one store front, faded Tina Turner t-shirts looked down at Winter, at another fish dried in the heat of the morning, but at every stand she passed Winter collected odd stares as she twirled in the aisles. Within a half hour they had completed the list.

"Winter, over here!" Alexis called out.

She jogged to keep up with the other two, the novelty had somewhat worn off of them. They walked through like they would in any other venue, but every corner intrigued Winter. Every stand filled with cooked crickets and Ugandan ornaments drew her gaze. Pieces of clothing and trinkets that had traveled from around the world and ended up on stands next to handmade jewelry demanded her attention. Winter decided that untold stories lingered here, waiting to be told and released into the world. But for now, she followed Michael and Alexis out of the market.

The cafe was full when they arrived. Sandy bustled around in the kitchen throwing ingredients into pots and pans.

"Alexis," Sandy said, smiling. She cleaned her hands on a fresh towel, and held Alexis' face between her palms. "How are you?"

"Wonderful. We have your groceries from the market," Alexis said, beaming at Sandy's greeting. Michael handed over the bags.

"Hello Michael! How did you enjoy my cake?"

"Best I've ever had," Michael answered with a grin. Sandy patted him on the cheek.

"Thank you, both. And who is this?" Sandy asked, looking at Winter.

"This is Winter. She's the new volunteer."

"Well I hope you are liking your time in Uganda!" Sandy said.

"I am! We went rafting on the Nile yesterday, and I'm excited to work here in the café."

Sandy turned off the fire beneath her cooking food and said, "Come, I'll show you around. You two already know what to do." Michael and Alexis dispersed and Sandy scooped up Winter's hand in her own and left the kitchen.

"So, here is the café. You must try my food while you are here!"

"I had some of the food you sent upstairs. I loved it."

"Why, thank you." Sandy waved her hand in the air coyly, but her eyes burned bright with pride. "The store is just there. Some days you will work in the cafe shop. Customers come from all over," she said with accented English. "Everything in the shop is made in the courtyard by women affected by AIDS who need ways to support their families." Sandy patted Winter's hand as she spoke. "The library is very, very dusty. Most volunteers do not like cleaning and sorting books, but I find it calming."

Sandy's eyes moved to the door where a boy stood begging. Sandy walked to the doorway. "No! I'll have no begging outside this cafe!" Sandy said. The boy scuttled off, and Winter's heart shredded. "You think I'm awful. But sometimes young ones are sent into the city to get money that is used for bad things. In some places of the world, children are mutilated to bring in more money. I will not have it."

"Their realities remain unchanged," Winter said.

"Yes. People want to throw money and agendas at things when they need to throw ears to listen, opportunities for partnership. Sometimes I feed the begging children when the cafe is closed, and I've talked to Simon about making a new program, one that funds the street kids to have meals, but there are other ways to help. Now, back to work. Some days are slow. If you want to read or something, you can. We also have a computer where you can check your email. It runs very slow."

Sandy looked at the clock in the café dining room. "I need to go and cook again. This morning you can work in the cafe and later you can sort out donations for the library."

"All right," Winter said to her retreating figure.

Winter spent the afternoon cleaning dirty dishes and sweeping in the courtyard. She carried stacks of plates from tables and refilled empty glasses with water. She imagined talking with a bevy of world travelers, but the extent of the conversations she had with anyone was, "Are you finished with that?" and "Would you like some more of this?"

She occasionally ran into Alexis and Michael while carrying plates to the tables. The two of them played a game. Whoever had less dishes on their tray would get punched by the other. "You're welcome to join in the games, Winter." Michael had said while passing her on his way to the courtyard.

"Maybe later," Winter replied.

By the time the rush died down, Winter was sweaty, and her feet ached, but she brushed sweat from her brow with the satisfaction felt after a day of hard work. Over the next week Winter fell into a routine at the cafe. Winter's least favorite work days were when she sorted books in the dusty library. Her skirt pockets usually filled with tissues by the end of her shift. The days were much the same, cafe work followed by sorting book donations in the library; except for one.

"Sandy, it smells intoxicatingly good in here!" Alexis said as she gave her a hug. It was early afternoon, and Winter had spent the day stocking books in the library.

"You ready to go, Winter?" Michael asked.

"Where?" Winter asked Michael.

"We're heading out to a different village today," he said, scratching his jaw. Stubble grew on his face. "I was supposed to tell you, but I forgot. Sorry about that."

Winter felt her anxiety rise. Would today be like her first? Winter waved goodbye to Sandy and crawled into the suburban. The glances from her new friends made it seem that their minds were not far off from her own.

"Hey, Winter!" Simon called from the driver's seat. "I assume Michael forgot to tell you about our plans for today. Sorry about that. Next time I'll ask Alexis or find you myself."

"Good plan," Winter replied with a smile.

They arrived at a village in the late afternoon. Winter's eyes were met with a landscape of vibrant green and gold. Sugar cane stalks blew in a calm breeze. Corn stood shimmering in the light of the crisp day. Winter could hear the waters of the Nile moving. They sounded less threatening then they had when she rafted them.

The yard they were in had a church building built with handmade mud bricks. It stood to the east, next to the plants. A small one room house made of cement lay to Winter's left, and animals ran free in the yard. A turkey that was half Winter's height, and looked perpetually angry, started making its way toward her when a man emerged from the house and shooed him away. Two little boys and a short woman carrying a baby followed him.

"Ah, Simon, you have returned," the man said.

"I have, Wendell, and I've brought a few people with me. This is my brother, Michael, and our friends Alexis and Winter. The three of them are volunteering at the cafe."

"You are all most welcome," Wendell said to them. Benevolence lived in his voice. "These are my sons Aaron and Joseph, this is my daughter Lena, and my wife, Esther."

His wife smiled bashfully. The boys were young, between four and six, and the baby was only months old. She gurgled and cooed, melting everyone's hearts. "Have a seat. You all must be hungry."

Michael pulled out a bench and placed it near Alexis and Winter. The four of them sat down and washed their hands in a large basin. Afterwards, they were served maize, millet and fish. When they finished, Michael turned to Alexis and Winter.

"I brought some bubbles for the kids," he said, digging into his bag. "Simon said it wouldn't hurt to give a small gift to them for hosting us today." Michael passed two containers to Winter and Alexis. The three of them stood in the center of the yard and began to blow. Wendell's little boys leaped up from their chairs at the sight of the bubbles. They jumped high as they swatted at them.

Soon the number of children began to multiply as the boy's laughter lifted into the air. It seemed like every child in the village had gathered. All of the children looked up at Winter and her friends, smiling so intensely, so openly and intimately, that it made Winter want to reflect their openness into her own heart, into her life.

As the thought settled, another little boy came into the yard. He wasn't more than six years old, but he had a baby wrapped in cloth against his body. His face was shy and sweet and his golden skin bright. Upon seeing the bubbles, his features lit up. The children scattered as the wind carried the bubbles around the yard. When the bubbles disappeared, Michael, Alexis, and Winter blew more. The children's faces were expectant, waiting.

Winter lifted the soapy wand from the plastic container and glided it through the open air. Long, clear bubbles shone beneath the setting light of the sun. Smiles erupted onto their faces as they played under the sky. It was a surreal moment. Never in Winter's wildest imaginings could she have predicted what a moment such as this one could feel like; it was pure peace. They jumped and gently hit at the dozens of bubbles that poured down.

Winter wanted to capture the joy she saw spread across their faces. They smiled widely and freely, deeply, as they popped glistening bubbles while all of them avoided the angry turkey's territory. What they were doing was simple. As Winter pulled the wand through the air, she was reminded of what some people asked her before she came to the country. When she met people in the airport terminal, and they found out where Winter was going, many asked what she was coming to give to Africa, what she was going to bestow on an entire continent.

But Winter was only going to Jinja, Uganda, and she wasn't coming to give anything, but she could feel herself receiving something remarkable, indescribable. Winter was so struck by the people she met. The little boy who held his younger sister in one arm, and popped bubbles with the other, had more responsibility than she had at the age of twenty-four. The peace with life Winter was encountering in the people she met was more than up-lifting. All they were doing was playing with bubbles, but sheer joy was evident on their faces and after years of fear clouding her heart, Winter was beginning to feel that joy within herself.

After a couple of hours, they hopped back into the suburban and headed to a restaurant in town. They sat down at a white, plastic table inside a narrow restaurant. Winter didn't know what the menu said, but when she saw the word samosa, she knew she'd found her meal. Winter wanted to figure out if she could freeze boxes of samosas and bring them home with her.

"How have you liked working at the cafe?" Simon asked.

"It's quiet, only mildly less hectic than rafting the Nile," Winter said. Simon grinned and Winter noticed Michael trying to get his brother's attention. Michael eyed Alexis' plate of food. His fork moved towards her chapati.

"Michael!" She slapped his hand. "Avert the route of your fork!" she shouted.

"I didn't get any and I want some. Simon, you had one job! Keep her attention away from me," Michael said with exasperation.

"I'm not even brave enough to take food away from Alexis. You're entirely on your own," Simon said. Alexis ripped off the tiniest piece she could and teasingly gave it to Michael.

Winter laughed at them and bit into her food. At the end of the night, they walked out onto the curb, ready to head home. The heat outside the restaurant felt thick. Alexis closed her eyes and tilted her head back.

"I love this heat. I could move here for these hot days," she said.

I could run away because of the heat, Winter thought. To the touch, her skin felt overheated. The occasional cool nights gave Winter the relief she needed.

Simon stepped up to the curb and a slew of men on bikes rushed towards him. The drivers argued amongst themselves over who would drive them until some of them spotted a group of tourists.

I will get used to this, she told herself, eyeing the bike. Michael, Alexis, and Simon got on their bikes with minimal effort. Winter could hear the crunching sound of tire on rock and dirt as their bikes began taking off. Her bike was about to do the same when she felt a hand tap her elbow.

She looked down to see two little boys with open palms outstretched to her. She took them in as they stood before her. Their clothing was brown, worn from years of wear not inflicted by their bodies. The clothes they wore were probably once crisp and clean. Perhaps they were neatly creased shorts in another life. But here, the clothes sat draped on shoulders that looked too thin. Standing there in the skirt she bought for the purpose of coming to Jinja, Winter could sense her privilege. Was it guilt that sat in the pit of her stomach? *No, that's not it.* It was simple human empathy that made her heart heavy.

Their hands were still outstretched before Winter. A thick lump was forming in her throat. *What had I been doing when I was their ages?* She thought. Winter remembered Sandy's words. Sometimes children are sent out into the streets to beg for coins and shillings, only to return them to people who make a living off their standing under the hot sun in tattered clothing. Their realities remain unchanged, and yet their Winter stood. Debating. Saying no was more than difficult. *What if this situation is different?* She wondered, unsure of what to do. *I can't say no.*

Winter could see the bikes of her friends flying in between vehicles, so she searched in her bag and realized that she had one coin, just one. It was the exact cost of her bike ride. Winter had nothing else, and she was in the middle of a random street in Uganda. This was all happening in one moment, taking place over the span of seconds that seemed to drag on for a millennium.

Winter took the coin out and began to hand it to the driver. She could see a glimmer in the older boy's eyes, but she tried to relay the message that it's all she had, that she needed to get home. He seemed angered or disappointed, maybe both, perhaps neither. She passed the silver piece to the man with her eyes fixed on the boys. But Winter's hands, slick with sweat from the heat and shaking from the frantic beating of her own heart, faltered. The coin slipped from between her fingers. It rolled over the curb and hit a patch of tan dirt. The younger boy's hand reached out quickly, with a dexterity she never possessed at his age.

He locked the coin between his pointer finger and thumb and stopped it from rolling around in the dirt at their feet. He held it in his hand and without hesitation, the boy placed the coin in his palm and held it out for Winter to take. The older boy nudged the younger one, his eyes growing big with irritation and chiding. Someone called out Winter's name, but they were unaware that her feet were welded to the spot.

His hand was now outstretched, and Winter was the one taking the coin. Looking into his young eyes, she deeply wished she could enclose his fist around the coin and say, "Take it. It's yours," and though they spoke different languages, their souls would connect and he would understand. With the threat of tears in her eyes, she turned and gave the driver his money, and they took off. As they drove, Winter remembered she did have something she could give. She tapped the man's shoulder and asked, "Can you turn around?" He listened, weaving the bike back up the path toward the boys.

She jumped off and pulled out a small tin of candy she bought at the airport. The older boy seemed perplexed to see Winter again. She felt absurd, useless, handing out what was the equivalent of a breath mint. The younger boy raised his eyebrows in surprise when Winter stooped in front of him. She gently reached for his hand and placed the candy in his palm. The boy looked up at Winter, astonished, but then his brown eyes shone with gratitude. As he looked up at Winter, he smiled the most radiant smile she'd ever seen. Bright enough to light a thousand worlds. Winter turned and climbed back on the bike, not wanting them to see her cry. She waved at the boys and the driver took off.

It was nothing to give. It didn't do anything for the situation, and part of Winter felt that it was done to appease a sense of unease and guilt in her soul. But as she rode away, she realized that wasn't it at all. She wanted to say thank you to the little boy for teaching her something invaluable. Winter hoped that little boy felt some sense of the innate awe he had inspired deep within her soul that day, while standing on a corner under a blazing sun, waiting for a bike to carry her home. After she met that boy, Winter hoped their paths would cross again. But she would never see him, not during any of the days that followed his.

CHAPTER TWENTY-TWO—ANNA HERALD

A few days later, the four of them sat outside on the porch listening to music on a record player Alexis bought at a street shop in Denmark. Her playlist ushered them into relaxation after a long day in the cafe. Michael broke three glasses and two plates, prompting Simon to wonder if his brother volunteering at the cafe was actually costing more money.

"I'm done with the computer if anybody needs it," Michael said, holding Simon's laptop in the air.

"Can I check my email?" Winter asked.

She sat on the lawn, using her camouflage jacket as a blanket to shield her skin from the dewy grass. Michael handed the computer over. In her inbox, she had a couple emails from her parents that she'd already answered, but then Winter's hand froze. An email from Anna Herald sat at the top of her inbox. Winter hesitantly clicked open the email and read Anna's words.

Hi, Winter.

It's Anna Herald. I got your email from your mom. She told me you're traveling in Uganda right now. I was glad to hear that you're doing well. I'm sure you know why I'm emailing. I left a note with your sister a little while ago. I don't know if she gave it to you or not, but I asked you something, and I need an answer. I've done a lot of growing up since we last saw each other. I don't know how much you blame me for what happened that day.

I just wanted to let you know that I've changed. I have, and I'm sorry for the years of torment I put you through. It would mean a lot if you could forgive me. My number's at the bottom of the email or you can just respond to this. Thanks, Winter. Have a good trip.

-A.H.

Winter thought about her Grand Failure. That was the last day she'd seen Anna Herald. She did blame her. She blamed her almost entirely, but Winter was more disappointed in herself than anyone else.

"Are you all right, Winter?" Michael asked.

Winter looked up to find the three of them staring at her. Her face must have given away what she was feeling, even though she couldn't pinpoint every emotion Anna brought forth. Winter did know how much anger she felt towards Anna. Winter thought Anna had no right to ask for forgiveness for the pain she left like white hot brands, in Winter's brain. Winter felt guilt, too. Guilt because she could not muster up any part of her that wanted to forgive Anna though she felt she should.

"I just got a surprising email," Winter said.

"Oh, what does it say?" Michael asked.

Alexis threw a pillow in Michael's direction, and Simon said, "Michael, you can't ask people what their personal letters say." He sounded like the quintessential older and more mature brother.

"You don't have to tell me if you don't want to," Michael said.

"It's from a childhood bully I had. She wants me to forgive her."

"Woah. That's interesting. Do you think you could find it in yourself to forgive her, or would it be too hard?" Alexis asked.

Winter thought back to the days leading up to her Grand Failure and swallowed hard as the memory came crashing back.

Winter wasn't always a gifted student. She had countless insecurities that touched most facets of her life, but at the end of her junior year in high school Winter was presented with an opportunity, a chance for Winter to prove herself.

In the middle of her junior year, everyone was talking about the colleges they wanted to attend, and Winter secretly had a dream of attending a top school. It was why she went to extra tutoring after classes, why she tried out for sports; she wanted to live the dream of getting through doors she'd been told by classmates, and even a few teachers, were closed to her.

When Winter told her guidance counselor about her aspirations, he suggested Winter think more realistically. Winter was used to not being believed in, but she decided that mindset needed to change, starting with herself. So when the Illinois chapter of the prominent foundation, 'Trailblazers: Empowering Today's Youth for a Brighter Future,' announced a writing competition, Winter was determined to win it.

The winner would receive a substantial scholarship, and have their essay printed in the foundation's respected academic magazine. It was the most future boosting opportunity Winter had ever encountered, and she firmly believed this was her chance. Winning this would enable Winter to walk through those doors.

The application was due in October, which gave Winter nine months to write it. Winter worked on her essay all spring of her junior year and over the summer leading into her senior year. In the fall, she marched to the main office at school to turn in her work. High schools across the state would mail in the applications together, and two winners and ten semifinalists would be announced by district principals. Winter's hands shook as she dropped the paper into the bin.

The topic of the essay was deeply personal. It was about a time of struggle or strife in your life, and Winter wrote about her first encounter with prejudice and the years that followed: losing all of her hair in the pursuit of an ideal of beauty, of assumed worth, in which she'd not been included. After she dropped her application off, she turned and ran into someone.

"Oh, sorr-" Winter stopped talking when she saw Anna Herald looking down at her.

"Where are you going, electro-girl?" Anna asked.

Winter bit her bottom lip and kept walking.

"But I guess I can't call you that since you don't have hair anymore."

"That was years ago, Anna. My hair is growing back," Winter retorted.

"Doesn't look like it to me. Maybe you should go for the shaved look again."

"My hair is tightly curled, so length takes longer to show," Winter said, unsure why she was trying to explain anything about herself to Anna Herald.

"Whatever." Anna remarked, examining her polished fingernails. Then she frowned and pulled Winter's application out of the drop box. "You're trying to win this award? Ha! Winter, every time we face off, I win. Do you want to take this sad excuse for an essay with you now or later?"

Winter hated that her eyes welled up with tears when she was angry. It made her feel weak and exposed at the moments when she most wanted to feel strong and untouchable. Anna Herald had elicited too many tears from Winter over the years, and Winter didn't want to shed anymore tears over her.

"Don't you have anything better to do than harass people?" Winter asked.

"But you're not a person, are you, Winter? Not you, not your weird little freaky friends. Tell your identity confused friend to stop bringing that weird crap for lunch. I can't stand the smell."

"She's not identity confused, she's multicultural. A person can identify with multiple backgrounds. Your insults haven't matured much over the years, just like you, Anna. You're still using the same material to talk about Sienna."

Anna stared at Winter and asked, "Why are you still talking?" And then Anna threw Winter's application into the space between them. It fluttered to the floor.

"What's wrong with you?" Winter shouted, but Anna wasn't taken aback.

"I wondered when I'd see some fire from you, Winter," she responded, looking Winter over with icy eyes. "Nothing is wrong with me. I just don't like you. I don't like how you're afraid to speak in class. I don't like how you walk around like your feet don't know where they're going. I can't name one thing I like about you, except the fact that I can see over your hair now, Malcolm," she remarked forcefully. "You're going to lose."

"We'll see, Anna," Winter retorted, walking around her nemesis without looking back. Winter was committed to winning that competition.

It was late October when the principal's voice came over the intercom. Winter looked to the trees outside the classroom window. An array of deep auburn and bright yellows painted the dark branches. She shifted her gaze when she heard the topic of the announcement.

"I am pleased to announce that the winner and runner up for the Trailblazer's Essay Competition have been chosen from our very own school! They will be sent to a conference in Chicago where the winner will read her essay aloud, and have a feature in the foundation's academic magazine, *Trailblazing Leaders*. This is an amazing accomplishment! Let's give our finalists a hearty round of applause. Congratulations, to our runner-up Anna Herald and our winner, Winter Wright!"

Winter grabbed the sides of her desk in utter shock. For the first time in her life she'd beaten Anna Herald, but it wasn't the fact that she'd had won over her that impacted Winter; it was being told she had a voice worth hearing that made her sit up in the seat in disbelief. She was so elated she could cry. She'd been picked. Her, Winter Wright, introvert and anxiety filled girl had been chosen. Chosen.

In preparation for the Chicago gala, which all semi-finalists attended, Winter's mother let her pick out a dress though money was tight. The dress Winter chose to wear to the gala was a shiny emerald color with flowing fabric that swept the floor as she walked. Winter tried the dress on every night in anticipation of the evening when she'd read her essay aloud. It was going to be her moment, her dream come true. Winter was in the clouds.

The feeling of affirmation wouldn't last long.

Winter shut the lid of the computer and pushed the rest of the memory away from her conscious mind. She wasn't ready to relive what happened between she and Anna, not yet.

"I don't know if I can forgive her. I know I should try, but I've spent so much of my life worrying about her and what she might do to me. But that's not what I want to focus on anymore. I can't focus on it right now. It doesn't put me in a good place," she said.

"What do you want to focus on now?" Simon asked.

"I want to focus on figuring my life out. I've been in limbo for so long, directionless for months, but if I'm honest it's more like years. I'm tired of feeling like a failure. Do you all ever feel that way?" Winter asked, feeling immensely vulnerable.

Michael shifted in his seat and said, "I'm the king of directionless. For as long as I can remember, I wanted to play baseball. I was always one of the top players, and my senior year college scouts came to watch me play. It was a rough game, but in the last inning I hit a home run. I won the game, and all these scouts were there to see it happen. Instead of running it home, I decided to show off and milk that moment. I wanted to do a slide into the home base because I had the time. I raised my hands into the air, soaking in the moment. The crowd cheered and then I went into the slide. But my cleat went one way, and my ankle went the other. I ended up breaking my left ankle, and I was inches away from home base; the other team won the game. I felt my humiliation and shame far more than the pain of my ankle. I missed out on that chance and lost the game for my team. Nobody wanted a player who got injured doing something as stupid as that. I had ended the dream of my life before it had a chance to begin. I felt like the biggest failure on the planet. But I've recovered, almost, from the loss. I'm doing other things I like to do. Part of my thrill-seeking has increased since that dream died, and I've found other things I enjoy, like living in Uganda, and just experiencing life. I just try to hold on to the belief that I'll find a new direction. And while I figure out what to, I'm purposefully being appreciative of exactly where I am in my life. That baseball goal, at that moment, must not have been the right time for me, and that's all right."

"Michael I think you're a deeper person than you might get credit for being," Winter said.

"Winter, don't tell him that or he'll have to start buying shirts with an extra-large opening for his head, "Alexis said.

"Alexis, answer Winter's question. I know you can relate to failure," Michael said, grinning.

"Dude, one day! Give me one day where you only say wonderful things about me."

"Only if you can do the same for me," Michael said.

"Forget I said that then," Alexis retorted, laughing. "But he's right. I can relate. I come from a long line of lawyers," Alexis said. "My mother always thought I'd join that profession, but when I told her I want to travel and find odd jobs, like working at a cafe around the world, she thought I was joking. She doesn't understand why I love what I do, and whenever she tells her friends about me, she embellishes. When I was in Italy, and I told her I was learning Italian, that translated into me studying abroad. When I was in Europe working as a camp counselor, I was learning about impoverished youth's access to enrichment programs. I tried the lawyer thing, and I failed, and I thought I was making the adult decision by going after this profession that felt big and hard. I thought I was doing the right thing by doing what other people expected of me. I thought it was brave to push forward, but I wasn't brave at all. I began being brave when I started listening to the whispers of my heart."

They all sat in silence for a moment. "What about you, Simon?" Winter asked. Simon leaned forward in his chair and started to share his experience with failure.

"I'm the oldest one here by about seven years, so I've had seven more years to fail. If you told me when I was seventeen that I'd be working for a non-profit in Uganda, I wouldn't have believed you. It wasn't on my radar, but a lot of other things were. At one point, I was in a band—"

Michael began to laugh loudly. "I forgot about that! You were! I still have the pictures somewhere in my room at home. Do you remember your spiky hair? You practically used a million jars of gel to make your hair stand up. I swear your hair was so hard you could have cut through cement. You were a great drummer, but you looked ridiculous!"

"Michael, you are a truth teller to a fault. I did look pretty interesting, though," Simon admitted before continuing. A smile of remembrance settled onto his face. "At other times in my life I wanted to be a psychologist, pediatrician, and park ranger. I've failed at least three times at every aspiration I've ever chased. The first time I applied for the internship at The Life Cafe, I didn't make the cut. I tried for three years and was finally accepted. Over that time, I wanted to give up so much because I felt jilted and embarrassed, but I knew I wanted it. On my fourth attempt, I was accepted, and now I live here. I feel like people associate failure with weakness, with not being good enough, but I believe it's the opposite. Failure takes strength. It takes fortitude, resilience, and unwavering belief to relentlessly work towards a goal you have; and that's the only way you'll achieve it. Setbacks will always come." Simon's blue-green eyes shone fiercely and Winter knew this next line was meant for her ears. "You just have to stay the path."

CHAPTER TWENTY-THREE—DIVE LIKE A SWAN

After a couple weeks of being in Jinja, it hit Winter that her birthday was coming up. June 17 was not far off. It was just a week and a half away. Michael and Alexis made every day lively for Winter, so much so that her birthday had slipped her mind. She spent her days at the cafe sweeping and mopping, working the cash register in the shop, and serving food. She, Alexis and Michael all felt like they'd run half marathons by the time they closed the cafe doors.

"Well, ladies," Michael said one night after locking the doors. "I'm heading out soon. I was offered a job back home," Michael said.

"That's wonderful!" Alexis screamed, hugging Michael.

"Michael, that's awesome! I'm happy for you," Winter said, hitting him with a dish towel.

"I'm going to be an adventure tour guide in Colorado. I'll take people rock climbing, kayaking, backpacking. You name it and I'll probably be doing it!" He said, puffing out his chest.

"We need to celebrate!" Alexis said. Winter nodded in spirited agreement.

"I already know how I want to celebrate," he said.

"How?" Winter asked. Michael's face spread into a wide grin.

"Oh no," Alexis said. "He wants all of us to go bungee jumping with him."

Simon walked in then, carrying a stack of papers. "Have you all heard the good news?"

"Yes, and we heard the other news as well," Alexis said.

"What are you talking about?" Simon asked, confused.

"Michael wants all of us to go bungee jumping with him," Winter answered.

"Come on, brother," Michael said, lifting his eyebrows.

"Michael, I have a feeling you are going to be my destruction one day," Simon said, rubbing his forehead.

"Yes! I knew I could count on you," Michael shouted.

Before Winter ever left for Ireland, when this journey was still just a thought in her mind, this was how she'd envisioned facing her fear of heights. *What a way to end my time here.* Winter was taken aback by the thought. She'd not planned on leaving Jinja quite so soon. She'd been gone from home for almost six weeks. It felt early to uproot and go to a new place, but Winter was spurred by Michael's news. She wanted to face the rest of her fears and go home triumphantly changed, but she still had most of her list and that fact was never far outside of Winter's mind. Though she loved being in Uganda, she wanted to leave and challenge herself with more fear conquering. Her budget would only stretch for one more city and Winter already knew where she was going.

"Fearless One?" Michael asked, bringing Winter back to the conversation.

"I'll go for you, Michael," she said. Michael pumped his fist in the air.

"Alexis, are you going to go?" Winter asked.

"I don't know about this one. Michael, I love you, man, but the way the cord snaps your body gives me chills," Alexis said. "But I'll watch!"

Michael put an arm around Alexis and said, "Fine, I guess you can take pictures."

"Great! Now, there is one way I know how we can all celebrate!" Alexis said, leading them all upstairs to the living room.

She pulled out an old vinyl and placed it on the record player. The rhythm of multiple drums filled the room. Alexis twirled around and lifted her arms into the air, shaking her head back and forth. "I'm not going to be the only one who dances here today," she said. Alexis jumped in between the other three and put her face in each of theirs as she snapped her fingers. "Come on!" She yelled to the beat of the song.

Slowly each of them began to dance. Michael and Simon heard a different beat than Winter and Alexis. Michael tried to moon walk and tripped over the side table. He fell over it and knocked a cup of water onto the floor.

"Walk it off! Walk it off! Alexis called out through bouts of laughter. Without a trace of embarrassment, he got right back up, swung his arms to the sides, clapped his hands, and rejoined the dance.

***

The morning of Winter meeting the last fear she'd encounter in Jinja, she woke up cursing Michael. *What if the rope snaps? What if they miscalculate and send me diving to the depths of my untimely death? What if....* The morning went on and on like this, her brain rattled off irrational yet understandable fears about what could potentially happen. Michael was the picture of calm. The only time Winter saw his emotions change was when they walked up to the bungee jumping platform. Simon kept muttering over and over to himself these words: "I can't believe I'm doing this. I can't believe I'm doing this. Michael this is for you, but I can't believe I'm doing this."

"I'll take your pictures," Alexis said, turning on her camera.

Michael clapped his hands together and kept yelling, "Yeah! Woo!" before he was even tied to the cords. Two employees stood on the platform suspended in the air, and asked three terrible words; "Who's going first?"

"I do not like that question. I might even despise it," Winter said, shaking her head back and forth.

"Why not?" One of the instructors asked, bemused.

"Because it means I'm going at some point," Winter said in a manic tone.

Winter started to step back, trying to get out of going first, but possibly sensing the fact that she might sneak out of it all together, Michael and Simon both pointed to her.

"Get her ready, guys," Michael said.

"Really? I'm not going to run away! There's nowhere to go!" She yelled at them. They both pushed her forward.

"We insist," Simon said.

Michael looked at his brother and said, "Hey, don't think you're getting out of it. I might make you go next. Now, Winter if you could raft the Nile I have complete faith in you to do this, too."

Winter stepped up to the platform as the men wrapped thick cables around her ankles.

"They just don't want to admit that they need you to go first," Alexis called out.

"Is this your first time bungee jumping?" One of the men asked. He had an Australian accent.

"I must be the most obvious person to read in the universe."

"Even some of the regulars get that rush of nerves before the jump," he said. Winter half listened as they spoke reassuring words of how safe she'd be.

"Do you want to be dipped into the Nile on your way down?" The other instructor asked.

"No. I'd like to come back up alive today. Maybe tomorrow, though."

They stood Winter up and walked her to the edge of the board. The idea of jumping from it made Winter light-headed. The dark green board was rusted looking, but sturdy.

"Okay, love, see that building out there?" Asked the Australian instructor. He pointed his finger into the distance, and Winter could make out a yellow arrow on the top of a building.

"I do. Why?"

"Just swan dive out towards that arrow," he said.

"You have far too much confidence in my abilities," Winter told him.

"You can do it."

Winter was supposed to nod in agreement, but she shook her head in the opposite direction. The word 'no' began to form on her lips.

"I'm not a bird. I can't swan dive off this thing."

He hid a burst of laughter under his breath. The other man walked over and stopped next to Winter. "How would you like to do it?" He asked.

"I want to close my eyes and fall forward," she said softly.

"That seems scarier to me, but I'm not the one jumping," he said.

The Australian guy spoke again, "We'll count down from ten and then you can go."

Winter gripped the side railings, and they each placed a hand on her back, which she eyed suspiciously. Michael, Simon, and Alexis walked over and said, "We'll count too." The six of them counted down together. Ten. Nine. Eight. Seven. Six. Five. Four. Three. Two. One.

"Here's to seeking a bigger life," Winter whispered to herself.

She let her body fall forward. The intensity of the wind in Winter's face made tears pour from her eyes. She let out a scream as her momentum increased. The wind blew Winter's cheeks back. She was barely able to keep her eyes open. The water below was rising to Winter at an amazing speed. But after that initial yell of undiluted fear, Winter looked around as her body defied gravity. She could see the city of Jinja for miles and lush treetops stretching the length of the Nile beneath her. Buildings in the distance stood tall. She was as high as free-flying birds in the sky, and it hit Winter, fully, where she was and what she was doing.

Then she screamed again, not out of fear, but out of wonder for the world she saw around her, for the heights she'd climbed over the last six weeks, and for the beauty of that moment. When it was over, Winter was pulled into a boat with two Ugandan men waiting to help her out of the cables. Her hair was wild, her face whipped by the wind, and Winter was floating in the contentment that comes with living life.

Michael went next. He swan-dived off the platform, flying high into the air before falling downward. He was an obvious veteran. His ecstatic yells echoed all around them. When Michael reached the boat, he and Winter watched Simon from below while Alexis took pictures. Simon would walk to the tip of the plank and then retreat to the safety of the platform. He did this five times before he finally jumped off. He screamed the whole way down, but then his shouts transformed as he too became filled with wonderment.

***

That night, after spending time on the porch with her friends, Winter climbed into bed and wrote in her journal gifted from Sienna.

I bungee-jumped today! It made my stomach reach into my throat, but I can honestly say that I've never felt more alive. It's not just the rafting and bungee jumping or even the traveling. It's the people I've met along the way, even the brief encounters with faces I won't ever see again, and can't fully recall now. They've all given a personal touch to my trip and connecting with them, hearing their stories of trial and triumph, has imbued in me a brighter sense of life. I guess that's what this existence is about, the people you meet and the contributions you make to one another's lives.

After we bungee jumped, the four of us sat on the back porch. Simon strummed the guitar, Alexis meditated in the distance, and Michael read a book about mountain climbing, and I just kept thinking about how grateful I am for everyone I've met on this adventure. I've loved getting to know these people. Tonight I have an overflow of gratitude for those who surround me, and I want to settle into the sensation of this feeling. So, here's to seeking a bigger life.

Until then, Winter

CHAPTER TWENTY-FOUR—THE BLESSING

"For people's last night's we usually have a little something planned," Simon told Winter a couple days later.

"I don't know if I like the idea of a blessing ceremony, Simon," Michael said as he plopped himself onto the couch.

"Michael, you're not supposed to give it away," Simon told his little brother. "But I'm faithful I'll have you reformed by the end of tonight. There are usually candles, but you can all use your imaginations," he said. They all sat in the living room together in a circle. "A blessing ceremony is simply me saying thanks to you all and offering a bit of encouragement as you leave us here at The Life Cafe. I'll start with you, Alexis."

"I'm not leaving for a couple of weeks yet! Are you trying to get rid of me, Simon?"

"No," he laughed. "Not a chance. But blessing ceremonies are meant to happen with a lot of people."

"Good," she said. Alexis rolled her thumbs, one over the other as she waited.

"When I first received your email asking about volunteering here, I knew I had to say yes. You are the epitome of a free spirit. Everyone who meets you can see that you have a passion for life that is rare, and a natural friendliness that is unsurpassed. You're the person people want to meet because you make them feel safe, welcomed, and seen. You've brought smiles to the customer's faces, you've kept Michael in check, and you've been so open to wherever we took you. As you leave Jinja, I'd like to encourage you to never lose your ability to seek out the good in each new place you find yourself, and to hold on with a death grip to your fierce love of other people who cross your path. I believe it's something needed in this world.

"Aw, goodness, Simon," Alexis said.

"I mean it," he said. "Michael, my dear, annoying little brother, you are one of the most hyper people I've ever known. You're always up for a good time. From bungee jumping to skydiving, to rappelling. My life has flashed before my eyes too many times since knowing you, but it's your sensitivity to other's needs that I hope you never let go of. You may not always have the perfect words to convey that, but you always seek to make other people feel at ease, to calm their nerves. Maybe you understand how to do that because you find your comfort in discomfort. You live off your heart beating faster, and you're drawn to those whom that doesn't come naturally to. I encourage you to never lose your heart for other people, and to cherish your ability to make them breathe a little easier."

Michael smiled gently and nodded his head. His eyes were soft, giving away how touched he was by his brother's words.

"Winter, you haven't been with us as long, but I feel I gained a friend. I've watched you silently endure through your struggles since the day you arrived. As you dealt with nuanced cultural histories that define people's interactions today, and sometimes resulted in you being ignored, disliked, or a person of intrigue, you still came out each morning with a face full of hope for the start of a new day. I'd like to encourage you to become a storyteller, to start sharing those words that live in your mind and put them out in the world for other people to hear. You might have to fight to be heard when you're overrun, but I sincerely believe that when you speak, people will listen. I can honestly say that I've learned from you, been impressed by you, and am proud at having witnessed your journey for a brief time. I'll miss your legendary facial expressions."

Simon's words settled into Winter. Become a storyteller. "I really appreciate your words, Simon," Winter said, feeling tears wet her cheeks. Simon's words struck a deep chord. Gratefulness welled up in Winter's core.

"Simon, stop making people emotional!" Michael shouted.

"Sorry, I'm done now," he said with a gentle smile.

"So what should we do for the rest of our last night together?" Winter asked, changing the subject.

"I've got that covered," Alexis said, and then she hooked up the projector and pointed it to a blank wall. Alexis put up the pictures from bungee jumping. Simon made chai and coffee for the picture show. They all held their stomachs from laughing so hard at the images of Simon and Winter's petrified faces and Michael's blissful one.

"Where are you all heading next? Do you know?" Simon inquired as they scrolled through the photos.

"I think it might be time to head home for me. I want to see my nieces and nephews," Alexis said.

"Have you already forgotten that I'm going home for a job?" Michael asked in jest.

"Are you kidding me? I'm counting down the days. I'm excited to see where you go in life," Simon responded.

A smile lifted Winter's lips. She always knew where her last destination was going to be, the last place she would face the rest of her fears before returning home. The scents of her childhood babysitter's house wafted into her memories. Cinnamon, coriander, cloves, ginger, cardamom, and the vivid colors of turmeric and red chilies. Her mouth watered from remembering Mrs. Kapoor giving her a taste of her immensely sweet rice pudding, as she cooked it over the stovetop. Winter adored her time spent next to Mrs. Kapoor in her kitchen.

The Kapoor family moved away when Winter was ten and she'd not seen them since then. But Mrs. Kapoor's stories lingered still. She always told Winter tales about Mumbai. Mrs. Kapoor had laid out the land so intricately that whenever Winter recalled her stories, she felt she was walking down the streets of Mumbai herself, and now Winter wanted to put real life images to the wonderings of her young mind.

"I'm going to India."

***

Winter worked her last day in the cafe. Michael left for America the day before.

"Make sure you face the rest of your fears," he'd said, gently nudging Winter.

"I'll try."

"And Alexis, don't replace me."

"Never could. There is no one that gets under my skin like you, friend."

Michael pulled the two of them into a rough hug and then Simon drove him to the airport in the big, white suburban.

On Winter's work breaks during her last day's in Uganda, she researched well-reviewed hostels in Mumbai. The winner was near a university, and Winter thought that would be helpful for meeting people when she arrived. She paid for a double room and released a quiet, steady breath and stepped back from the computer.

The night before leaving for Mumbai, after spending the evening with Simon and Alexis on the back porch drinking chai, Winter packed. She folded up her clothes and tucked them into the suitcase. Winter picked up her camouflage jacket and held it out in front of her. She didn't think it possible for the coat to look more weathered, but it did. After a moment, Winter sighed, rolled up the jacket, and placed it in the bag with her other belongings. It was almost midnight, but Winter knew sleep would not come swiftly. Her departure to India was mere hours away and she was full of nervous energy. She searched for the stack of letters from Sienna.

"I haven't read one in a few days," Winter said as she pulled out one more letter from the dwindling stack.

Winter,

I don't have too much to say except this: I know it was you who found my salted caramels! You've always known where to look to find the best of my stash. Even when you were young, you had a talent for seeking out what you wanted. You wouldn't stop until you found what you were searching for. So, it shouldn't surprise me that your penchant for seeking hasn't left you. You've set off to find the best of what lies beyond, beyond what you're familiar with, beyond what you're comfortable with. My darling daughter, don't give up when things get difficult. Life is sweet, and sometimes we just have to work a bit harder to find that enjoyment. I know you can understand that.

Love Dad

P.S. I've changed the location of my stash. Good Luck!

***

When the afternoon arrived for Winter to leave Jinja, she sat on the porch writing in her journal. A gust of wind blew around her, lifting the pages of her notebook. Winter was enjoying breathing in the scents and sounds of that early Ugandan morning when a shadow moved in front of her, blocking the sunlight. She looked up and saw Alexis.

"Let's stay in touch, all right?" Alexis said.

"Without question," Winter replied before standing to hug Alexis.

Simon drove into the driveway and jumped out of the suburban. "I have chai in portable mugs for our ride."

"Good man," Alexis said.

"Thank you for noticing, Alexis."

"Anytime. Well, I better get back to work. I'll be waiting for an update, Winter."

"Same here," Winter said. The girls hugged one last time before Alexis walked into the cafe. Simon turned to Winter.

"You ready?" He asked.

Winter looked around the cafe lawn, at the wooden sign that read The Life Cafe, and said, "Yes."

As they spoke in the yard, Sandy walked down the road heading towards the café. Upon seeing Simon her eyes lit up.

"Oli otya, Simon," she said. "How are you this morning?"

"Bittersweet, Sandy. All our volunteers are leaving us. My brother left a couple days ago, and Winter is leaving now. Alexis won't be far behind." Sandy's eyes moved to Winter. Their warmth made Winter wish she'd talked to Sandy more.

"And how have you enjoyed your time in Uganda, Winter?" She asked.

"I'm not sure I have the words to describe it," Winter said honestly. She'd experienced joy in its most rare and raw form, but she'd also met new kinds of need that left her with unanswered questions.

"I think you've got the words hidden somewhere," Simon smiled.

"It's been an adventurous and eye-opening time," Winter settled on saying. That fit.

"I was hoping some of the volunteers might take language classes with me," Sandy said.

"I'm sorry about that. We'll definitely make time for the next group," Simon replied. "They should be staying longer so they'll need them."

"You teach languages?" Winter asked. Sandy raised her eyebrows, signifying yes.

"How long have you been a teacher?"

"Many years," she said with a smile. "I used to teach numerous subjects, but now I am strictly a teacher of language when I'm not here cooking and running the cafe."

"What drew you to teaching language?" Winter asked.

She inclined her head towards the bit of sky that peeked through the clouds. Then she raised her finger energetically and said, "Because language is life, but it changes across the world! For example, when a group of men climbed Mount Everest, every country perceived the feat differently. In one country the papers read: 'Man conquers mountain.' In another country it said: "Mountain Befriends Man.""

She looked down at Winter and grinned, her hands still in the air.

"Perception is everything. It shades our societies and colors our beliefs. Words are special. They are the life-breath of thought; the root of perception," Sandy said.

Winter nodded, entirely lost in Sandy's words.

"If you take nothing else from this place, take this one piece of knowledge. It's the only thing I know," she said to Winter. "The world turns, and we don't feel it moving. The sun, though millions of miles away, rises and gives warmth to nations. The moon, though over 230,000 miles away, has the power to shift oceans. How much more can we do living beside one another?" She smiled, told Winter it was nice to meet her, and with a sharp wink, she turned and walked into the cafe.

Simon looked to Winter and said, "Sandy is one of a kind."

At the airport, Simon lifted Winter's bag from the car. "You'll need to get that wheel fixed," he said, pointing to her luggage. Winter shook her head as she stared at the broken wheel on her suitcase.

"I don't think it'll survive the trip," Winter said with a chuckle. It had progressively worsened along the journey.

"Make it to Mumbai safely," Simon told Winter, sounding very much like an older brother.

"I've already arranged for a driving service from the airport," Winter said, lifting her eyebrows.

"Look at you," Simon said.

"I know, right? I picked up some tips from Alexis." Winter's smiled faded. She breathed in deeply. She wanted to go and see what else existed in the world, but the unknown, though she longed for new adventure, still scared her. Simon reached out his arm for a side hug and rested his head on Winter's.

"I expect good things from you, Winter." She snorted in his arms.

"We'll just have to see about that," Winter said.

"It's like Michael said," Simon spoke, looking down at her. "We've all got unique contributions. Callings. I'm interested in what some of yours will be."

"Me too," Winter said genuinely. The friends who surrounded Winter throughout her life, like Sienna, seemed to be masters at answering the age-old question of What-To-Do-Next, and she wanted to at least be adequate in the field.

"Do you think you've found one of yours?" She asked.

"I do. Being here, learning and working with the people from the cafe over the last five years has been a part of it, but I think we can have more than one gift to give. Whatever it is that makes you burn with a desire for life, is a decent place to start. You might wander along the way. You might find that you have countless paths to choose from, but we all have purpose, no matter the size, that we can fulfill every morning we breathe fresh air. It could be connecting with the people around us, rooting ourselves into a community, spreading goodness, raising a family, being an ear when someone needs it, giving a voice to the voiceless, or winning the Nobel Peace Prize. Your passions can alter every day, and new purpose can fill your spirit each week. Just remember they are there waiting to be found. I could be wrong; it's happened a few times in my life. But I believe we each have a God purpose, a course in life tailor made to fit each of us, that will make this world more accepting, more beautiful, more human."

"I do believe we each have a purpose. I can't say I'm close to finding mine, but I'm trying to be present along the way.

"I think that's the best any of us can do. And don't forget the importance of living each day as you discover your dreams. I wish you luck, Winter. And Godspeed in India."

Simon waved to Winter as she walked through the automatic doors at the airport. On June 10th, she stepped into the fluorescent lighting and took the first step of the last leg of her journey.

CHAPTER TWENTY-FIVE—MONSOON SEASON

The plane landed smoothly. Passengers stretched and grabbed heavy loads of luggage from above their heads. Winter slept during most of the six-hour flight. She walked outside the airport as rain poured down from the sky and onto the billowing canopies of Mumbai's International Airport. Winter scanned the crowd and found her name written on a white board. The hostel she picked was a long drive from the airport, but Winter learned in Uganda that distance proved to be a positive thing for newcomers.

Winter was mesmerized by the scenes taking place outside the car windows. She was utterly enmeshed in what she saw. Small buildings with slanted tin roofs, fading tarp, and other makeshift materials hovered above the heads of groups of people speaking Marathi. Piles of brightly colored garbage sat in mounds on the ground. Dogs with protruding rib cages sniffed the piles hopefully, as bright lights and honking from surrounding cars filled Winter's senses.

Handkerchiefs covered the faces of passerby on vehicles wanting to avoid the fumes and exhaust that circled the roads in shifting clouds. Motorbikes squeezed by cars and vans, and rickshaws weaved in between vehicles with an unearthly agility Winter didn't expect machinery to be capable of performing.

Streetlights seemed more like suggestions than carved out rules. Honking was used not out of anger, but as a friendly spatial reminder to your fellow cars. As they neared the city, Winter could see the gentle curves of Hindu temples come into view. Standing out against the pale blue sky. Street stands with decorated elephants, candle holders, and newspapers filled the sidewalks. Signs written in elegant, looping Hindu letters guided large buses carrying heavy passenger loads.

Winter soaked in her first few moments in Mumbai, transfixed by the vibrancy of this new place. The whole city seemed to buzz, like the gentle hum of a rhythmic song. If Winter listened closely she could hear the steady beat of Mumbai life surrounding her.

The taxi driver couldn't speak English and Winter couldn't speak Marathi. So they rode in silence, occasionally smiling in the other's direction. When the car stopped in busy traffic, small children asking for money would crowd around the taxi. Winter smiled lightly at them.

They pulled up to the hostel an hour later. "Thank you," Winter said, not sure if he understood. She passed him the money, and he bobbed his head.

Winter stepped out of the car and stood outside on the street. The smell of hot spices on cooking food filled the air. Winter inhaled and then moved brightly forward, over the uneven concrete, and then she felt a tug and heard a popping sound. Winter looked down at her luggage. Her one good wheel had snapped off her bag.

Winter shook her head as she stared down at the suitcase. She knew it wouldn't survive the trip. Winter picked it up by the handle and pushed open the doors to the hostel. The inside of the hostel had white walls and wooden fixtures. It was narrow and extremely hot. Monsoon season had arrived, along with its signature heavy rains and searing heat. Sweat began to trickle down Winter's face. Winter carried her suitcase up to the counter and set it down on the floor with a hard thud.

"Hi, I'm Winter Wright. I have a reservation for a room."

"Welcome to Mumbai, Winter," the woman at the desk said. Her long, radiant hair was braided. A red sari with gold accents draped her body. Her rose-gold nose ring glinted, catching Winter's eye. "I just need identification and then I can give you a room key."

Winter dug in her bag and pulled out her license.

"You will love Mumbai. The city is so lively!" She said with enthusiasm.

"I'm sure I will. Thank you," Winter said, taking the room key. She carried her things up three flights of stairs to her room. Winter unlocked the door, kicked it open, and a wave of heat hit her. She dropped her heavy, useless bag onto the floor and looked around the room.

Clothes hung to dry on the window sill, and open bags were strewn across the floor. Winter stepped over the debris and went to a thin cot perched above the cracked floor. Winter noticed that whenever she left somewhere familiar, she had a small moment of mourning. She'd miss the friends she'd made, the room she slept in, the comfort of knowing a space, a place, and the people who occupy it. The hazardous room only amplified those feelings.

Suddenly, the room door flung open, and a girl around Winter's height strode inside. Mehndi covered her hands and arms, a beautiful hand-painted design of shapes and flowers. The girl wore multiple silver rings she'd found at various street shops. Her large hazel eyes widened with excitement when she saw Winter.

"Hi! You must be my new roommate. The other girl just left. I'm Lucie! Sorry for the mess," she said. She walked over to the window and started to pick up the underwear she'd hung to dry, stepping on a mess of clothes as she went.

"Oh, no problem. I'm Winter."

"Are you just traveling through or we will be roommates for a while?" Lucie asked.

"Not sure yet. I might be here for a few weeks. I'm just doing a bit of traveling on my own," Winter said, examining the messy floor.

"I do that all the time! I love traveling solo and then meeting up with friends in different places. Are you meeting anyone?" Lucie asked.

"I don't know anyone here," Winter said. Lucie's eyes grew large at Winter's words.

"You don't know anybody at all?" Lucie asked Winter with pity in her eyes. Winter shifted uncomfortably.

"Sorry, it's just that I've spent my life moving around. I'm the only daughter of parents who were traveling doctors. My family was always on the move. Growing up, I absolutely hated it. I'd always be going different places, and the first few weeks could be rough cause I didn't know anyone. When I got older I saw what a blessing it was and now I adore moving and finding new homes around the world. I did a study abroad here in Mumbai during college so I have a few friends in the area."

The entirety of Lucie's life had been spent moving, making friendships that sometimes only lasted for a moment. She'd had to say goodbye to friends from the farthest reaches of the world when her family moved to a new place. Lucie knew what loneliness in a new country entailed. She shook her head with vigor.

"I can't let you be completely alone in a new country! You can be my friend— and my friends will be your friends. I came back to grab a couple things and then I'm heading out for a dinner party, but before that I'm going to a free yoga class. The school across the street offers it once a week. You should come, too!" Lucie stopped talking and looked Winter over. Winter wore torn jeans and a wrinkled, white t-shirt.

"You might want to wear something more comfortable. I have clothes clean if you want to borrow something," she said, pulling at a pile of clothes on her bed, some of which toppled to the floor. "Get whatever you need. We won't be back for a while," Lucie instructed. Winter stared at Lucie. She was like a miniature tornado in every way. Lucie moved through the room, tossing things into the air as she searched for a change of clothes. Even the way she spoke was rapid and unpredictable.

"Is there some place where I can get some rupees?" Winter asked. Lucie put a hand on her hip and thumped her foot against the cluttered floor before answering.

"Oh yeah! There's an ATM that we'll pass on the way to the school."

"Great. So, do you ever plan to live in one place? Or will you travel until the end of your days?" Winter asked with a dreamy smile.

"I'm gonna see as much as I can while I can, but I'll settle where my roots are."

"Where are your roots?"

"I'm from the West Coast, baby! It was our home base every time we came back to the states." She said, raising a peace sign into the air. "My grandmother is from the Czech Republic, and growing up I'd spend every other summer there with her and my cousins. So I feel like I'm from two places, but I live in California. Oh, and just so you know, there are some creepy dudes in this hostel. Avoid them at all costs. Sometimes when I don't want a weird guy talking to me, I pretend I can only speak Czech," she said.

Winter burst out in laughter as she searched her degenerating bag and found a change of clothes at the bottom of the suitcase.

"By the way, there's a girl's only bathroom here. It took me two days to figure that out. One morning I was brushing my teeth next to two half naked, smelly guys, and realized there had to be a better option that I was unaware of. There was."

"Thanks for the heads up!" Winter said.

"That's what I'm here for!" Lucie remarked brightly.

They left the hostel and headed for the university's gym. Winter and her new friend collected a bevy of stares from locals as they waited to cross the busy traffic.

"Is there a crosswalk light we should wait for?" Winter asked Lucie. Lucie laughed so hard Winter thought she might have stopped breathing.

"No, no," she said in between labored breaths. "There isn't." Winter wondered if Lucie's laughter would cease, but then she wiped her eyes. "You're a funny one. I'm going to have to keep you around. I know the roads are intimidating, but you just have to go for it. You'll get used to it fast, though, because you have to."

With that, Lucie grabbed Winter's hand and raced across the four lanes of traffic that seemed to move in six different directions, without an accident occurring. A speeding black and yellow rickshaw swerved just behind them as their feet landed on the curb.

"What was that?" Winter asked, staring at the three-wheeled vehicle with open doors that sped past them.

"Rickshaw," Lucie said. They're great for short distance traveling."

"That looks a bit more comfortable than riding a boda-boda," Winter panted on the other side of the road.

"A what?" Lucie asked, wrinkling her nose.

"A bike taxi," Winter said.

"Interesting. I think I'd like that if I could be the driver." Lucie put her hands into the air and pretended she was driving an imaginary boda-boda through busy traffic. She raised one of her eyebrows and asked Winter, "Would you like a ride, pretty lady?"

"I'm okay. I think I'll walk," Winter said with a laugh.

They walked underneath the campus' entry way, and Winter's gaze was taken by women who hunched over with handmade brooms, sweeping dirt on the ground. A few stray dogs and a couple small monkeys ran past the women, disturbing their work.

"Have you done yoga before?" Lucie asked as she applied lip balm. Winter turned her attention to her new companion.

"Yeah, I have. Two of my friends, Sienna and Ali, were my college roommates and we practiced together. We'd move all the furniture and stand in a circle to do yoga between studying. Just before we finished college, Ali became a certified yoga teacher, and I went to a few of her classes. I'm not great or anything, but I'm familiar."

"You're ahead of me! My first time in a yoga class, I fell over multiple times. I undoubtedly passed the acceptable amount of times to knock over your yoga neighbor, but so many of those movements are difficult! The teachers stand at the front of the room, and they're like, 'Fold yourself into a pretzel and smile, and breathe and unfold, and stand on your head and smile and breathe.' The teachers make it seem as if it's easy to fold yourself in a million directions and breathe calmly. For me, it's one or the other. That's not even true. I can only do the breathing calmly part," she said as she hopped over a puddle of murky water.

Winter hadn't stopped smiling since she met Lucie. Winter knew this was presumptuous and romanticized, but part of her envisioned India to be the place where she'd heal her core and experience a sort of spiritual transcendence. *And where better to start than with yoga—the practice of mental, emotional, physical, and spiritual balance—in its birthplace?* Winter thought. Lucie and Winter entered the L-shaped room where the class was being held and grabbed thin rugs with tasseled ends from against the wall. Lucie started for the front of the room and laid her mat down.

"You don't want to go to the back row?" Winter asked, hoping she didn't sound too obvious.

"I prefer to be right in the middle of things. Also, when I fell, I hit my head on the wall. So it's for safety reasons as well. Don't get too close," she warned with a lopsided smirk.

Winter wiped a bit of sweat from her head. The heat was overwhelming. Outside, it was a threatening eighty-eight degrees, weather too hot for a girl from Midwestern America who lived beside the air conditioner during the summer months. She adored the cool of fall, the changing trees, and sweet air.

The teacher came into the room while Winter sat fanning herself. She wore a pink sari wrapped around her plump body. Her presence brought with it the faint smell of jasmine. She rose her small hands to brush away a piece of pitch black hair that shone even in the darkened room. The woman tucked the fly away strands that had fallen from her messy chignon behind her ear. The air was so humid Winter felt it stuck to her skin, creating another level of heat that even the falling rain outside could not rinse away. A fly buzzed in front of her face, taunting Winter. She swatted at the bug, but noticed that everyone around her sat with legs crossed, looking serene despite the loud buzzing. Winter quickly adjusted herself in an attempt to appear calm.

"We will begin," the woman said with her hands in the prayer position. "Take a deep breath in, and out, in and out," she said.

Winter followed the movements and felt the air expand her chest. The slow release calmed her thoughts. This was exactly the moment she had been looking forward to, practicing yoga in India.

"Stop!" The teacher's voice cut through Winter's rumination, making her eyes pop open. "Now rapid breathing. Follow my example."

She raised a hand to the right side of her nose, pressing her nostril inward as she breathed quickly in and out the left side of her nose. Winter glanced around the room, still rattled, and followed suit.

"And stop!" She shouted out to the room. Winter couldn't help it. She let out a small bout of laughter. When she'd envisioned yoga in its homeland, Winter imagined being surrounded by lush green plants, the scents of essential oils, and calming voices that practically sang the instructions to you as you folded your body into positions that would infuse ancient healing into your bones.

This was not close at all. The chasm between her daydream and reality was so far off it made her stifle fits of laughter whenever the teacher yelled instructions at her. The room Winter sat in didn't have a plant in sight, and the only smell that filled the room was eighteen hot bodies. Thin mats lined every available inch of the room, and the instructor's voice made Winter jump and feel slightly chastised every time she spoke. So Winter laughed at how wrong she'd been, at the perfect image she created in her mind and the experience that lay before her. Winter found she preferred the reality.

"Now, take your hands and rub your palms together," she spoke quietly then, for the first time since the class began. Everyone rose their hands to their chests, just above their hearts and began to create friction between their palms. The room filled with the low rumble of deep breaths.

"Heat," she said, as she sat incredibly still, "is healing for your eyes. Place your hands over your eyes and let the warmth sink into your skin," she called out.

Winter followed, letting the heat created from her skin move over her eyelids, and she began to feel calmness rise. The rest of the class was filled with the small instructor shouting out a range of demands. Some Winter recognized, not by their ancient names, but by the familiarity of the movements. At the end of class, Winter felt more aware of her body, more settled in it. She folded up the slim, hand woven rug. Red, purple, and white threads interlaced, forming a rainbow of shades and patterns.

"When I do yoga at home I never sweat," Lucie said, wiping at her glistening forehead. The smile on her face reached her ears. It was almost perfectly symmetrical except for the right side of her mouth which slanted downward, making her smile distinctly crooked and entirely memorable.

"Whenever I come to this yoga class I'm reminded I'm not doing it the right way. Oh! There's Amala," Lucie shouted. Her finger pointed out the window onto the campus. A short Indian woman with shining black hair, deeply sun-kissed skin, and onyx eyes filled with life, walked on a pathway. Lucie ran outside and called out to her friend.

"Yo! Amala! I've found another person to join us tonight. This is Winter! She's my hostel roommate. She has no friends, so we have to be her friends while she's here," Lucie called out.

A few people stared at Lucie as she yelled across the campus, which only made her yell louder. Winter wished she could shrink into the shrubbery. Amala turned and started walking towards the two of them when Lucie began singing, "Woah, girl! Amala, you look so good. Tell me all your secrets!" Amala laughed at Lucie's greeting.

"Thank you, Lucie," Amala said in a musical accent before turning her attention to Winter. "That's a beautiful name."

"Wish I could take credit for it," Winter said.

Amala smiled and said, "I'm glad you'll be joining us. Are you veg or non-veg?"

"Am I a what?" Winter asked.

"Do you eat meat or are you a vegetarian?" Lucie asked.

"I do. Not a lot, but I do."

"There will be both at the party, and Lucie, I've made rice pudding for tonight as you requested."

Winter felt this trip was meant to be when Amala spoke those heavenly words.

"You're amazing! I'll buy you anything you want. Sky's the limit! As long as it's under $20!" Lucie shouted.

"If you think rice pudding is worth it, be my guest. I'm sorry to say I can't stay out late tonight. I'm working on a story tomorrow."

"What story?" Lucie asked. Before Amala could answer, Lucie turned to Winter and said, "Amala is an amazing journalist. She's had several pieces published. Her work is usually centered on human right's issues. Amala makes me feel like I'm slacking in the life department. When she tells me about her journalistic endeavors, I feel the pressing need to do more with myself."

Winter laughed. "I know the feeling. I don't have a job or anything back home. I feel so useless sometimes."

Lucie placed a hand on Winter's arm and said, "Oh my gosh. I can relate to that. I just got fired from my waitressing job because my boss said I talked so much to the customers that I forgot to bring other people their orders. Back home, I'm the enigma in my group of friends. They've all known what they wanted to do since an abnormally early age. I'm like, look, when I was seven I was digging in the dirt like a normal child, not planning out my future!"

"We can join in angst over our clouded futures," Winter said.

"I'm sure you'll both see clear skies soon," Amala interjected.

"Which story are you working on tomorrow?" Lucie asked again.

"I'm going to Dharavi slum."

Winter's brows furrowed as she asked, "What's that?"

"It's the largest slum in India. Over a million people live in one square mile."

"Amala told me that only one percent of people in that slum have a private toilet," Lucie added.

"How do other people use the bathroom?" Winter asked.

"Others use a communal toilet if it's working properly. Some people use toilets you have to pay for but the fees are unreasonably high. A lot of people have to use open spaces. For women it can be dangerous because in public restrooms there is fear of assault, and night time brings so many worries. Often the facilities aren't sanitary either. The issue presents many health problems and fear just to do something that is a part of our human makeup.

"I can't imagine what that would be like. Is that the story you're working on?" Winter asked.

"No, I'm working on something different. A small group has been pursuing a water shortage in their community. Each province is allotted a certain amount of water, and they are getting less than half of theirs. In the process of uncovering the missing water they've had death threats from people in positions of authority. I'm covering what they've found out so far. I hope to get them some aid."

If Winter ever doubted her belief that a life should serve more than oneself, she would have been reformed standing next to Amala listening to her talk about people's struggle for water.

"After that I'm covering a story about a group of young orphaned boys who lack proper identification. They don't have birth certificates and can't get government aid because it's as if they don't exist. Then I hope to talk about squatter settlements."

"What are squatter settlements?" Winter asked, wanting to learn as much as she could.

"Sometimes new arrivals will set up homes on the edges of slums. It's illegal to do so, but they have nowhere else to go. They build homes on wastelands, because that's often the place available to them, and when monsoon season comes, along with its heavy rains, they face so many problems because they've constructed homes on low lying ground. I want to cover a story about the factors that contribute to squatters wanting or needing to migrate and the rights they have."

"How long have you been a journalist?" Winter asked, wondering what other stories Amala had unearthed.

"I went back to school a year and a half ago to finish my degree. I had to take a couple years off to help with my family. I like to think that I've always been a journalist in my soul of souls, but I'm still studying. I'll finish at the end of next year," she answered with a smile.

"You're passionate about journalism," Winter said, making an observation. Winter was inspired by Amala's sense of purpose, by the way she talked about her dream.

"Oh, yes. Stories connect people. You don't have to know the person to feel touched by their plight. That's why I love journalism. It enlightens. On the outside it asks, hopefully, unbiased questions, but at its heart, it seeks to uncover and tell a story that will help shine light into dark places."

Lucie looked at her gold wristwatch. "We better get going, or we are going to be late, and we have the best dish."

And so Winter, joining two new friends, began to walk to an apartment on campus next to monkeys that danced in the Mumbai heat. Winter walked with a lightness in her step, because she didn't know what was coming.

CHAPTER TWENTY-SIX—BROKEN PIECES

Winter woke up the next morning with her list of fears circulating in her mind. Lucie had already gone, so Winter turned on the television as she threw her belongings into a shower caddy. Since being outside of America, she'd developed a fascination for other country's television commercials. Winter finished collecting her toiletries for a shower when an advertisement caught her eyes.

A dark Indian man sat alone on the curb hunched over. Passersby took no notice of him. The girl of his dreams couldn't see his lonesome figure, but then a heavenly light entered the screen. A stranger passed him a bottle containing a miracle cream. The man stood up brightly with the feverish sensation of shallow hope. He applied the cream, and it lifted the sun's kiss from his skin, no longer was he invisible or unworthy of attention.

Now he was the man of the moment. His love for the woman who never saw him before was returned tenfold. Strangers stopped walking past him without a glance in his direction; now he drew their attention in hordes. Winter sighed and shook her head back and forth. It was the same message repackaged for a new region.

His worth had increased as his skin was made lighter. She'd not realized how far reaching this notion was. Winter took a quick shower, the images from the commercial rolling around in her mind. In Jinja she'd seen billboards for skin lightening, too. Winter sighed deeply. Chemicals to alter the color of your skin were everywhere. Winter Wright wasn't the only one who'd been told her inherent being was wrong. Winter returned to her room and found Lucie inside.

"I went down to get breakfast in the hostel common room while you were asleep. I was thinking of going to Colaba today for some shopping. Want to come?" She asked brightly.

Winter wasn't feeling up for much sight-seeing, but then she thought about her list of fears. She wasn't going to get any further by sitting on a weathered cot alone.

"Definitely," she said.

The two of them walked down into the hostel lobby. A peeling wooden table held an assortment of foods. Winter took a couple pieces of bread that were similar to the chapati she'd loved in Uganda.

"We can take a taxi if you want," Lucie said. "But I feel very strongly that the train is an experience you have to have."

"Then I have to choose the train," Winter said.

They walked to the train station in Mumbai. Upon arrival, Winter saw women selling wrapped parcels of food from baskets at their feet to train passengers. Their hands were rough and slender. Years of work could be seen on the surfaces of their fingers, the callouses on their knuckles, the wrinkles on their faces. The veins beneath their skin pumped as they tried to sell their wares.

Winter could hear the sounds of a distant train nearing. Seconds later, a train rolled in with multiple cars, each labeled by class and gender. The train came to a stop, and the doors flung open as hundreds of people pushed their way out onto the platform. A young boy got caught between the influx of passengers trying to force their way on and off the open car.

Lucie turned to Winter and said, "You've got to push a bit to get on, or you won't make it. Ready?"

Winter was about to nod when she felt an odd sensation, a macabre tingling down her spine.

"Winter, we won't make it if we don't go now," Lucie warned. But Winter could feel hostile eyes upon her. She sensed tension rising in the air, growing thick as it had when she was a little girl facing a man across the street. Winter looked up and locked eyes with a man on the train. His deadpan stare sent chills throughout her body that made her wish she could exit her skin.

He stared at Winter, singling her out from amongst the crowd, his nose turned up. He hung from a bar on the train door and jutted his fist out forcefully, and then he lifted his middle finger into the air, thrusting his arm towards Winter. Fear and hurt clouded up her lungs, leaving her taking in shallow breaths as his hatred aligned with where she stood. *He can't reach me*, Winter told herself, only half believing.

The train began to pull away, but Winter couldn't let herself exhale, not yet. The man hit his friend and pointed at Winter, continuing to make the gesture with such force it kept her gaze transfixed on him, locked upon his figure as it receded. Winter was too familiar with the look on his face.

She'd seen it before as its owner attempted to conceal it. She'd seen it displayed loudly and with pride. Winter tried to dissect his curled lips and upturned nose, his lifeless eyes filled with disgust, violence, anger, ignorance, and intolerance: hate. That's what Winter saw reflected in the features staring back at her. That's what she saw on his face. Standing there on that platform, Winter couldn't understand the hate her complexion invoked in people. She couldn't fathom the broken humanity it exposed. His eyes moved to Lucie then, he lowered his finger, his gaze softened, and anger flared in Winter's heart.

Lucie turned and placed her hand on Winter's arm.

"Don't take it personally," she said. "All right? He doesn't know you. It's not meant for you."

Winter nodded her head at Lucie, unable to keep eye contact with her sympathetic gaze. Her encounters with prejudice always made her feel ashamed of the skin she lived in, they made her want to hide away. She couldn't count how many of those looks she'd received throughout her life. Winter whispered, "I just need a moment."

She stepped off the platform and into a grassy spot, turning her back to the train. Winter swallowed hard and bit her bottom lip. She told herself it didn't matter how many billboards she saw for skin lightening cream, or how many people didn't see her when they looked into her eyes. She told herself that it didn't matter who hated her. Winter stood alone and unsure with her feet planted in solid earth.

"Do you want to go still? We can stay around town if you'd like," Lucie offered kindly.

Winter didn't want to do anything but disappear. Despite the heat, she longed for her jacket and the protection isolation provided. Winter tried to self-talk herself out of the pit she was sinking into. *I have so much. Look at what you've seen of this world, Winter. Think of the poverty that claims lives. Injustice has engulfed your senses*, she muttered to herself, trying to will her mind out of pain. And yet, she could feel herself beginning to fade, to crack in places that had been rebuilt too many times. Already worn down, her resolve was beginning to collapse.

As she stood next to poverty that made her question the power of good, and with the image of that man's hate fresh, it was then that Winter Wright knew with undeniable certainty that this time in India would break her, or force Winter to be stronger than she'd ever been in her life. It'd be her final undoing or her point of resistance, her time of strength. Winter didn't know where she'd fall yet. She only knew where she hoped she might land.

"Winter," Lucie said softly. Winter collected herself as best she could. She didn't want his hate to touch Lucie's day, too.

"Let's go," she said. Lucie's face was full of concern, but they stood on the platform and waited for the next train. One pulled in after a while and for a second, Winter wished she'd said taxi when she saw the crowd. Lucie charged forward, but Winter was becoming feebler. She only got pushed further away from the train doors. Lucie turned and saw her falling behind.

She came back for Winter, grabbing hold of Winter's arm she pushed a clearing through the crowd. When they finally sat down, Winter was out of breath.

"I don't know if I'd ever get anywhere if I had to do that by myself," Winter said.

"You'll adapt. Believe me. When I came here, I missed my first three trains because of the crowd pushing you around. Now I don't miss any," Lucie said with pride.

They sat in the female-only car. It was a pale blue color with rusted walls and thin, metal bars covering some of the windows. Through the holes in the metal bars, Winter could see outside. She could see the large piles of garbage that lay next to the train's path, and the homes stacked on top of homes that rose into the sky.

"Is there anything I can do?" Lucie asked, breaking the silence that had settled.

"That means a lot to me that you'd ask, but I don't even know how to deal with it," Winter replied. She took a deep breath. Her anger was swelling, and finally Winter snapped. Her eyes narrowed and her voice became louder as she said, "He doesn't know me or the type of person I am!"

Winter shook her head back and forth and sucked in a shallow breath again. "But that's what prejudice is," she said, shrugging her shoulders in defeat. "Assumptions of various levels are made based off the exterior about a person, and then the decision is made that somehow, because of complexion, or religion, who you love or whatever, that you are less human, less alive than them. Your existence is innately less right."

Winter looped her fingers around the bars covering the window. "It inherently enables them to strip away a sliver of someone else's humanity in their minds, and the next cut against them can be larger and deeper while the person remains justified in their minds. Because over time, the idea of another person's humanity has eroded. So their actions, by nature, remain not at all inhuman."

Lucie could see past Winter's anger. Beneath her fury Lucie saw exhaustion and pain. She scooted closer to Winter and wrapped her arm around her frame. Though Winter barely knew Lucie she rested her head on her shoulder.

"I just...I need to know that there is something redeeming, something life-giving woven into the experiences I've had. I have to believe that something good can from them, or I know I'll crumble." Winter's voice cracked as she finished speaking. She lifted her head and looked at Lucie.

Lucie's eyes were soft, filled with empathy and compassion. Their warmth made Winter feel heard, seen, understood.

"I can't stand that kind of ignorance. What's the point of it?" Lucie asked loudly, frustration replacing the kindness in her eyes.

Winter shrugged her shoulders in response, unsure of what to say. It was almost thirteen years ago to the day that Winter had first encountered that brand of hate. Her birthday was just around the corner, and she didn't want to spend it in an unfamiliar place.

"Thanks for listening," Winter said.

"Of course, Winter," Lucie replied wholeheartedly.

After an hour on the train, Lucie and Winter got off in Colaba and stepped into the light of day. They spent the afternoon touring the city. Lucie filled her arms with rich colored fabrics from a popular store filled with teas, clothes, and furniture. Winter glanced at racks of saris, admiring the designs and vivid colors. Lucie bought mounds of fabric and Winter settled on a tin of tea. On the streets of Colaba, Winter and Lucie found stands offering different trinkets and books. Maps and handmade goods lined the sidewalks. Street vendors called out to the girls, trying to persuade them to come over to their stands. They walked arm in arm along the crowded roads.

"Amala told me she did a story on these street shops. Everyone has to close down their stands at a certain time each night." Winter looked at the stands that housed hundreds of earrings, necklaces, and bracelets. Having to pack and unpack the whole stand seemed more than a hassle.

"Sometimes people can bribe police so that they can stay open a bit longer," Lucie finished.

"Lucie, the woman I saw yesterday on the campus who was sweeping the ground, is she a janitor?"

"No. She is Dalit. Are you familiar with the caste system?" Lucie asked, her natural merriment lessening.

"Not fully," Winter confessed.

"Amala explained some of it to me when I first arrived. The caste system divides Hindus into four main groups. One group is considered so low that they're not even included in the caste system. They're known as the untouchables, and they have some of the most dangerous and dirtiest jobs in all of India." She squinted her eyes as her mind worked, recalling what Amala had shared.

"Amala said they renamed themselves 'Dalit.' It means broken or oppressed. Some of their jobs include sweeping the streets or climbing underground to remove human waste from public latrines by hand. It's dangerous work and it affects their health. On top of that they face so much discrimination because they were born Dalit. Many of them don't get a chance to receive an education or face a lot of stigma and prejudice in school. It's just crazy. I used to fight my mom to stay home from school, but kids across the world don't even have the opportunity to go. I don't totally understand this part of it, but the caste system has a weird relationship with skin color. Usually people with lighter skin are in the higher castes and people with darker skin are in the lower castes, or they're Dalit. The part that really struck me when I spoke with Amala was this: It's so difficult for Dalit's to get out of these jobs because their caste is expected to this do work. This is life for millions of people."

Winter knew she'd learn a few things going outside of her country, but this was more than she presumed. The girls walked throughout Colaba, past colonial-era buildings and hordes of tourists. Colaba was a mix of old and new. The Arabian Sea was in front of Winter and Lucie, and its surface was sprinkled with trash from a ferry boat carrying passengers to Elephanta Island, the home of ancient archeological remains. The island was an abundance of ancient history and ruins, of old stories kept alive by the visitors who gazed at the broken shapes and aged stone.

"It's too hot here. San Diego's perfect weather has ruined me for climates that are less than ideal."

Winter nodded, trying to focus on this present moment, but she was unable to fully immerse herself in the bright scarves and fabrics that hung from sidewalk shops, in the smell of sweet spices coming from nearby street food stands, in the sounds of India. Her heart ached after hearing Lucie's words. All day she felt as if she were under water, in need of air but unable to breathe. That man from the train that morning never left her mind, not as she explored shop stands, not as she walked the streets of Colaba. The incident weighed on her heart with unceasing heaviness.

"I'm craving a mango lassi. Want to get one? It's like a sort of yogurt drink. If you eat yogurt, then you should like it."

"All right," Winter answered.

They grabbed mango lassies and headed back toward the train. Winter drank the tangy, fruity drink absentmindedly as they walked. A craftsman across the street, carrying a tray of handmade clay elephants painted black and gray, came up to the two of them. Little jewels complimented his craftsmanship. He presented the tray to the girls.

"Those are beautiful, sir, but no thank you," Lucie said, and then the man looked at Winter.

"Oh. No thank you," Winter said. The man was persistent and showed them the best of his handmade stock.

Winter smiled, but her smile was hollow, strained from heartbreak, and that was evident to the man. It was a struggle far different from his own, but he recognized pain nonetheless. He searched in his box and retrieved an imperfect elephant. Some of the jewels had fallen off, leaving the elephant with half a face. It was a broken trinket he couldn't sell, so the man passed the ornament to Winter.

"For you," he said, looking into Winter's eyes.

Then he walked down the street towards a group of travelers to sell his untarnished handmade work. Winter stared down at a piece of that man's livelihood he'd given to her. Winter could see the outline of glue where the man had tried to repair the trinket. As she stared at the evidence of the man's honest attempts at reparation, Winter realized that during her journey she'd done the same thing as the craftsman.

She'd been trying to fit back together broken pieces of herself, but the broken pieces weren't meant to be reunited. New, abundant life was waiting for her. Winter had to learn to let go of the brokenness that took life from her, causing cracks and voids in her existence. Winter turned the elephant over in her hands, and she finally understood that her broken experiences did not make up who Winter Wright was. Her scars and imperfections from the life she lived didn't make her unlovable or unworthy. The skin she was born in didn't make her less than. It was the opposite. *I have to make peace with myself, with the life I have. I can't internalize other peoples warped ideas of me. My humanity is not dependent upon who chooses to see it. I will make peace with myself.* Winter believed that was the only way to bring healing into her life.

CHAPTER TWENTY-SEVEN—THE GRAND FAILURE

Winter, Lucie, and Amala took a rickshaw to a coffee shop for breakfast the following morning. Winter couldn't overlook the mixture of wealthy hotels, shops, and restaurants neighboring some of the most severe, poverty-stricken places in the world. At the air-conditioned restaurant with glass walls, Winter was able to order chocolate cake and a cappuccino. She picked up her mug of coffee and took a deep breath. It was as familiar to her as an old friend.

"How was your day in Colaba?" Amala asked.

"I found a ton of beautiful fabrics. I want to make something unique with them, but I haven't decided what yet," Lucie said as her eyes darted from Winter to her plate of scones. Amala stared between the two of them.

"What else happened, you two? Lucie, what did you do?" Amala asked.

"What?! I didn't do anything," Lucie said loudly.

Winter wiggled in her chair. "Someone flipped me off, an early birthday present," Winter said, trying to make light of it, and failing.

Amala's eyebrows furrowed with concern at the news, but then her features softened. "It's your birthday?"

"Soon, this weekend actually. June 17."

"How old are you going to be, Grandma?" Lucie asked.

"The big 25," Winter said, trying to sound full of excitement, instead of worn down.

"Well, what he did was terrible. But we should celebrate your birthday! That's shameful behavior. Please don't let it alter how you think of Mumbai," Amala said.

"I won't," Winter said. "Can't judge an entire place and the people who live there by one person's actions. Besides, prejudice seems to be everywhere," Winter said with a sigh. Her state of mind made her share more than normal. "I just want to live life comfortably in my skin. That's it.

I'm searching for the pockets of hope. That's why I'm traveling. It's been harder to find than I anticipated."

"You're traveling to find hope?" Amala asked.

"I started traveling to face my fears. I call it my list of illogical logical fears."

"Winter, how could you keep this information from me?" Lucie asked as she polished off her first pastry.

"That is an intriguing idea," Amala said, her dark eyes twinkled as she leaned forward.

"Are fears illogical?" Lucie asked, her forehead wrinkled as she posed the question.

"I don't think all of them are, but some are granted too much free reign over our lives and our minds. I think that's when they become unhealthy," Winter said.

"I wonder what some of mine are," Lucie said, tapping her chin with her pointer finger.

"How have you done?" Amala asked.

"My list has been getting smaller, not at the rate I imagined," Winter said with a small laugh. "It's a bit strange, though. Each place I've gone to seems to fit with the fears I need to face."

"What fears line up here?" Lucie asked, biting into her second scone.

"Uh, my largest fear. It keeps coming for me," Winter said, licking chocolate frosting off her fork. "In every place I've been." Winter remembered the billboard in Northern Ireland, the woman who passed her over in Uganda, the man on the train. But Winter had to remind herself of the people who had given her strength and hope along her journey, not just on this trip but throughout life. It was harder for Winter to focus on the good because the bad seemed unconquerable.

"What's your largest fear?" Amala asked.

Winter took a breath and said, "Prejudice in any form. It makes me lose hope and faith in people. It makes me question every interaction I have before I have it. I'm always on the lookout for someone to show me hate. But in the end, I'm the one losing out, because I'm not really living. When I was twelve, I bought this camouflage jacket after my first encounter with overt racism. I wanted to hide. I was so afraid of people, of hate, finding me. I was ashamed of who I am. I wore that coat for years. I still wear that coat. It's in my bag at the hostel now. I guess I'm afraid that I'll always live my life like that: hiding, afraid to be seen. I'm worried that I'll fade away into my fears until I just cease to be."

Winter's voice had quieted before she found it again. "Whenever I think I've finally unraveled my fears, I turn around, and they're chasing me. I don't want to run anymore. I want to pick a spot, a good spot, and stand my ground and live my life," Winter concluded. It was what she wanted, but putting it into action was proving to be more taxing than she'd hoped.

The part about prejudice that always embedded itself deeply within Winter was the shame. Shame at being considered different, less than. Shame at making other people uncomfortable when she recounted stories. *But why should I feel shame?* Winter thought with exasperated anger. *I can't let shame be the banner under which my life is lived*, she thought in her head.

"Winter, I can't pretend to understand what you're going through. I don't have any idea what it's like. I know we've only just met, but you also know I say pretty much anything that comes to my mind. I don't have a filter. I tried it once, and I thought my head would burst open. I don't know if this helps or not, but I just wanted to say that I'm here if you need to share. There is too much negativity in the world. We need to pull together and celebrate what makes us different, not demean it. I guess what I'm trying to say is this: I'm here if you need someone to listen to you or if you want a friend to cry with. I can't pretend to understand, but I can try to be human alongside you. That's what I can offer."

Winter nodded her head rigidly, not wanting her tears to fall, but then she threw the notion out of her mind and pulled Lucie into a hug.

"Thank you."

That's what Winter wanted, and she didn't even know it. Having someone offer to share the burden, to try to understand the weight of it, lifted some of it from Winter's shoulders. Hope was a mighty companion.

"Thanks," Winter said again, roughly. She was getting used to being emotional around people she'd only known for twenty-four hours. Winter couldn't ignore the fact that when she put herself in vulnerable places, when she shared her own heart and listened to others, she could feel her life expand.

Amala looked to Winter and said, "You and I are the same."

Winter gazed into Amala's dark eyes, which twinkled with understanding. And Winter knew Amala was speaking truth, that somehow between the two of them existed shared life experiences.

"I can relate to you so much, especially about wanting to live comfortably in your skin. Here in India, there is such an obsession with fair skin, and people look down on those with a dark complexion. We say we don't, but it's so apart of our culture that it's become a norm. I know part of that is colonialism's impact on our culture and psychology. Whiteness is associated with power and position because of our history with colonizers. Upholding lightness is ingrained in minds and generations. I've had family members tell me I'll have a hard time getting married because of my dark skin. My aunt, who also has dark skin, always told me as a child to stay out of the sun, and she favored my cousin who is lighter than me."

"She was always telling my cousin how lucky she was to have a beautiful complexion. So many of my family, friends, and girls at school would buy skin-lightening creams. When I was younger, my mom would put skin lightening lotion on me every night. It was a part of my bedtime routine. When I got older, I wanted to get light quickly, so I covered myself in any bleaching agent I could find. I burnt my skin pretty badly. I still have the scars."

Her voice trailed off for a moment as she rubbed her side. Winter thought about the scars left on her knees from that distant summer day. Prejudice had left both of them with scars on their skin and marks on their souls. "It used to be a daily struggle for me to accept myself because everyday everything around me tells me I shouldn't. We might not have racism here, but we have colorism, and it's just as destructive." Amala sat up straighter in her chair. "Can I show you something that helped change me?"

Winter felt ravenous for any morsel of aid. What had changed Amala? What had altered her so clearly that it *used* to be a struggle to embrace herself?

"I have a story to complete over the next few days. But this weekend I want you and Lucie to come with me."

"I'm definitely up for that," Winter said.

"I actually need to go work on my water story in Dharavi right now," she said, glancing at the watch on her wrist. "I'll see you both this weekend! Yes?"

Winter smiled and nodded her head.

"Yes!" Lucie agreed. Lucie finished her coffee and said, "Winter, I'm going to go to the seamstress in Chambra to pick up a piece of mine. You wanna to come? Or we can do something else."

"Thanks, but I think I'll head back to the hostel," Winter said with a small smile.

The three of them rose from their table, paid their bill and walked outside to the curb. Winter parted ways with the others and began her walk to the hostel. During the walk it began to rain, not lightly, but torrentially and Winter's thoughts moved to Anna. The downpour reminded Winter of her arch-nemesis leaving her out in the rain in high school.

She's still waiting for an answer, Winter thought.

She still didn't know if she could forgive Anna, but Winter knew it was time to be honest and examine the possibility. It was time to face the past she was running from, and revisit the memory of the Grand Failure

Anna was in shock when she learned Winter had won the writing competition. After the principal's announcement, Winter crossed paths with Anna, but Anna said nothing. She walked past Winter without uttering a single word, which only made her worry. At the end of the school day, Winter grabbed books from her locker and placed them in the bottom of her bag.

Maybe Anna doesn't care that I won, she thought.

Her face had a huge smile across it as she shut the locker door and walked down the long, stone steps outside. Out of the corner of her eye Winter could see Anna and her group of friends. She contemplated turning around and going the long way home to avoid Anna, but that day Winter didn't want to cower. She stayed her course.

Anna and her friends' gazes turned toward Winter as she passed. Winter was almost clear when she heard Anna's voice. "I wish I had a sob story like you," she said, jumping off a bench. Her friends followed, making their way towards Winter. "I don't like that my face isn't perfectly symmetrical. Do you think I can get a full ride to college?" Anna barked. Anna's friends were now encircled around Winter.

"Why is your gang surrounding me?"

"You're so funny, Winter. You know what else is funny? This: you won because the judges felt sorry for the minority girl. You won because they felt guilty and I'm losing out on my dream because of it."

"It's my dream to go to a top school, too."

"With your grades?"

"I work hard, Anna. I get good grades."

The eyes of students leaving to go home fell upon Winter. In some eyes she could see pity or shock, in others she saw relief, but she also saw fear. No one wanted to be that person, the one who spoke against the girl who commanded the attention of an entire room. Winter tried to stand up for herself. She pushed her shoulders back, making her appear more self-assured than she was.

"Besides, my essay is not just about not liking a feature. It's about being told that what you are innately isn't valued, that it's less than something else. Tons of people can relate to that. It's not a small thing to be told that what you are isn't good enough."

When she finished, Winter thought she might have gotten through to Anna Herald, but Winter could see something brewing behind Anna's eyes. She bit her bottom lip and turned to leave, when Anna said, "It's because they felt guilty. They had to give the award to you. Remember that. You took my spot because they felt sorry for you." And then she turned and started talking with her friends.

That night, Winter's parents, and Ella, took her out for a celebratory dinner, but during the meal Anna's words played in Winter's head. "You won because they felt guilty." Winter picked at her food and chewed the inside of her lip. She knew Anna wasn't right, but the seed of doubt had been planted in Winter's mind. When the night of the gala came, Winter pulled out the dress her parents bought and her whole family piled into the car to drive to Chicago.

"I can't wait to hear you read the essay," Marie Wright said to Winter as they drove.

"I brought my camera and I'm going to record it," her father said proudly.

"I'm not even going to mess with you tonight, little sister," Ella added.

At the hotel Winter changed clothes, placed her hair in a neat bun, and went to the common room to wait with the other students who were runners-up, and had been invited to the event. As Winter walked inside the common room, numerous heads turned towards her. Winter thought she was being paranoid and self-involved to believe that many people were paying attention to her, but then she saw her. She saw Anna Herald sitting on a lounge chair.

"That's her," Anna said, and then she leaned low and whispered into the ears of the new friends she'd made. Winter turned her gaze from Anna, and tried to ignore the low whispers. She walked to the side of the room, pulled out her essay, and began reading over it. One of the girls in Anna's group started pointing in Winter's direction, laughing. Winter took a deep breath and forced her eyes to stay on her essay. *Focus Winter,* she told herself. *You're almost there. Your dreams are coming true.* She was going to be featured in a prominent academic magazine, meet with prestigious schools, her future was coming together.

"Hey, Winter! You forgot something!" Anna yelled.

Winter turned and one of the girls in the group, a black girl, called out, "Your hair!"

Winter swallowed hard and kept going over the lines of her essay. They laughed so hard tears fell from their faces. Winter glanced around the room, but everyone was avoiding her gaze. No one was willing to lend their voice and risk being put on the spotlight like Winter. She couldn't take anymore. She walked out into the hallway as Anna yelled out to her, "Winter, I hope tonight isn't a repeat of your chorus solo!"

In the hall, Winter leaned against the wall, collecting a couple stares of pity as she left. She needed a friend. Winter pulled out her phone and dialed Sienna.

"She did what?" Sienna asked after Winter recounted the incident.

"Sienna, I don't know if I can do this. What if everyone in that room agrees with Anna? I'm positive the majority of the semi-finalists think my paper is a joke. Anna has already recruited them. How can I face a room full of people who might agree with her?"

"Winter, if Anna's words were true, you wouldn't have made it this far and you know it. She's mad because some dorky, outsider girl was chosen over her."

"Hey."

"The best people are dorks. We make the best friends," Sienna said. Winter smiled hesitantly before speaking.

"Sienna, I'm sharing my soul. I know rejection is a part of life, but I can't stand any more rejection in this particular area of life," she said in panic as tears rimmed her eyes.

"If people took a moment to experience life from a place contrary to what they've known, ignorance and prejudice would be eradicated. Don't pay any attention to Anna. You got there because you worked hard, not because of someone feeling guilty for you. This is your accomplishment. Now go get on that stage so that I can hear about how amazing your reading went when you get back."

"Thanks, Sienna."

"That's what best and truest friends are for."

After hanging up, Winter sat through an hour and a half long dinner with the other students, but she chewed on her bottom lip more than anything else. Anna was the rising star of their table. She flawlessly made conversation with everyone there, while Winter awkwardly attempted to speak with the intimidating strangers. Winter stumbled through the conversations, and then it was time. It was time for her to read the essay in front of two-hundred people. Winter nervously stood up to go backstage, and as she passed Anna, her arch-nemesis said loudly, "Good luck, Winter. You've worked really hard. You'll do great. You're a natural on stage." She flashed a dazzling smile. Winter wanted to hit Anna with the steak on her plate, but the eyes of those at the table were on Winter, waiting for her response.

"Thank you, Anna," Winter conceded.

"You're so very welcome."

Anna's runner-up grace was perfect, without a trace of Anna's true motives. *I can't believe I have to thank her for insulting me!* Winter left the table and walked up the stairs to the stage with shaking hands that crumpled her essay.

"Winter, ready to go?" Someone dressed in all black with a headset attached to their face asked her.

Winter took a step forward, but her hands trembled harder.

"Winter, you're on in five…four…three… two…go."

Winter could see Anna at the front table, that same snide smirk on her face. Slowly, Winter began backing away from the stage entrance. She shook her head no. "I can't. I can't do it."

The woman rushed towards her, urgency and care alive in her voice.

"Oh, honey, of course you can. Just go out there and read it. That's it."

The woman placed a hand on Winter's back and guided her out to the stage. Winter wished this could be the last time Anna sat front row waiting for her to mess up. Winter moved her eyes away from Anna and looked around the room. A sea of faces stared back at her and it hit Winter that once she shared her words she'd be exposed. Some of her most intimate fears were written on the pages she was about to read aloud. What if people agreed with Anna? What if they thought her heartache void and lacking? Winter stood at the podium and opened her mouth to speak.

"I'm Winter. Thank you for...for having me," she said with a shaking voice. My essay is entitled, "What's the definition of humanity?""

Winter took a deep breath and looked out at the crowd. "When I was six I took a ballet class and I remember...I remember being scrutinized for the way my hair...for the way..." Winter stopped speaking. She could see Anna and some of her friends talking. With wide eyes Winter tried to find her family in the crowd, but couldn't spot them because of the bright lights. She searched for encouragement or comfort outside of herself, but couldn't find it.

"Um...sorry," she laughed anxiously before continuing. "I first realized...I mean, when I first realized. Wait. Let me...let me start again," Winter said, wiping sweat from her brow. She searched for parts of the essay she believed other people wouldn't ridicule. "As a young girl, I rode down empty lanes to my friend's house and one day I came face to face with a man who...who..."

Winter's eyes became wide as realization set in. She couldn't share her soul's pain, not in front of Anna or these strangers. She couldn't give a part of herself away when people might disregard the words shared, the experiences lived. Winter was already too broken and she was so afraid of being shattered.

"I can't, um, I can't finish."

The words were amplified by the microphone she spoke into. Winter said them more to herself than anyone else. Winter took a step back from the podium and stared at the crowd. She couldn't breathe, and the single thought in her head was, *I'm too scared.* The stage lights made her emerald dress shine with each step she took away from the platform. Winter's moment was over before it began. The woman in black motioned for Anna to get up as fast as possible. Anna walked to the stage and took her spot at the podium. Winter stumbled back to her seat, wishing she could dissolve.

Anna cleared her throat and said, "Before I begin, let's give Winter a round of applause for her essay, which I know was brilliant."

Everyone clapped, but none more fervently than Anna, and then Anna read her essay. She read with passion and clear story telling ability. The audience was in rapture, utterly enchanted by Anna. Winter sat and watched her receive a standing ovation. At the end of the night, Anna was interviewed by press and met with representatives from top schools.

Weeks later, Winter received the magazine in the mail with Anna's feature inside. She'd done it. Anna had done what Winter couldn't. She'd just secured her future and Winter had just ruined her own. She was mortified and broken hearted, but more than that she was angry and disappointed in herself. She'd finally been chosen and she'd failed. Epically.

Anna's words had seeped into Winter's heart like a poison, and Winter was angry with herself for not seeking a remedy, for giving in to the pain instead of fighting for her hopes. For weeks, the same words replayed in Winter's mind. *I didn't fight for my dream because I believed in Anna's arsenic covered words, instead of myself. I let her win. I let fear take over and I was so close.*

Something broke in Winter in those weeks following the gala. It wasn't just that day which made her crack. Winter felt her shame so keenly at failing so spectacularly and losing out on her dream. If only she'd been brave enough to take a stand for herself, to believe in the words she'd written, the experiences she'd lived. When Winter's family left the gala early, even Ella had no jokes.

"It's all right, Winter. It's not the end. It's just a chance for a different beginning," Marie Wright said. Winter's mother held her daughter as she wept into her green, camouflage jacket, and that night Winter felt her tears would never diminish. Despite her parents comforting words, Winter only heard one; Failure.

Her tears that day had streamed down her face like the torrential rain pour in Mumbai that now soaked Winter through. She walked into the hostel dripping water from her clothes. Questions burned with urgency in her mind.

How do you let go of a past that still affects your now? That changed your future? How do you forgive? How do you defeat your fears? Winter felt hot tears in her eyes. Both ideas seemed preposterous to her. *I'm going to fail.* In her hostel room Winter stared down at the list in defeat.

My List of Illogical Logical Fears

1. ~~Bodies of water (and being lost underwater)~~.
2. ~~Heights that are above my own.~~
3. The future. Where am I going?
4. ~~Singing in public.~~
5. ~~Being alone in a foreign country where I don't know anyone.~~
6. Getting rejected and being vulnerable.
7. Not finding true happiness.
8. Looking and sounding incredibly stupid.
9. ~~Getting out of my comfort zone.~~
10. Self-consciousness growing larger in my life.
11. Failing to find the road that leads to the path I'm meant to be on in life.
12. Never accomplishing my dreams.
13. Reliving the sadness of my past.
14. Living a small life.
15. Having hate find me again.

She rose from the bed, stepped into the hallway, and went to the showers. It was usually Sienna who helped Winter through her tangled memories of Anna. It was Sienna who first befriended Winter after Anna's taunts, when everyone else decided it was better to ignore the girl with the weird hair.

In the hostel bathroom, Winter walked into the last stall and turned on the water, letting it slide over her tense muscles. Before she knew it, she was shaking. Nothing was changing on her list since coming to Mumbai: it was only growing.

Fear surrounded Winter. It enveloped her, constricted her throat. *I'm failing*, she cried. It wasn't the list being checked off that worried her, it was the idea of living life the same lifeless way. That's why she had to make it. That's why she couldn't fail. Winter had to change her life by entering it, she just couldn't find a permanent way inside. Her body heaved as her chest rose and fell unevenly in the empty room. Water splashed over her skin and Winter was thankful for it because it masked, even to her, how many tears fell from her weary eyes.

Everything, it seemed, was rising up. Every memory from her childhood, every tarp-covered home, and hungry child, every hope she'd had for herself that seemed a cruel, practical joke against the reality of her existence. Winter was broken. Her heart felt as though it no longer beat as one, but in disconnected fragments Winter wasn't sure she could mend. Her soul ached for the hurts of her past, the fears of her future, and the way injustice lived in the lives of people she'd met, encountered, or loved in her life.

Winter sunk to the floor of the bathroom, limply, and sat at the bottom of the shower as she cried. Winter cried until she thought her muscles would ache and never recover from her heaving, from the pain that embodied a physical form somewhere nestled roughly and deeply into her chest.

As a girl, she wouldn't allow herself to cry. She thought that meant she was giving in, and she wanted to be strong. *But maybe there is strength in admitting to yourself when you're hurt*, Winter thought. It only made sense because she wasn't getting any stronger attempting to appear unbreakable. She couldn't reconcile the brokenness she saw, the need, the poverty, and Winter felt impoverished in her soul.

She bit her lip as she laid on the sunken in floor. As Winter lay there, it occurred to her that she didn't know who she was. She had a list of the things that had happened to her, how they made her feel small, how she longed to feel significant, worthy, how it angered her that she was seen from a place of a deficit.

Winter had unintentionally compiled stacks of grievances at the cost of her identity, of her sense of self. In her desire to keep hurt at bay, she had indeed let herself become the sum of what had happened to her, like Sienna had warned. Winter didn't know how to separate who she was from the pain she'd lived through, from the trauma endured.

Winter only knew the brave thing to do, which was to become everything she ever wanted to be, everything she'd always hoped for, and then keep striving towards embracing more of herself. She would become what she always longed to embody, but felt disconnected from. Winter dressed in the bathroom and threw her old clothes inside her bag.

Despite the heat, Winter was cold. Back in her hostel room, she pulled her camouflage jacket from the depths of the bag. As she did so, her finger slid quickly across a piece of paper, separating her skin. She lifted up the paper to see what it was as she wrapped the coat around her body. It was the note from Marieleen. Winter peeled back the paper and read it.

Hello, Winter!

How is your time going? I hope you've finished your list! I just wanted to write to you to say I'm so happy we had the chance to meet. I believe it was meant to be! Winter, I wish you success on your endeavor. Sometimes it's in the hardest moments of life that we find ourselves, and you're seeking out your hardest moments. Seeing you do that has made me want to go after some of my own. I decided I'm going to try to become a professional photographer. I know there will be hard times while I pursue my dream, but isn't that why we are here? To listen to our soul's yearnings, to be our best selves so that we can invite others to do the same?

I'm going back to India to hike the Himalayas. Sometimes that's when I feel the most alive: when I'm traveling, when I'm around other people, when I see the soul of this thing called life. Well, this letter is becoming too long. I'm sure you are having a good time and want to get back to it. But if you're not enjoying yourself, if you are having your hardest moment right now, know that you will come out better on the other side of it. That's why we have those times that seem like they will shatter us, so that we can come out more whole than before. One last thing, Winter, you taught me something whether you meant to or not. You taught me to hope in my dreams. You taught me that nothing was out of my reach, so long as I extended my hands high enough to grasp it. Remember to reach.

Love, Marieleen

This was Winter's hardest moment, and she desperately wanted to survive it.

CHAPTER TWENTY-EIGHT—A RIPPLE OF HOPE

The next few mornings Winter ventured out on her own to occupy her mind. She went to a cafe and wrote in the journal given to her by Sienna. Her nerves calmed as she put her thoughts to paper.

I don't feel brave right now. To be honest, my hope has been diminishing. I don't understand the state of the world, the suffering. I'm broken when I want to be whole. My time away hasn't gone as planned, but I'm holding on to the wish that things will turn around, that brighter days will come.

Here's to seeking a bigger life.

Until then, Winter

When Friday rolled around, Winter packed up all her belongings for the weekend. She didn't want to leave anything behind. They had to check out of the hostel since they'd be gone for a few nights. Winter shot a text to her family to let them know they wouldn't be able to reach her and then she scrolled through her funds. At most, Winter could do another week and a half in Mumbai. She only had enough money left for an emergency ticket home if she needed it. It would be more than disappointing to Winter to return home more broken then when she'd left.

Late Friday afternoon, Winter lugged her dilapidated bag down the hostel stairs. Lucie ran through the doors of the hostel from the street out of breath. "I just have to grab my things, and I'll be ready to go! Any idea where we're going?"

"Amala hasn't let a single word slip," Winter said.

"Ahhhh, I'm so excited," Lucie said through her teeth and then she stopped walking.

"Is that your bag?" Lucie asked.

Winter looked down at the luggage. "Yeah, um, it's been through a lot."

"I don't think it can even be called a suitcase anymore."

"Probably not. It's a bit of a stretch."

"I have an extra I've been carting around. I was going to use it for souvenirs, but I don't need to buy anything else. You want it?"

"Really? I'd appreciate that so much!" Winter said.

"Let me grab it." Minutes later, Lucie returned with her things and an extra suitcase for Winter. It was smaller than her original, but it had working wheels, something Winter had not experienced for quite some time. Winter rolled her new luggage outside where Amala met them on the curb.

"Ready?" Amala asked. Her face was full of light.

"I'm ready. All packed up," Winter said, hitting her new bag.

"Before we go, I have to retrieve something important from some friends of mine who live in Dharavi."

"That's one of the slums, right? They're the people trying to get their water back?" Winter asked.

"It is. It shouldn't take too long, but then again hospitality is an essential part of my culture. So, we could be there for hours being fed," Amala said with a smirk. The three of them headed to the slum, and when they got close, a woman called out.

"Amala!" The woman began walking toward them, energy alive in her limbs. Amala smiled as she approached.

"Oma, how are you dear one?"

"Very well," she said as her eyes fell on Winter and Lucie.

"Lucie and Winter, this is my friend, Oma. My friends and I are leaving for a few days."

Oma's eyes widened as she said, "You'll need to eat before you go! Come along." Amala cast her friends a smile, and then Oma began to lead the way to her home with Amala keeping pace next to her. Lucie and Winter grinned at one another and followed.

"Amala is helping us to fight corruption. Someone has been taking bribes for our water supplies, and we are standing against it," Oma said as she led them into Dharavi slum. The slum was unlike anything Winter had come across before. Narrow alleys and streets lay between houses. Pipe and metal fragments jutted out along the walkways. The slum demanded that your senses be on high alert.

Winter watched Oma's careful, yet familiar steps as she stepped around jagged metal and onto wooden beams serving as permanent bridges across deep puddles of murky water. The slum was downwind of a garbage dump, and numerous flies had taken over the open air. Winter swatted at the bugs and watched as children kicked a ball with fun-filled smiles covering their faces. Oma turned down yet another narrow passageway and then stopped walking.

She pushed open a fading, crooked door, turned to her guests and said,

"Welcome, welcome."

Winter followed the other two through the doorway. The house was as large as Winter's parents' living room. Two young men sat on a bed inside the one room home. They hopped up at the sight of guests.

"These are my sons, Sachet and Joseph," Oma said, a proud look across her face. The boys walked over and extended their arms, saying hello to their guests with gentle head bobs.

"Please sit," Joseph said, gesturing to the bed that also functioned as a couch.

"Yes, please have a seat," Sachet echoed.

Oma passed the girls tin mugs filled with pop and set out a tray with cookies. Winter took a drink as her eyes moved around the room. Sheets hung down from the ceiling separating the kitchen from the living space, the floor slanted in the middle, metal plates sat on empty, broken crates.

"What has brought you both to India?" Sachet asked.

"We're both traveling. I came to India in college and knew I wanted to come back one day. I saved for a couple years and then came," Lucie said.

"That's wonderful. I'm glad you enjoyed your time in India so much that you came back," Joseph said with a proud smile.

Sachet's brown eyes looked to Winter.

"I had some neighbors who were from Mumbai when I was younger. They made Mumbai sound so amazing that I wanted to come," Winter said, taking another drink.

Joseph shook his head from side to side and said in a warm accent, "You are both most welcome."

When Winter's drink was halfway gone, Sachet filled it back to the rim. "Thank you so much," she said, taking another drink. Winter looked around the room as everyone talked, feeling incredible awe. The people she sat with were fighting to get water and yet her cup never emptied the entire night. Cookies constantly found their way to her lips and warm smiles filled her field of vision. Winter still felt utterly broken, but she also felt humbled and inspired by the strength and generosity of the human spirit.

***

After visiting Oma, the three friends took a taxi to a bus stop forty minutes away for their secret weekend. They rode down dust covered roads amid traffic that seemed to loop and turn at times Winter didn't understand. Motorcycles weaved between buses and rickshaws, some barely making it. Winter stared out her window at the mountains that began to form the further away they went from the city.

Within a few hours, they'd made it to their destination. The bus stopped abruptly at a small station next to green grass fields that danced and swayed in the wind. Winter looked up at the sky from her window. For the first time since arriving in India, she saw soft blue sky peeking through white, luminescent clouds.

Amala stood from her chair and put her arm out to the side. "After you, ladies." They came down the bus steps, and Winter inhaled the fresh, unpolluted air. She and Lucie followed Amala past streams and through mountains covered in green foliage. When they reached a clearing, Amala stopped walking.

"This is my parent's home. They are away for the weekend but have agreed to let me use it for my own personal devices." She rubbed her hands together. "Come in and we shall prepare a meal together." A white and beige house was tucked into the green landscape.

Before walking inside Winter stared at the setting sun, at the mountains that seemed to swallow the sunlight. Winter couldn't believe her wanderlust had led her here, wherever here was. Inside, Amala set to work. She grabbed milk and tea bags out and placed them into a portable water heater. She put the steaming liquid into three light yellow mugs and poured sugar over the vapor reaching out of the small cups. Amala placed the remaining tea in a teapot and set it between the three of them.

Winter took a sip from her mug and her taste buds instantly recognized the liquid that ran over them. It was chai. She savored the comforting creaminess of the drink. It transported her back to the porch at the cafe, to lazy nights with Simon playing guitar and Michael and Alexis arguing beneath the moon.

"Ladies, tomorrow you will find out why we're here. Winter, it will be a wonderful way to celebrate your birthday," Amala added with a smile. "But tonight, as a prequel to tomorrow, I want to talk to you both about what drives you," Amala said, resting her chin on her folded hands. "What are your hopes, girls?" Amala asked, looking between them. Winter narrowed her eyes, and Lucie sat up straighter at the mention of what drives she and Winter.

"I've got this," Lucie said. "For as long as I've been able to move my legs, I've wanted to be a gymnast. That may seem like an exaggeration, but it's not. I've wanted to fly from the high bar, stick a perfect landing on the balance beams, and flip till the audience falls over with dizziness. That's more of a lofty, childhood goal. In my old age—"

"You're twenty-five," Amala interrupted.

"Don't be rude to your elders," Lucie quipped back. Amala snorted.

"In my old age, I realized it was just praise and attention that drove the ambition. I grew up in a house where I felt ignored. Other people's problems took precedence over my own. Being traveling doctors meant my parent's always had a lot on their plates, and we were always moving around. So, one of my real life desires is to do what I'm doing, to meet people and be engaged with them in the ways I often wished my family would be with me. I can't stand when people look through you instead of into your eyes."

"I can see that in you," Amala said, bobbing her head. "My hope," she began, placing a hand over her heart, "is to tell the world's stories through my journalism. I want to find the roots of oppression and upturn them."

"That's a valiant, selfless dream," Winter said. Lucie and Amala both looked at Winter. It was her turn to share now, but she still couldn't make herself say her hope out loud. She thought about the journal Sienna had given her, the reminders to write inside its pages. Sienna knew Winter well.

"Winter, don't make me force it out of you!" Lucie joked.

"I don't know," Winter said.

"Yes you do. I can tell," Lucie said with a confident smile.

"It's not something I can achieve very easily, but I think one day it'd be, I don't know," she shrugged her shoulders, "kind of cool or whatever, to you know, maybe, write a book. I'm sure my chances for getting people to read it are probably slim," Winter said.

"What kind of book?" Amala asked.

"I don't know. Who knows?" Winter said.

"You should probably have a topic!" Lucie said. "We can brainstorm tonight and then when it's finished you can thank me in the acknowledgments section," Lucie said, beaming.

Amala laughed at Lucie's speech and said, "You can think about the topic while we make dinner."

The three of them prepared spiced tandoori chicken, rice pudding, naan, and root vegetables fried in a bevy of savory flours. Amala instructed them on which seasonings to use and how much of each. By the time the food was done, Winter was aching to try it. They sat outside under the starry sky and ate. The spicy food enlivened Winter's dulling senses. Her nose and eyes ran as she placed food on her tongue.

When the moon rose into the sky, Amala said, "I have a story to share with you both. It's an old tale, and it's one of my favorites. Would you like to hear it?" Both girls nodded their heads as they filled their mouths.

"One day, long ago, a man walked past a barren tree. Its shallow roots could not push through the soil. The tree was void of life and beauty. The man's family told him to let the tree die or chop it up for firewood to make it useful, but the man didn't listen. Instead, he told them, 'The shade of a good tree offers refuge to many.' The man decided that day that he would not chop the tree down. He said, 'I will care for this tree. I will water it and bring life back to it.' His family told him he was foolish, but he had made up his mind.

His goal was to water the tree every day, but sometimes he forgot, and other times he overcompensated. But he always returned, even when the tree still looked like it was decaying, he kept coming back. Day after day, slowly, the tree improved. It's bark, once stripped, grew hard and sturdy. It deepened in color and on the branches, buds began to grow into full bloom. The man didn't even know what kind of tree it was when the white and pink flowers grew from green leaves.

It wasn't the water alone that gave new life to the tree. It was his dedication to it, his love for it. The seeds fell on the ground and were blown by the wind. They rolled upon the earth and new trees sprouted. An endless ripple of life had been given, a ripple that only grew and expanded to infinite lengths. The point of this story is that we are all ripples. We all can give life or halt it. We only have to choose."

CHAPTER TWENTY-NINE—A BEACON OF LIGHT

On June 17, Winter's birthday, she woke to Amala and Lucie banging on her door. Winter sat upright in her bed as a familiar song was sung to her.

"Happy Birthday to you! Happy Birthday to you! Happy Birthday Dear Winter, Happy Birthday to you!" Winter got up and opened the door.

"That was beautiful. You two should consider going professional!" She said.

The girls devoured warm bread and fresh chai tea for breakfast that morning. Before leaving, Amala said, "Bring your jackets ladies. It's hot now but it will be cool tonight." Amala picked up a back pack and the girls eyed it with curiosity.

"What's in there?" Lucie asked.

"You'll see," she remarked with a grin.

The three of them hiked for most of the morning, and had a picnic outside for lunch. Winter felt her skin might melt off, but when evening came everything cooled down as Amala had cautioned. Winter slipped her jacket on as evening descended. When the sun began to lower, Amala stood from the ground they sat on and said, "It's time." She wrapped the backpack around her body. It clanked as it settled on top of Amala's shoulders. Winter tried to get a peek of what might be inside.

"Do you want me to carry that?" Winter asked. Amala cast her an accusatory side glance.

"Thank you for that offer, but no. Girls, it's a bit of a trek. You'll need to watch your step."

Along the path Winter could see the wheels of bikes and the staggering footprints of former passerby in the dark, hard soil. The setting sun cast an orange glow across the landscape, bathing everything in a peaceful, honey-colored light. Winter could hear a river flowing over rocks embedded beneath its rippling waves. Amala led them to a stream of water where small, colorful fish swam.

Amala turned around to face them, her arms out to her sides, "We've made it." She took the bag from her back and set it on the ground, but she didn't open it. Winter looked around for a hint or clue of what to expect but found nothing. "Winter, you told us you came here to get rid of your fears. I can relate to that. This night won't solve society, but it if you let it, it might be able to help you heal, and then you can spread that to others. When hate is present in your life, you need healing. Don't ever, not even for a moment, forget how important it is that your heart be mended. So, this is my idea," Amala said. "I thought that perhaps, instead of thinking about your fears, we could shift the focus to our hopes and our wishes. I have a special ceremony planned for the three of us."

Amala pulled open the bag and took out what looked like several sheets of paper with bits of wood connecting them. Winter still couldn't make out what she had planned.

"There is a custom in my heritage called the Diwali Festival. It is all about hope and togetherness; the triumph of light over darkness. Tonight, I'm taking inspiration from this ancient spiritual festival." Amala took a breath. "Light is special. It symbolizes that even in the darkest of times, during the most difficult problems you face, that your soul's light will find a way through it. Tonight, we'll write our fears down on this piece of paper. We'll say goodbye to those things that have threatened to rob us of our light but have not succeeded."

Amala stood in front of the mountains as she spoke. A soft wind blew her dark hair. Her black brown eyes twinkled as brightly as the glowing sun.

Amala picked up the folded paper and said, "Inside these lanterns, we'll write our dreams, and as they float away into the sky, we'll reflect on the waves we hope to create in the world," she finished.

Amala passed a lantern to Lucie and Winter. They put them together under the changing sky. Crisp, mountain air encircled them. "Have either of you built a fire before?" Amala asked as her fingers worked.

"Not since a family camping trip when I was nine," Winter said.

"I can," Lucie called out. "I could be a survivalist!" She said with lively animation.

They put down bits of wood and lit a match. Amala and Lucie blew softly. A smoke formed and the flames burst to life. "You first, Winter. Write your fears," Amala said encouragingly. She passed her the piece of paper. Winter wrote her fears on the paper in deep ink. She knew them by heart now. She passed the paper and then Lucie wrote hers down, too. When she finished, Amala scribbled her fears across the white paper.

"Let's do this together," Amala said.

They held the paper out over the flames and let it drop. The girls watched the flames burn and blacken the paper until nothing remained of the fears on the list. Though it was a simple act, Winter felt a release as she watched her fears burn in the fire.

I'm going to make it.

Winter looked at the girls she was with and recalled the string of people she'd met abroad that had woven themselves into the tapestry of Winter's life. Each had changed Winter in their own way. Their openness altered her being. They helped to lift her out of the despair that had been building over the years. Winter wanted to live a lifetime in that finite moment, make an eternity out of those brief moments when she felt hope brewing in her soul.

Winter looked down at the camouflage jacket she wore and she knew it was finally time. Her eyes grew misty as she stepped toward the fire. Fear was present as Winter realized she was going to part with this thing that had offered comfort and protection to a young girl trying to understand prejudice.

She ran the tips of her fingers down the fabric her twelve-year-old self picked out. She remembered the desperation deep within her. But now, this fear of hate grew to hide Winter from her own life. Winter knew she had to take this step. Winter had to trust that her life would be all right, that people weren't as bad as she once feared, that hope is always possible.

"It's time," Winter said, reassuring herself. *Don't hold on to it. Not anymore. It's the first and last piece,* she thought.

Sleeve by sleeve Winter slipped her arms out of the jacket. It slid slowly down her body and into her hands. Winter held the jacket in her palms and examined its holes. She could trace her youth through the fraying, discolored lines of thread. There were moments of happiness interwoven with trials of doubt in the human spirit, and now she stood at the edge of a river in India saying goodbye to her fears.

Winter was shedding away her prison of captivity. She didn't need it, nor want it, any longer. It scared her and left her vulnerable, but Winter knew when she stepped away from what was comfortable, that was where life would take off. She dropped her camouflage jacket into the fire. The flames wrapped around it, breaking down fibers, and further freeing Winter. As she watched the fire envelope the jacket, she couldn't help but feel that the embers from the flames were giving her new life, igniting old hopes that had been dimmed.

Winter inhaled sharply. "It's done," she said. Though she wasn't without fear, in that moment Winter felt that the mountain of turmoil that had been laying on her chest had just shifted beneath her, and instead of being crushed by the mountain's weight, she realized that mountain strength resided within her.

Both girls placed an encouraging hand on Winter's back, understanding in their own way the significance of what she'd done, and then Amala said, "Winter, the thing I wanted to tell you is probably nothing you've not heard before, but I believe it's worth repeating. Living life from a place of love is the key. Surround yourself with people who do the same. That's the answer. It won't change injustice right away, but it will begin to heal you, and then you can start the ripples you hope to achieve."

Winter nodded her head slowly, taking in Amala's words.

"And now for the pinnacle of our night," Amala exclaimed.

They opened up their lanterns and Amala passed each of them a match. Before lighting them, they cradled the lanterns next to their hearts, imbuing them with their most illogical logical dreams.

As Winter held the lantern to her chest she whispered, "I'm ready to live the life meant for me." And then they raised their arms into the air and let the wind catch their hopes and lift them high into the sky. With soft smiles, Winter, Lucie, and Amala watched the lanterns float away, small beacons of light amid darkness, silent prayers lifting up to the heavens.

CHAPTER THIRTY—A FIGURE FROM THE PAST RETURNS

Early the next morning, Winter walked back to the river to write in her journal. Words spilled from her mind and onto the page.

Sending our lanterns into the sky last night was beautiful, and it helped me realize even more that I have the right to exist fully, with arms spread wide in open abandonment. I have the right to stand, to occupy this space, this time, this place, this body. I want to believe in hope again. Instead of fearfully expecting the worst, I have to be bravely open to the best. It's like I've been lost all this time, but I've found a way. I've stumbled upon this bountiful path to transformation and crossed over into the land of the living. I just had to be open to where the path of my life led, and I'm willing to travel down it. I'm willing to begin to love myself uncompromisingly. It's long overdue, but I'm ready. No more seeking to live a bigger life, by seeing that, I already am.

Winter stood and lifted her arms into the sky, high, reaching to the heavens above her. In this broken place, she'd found herself. In the depths of despair, though difficult, she found infinite reserves of hope, waiting to be unlocked, to let light shine upon them and be released into the world. Winter stood at the edge of the mountainside, no longer the girl she once was nor ever would be again.

She'd been stretched to the point of surrender, so thin a soft wind could end her. And yet, there she stood, more alive than ever. It was then that Winter knew she hadn't just taken a trip or simply embarked on an adventure; she was in the midst of a revival, of life, of hope, of her.

Back at the house, Amala, Lucie, and Winter packed up and headed back to Mumbai, and when Winter's phone reconnected to the internet her heart's beating picked up. Her phone was flooded with messages. Sienna was in the hospital. There had been an accident on the lake. A jet ski hit her. She was pulled out of the lake unconscious.

Home.

The word filled Winter's senses. "I have to go," she said out loud. A plane flew overhead and Winter longingly wished it was her flying home to see Sienna.

"What?" Lucie asked, confused.

"There's been an accident. I need to go home. My friend was hurt."

"Winter, take a breath. We'll help. I'll get a taxi. Wait here." Amala crossed the street and ran into the taxi lot. Minutes later a blue and white taxi pulled up to the curb.

"Are you sure you want to go now?" Lucie asked Winter.

"Yes," Winter said with assuredness. "I'll get the first flight out I'm able to," Winter responded as she checked her phone for flights. If she left right now, she might be able to make a flight leaving in two hours. Winter threw her brand new luggage into the car and looked at Amala and Lucie. She shook her head as tears fell from her clear, brown eyes.

"Thank you for everything," she said shakily.

The three of them hugged and then Winter got into the cab and pulled away from Mumbai on her way to go home.

***

Winter was able to make it on the next flight out. She had just enough funds left for an emergency ticket. Her legs shook up and down anxiously as she waited in the small, hot terminal for her plane to board. She sat gnawing on her lip and twisting her fingers until she was in her seat on the plane. In the air, Winter turned her phone to airplane mode. It was torture not to have a signal, to know updates were being sent while she was in limbo. Winter arrived in Chicago fifteen hours later and was glued to her phone. She felt she'd fallen into a black hole for the plane ride. Once the plane landed, Winter read the texts from her sister, Ella.

Sienna was moved from intensive care. The drunken teenage driver who crashed into her is fine, but Sienna took a hit to the head and fell into the water. I'll pick you up from the airport and bring you to see her.

Winter prayed. Over and over again, she reminded herself of Sienna's strength, of her resolve. *She is going to be all right,* Winter thought. Sienna had always been there for Winter, and Winter needed to be there for Sienna now. The plane doors opened and Winter rushed out into the terminal, thankful her new luggage rolled smoothly on the floor tiles. Winter made it to the curb and searched for her sister's car. In that brief moment of stillness, Winter realized her trip was over.

The first day Winter came to the airport, she was a bundle of nerves. She'd never flown by herself, and now she'd crossed the ocean and not thought about it once. Ella pulled up to the curb and Winter breathed out in relief at the sight of her sister. She tossed her suitcase in the back before getting into the car.

Ella reached across the console and hugged Winter. "Hey, adventurer. I'll take you to the hospital."

"Tell me everything," Winter said to Ella, needing to understand exactly what happened.

"It was some idiot drunk kid who took his jet ski into the water. He crashed into her side and pinned her leg between the two jet skis. She fell into the water, but he kept going. Somehow she hit her head and was knocked unconscious. Luckily, he wasn't going extremely fast. At least, that's what some of the people who saw what happened said."

"How is she doing?" Winter asked with desperation as she pulled the seatbelt across her body. Ella's gaze stayed marked on the road.

"There was a rough period. They were concerned she might have been under the water, but it seems like she was facing upwards when she was knocked out. She had a life jacket, which saved her, but she got a nasty concussion and her leg is fractured. The doctor is hoping that the trauma is no more severe than that, but they need to run some tests. The doctor's staying on the positive side."

Winter nodded her head, trying to digest the information. She clutched the journal Sienna had gifted her in her hand. Winter wanted to show Sienna that she'd listened, that she'd written in it, that it had helped her to stay sane.

Winter closed her eyes and exhaled slowly.

"Mom and dad have been remodeling the kitchen," Ella said, trying to keep her sister calm through mindless updates. "A pipe burst and they took the opportunity to update a few things. The house is full of wood, discarded countertops, and general remodeling debris. The banging starts bright and early. Construction workers have been in and out of the house for the past few weeks."

They arrived at the hospital an hour later. Winter's parents sat in the waiting room next to Sienna's family. Sienna's little brother sat staring blankly at a white wall.

"Hi, Winter," Mrs. Magan said, rising from the hospital chair. The Magan's walked over and hugged their daughter's childhood friend.

"Hi Mr. and Mrs. Magan," Winter said. "How is she?"

"The same right now, which is a good thing they tell us," Mr. Magan replied as his wife wiped her eyes with a tissue. Sienna's brother still sat staring straight ahead, so the Magan's went and sat with him. Winter turned to her parents and hugged them.

"It's been a while," Winter said with a small smile.

"We're glad you're back," her mother said, holding her daughter in a long hug.

"You don't look any different to me. Maybe you should go back,"

Christopher Wright teased. Winter thumped her father on the arm and then turned to everyone.

"Can I get anyone anything? Coffee? Food?" Winter asked.

"A coffee would be great," Mr. Magan said. He reached into his pocket for change.

"No. Don't even think about it," Winter said, remembering the Irish warmth she'd encountered abroad, the family at The Gregory who paid for Winter's bus fare and wouldn't take anything in return.

"I'll help," Ella said, rising from her chair.

She and Ella walked to the hospital cafeteria to find refreshments for everyone. The hospital cafe had slim pickings. Winter breathed out heavily. Beneath bright white lights sat an abundance of cold sandwiches, soggy bread, and stale chips. They settled on frozen pizza and canned juice, and grabbed coffee from a vending machine for Mr. Magan. The sister's walked slowly back to the hospital waiting room.

"This probably isn't the best time to ask, but how was your trip? I guess it got cut a little early."

"I'm just glad I had the money to get back." Winter said, not wanting to imagine being stuck in another country when her closest friend was confined to a hospital bed.

"But my trip...it was...it was a revival, Ella," Winter said.

"So is it safe to say you're done with pantries?"

Winter laughed half-heartedly, her mind still on Sienna. "I think we can safely say that, yes."

Ella pushed open the door to the waiting room. The sisters divvied out the food and then they sat and waited until Sienna's doctor came out. His long white coat reminded Winter of floating lanterns, of hopes being heard, and that's what she longed for now for Sienna.

"There hasn't been much of a change. However, she is stabilized. We have to be very cautious with head trauma. We have a few more tests we need to run. She's asleep, and right now she needs rest. If you all would like to go home and get some rest yourselves, now is the time."

"We'll give you all some family time, but call us if you need anything at all," Mrs. Wright told Mrs. Magan. "And I'll bring breakfast to you all in the morning."

"We so appreciate it, Marie," Mrs. Magan said.

"Thank you for coming, all of you," Mr. Magan added.

That night, Winter slept in her childhood bedroom and in the morning she was the first to wake. The house indeed looked as though a small storm had torn through the kitchen and exited the sliding glass doors, leaving the rest of the house intact. Winter needed something to do, something to occupy her mind. So she grabbed her car keys and drove over to Mariah's Home Bakery that cool morning. She ordered coffee for her family and the construction workers who would be arriving soon to work in the kitchen.

The smell of Mariah's pies made Winter's mouth water, so she ordered an extra one. At home, Winter had a hard time getting the front door open with her hands full of pie, but she managed. Winter opened the door, and the noise of construction filled her ears: clanging nails, walls being sandpapered, and the sound of drills. It smelled like a construction store filled with wood and fresh paint. She carried the pies in, set them on the table in the foyer, and went back for the coffee. Winter heard banging coming from the kitchen and made her way there first.

"Hello, I've got coffee for anyone who wants…" Winter's voice stopped. The face she was looking at, she hadn't seen in years, but no amount of time could distort his features. It was him. The man who first made Winter fear.

She looked him over, stunned. He seemed smaller in every way to her. *What is he doing here? He didn't want me on his street, and now he's in my house.* The answer came swiftly. *Perhaps he'd changed.* And then she caught something in his gaze, the light of recognition and something else. Winter could undoubtedly see something in his eyes.

"I heard your parents needed some help with a pipe that burst. I've always been pretty handy," the man said.

How long has he waited to see me? Weeks. How long have I been imprisoned? Years. Winter knew why he had come. Just like Anna, he wanted forgiveness. Forgiveness from the twelve-year-old girl he'd wronged, from the child whose life he'd injected his hate into, from the one he wounded. He longed to erase the translucent scars left from his weapon of prejudice.

And there stood Winter, left with an all-consuming choice. She had the power to wound this man back, not on the same level of hurt inflicted upon her, but still. Or she could do something else. She could forgive him and release them both, forever. Though it seemed obvious, though the decision appeared clear and the right path evident, Winter couldn't help but wonder why it was ultimately left to her to put right the wrongs of his life. Why must she be harmed one and forgiver? That was her role, and it was one with which she struggled. Try as she might to understand its complexities, it simply threatened to choke her.

Winter felt something hot dripping down her hands. She looked down at the coffee cup she held in her right hand. Winter had been squeezing the cup so tight that its contents burned her skin. Her hand screamed out in fury, but none to match that which resided in her heart. But had she not released herself? Though it wasn't right or fair, though it made no sense to her, perhaps she had to do it. Perhaps forgiveness of those who hated her was her responsibility and her burden. To remain human in the face of inhumanity. Winter would not pretend that those words came from her mouth with ease. They fought to rise to her lips, to be spoken into the tension filled air between the two of them, but they emerged.

"I forgive you," she said.

The man's eyes softened. He looked down at his feet and when his gaze returned to Winter she knew she wasn't looking at the same man who stood before her thirteen years ago.

"Thank you," he said. "I know I don't deserve it, but thank you for giving that to me."

When those words were released, Winter didn't feel immediate relief. Part of her shouted for justice, or for him to rot away as she had, but she'd learned something since she left home. Winter knew the kinds of ripples she wanted to leave in the world. So in the final act of saying goodbye, of shedding that last bit of hate from herself, Winter forgave him. Seven times over she spoke the words, to remind herself, to embed them within her soul, and give flight to his.

CHAPTER THIRTY-ONE—FORGIVENESS

Winter left the house. She walked and walked until she came to a clearing in her town. Fields and farmland stretched far. Winter closed her eyes. The sky was cloudless, the breeze soft. During her journey, Winter learned what part of her driving force was. She just wanted to belong as she was: to a community, to people, joined by love and abiding in peace, seeking to find their unique place in the world. *But don't we all?* She thought. *Don't we all long to belong and be able to step outside and feel that your existence won't be questioned, or judged, devalued, or negated? Don't we all long for connection?*

She rested her hands on her upper arms and hugged herself as she stood in the swaying wheat stalks. But no person could give her that sense of belonging. Winter thought of the places in her life where reconciliation called out. If Winter was going to forgive that man, then perhaps she could forgive someone else, too. Winter closed her eyes for a moment and took a deep breath.

Winter had lived a caged existence, and she was ecstatic to be free, and now she had to give Anna Herald that same chance. Winter glanced up at the sky. *I'm going to regain everything I lost and more*, she promised herself. Winter didn't want any residual hate left in her life. She was finally ready to make the call. Winter retrieved her phone from her pocket and found Anna's contact information from the email she'd sent. Winter dialed Anna Herald's number.

"Hello?"

Winter took a breath. "Is this Anna Herald?"

"Yes, who is this?"

"It's Winter Wright." There was silence on the other end of the line.

"…Thanks for calling me," Anna said.

Winter's jaw tightened. Doing this was going to be difficult.

"Before we talk about anything else, I have a couple questions for you."

Winter said. She could hear Anna sigh.

"I might not have a right to the answers, but I'm going to ask anyways. I'd like to know why you did all those things to me…and what made you change."

Winter waited, unsure if Anna would divulge that information.

"I was expecting that question, but I still don't feel prepared to answer it," Anna said, and then she laughed softly. The sound was odd to Winter. She'd never heard Anna laugh without malice in her voice. "…I don't want you to think this is a cop-out answer, but I went through some things in my life."

"Like what?" Winter asked. She could hear Anna's discomfort.

"My family looks ideal from the outside, but my father had alcohol problems, serious alcohol problems. I guess ruling our school," Anna lowered her voice, "and you made me feel in control. I wanted control. I needed it, and you were always so timid. When you won that competition, I was livid because it showed me that I wasn't as in control as I thought. And I was always worried that you'd find out about my family's problems and tell people. You were just a few houses down. If anyone was going to find out and tell people, I was sure it would have been you. It doesn't excuse my behavior, of course."

"What about your constant taunting? You put down everything I am."

"I know. I didn't realize how damaging some of those things I was saying were, and I did believe them. I did believe that you won unfairly, but I know better now. My mind was full of anger and insecurity and ignorance." There was a pause and then Anna said softly, "I'm sorry about the competition. I shouldn't have done that."

Winter recalled her Grand Failure, the first major dream she abandoned. "It wasn't the kindest thing to do."

"No, it wasn't. I know it's a late apology, but it is sincere. Your other question is what changed, and I guess the biggest reason I reached out to you is because I'm engaged. The man I'm marrying is black, and now I'm going to be the mother of children who might have similar experiences to you. How ironic," Anna said.

Winter could hear how nervous Anna was.

"I made fun of you because you were different. You stuck out. I teased you about the way you looked, because of your hair, and then I belittled your experiences because I didn't understand them. The things I said to you, someone could say to my future children. I don't want anyone thinking those things about my kids or making them feel bad about who they are because they'll be perfect just as they are. I'm sorry, Winter. I'm so sorry, and I'm so ashamed. That's why I need your forgiveness. I want to be able to look my children in the eyes, and to do that I have to lay this down to rest. I'm ashamed."

And then Winter could hear Anna crying. Her muffled sobs reached Winter's ears and melted the last bit of animosity Winter clung to in her heart. People indeed can change.

"Anna," Winter said. "I forgive you. I forgive you. Have a good life and don't ever come to any of my future public speaking events." The girls laughed together for the first time in their lives. Anna's voice was thick and full of emotion as she said these last parting words to Winter. "Have a *great* life, Winter Wright."

***

Back at home, once all the workers had gone, Winter flipped through her steadiest of companions on the trip. The journal Sienna had given her was worn from use. She sat down at the desk in her room. Above it, were memories from the last ten years of her life. Pictures of she and her friends stared down at her, and in one photo Winter saw that old green coat. Winter pulled the journal closer and began to write. Words resounded in her heart and tumbled from her pen. They filled the blank pages until they were covered in scratchy, black ink. In the evening, Winter heard her mother's voice calling upstairs.

"Winter! The Magan's just called! Sienna has been released from the Intensive Care Unit! She's doing well!"

Winter had never moved so quickly in all her life. She and her family rushed to the car and drove over to the hospital. Sienna could only have visitors who were family, but Winter wanted to be there, even if she couldn't see her. The Magan's faces were still red from tears when they arrived, but this time they'd been cried in joy.

"We got to talk to her," Mrs. Magan told them. "It's looking good. Sienna asked to talk to you, Winter. I told her doctor it was fine," her mother smiled. "I told him you were family."

Winter followed Sienna's nurse to her room. She twiddled her fingers nervously. *Why am I nervous?* Winter asked herself.

"She's right in here," the nurse said, extending her arm towards Sienna's room. Winter turned her eyes to room 304 and looked inside.

"It's all right. Go ahead," the nurse said encouragingly.

Winter told her legs to move. She was nervous to see Sienna, her unfailing rock, the girl with quiet strength, weakened. Winter walked into the room and laid eyes on her friend. Sienna's head had bandages, her bottom lip was swollen, and she had a long cut on the side of her face.

"You look purple," Winter said. Sienna turned and smiled, before grimacing.

"It hurts to show any emotion other than a blank one," Sienna said.

"Hi, Friend," Winter spoke quietly, feeling her throat constrict.

"Hi, Friend. I won't break if you come closer."

Winter walked over and sat on the chair next to Sienna and held her hand.

"How do you feel?"

"Like I'm healing. Believe it or not, this is not the worst injury I've ever had," Sienna said with a laugh before she started coughing. Winter grabbed a cup of water and helped Sienna take a drink.

"You wanted to talk to me?"

"I did. How was your trip?" Sienna asked with a grin.

"Are you kidding me?" Winter asked, shocked.

"No, they told me you came back, and I was curious."

"Sienna, how are you?"

"I'm good, really."

"You are?" Winter said, tears falling from her eyes.

"When I saw him coming I was so scared, Winter," Sienna said, her eyes had moved to the ceiling, but then she focused them on Winter. "I knew it was going to be bad, but you know the first thing I thought?"

Winter shook her head no.

"I always judged myself according to how well I did in school or at my job. I wanted all of my relationships to be tidy and neat. I told myself to try my best at everything, but right before he hit into me, I didn't think about those things. All I wondered was, did my life have meaning? Did the small amount of time I had on this earth make any kind of difference? Could I have loved more deeply and lived more fully?

"You touched my life, Sienna. You've impacted everyone who knows you," Winter said. Sienna smiled that way only she could. Gentle and unassuming, yet filled with a strength Winter rarely saw.

"I can tell you're different. Your trip must have worked."

"What do you mean?"

"I can see a change in you," Sienna said, squinting her eyes.

"What?" Winter asked, wanting to understand, but Sienna ignored her question. With fiery eyes, she asked Winter a question of her own.

"It's a beautiful thing isn't it?"

"What's that?" Winter asked.

"To believe in people."

***

Winter returned home that night more relieved than she'd ever been, more grateful than she'd ever felt. Sienna was going to be okay. She'd have to take time off work and move back home for a little while, but she'd be okay. Winter prayed out of gratitude. She did believe in people again, and that started with herself. She believed in her own voice, in her own purpose.

As Winter reveled in happiness, she realized that there was one fear on her list that she'd misnamed. She still had almost a month and a half left of her three-month period, so Winter set herself a new task, a new list, with just one thing on it. Winter Wright no longer wanted to live a fearless life;

she wanted to live a joyful one, and the first thing she wanted to do was achieve her greatest dream, and she knew exactly where to start.

Winter revisited the mental list of dreams she'd made and set hopefully onto quiet winds. There was one longing disguised as a fear because Winter worried it might never come true. She pulled out a stack of blank paper and an ink pen and turned on the light above her desk. With trembling fingers, Winter got to work. Sienna already knew what Winter's long-held dream was, and now she was brave enough to admit it completely to herself.

Winter was through with striving to be someone or something different. Instead, she wanted to be the person only she could be, the person she was destined to become. And she was going to focus on being the fullest version of that self. Simon's insightful words carefully drifted back to Winter: become a storyteller. Winter was going to reach for her dreams. That was it, and she knew it, and for the first time she didn't want to run.

For the next couple weeks, Winter locked herself in her room, in Mariah's Home Bakery, at the local coffee shop. Using her journal as a guide for the story she wanted to write, Winter wrote the story she was meant to tell. Winter wrote by moonlight and thought of lanterns. After a few weeks of Sienna being back home, she was on the mend. Winter visited her every moment she could. One sunny afternoon, the two life-long friends met for coffee, and Sienna proclaimed she'd get back out on the water again. Not anytime soon, doctor's orders, but one day.

"When you do, I might have to come with you to supervise your safety," Winter said. "I can't believe you're out and about."

"Crutches aren't new to me. This is not the first time I've broken something."

"That's true."

"Besides, I can only stay housebound for so long before I go crazy. What have you been up to lately? Any luck on the job search?"

"A little. I found an organization that works to bring affordable healthcare to low-income neighborhoods. I've had a couple interviews, but I'm still in the waiting phase."

Winter took a sip of her coffee and then remembered the news she wanted to share with her friend. "I'm writing a book, Sienna! I'm using the journal you gave me as the bones of my story."

Sienna swallowed her coffee and sat up. "I'm glad to hear that. I had a feeling you might realize it one day."

"You know me too well, better than I know myself. You're the one who got me started." Sienna proceeded to pat herself on the back. "It's true, Sienna. While I was away, I would have failed so many times if it weren't for the letters you gave to me and the people I met. And I never would have gotten started if it weren't for you pushing me to go somewhere that day at the lake."

"Life is about people," Sienna smiled. "Can't do it without them, even though we might wish we could at times."

"It is," Winter agreed. They left the coffee shop together and drove to Winter's house. The street was full of parked cars. "Someone's having a party," Winter said, shutting the car door.

"Somebody is," Sienna said. Winter opened the front door to her house and heard a clattering mass of voices.

"SURPRISE!"

Winter collapsed to the floor. Sienna laughed loudly at her friend as a sly smile began to cover her face. Winter stood up and looked around the room. The theme of the party was global travel. Pictures of the earth hung from the ceiling, blue and green streamers covered almost every doorway in the house. Pans and bowls filled with diverse and aromatic foods were next to a large cake dripping with chocolate.

It took Winter a few minutes to notice that question marks were hanging around the room. Question marks of various sizes and shapes, shades, and dimensions, hung alongside banners and covered the floor next to multicolored confetti.

"That was my touch," Sienna said. "Because you embraced the unknown. You haven't talked much about your trip, but we wanted to hear."

Winter's face broke out into a smile as she was led to the backyard by her closest friends and family. One long, rustic table sat in the yard beneath hanging lights suspended from tree limbs. The table was decorated with tall glass bottles cradling candles burning with bright flames, colorful plates, sparkling silver utensils, and soft cloth napkins. Winter spent the night talking about rafting the Nile and bungee jumping. She talked about crossing the Carrick-A-Rede rope bridge and seeing the most divine sunsets of her life.

Underneath a sky of stars Winter told stories, stories she couldn't believe were hers to tell. She'd set out to face her deepest fears, and she was finally free. Isn't that what fear is at its core? Running from the things people think will break them to the point of no return. Winter's fears had come, shown themselves to her, and made her crumble, but here she was at the end of it all. And she was better than okay, she was revived.

CHAPTER THIRTY-TWO—A LETTER FOR YOU

One Year Later
Winter's letter to you

It took me months of navigating through a forest of doubt to finish this book, but I'd found one of my hopes. I believe that everyone should look, as if the sun rising depends on you finding your illogical logical dreams. I believe my dreams were intertwined with part of my purpose, and I'd never have uncovered it if I hadn't faced the things that held me back.

They don't have to be large, just live your life the best way you know how. Live with abundant hope and seek out the things that set your heart ablaze. Somewhere, someone, is in need of something you're going to create. It might be you alone who is changed, but it might be millions who are need of the dreams that live in your soul.

Instead of daydreaming, let your actual days be filled with your fulfilled dreams. Build beautiful relationships, and invest in the world around you. As you move in life, be grateful for every season you live through, for every season of expansion, of trial, of opportunities, and through it all remember to feel joy.

During my adventure I never, not even once, stopped feeling fear. But I learned to live beside it more boldly than I ever had before. I thought I'd trample my fears, but it was meeting them along the way, along the path of life that strengthened me. Perhaps that's where the beauty lies, in deciding to live fully despite those confines of fear, and as you do, you break them apart.

As you grow, they fly in pieces through the air, and you stand on top of the shards. It doesn't mean they won't occasionally hurt you, but that's life. Your fears keep coming up, and you've got to grow and speak to them, lay them down, and walk over them. That's the overcoming.

Meeting mine, standing to look my fears in the face, instead of cowering beneath them was the bravest thing I knew how to do. And if you've got any fears, I hope you'll tell them to live on the sidelines as you become more a part of your own existence. I know others will come as life moves and shifts, as new challenges emerge and attempt to alter your being. Some of them you'll grow from, and some you might feel will grow too big for you to see over, but know there's another side, a side waiting to be lived and full of dreams eager to be found.

I've found memories can be rewritten, from pain, from happiness, from perspective. I decided to turn my memories of hurt into fuel, hope, and possibility. If I learned anything from my revival, it was to always see hope, to forever strive for it. So I did, and this is my letter to you.

The end of this story is nearing. I think I've shared most everything I can, for now, about how I learned not to become hostage to my trepidations, bogged down by the suffocating force that fear is. And this is my last fear turned to dream. In your hands. That's what this is; my last fear met. My first dream lived.

I wanted to put down everything I'd seen and done, the lessons I learned because maybe it meant that someone else might have a little less pain. One of my favorite authors said, "Better one heart be broken a thousand times in the retelling...if it means that a thousand other hearts need not be broken at all." I didn't need to travel the world to find myself, to learn to love myself as Ella said, uncompromisingly. But that's what I did, and I learned so much more than I could have hoped. My journey was also about finding my unique contribution. And this is it. The thing that only I could do.

I don't know where or when a revival will occur in your lifetime, maybe it already has, who knows how many times you'll experience it. But I hope you'll find one of your gifts; one of the gifts that will make the world different. I believe you'll find yours. I know you can, and I can't wait to find out what it is. It could be something that seems simple but ignites your soul. I suspect it has something to do with living in love, with fiery compassion, and an enduring devotion to being grateful for life.

Sienna called me a couple weeks ago and invited me back to the lake house to join her on the jet skis. It was almost one year ago exactly that I started this journey. Before, I had been too afraid to take that plunge into the cool waters from the black diving board in the middle of the lake. But today, as I look down at shifting waters below me, I know I won't always know where I'm going, but I do know I want to take the leap. I hold my breath, bend down, and jump.

Here is to living a bigger life, Winter

timeless.
for dreamers who journey
who dare to reach out and touch the gentle giants
who awaken the hidden fears living within their conscious
who go. and see. and do.
who confidently understand your own healing power
who lift up your hopes like lanterns floating across a black sky—
it is these small communities of people who tell unknown stories
and travel the vast expanse of our universe— it is you who
through small steps
stumble upon some bountiful path to transformation—
Who have the courage to Meet your Life.

"Better one heart be broken a thousand times in the retelling...if it means that a thousand other hearts need not be broken at all"

Quote by: Elie Wiesel

Stay tuned for the musical companion to the novel! Coming soon!

In the meantime, stay connected by visiting the following:
sherie-james.com
Instagram: sheriejames
Twitter: sherie_james
Facebook: Sherie James

ABOUT THE AUTHOR

I know this is supposed to be written in the third person, but this is self-published and we all know I'm writing it about myself, which can be super awkward! My sincere hope for this book is that it encourages you in your life journey. It can be so easy to become discouraged and to feel trampled by life's hardships, but I also believe that connecting with each other and living in love can alter our lives and so many others. So, if you've faced some deep trials I hope you find strength within these pages. May hope and light lead you to live beautiful lives, even in the face of hardship. You've got a gift we are all waiting for and I hope you know that to your core.

For those of you who prefer traditional third person bios, this is for you: Sherie James is a social worker by training and a writer through love of the medium. Her sincere hope for this debut novel is to encourage its readers to seek out their truest selves and live abundant lives.

ACKNOWLEDGMENTS

Foremost, I'd like to thank God for allowing me to take a risky leap of faith and land into a hopeful embrace. I'd also like to thank my three parents, Christopher, Donna, and Felicia for their unwavering love and support. Thank you Dr. Sara Barton for your mentorship and for encouraging my storytelling. Dr. John Barton, thank you for encouraging this journey and giving me renewed hope during a time I needed it. Beth VanRheenan, thank you for your insight, guidance, and support. I'd also like to thank the editorial skills of the Writer's Beacon, headed by my sister, Joy. Joy, thank you for supporting me in every way.

Crystal, thanks for always believing and being a champion of this novel before it was even finished. Sierra, thank you for your willing, enthusiastic heart and for always teaching me. Brother (Chris), thanks for staying up late to listen to my hopes. Kristan, thank you for your encouraging spirit. Lianne Lang, thanks for your loving support, and Greg Avey thanks for helping me to go on my first abroad excursion which ignited my love for travel. Valinda and Vivian, thanks for all you've done. Grandma and Aunt Eloise, I'm grateful for you both.

Stephanie Beason, thank you for encouraging me to write my story in the first place, and Shalmar, my fellow writer, thank you for reading some very rough drafts. I'm grateful to you both for your love and guidance! Sita, thanks for never making me feel crazy for beginning this adventure. I'm grateful for the advice and love you've given. Leti, thank you for always believing right from the start. I'm thankful for your love and support, and don't forget we have a NPP to win! Pia, thank you for your unceasing prayers during this season of life, especially when doubt crept in, thanks for always being an open ear, and for your support and love. Sarah Schewe, thank you for being my singing partner and fervently supporting this endeavor, grateful for the love you give so openly. Thank you for your amazing love, support, and friendship over these years, and for our lake adventures: Katie, Liz, and Jen. Thank you for the light and encouragement and wonderful feedback you gave: Stephen Lamb and Karina. Thank you Garners for being such an amazing host family during my time in Uganda, and thank you Bobby, for telling me to become a storyteller. To the teachers who gave me opportunities and developed my confidence, thank you: Ms. Clark, Mrs. Harger, Mr. Malizia, Mr. Golden, and Dr. Barton. I'd like to end this thank you by showing my gratitude for my Cousin Mike and Cousin Peggy of IH Productions for helping me record the musical companion to this novel.

Manufactured by Amazon.ca
Acheson, AB

12827814R00139